RUBBER SOUL

RUBBER SOUL

A NOVEL BY

Greg Kihn

RUBBER SOUL

Copyright © 2013 Greg Kihn

eISBN: 978-1-62467-093-0
Print ISBN: 978-1-62467-094-7

Published by Premier Digital Publishing
www.premierdigitalpublishing.com
Follow us on Twitter @PDigitalPub
Follow us on Facebook: Premier Digital Publishing

DEDICATION

This book is dedicated to Nate and Zuri, the next generation
of Beatles fans- may they grow up in as magical a time as I did.

ACKNOWLEDGEMENTS

I'd like to thank Judy Coppage at The Coppage Company for her invaluable
work getting this novel published. Her final edit really made it sing. I'd like to
thank Pete Heyrman and his fellow editors at Bear Press for the initial edit.

Thanks to my long time manager and business partner,
Joel Turtle and his son, Skyler, and the Greg Kihn Band.
I'd also like to thank my wife, Jay, my son, Ry, and my daughter, Lexi.

I'd like to thank the Beatles that I was lucky enough to interview.

I'd like to thank all the Beatles fans around the world.

FOREWARD

HOW RUBBER SOUL HAPPENED

Let me begin by saying that this is a work of fiction. None of it really happened. Dust Bin Bob never existed, and the words I put into the Beatles mouths were never spoken. I invented it all.

I was one of the 73 million viewers who watched their first magical appearance on the Ed Sullivan Show. The effect the Beatles had on me was incredible. They changed my life. I became a musician.

Over the course of sixteen years hosting the morning radio show on KFOX in San Francisco, I had the privilege of interviewing many people in the Beatles universe including Paul McCartney, Ringo Starr, Pete Best, Beatles driver Alf Bicknell, and Abbey Road recording engineer Geoff Emerick, as well as Patti Harrison and Yoko Ono.

I always wondered where the Beatles got their records: the music that constituted their early repertoire and influenced their songwriting. I asked all of them about that, and they all gave me the same answer. They got those records from friends of Merchant Marines traveling back and forth between Liverpool and the States. That gave me the idea for "Dust Bin Bob."

Pete Best was particularly helpful. He was able to pinpoint where and when Stu Sutcliffe was attacked and kicked in the head. (Stu would die of a brain aneurism in early 1962.)

Paul and Ringo's memories of the Manila Incident were still vivid, and I was able to color the story with unpublished details. I tried to keep this novel as historically accurate as possible. You know it's funny, you do research on a book like this, but I didn't really do that much. I remember it all like it was yesterday. I lived it. Using the Manila incident as the climax, the whole story just popped into my head. From one Beatles fan to another, I really hope you have as much fun reading this book as I had writing it.

CHAPTER ONE

DUST BIN BOB

Bobby Dingle looked down at water the color of Coca-Cola lapping against the pilings. The sagging pier smelled of fish and diesel fuel. The *Empress Baltimore* groaned and creaked against its mooring lines, a sleeping giant in Albert Dock, Liverpool. There were lights aboard, and the faint sounds of machinery. An icy fog hugged the waterline. Bobby's shopworn pea coat and corduroy cap shielded him from the cold yet he could still see his breath, and his ears stung. A whistle sounded from the deck. He looked up.

A backlit figure waved.

"That you, Bobby-boy?"

"Yeah."

"Come on up. I left the gangplank open. Hurry, now. I could get pinched for this."

Bob hastened his step up the narrow passageway, careful to mind his footing. He was well coordinated for a gangly eighteen-year-old.

"Nip along smartly, lad. Come on, come on, that's it."

Bob legged it the last twenty feet. An unshaven, middle-aged, Merchant Marine named Hank the Frank grabbed his arm and swung him over the rim and onto the deck. The man's short gray hair looked metallic in the half-light. He had a mad gleam in his eye, the kind of gleam Bobby knew from the movies – a Dr. Frankenstein gleam. When he spoke, a prominent bad tooth flashed in his mouth.

"Steady there, mate. Follow me."

The deck seemed deserted. Except for the sounds of machinery below and the constant creaking of the old cargo ship, the waterfront felt weirdly still and silent. Hank led Bobby through a hatchway into a warren of tight corridors, down a ladder and into the crew's quarters. He unlocked a metal door and opened it with a chalkboard screech.

"In here."

They entered a cramped cabin with two bunks lit by a single caged, 40-watt light bulb. Its silvery light pierced the small space, forming sharp, elongated shadows. From beneath the lower bunk, Hank pulled out two square cardboard boxes.

"I got good stuff this time, laddie. Real good stuff. The best yet. I think you're gonna like what you see."

Bobby carefully lifted the lid off the first box. The smell of freshly pressed vinyl filled his nostrils. With the light behind him, he looked inside and gasped.

"Chess Records! Chuck Berry! My all-time fave!"

Hank beamed an uneven smile.

"Got that one in Philly. Go ahead, take 'em all out."

Bobby pulled the stack of thick 45-rpm records out of the box. The paper sleeves rustled through his fingers like bills in stacks of currency. Bobby knew American 45s better than most U.S. teenagers did. He knew they'd begun as disks for American jukeboxes, playing music in bars and roadhouses Bobby could only imagine. He knew that their huge spindle holes were a carryover from that original jukebox function which made it easier for a machine to handle them. But most of all he knew the music.

Bobby began sorting through them, reading the titles aloud in his mild Liverpudlian lilt.

"Little Richard, Fats Domino, Jimmy Reed. Oh, and what's this? *Money?* By Barrett Strong? I've never heard of him."

"One of my own finds. Great song, that."

Bobby held up another record.

"Bo Diddley on Checker Records. *Say, Man.*"

"Oh, yeah. *Say, Man.* Mr. Diddley sings about gettin' whupped with an ugly stick in that one. An ugly stick! Can you imagine? A stick, that once you're beaten with it, makes you ugly. Sheer genius. So... young Bob, what have you got..." he paused and raised an eyebrow, "-for me?"

Bobby felt in his pocket and pulled out a ball of twine. He deftly unraveled it to reveal a piece of hashish nearly the size of a golf ball. Hank's face lit up.

"Well, I like the looks of that."

"Red Lebanese. Very good stuff, if I do say so myself."

Hank sniffed the chunk of hash.

"Red Leb, eh? Hmm... I think we can do business."

Bobby sat down on the lower bunk. He emptied the two boxes of 45s, examined each, counted and recounted. When he was finished, he divided the records into two stacks. One stack of stuff he knew, one stack for unknowns. The new releases by Chuck Berry, Little Richard, and Fats Domino were worth their weight in gold. It would be months before any of the import record shops would have them... if ever. And the unknown pile was sure to contain nuggets.

Bobby tallied the value of the records based on his best guess, then figured what Hank must have paid for them back in America.

"What do ya reckon, then? About fifty records here? That piece of red Leb must be about an ounce, eh? I'd fancy a trade, straight up."

Hank chuckled. "A trade, he says. Well, now... You've seen the merchandise. You can attest to the quality of the selection."

Bobby said, "Hey, I don't know half of these guys." He picked up a record with an all-black label. "*Think*, by James Brown, on King Records. So, who's this James Brown, and what's his game?"

"That's a great record, take my word for it. A real corker, that one is. The guy screams like a maniac when he sings. It's unbelievable."

Bobby shuffled the records, reading more titles. The more he read, the more excited he got. He could only imagine the exotic sounds locked in those grooves. The Coasters, Johnny Burnette, Gary "U.S." Bonds, Jackie Wilson, Hank Ballard and the Midnighters, Ray Charles.

Hank coughed. "I could fancy a bit of smoke. It's a long voyage comin' up, and old Hank is feelin' the chill of winter a bit harder these days."

"Then you'll go for it?"

The sounds of the ship echoed through the superstructure. Bobby wondered how the big vessel sounded at sea with an ocean swelling and dipping beneath her rusty hull.

Hank gave Bobby the thumbs-up.

"What the hell. Deal."

"Bless you, kind sir," Bobby said, with cynical Liverpudlian lyricism. "I will now take my leave of this vessel."

Bobby and Hank shook hands. Bobby gathered the records and put them back in the two boxes.

"I can't wait to hear these."

"You won't be disappointed. This is the best batch yet."

Bobby pulled the gold-labeled Anna Records 45 by Barrett Strong out of its paper sleeve: *Money (That's What I Want)*.

"I love these American R&B designs."

He held the record up to the light and examined the spiral pattern of the grooves.

"Look at this thing. It's so... audacious. Who ever heard of Anna Records?"

The logo was a silhouette of a guy waving a baton against a gold background.

"It's like a flier for a strip club. The Yanks are so brazen. And look at the grooves on this thing. You can almost see how the song changes from moment to moment."

Hank pointed. "Be careful with that one, lad. It's a song about money. The lyrics are insane. Barrett Strong is not to be trifled with. It'll blow your bloody socks off."

Bobby looked down at his ankles.

"Better wait till I get home for that. Can't afford a scandal."

Hank chuckled. "That's what I like about you, Bobby-boy. Always sharp, always quick as a ferret. You're a smart lad. You'll go far one day. Mark my words."

"I'm just a businessman. Quicker than some, luckier than most. But thanks for the compliment. You forget that I'm stuck here in Liverpool. Nothing much going here, you know."

"Something will come up. You'll see. Life is funny that way. Back during the war I just hoped I'd live through the day."

Bobby tied the two boxes together with the twine and hefted the package over his shoulder.

"I'm off, then. Thanks, Hank. It's a pleasure doing business with you."

"Likewise, young Master Robert. Careful on the way out. Don't be spotted."

Bobby stole off the *Empress Baltimore* and faded into the gray streets of Merseyside. The package hung heavy across his shoulder blade, pounding his back rhythmically as he walked.

Harbor mist leached the color from the brick row houses, leaving a shimmer of translucent condensation. The sidewalk was slick under his shoes. Bobby's mind anticipated what the records might sound like. His expectations thrilled him.

When he got home, he went up to the tiny room he shared with his two stepbrothers above his father's shop. Again, he sorted through the records. Separating a pile of the ones he wanted to hear first, he inserted a spindle into the first, *Money*, by Barrett Strong. Placing it carefully on the compact phonograph, he dropped the needle. The piano started like a chain saw. A feverish voice sounded the cry, "The best things in life are free... but you can keep 'em for the birds and bees... I want money..."

Bobby felt swept away. Surely, this was greatness. *I've never heard a more honest song.* The song ended. Bobby played it again, not entirely sure he'd heard it right the first time. *Even better the second time.* The lyrics seemed to be sung in some incomprehensible, incredibly hip, American patois. *A song about money. Ingenious.* When the record ended the second time, Bobby tried another, then another, then another. Little Richard, Fats Domino, The Coasters, Ray Charles, Bo Diddley – all exciting, wonderful names. Bobby absorbed the rock and roll energy until he thought he would burst. The records were truly magic. Bobby's world expanded past all horizons.

Around midnight, he stopped listening and went downstairs to his father's second-hand shop. His two older stepbrothers, Mick and Clive, were there. The Dingle brothers drank Guinness and smoked. They looked at Bobby, nodded and went back to their beer.

Bobby was the true black sheep of the family. His mother, a dark-skinned Greek woman named Ariodni, had married Bobby's father late in life. She died when Bobby was eleven years old. He grew up under the badgering of older half-siblings. In the eyes of his stepbrothers, Bobby wasn't really part of the family. Then there was the issue of ethnicity. Bobby's mum was small and dark, with thick, wavy, black hair above breathtaking ebony eyes. She'd married into a family of Irish and Welsh descent. Bobby's stepbrothers were, like many of their father's ancestors, large, pale, and red haired. Bobby resembled his mother. That made things worse. "A touch of the tar brush," Clive called it.

Mick hit Bobby a half-hearted blow to the shoulder.

"Been down to the docks, little brother?"

"How do you know?""I have spies everywhere. So, what'd you nick?"

Bobby shrugged. "Traded for some records."

Clive belched. "Bloody waste of time."

Bobby looked at Mick.

"What's eatin' him?"

"Aw, he's just sore because somebody pinched his favorite pocketknife."

"The good one?"

Clive nodded.

"The one you stole from that German bloke?"

"The very one."

"We'll, I'll be damned."

"I had it out. I was showin' it around. Left it sit for one bloody minute. And... There it was, gone."

"There it was, gone?"

Clive's voice modulated up a key.

"What's the matter, don't ya speak English? I was havin' a pint and some little scut pinched it right out from under me nose."

Bobby didn't want to be around Clive when he sulked. Clive tended to drink until he turned violent, then aimed at the nearest target, usually Bobby. Clive made his living as a petty thief, working occasionally for one of the waterfront crime bosses. Mick worked as a stevedore and took part in countless wharf side heists, involving all manner of merchandise. The two older Dingles were almost always up to no good.

"Goodnight, dear brothers."

Bobby left the shop and climbed the narrow stairs to his room.

That night he fell asleep with the sound of Barrett Strong in his ears. He dreamt of money.

In Bobby's dream, Fats Domino was trying to hand him a big wad of money, but for some reason, Bobby wouldn't take it. It made Fats laugh.

"What's the joke?" Bobby asked.

Fats pulled a white handkerchief from his breast pocket and mopped his face, Satchmo-style.

"The joke's on me, young fellah. Me and the boys had a little bet goin'. Don't worry about it. It's cool."

Bobby stared at the rock and roll legend, dumbfounded. "But... why are you here?"

Fats seemed surprised by the question.

"Because something is goin' on here. Something big."

"Here? Are you sure?"

Bobby felt Fats' smile warm his skin like summer sunshine on a Butlins holiday. The big man nodded slowly.

"*Oh, I'm sure, all right.*"

"*I mean, are you sure you've got the right place? Liverpool?*"

"*It ain't exactly Beale Street, but it'll do. Now, are you sure you don't want*" *some of this here money? It's free, you know. Go on, take it."*

Bobby reached out and took the money. It felt right. Fats laughed again.

Bobby woke up suddenly, thinking, *That's the best damn dream I ever had.*

He looked out the window; half-expecting to see Memphis or Chicago, but it was still Liverpool.

*　　*　　*

The cramped flea market at Penny Lane hummed with energy. Most people Bobby knew lived a second-hand life, and here, where everyday barter took place, they felt at home. Bobby set up his father's stall in its usual place near the entrance. They sold an odd assortment of items; tools mostly, and some household goods. A large Moroccan prayer rug hung from a line. Some ostrich feathers jutted from a chipped vase. The air was redolent with the musty smells of old cloth, oily metal, and wood smoke. In the hazy light of a Liverpool Saturday morning, tough, pink, sniffling faces passed by. Some even smiled. Bobby put the two boxes of records right up front next to a case of cigarette lighters and old silverware.

A white-haired woman in her seventies, thin as an egret, moved slowly toward Bobby's stall. Bobby saw her, waved, and rushed to her side.

"Mrs. Swithins! How good to see you up and about today! How are you?"

"I'm flat as piss on a plate, La. Everything hurts and what ain't is about to. How's yer dad?"

"He's fine. Everybody's fine."

"I wanted to thank you for selling all of old Joe's stuff. You done me a favor and got a good price to boot. Here, I found these in one of Joe's drawers."

Mrs. Swithins handed Bobby a small stack of business cards. Bobby read the one on top.

"Robert Dingle, licensed retailer of antiques, curios, and previously owned merchandise." "He made these for my father?" Bobby asked.

Mrs. Swithins nodded. "Among Joe's many talents, he was a printer."

"I'll give them to dad when I see him. Joe was a good bloke. He had an eye for quality."

The old woman sighed like worn airbrakes.

"He died in his sleep just tryin' to get a bit of kip. I remember thinkin' he probably doesn't even know he's dead yet. He'll be in for quite a shock when he wakes up and finds himself deceased."

Bobby cocked his head, not sure he'd heard her right. Mrs. Swithins had poetic license, all right.

"I have a surprise for you."

Mrs. Swithins' eyes flickered like a pilot light.

"A surprise? Fer me? G'wan!"

"It's true. If you'll just excuse me for a bit while I look in the back of the stall."

He opened a steamer trunk and pulled out something the size of a football wrapped in a towel.

He brought it before Mrs. Swithins and pulled the towel away. She shrieked and threw her hands up in the air.

"Ahh! Bobby! It's beautiful! You didn't! You shouldn't!"

Bobby held up a hideous ceramic statuette of a toad playing a fiddle. Mrs. Swithins collected anything with a toad. She had toad salt-and-pepper shakers, toad teapots, toad lamps, and toad plates. The ceramic toad made her salivate.

"Oh, I must have it! How much, La?"

"I couldn't take money from you, Mrs. Swithins."

"What do you mean?"

"It's a gift. From me to you."

"A gift? That's daft. Come on, don't insult me, I got money. How much?"

Bobby handed the toad to Mrs. Swithins whose face suddenly illuminated like sunlight on dirty snow.

"Oh, Bobby. I don't know whether to laugh, cry, or burst out in pimples. A real beauty, this one is. Thank you, thank you so much, La."

Bobby grinned. The toad looked like something from a horror movie. It was easily the ugliest piece of ceramic artwork he'd ever seen. Bobby guessed its origins must have been promotional. Perhaps once, long ago, in another part of England, The Fiddling Toad Pub may have commissioned a hundred or so of the monstrosities. Bobby had seen other such figurines and estimated the cash value of the item to be quite modest. Hardly worth displaying. But, to Mrs. Swithins, it was a treasure. Bobby understood treasures.

"I just saw it, and I thought you might like it. That's all. No big deal. Your passion for toad art is an inspiration to us all. I got this particular piece in a trade with some other stuff. Go on, take it home with you."

Mrs. Swithins hugged Bobby.

"Such a nice lad!"

"There is one thing you might do for me..."

"Anything, La. Just name it."

"Could you keep an eye out for these?" He held up one of the records.

"Phonograph records? What for?"

"I collect 'em. Just like you and your toads."

Mrs. Swithins laughed.

"Well, God bless you, Bobby Dingle. If it's records you want, then it's records you'll get."

"Except I don't want the old fuddy-duddy ones. I only want American rock and roll."

"If there's any of those rocky-roll records out there in Merseyside, I'll see 'em before too long. You can be sure of that."

Mrs. Swithins left the stall as slowly as she came. Bobby watched her fade into the urban landscape.

Around the corner came two leather-jacketed young men, each with a pink-tipped cigarette jutting from his lips, and each with the swagger of someone who didn't give a damn. Two James Deans. Teddy boys. They stopped in front of Bobby.

"What's this, then?" the first one said with a thick scouse accent.

The second shrugged, looking at the prayer rug and ostrich feathers.

"A mysterious visitor from the east."

They eyed the records.

"Hold on. What's all this?"

Bobby noticed their hair; greasy, swept back, just spilling over their collars. They looked a bit scruffy with uneven sideboards and tight stovepipe trousers. The first one picked up a record and read the label.

"Chuck Berry!"

"Chuck Berry? No! It can't be! Let me see that!"

"Blimey! Little Richard! Bo Diddley! Where did you get these?"

Bobby smiled, letting the slight gap between his front teeth show.

"I have a special source, straight from America. Those are brand new releases. You can't get 'em anywhere else."

"Do you have any idea what you have here?"

Bobby nodded. "Actually, yes, I do."

"It's the bloody Holy Grail."

The two young men exchanged astonished glances.

"Are these for sale?"

"Yes, they are."

The two Teddy Boys shifted on their feet.

"I'll tell you the truth, mate. We're in a beat group, and this is just the type of music we do. You know, American rock and roll. I'm John and this is Stu."

John stuck out a hand. There was something in the way he stood that suggested a coolness far beyond anything Bobby had known.

Bobby accepted the hand.

"I'm Bobby. Pleased to meet you. This is my father's stall. He's got a secondhand store in Merseyside. We specialize in previously owned merchandise. A little of this, a bit of that; something that might have mistakenly wound up in the dust bin but is still quite serviceable."

John barked out a laugh, then slipped into a spastic impersonation. He looked like a juvenile delinquent Quasimodo.

"Dust Bin Bob! Dust Bin Bob! Your coming was foretold to us!"

Bobby eyed John. *Cheeky*, he thought, *very cheeky*.

"So, you're in a beat group, eh? Are you professional?"

John nodded vigorously. "Definitely professional. Oh, yes. The talk of the town, we are."

"So you must have lots of money to buy records."

John spat. "This is Liverpool, man. Look around you. The place is a bloody poorhouse. Nobody's got any money, least of all the beat groups."

Bobby shrugged. "If you don't have money, then you can't buy records."

John said, "I was wondering... You think it might be possible to just hear 'em?"

Bobby took the Chuck Berry record out of John's hand.

"This is not a lending library. Why should I let you hear these beauties?"

"Because we need the music, man. We're going to conquer the world, you'll see. To the toppermost of the poppermost, and beyond. Bigger than Elvis."

Nobody laughed. John pawed at the cracked pavement with the pointed toe of his winkle picker shoe.

"You aim to learn the songs in one sitting? That doesn't seem possible."

John smirked. "We're good."

Bobby turned to Stu.

"Is he always this cheeky?"

"It's worse than you think," Stu said.

Bobby rubbed his nose and looked the musicians over again.

"You say you play the music of Chuck Berry?"

"Like the man himself."

"Little Richard?"

"Mother's milk to us."

"That's bloody amazing. In all of Liverpool, Dame Fortune has sent me you. So if I let you listen to these records, what's in it for me?"

John hunched over, playing the spastic again. He twisted his face and spoke in a crone's voice.

"What's in it for me? For me? Something for me, sir?"

To Bobby, John's clowning mocked everything he stood for as an independent businessman. Bobby frowned, suddenly a shade more indignant.

"That's right. Something for me. Is that so wrong? Bloody hell. It's a hard life down here in the fleas. A fellah's gotta eat."

John straightened with a wry smile and a wink.

"You drive a hard bargain, Dust Bin Bob. How about a lifetime pass to all of our gigs, forever. That's gotta be worth a fortune."

Bobby snorted. "How about half a bar. From each of you."

"Bloody embarrassing, that is. You don't want the lifetime pass?"

"No offense, but... It can't be worth much."

John looked wounded.

Bobby sighed. "OK, I guess I'll take it along with the money."

John brightened. "Deal!"

"I'll need that in writing."

"Of course, of course. You won't regret this, Dust Bin Bob."

* * *

The musicians found Dingle's second-hand shop, and Bobby led them upstairs into his claustrophobic room. There was barely enough space for the three musicians, their instruments, and Bobby. Guitar cases had to stay in the hall. They squeezed in around the phonograph, three guitars poised to receive benediction. Stu was not among them. In his place were two other guitarists.

"Where's Stu?"

John made a sour face. "Bloody art school."

One of the guitarists, the one with the baby face, said, "Genius is like a crown of thorns. There's always a price, you know."

The remark struck Bobby as odd, yet extremely witty for a Merseyside musician. He picked up one of the records and held it out.

"This first one is my favorite."

Bobby put on Barrett Strong first. *Money* exploded from the lone three-inch speaker like a firecracker. John found the key on his guitar and played along.

"This is bloody great!" John shouted. "I gotta sing this one!"

"Can your voice handle it?"

"I don't know. Can't tell until I've done it."

The song ended, and John said to play it again. He showed his companions the chords and worked out the main riff.

"That's what it's all about, isn't it? Money? Everybody can bloody well understand that. I mean, you spend your whole life chasing after the stuff, and you still wind up skint and skinny. This song says it all, man. It's gonna be my anthem."

By the end of the second play, Bobby was amazed that all three musicians played along perfectly. When the song ended, John led them in another complete version without the record playing behind. Bobby was astonished.

"You blokes are pretty good!"

"Didn't think a couple of working-class lads from Liddypool could sound so authentic, eh? I told you we were good."

Bobby shrugged. "Merseyside is a wondrous place. It never ceases to amaze me."

"Hold on while I jot down the lyrics."

Bobby looked at the other two musicians. They seemed to be younger than John. Except for the one pithy "crown of thorns" remark, they hadn't spoken to Bobby at all, only muttering to each other in short incomprehensible phrases. John introduced them as his band: Long John and the Silver Beetles. The other two guitarists were Paul Ramon and Carl Harrison.

There seemed to be a spark between them- a kinship Bobby could appreciate. *These guys are closer than brothers*, he thought. *How rare.*

John wrote furiously in his notebook.

Bobby noticed the cover had been illustrated with hand drawn cartoons. "Did you draw that?"

"He's a crafty one," said Paul. "A cunning satirist with a mind like a refrigerator."

Bobby laughed. "Talent must be runnin' rampant in the streets of Liverpool."

"Rampant and naked."

John abruptly began performing the song again. Something wonderful happened. Bobby felt goose bumps rise on his arms and neck. The others came in one by one, layering each enthusiastic vocal on top of the next, building to a crazy crescendo. Musical energy crackled in the air like static electricity. Bobby's fingers and toes twitched. The harmonies were dead on, sung with exuberance. But it was more than that. The intangible quality he listened for between the grooves was there. What Bobby could feel in his gut were all the things rock and roll represented to him, all the reasons he liked it. The attitude, the passion, the feeling that there was a great big joke somewhere and only the rockers got it.

"The best things in life are free," John sang. "But you can give 'em to the birds and bees! I want money!"

"That's what I want," the other two answered.

"That's what I want," John repeated.

"That's what I want." Crackling dead-on harmonies

"That's what I waaaaaannnnnnnnt, that's what I want!"

John's cynical vocal style caressed the lyrics, played with them, teasing new inflections out. The fact that a guy Bobby had just met, a local lad, even had a vocal style, amazed him. It all amazed him.

Right then, Bobby wanted to stop time. The beauty of that moment felt like a pang in his heart, like the memory of his dead mother. A lump formed in Bobby's throat. These three couldn't possibly be from the same world he lived in; they had to be from somewhere else. People like this just didn't exist in Liverpool.

*   *   *

Long John and the Silver Beetles stayed for three hours, learning songs as quickly as they could play them. Bobby marveled at the skill with which they broke down each arrangement, substituting guitars riffs for horns, changing keys, adjusting tempos, and working out harmonies. Their level of musicianship was far beyond anything he'd ever witnessed up close. When they packed away their guitars and stood in the narrow hallway at the top of the stairs, Bobby didn't have the heart to ask for his money. John beat him to it.

John looked sheepishly at the others.

"Well... I suppose you'll be wantin' your money now, Dust Bin Bob. I'll have to take up a little collection."

They pooled their meager funds and handed Bobby a crumpled note and a fistful of change. Bobby held it for a second, then gave the money back.

"That's OK, I just want to be there when you play this stuff on stage."

Before John could answer, the floor shook. There was a commotion in the shop below. Glass broke. Something had been knocked over.

"Oh, shit. It's my stepbrothers. It sounds like they're pissed. You don't want to meet the likes of them. They're as mean as dockside rats. Hurry!

Down the steps and out the back door!"

Paul and Carl led the way with John behind. Just as Paul cleared the bottom step, two big bodies crowded the narrow hall, blocking his way.

"What's this? A couple of pretty boys?" Clive sneered.

He pushed Paul back.

"Musicians, is it?" Mick said.

"Leave 'em alone, Clive!" Bobby said. "They're friends of mine."

"Oh, I'll bet they are."

Clive grabbed Paul and pushed him against the wall. His guitar case banged, but he held on.

"Easy, friend," Paul said. "We're just on our way out."

"Not so fast."

Bobby said, "Come on, Clive. We don't want any trouble."

Clive pointed at John.

"Hey! That's the punter that nicked me knife!"

John looked worried.

"Wasn't me."

"The hell it wasn't. I never forget a face. You stole my knife, and I want it back."

John held up his hands.

"I swear I've never seen you before."

Clive released Paul who slid through the door. Carl ducked out after him, leaving John alone in the hallway with Bobby and his brothers. Clive stepped toward John eyeing the money in his hand.

Clive's meaty hand closed around John's, crushing the money and John's fingers.

"What's this? Money? I'll just take that."

Bobby boldly stepped between them.

"Let him go, Clive. He doesn't owe you anything."

"He stole me knife!"

"You've got the wrong man," John said.

"Bullshit!"

Clive twisted the money out of John's hand and shoved him back into the steps.

John instinctively raised his arms to protect his face just as Clive swung at him.

"Don't!" Bobby shouted and jumped on Clive's back. Clive threw Bobby over his shoulder and slammed him against the wall. John watched as Clive ruthlessly punched Bobby in the gut.

John lunged at Clive, fists flying. He caught the big man with a punch to the nose and droplets of blood splattered the faded floral wallpaper.

"What the hell? You broke me nose, ya little bastard! You'll die for that!"

Clive turned to face John who had backed up to the foot of the stairs. Blood ran from Clive's nostrils. Mick, who'd been watching, lurched toward John, his face twisted into an angry sneer.

John gripped the banister with one hand and pushed against the wall with the other. He swung his legs up and kicked Clive full in the face with both feet. Clive fell back. Mick tried to get at John, but the tiny hall had too many bodies in it, and Mick couldn't reach him.

Bobby, doubled over and holding his side, slammed his body into Mick, creating a space.

"Run!" Bobby gasped. "Run!"

John leapt through the hole and burst through the doorway. Paul stood clear, unsure of what to do next. John stumbled and went down, breaking his fall with the palms of his hands. From inside the door came the sounds of Bobby struggling.

"We can't just leave him here!" John cried.

John picked up a brick and charged back inside. Paul and Carl followed.

Bobby was on the floor in a fetal position, both of his brothers kicking him. John threw the brick at Mick's back. It bounced off him, and Mick toppled. Clive turned to John, enraged.

"You're gonna get it now!"

John, Paul, and Carl gang-tackled Clive, driving him back into the hall. They all went tumbling to the floor. Clive struggled to regain his footing, but John slipped his arm around Clive's neck in a headlock while Paul and Carl held his arms. Clive started kicking. Bobby picked up the brick and hurled it low at Clive. It struck him in the knee. With a grunt, Clive stopped fighting. Mick staggered to his feet, looking confused.

"Go," Bobby rasped. "They're crazy. They'll kill you if they get mad enough."

"What about you?"

"Think I broke a rib."

"Come on, you're going to the hospital."

They released Clive who had no fight left in him. He sat on the step, dazed, rubbing his knee.

John helped Bobby up and led him through the door. Mick and Clive did not try to stop them. But, as John stepped into the alley, he heard Clive's voice.

"I'll get you, so help me God. I'll get you and I'll..."

Suddenly, John flew into a rage.

"*You* attacked *us*, you stupid git! You stole our money and made us fight! What did you expect us to do? I should call the coppers!"

Bobby squeezed John's hand.

"No. Let it go."

*   *   *

The x-ray of Bobby's ribs showed a hairline fracture. A nurse bandaged him and sent him on his way. John sat in the waiting room with his band mates. He amused himself by drawing in his notebook. When Bobby emerged, they applauded loudly.

"Dust Bin Bob! Dust Bin Bob!"

Bobby blushed. "I want to thank you for pulling those scuts off of me. You could've gotten seriously injured. How can I ever thank you enough?"

John said, "After what you'd done for us? Letting us learn those songs? How ungrateful can we be?"

Bobby shook his head.

"I'll never forget it."

"How could your own brothers beat you like that?"

"Stepbrothers," Bobby corrected. "They've been doing it for years. They don't consider me part of the family. My dad doesn't seem to care as long as they don't actually kill me. Lately, for some reason, it's gotten worse. I'm scared to death of them."

"Why do they hate you so much?"

"Because they saw my mother as the Greek bitch who stole their father's heart."

"What happened to their mother?"

"She had TB. She died before I was born. My father met my mother shortly after that. They got married pretty quick. Clive and Mick never forgave him. That's why they hate me."

"You think they're going to come after us?"

Bobby shrugged. "They don't know who you are."

John lit a ciggy and squinted at Bobby through the smoke.

"They'll try to beat it out of you."

Bobby looked away.

"I'm not going back there."

John blew smoke through his nostrils.

"Poor old Dust Bin Bob. Forced out on the streets at such a tender young age."

Bobby sighed. "You lads should stay out of sight. At least for the time being."

The musicians exchanged glances.

"Well, it just so happens that we're leaving for Hamburg in a few weeks. We've got an extended engagement there. Four months of rock and roll madness in the Reeperbahn. By the time we get back everything should have blown over."

Bobby nodded. "Lucky timing. I've heard the Reeperbahn is a wild place. Trouble lurks around every corner."

"Not trouble, adventure," John said. "But I'm worried about you, Bob. You've got to go someplace for a while and mend. Have you got anyone?"

Bobby thought for a moment.

"No... Not really. I guess I could ask to stay at Strawberry Fields."

"That's a proper orphanage. They don't take in strays. I should know. If it wasn't for Aunt Mimi, I could've wound up there."

"I heard you could stay for a few months if you were in need."

John snorted. "You're too old. It's for kids. Listen, it's a long shot, but I'll ask my aunt Mimi if you could stay at Mendips for a few days."

Bobby looked at John as if he were a god.

"Really? That's awfully generous."

"It all depends on what Aunt Mimi says. I'll ask her, but I guarantee nothing."

"I understand. Thank you. Thank you so much."

"She's a compassionate woman. She might say yes. It's worth a try. Besides, I'm off to Germany in a few weeks. I should get the sympathy vote."

"When you play in Hamburg will you be using any of the songs you learned today?"

"Of course. But enough of that, Dusty."

John wiggled his eyebrows up and down. He tore the cardboard back from his notebook and handed it to Bobby. On it was a card-sized drawing of a garbage can with a cartoonish little man peeking out. Leaning against the can was an electric guitar with the words "Dust Bin Bob" beneath it. Bobby smiled, then began to read aloud.

"I, John Lennon, being of stout pine and knotty, do hereby grant a lifetime pass to Robert Dingle, also known as Dust Bin Bob, to all performances by the group known as The Beatles, whenever and wherever they may be."

Bobby looked up from the page.

"The Beatles? I thought you said the name of your band was Long John and the Silver Beetles."

John grinned. "I changed it. It's just 'The Beatles' now. Get used to it. Someday everybody will know our name."

The absurdity of that statement made Bobby laugh, but he was the only one. Paul and Carl stared back at him with Zen-like coolness.

"Look," John said. "It's been signed by all of us."

Bobby read the signatures.

"Paul McCartney? I thought you said your name was Paul Ramon."

Paul laughed. "Well, you know how it is in showbiz. McCartney's my real name. Ramon was just a passing fancy. If you see him, tell him I'm sorry."

Bobby shook his head.

"And George Harrison? You're not Carl anymore?"

George shrugged. "I can't live vicariously through the names of others. I mean, Carl Perkins is God... it'd be sacrilegious. From now on it's just plain old George."

"Don't forget the band name," John said. "That's different now too."

Bobby pointed to the page.

"Is this a misprint? You've spelled Beatles with an A."

"No. That's the way it's supposed to be. It's 'The Beatles,' as in beat, as in the rock and roll beat. Get it?"

Bobby winced.

"That's the dumbest name I ever heard. You'll never make it with a name like that."

CHAPTER TWO

THE RECORDS

John brought Dust Bin Bob home to 251 Menlove Avenue, Woolton. Nicknamed Mendips, the suburban Liverpool house seemed cheery; brick fence, broad green lawn, a tall hedge, everything a proper English garden home should be. A far cry from the cramped Merseyside two-up-two-down storefront Bobby called home. Bobby marveled at the wide thoroughfares and park-like setting of Woolton.

"You actually live here?"

"Yup, this is my Aunt Mimi's house. It's time for you to meet her," John said. "Be careful what you say."

John's rebellious nature sometimes strained his relationship with Aunt Mimi, but she loved him and almost always forgave his transgressions. He knew that her first impression of Bobby would be crucial. Bobby needed to appear to be the kind of boy she approved of. John felt good about that. Bobby didn't dress Teddy Boy-style like John did. Mimi was bound to like that. Also, he spoke well. Compared to most of John's other friends, Bobby would seem a step up.

John led Bobby through the front door of the prim suburban semi-detached. Aunt Mimi was in the front room.

"Auntie, this is my friend, Bobby."

Aunt Mimi eyed Bobby's bandages.

"What's wrong with him?"

"He's been roughed up by some hooligans. They broke his rib."

Aunt Mimi made a stern face.

"John, have you been fighting too?"

John blushed. "Well, Auntie... We weren't exactly fighting. We were defending ourselves. They jumped us. We were minding our own business, and they attacked us. We had to fight back, didn't we? Poor Bobby here took the brunt of it."

Bobby nodded. "It's true, ma'am. John saved me from far worse injuries than these."

Aunt Mimi looked at Bobby.

"Are you in pain?"

"Yes, ma'am."

Aunt Mimi studied Bobby's bandages.

"Why don't you go home to your mother? She must be worried about you."

"My mum's dead," he said softly.

"Oh..." Aunt Mimi stopped, glancing at John.

When John's mother suddenly died, the change in John had been dramatic. She knew first-hand about the pain and loneliness of a motherless child. Something in the intensity of Bobby's dark eyes resonated with her, something she'd seen in John countless times.

"I see. Well, how about your father?"

"My father's never home. He's always out collecting things for his shop."

Mimi brightened.

"Oh, he's a shopkeeper? Is it an antique shop?"

"You might say that."

John said, "Auntie, Bobby can't go home now because the guys that beat him up live in his neighborhood and they'll be looking for him."

John diplomatically omitted the fact that the assailants had been Bobby's stepbrothers. Mimi would have frowned on that.

"It's not safe there. But, I was wondering..."

Aunt Mimi crossed her arms.

"You were wondering if he could stay here," she said, finishing the sentence for him.

John managed a crooked, guilty smile. Aunt Mimi knew him too well.

"Just for a few days..."

"I see."

After an awkward silence, Aunt Mimi turned to Bobby.

"You really need a place to stay, young man?"

John watched the softening in Mimi's eyes. He knew that kindness lay at her core. It would all boil down to Bobby's conversation with her right now. John hoped he would say the right thing.

"Yes, ma'am. I would appreciate it greatly. I'm clean and quiet and I'll try my best not be an imposition. I'd even be willing to put a few bob into the food budget so it wouldn't be a burden."

Aunt Mimi studied Bobby.

"That's a nice offer, Robert. But it won't be necessary. We take care of our guests in this house."

John waited for the verdict. Aunt Mimi turned and looked him directly in the eye.

"All right, John. I'll let Robert stay for a week or so until he's well enough to go home. But, I'll not tolerate any bad behavior. First sign of trouble and out he goes."

John hugged Mimi.

"Oh, Auntie! Thank you! You're the best!"

"Thank you, ma'am," Bobby said. "Thank you for your kindness. I won't be any trouble, I promise."

"All right then. John, you'll have to clean your room and make a space for Robert. Use the cot from Uncle George's closet. Now get up there and wash yourselves for dinner."

*   *   *

Bobby couldn't believe his good fortune. Here he sat in a nice house in a nice neighborhood far from the dockside Teds and his evil brothers. John, Uncle George, and Aunt Mimi seemed like extraordinarily kind and generous people. Outside of his mother, Bobby hadn't known anyone like that. Just to know there were still people of that sort in the world gave him strength.

John showed Bobby his room. It was at least four times bigger than the one he shared with his stepbrothers. John's guitar rested against the wall next to a phonograph and a meager collection of records. A picture of Brigitte Bardot, clipped from a magazine, hung over the bed. It was as cheery a room as any he'd been in.

John closed the door and looked at Bobby conspiratorially.

"We've gotta go back and get your records."

Bobby laughed, but it hurt, so he stopped.

"You're kidding, right? I wouldn't go within ten blocks of that place right now."

"The records, man. They're priceless."

"It's not worth the risk of getting stomped again."

"That depends on how you look at it. We need those songs. They're a bloody gold mine. We'll double our song list. We'll be playing all night in Hamburg. The Beatles need a repertoire, man. Nothing can stand in the way of that."

"Are you willing to risk it?"

"Absolutely. I'll go it alone if need be."

Bobby shook his head.

"Alone? Well... I do have a set of keys. I suppose it is conceivable that you could go when no one's around and get away with it. But you would be taking an awful chance. If my brothers catch you, they're liable to kill you."

"They won't even know I've been there."

Bobby wrung his hands.

"All this for a stack of records?"

"I'm surprised at you, Dusty. It's more than just a stack of records. It's rock and roll. It's my future, man. It's the Beatles' future. It's all our futures. Your record collection is exactly the kind of musical foundation we've been looking for. It'll put us leagues ahead of the other beat groups in Liverpool. And it'll make you, my Dust Bin friend, a part of rock and roll history. Because, mark my words, someday the Beatles will be bigger than Elvis."

Bobby looked up. "You don't lack much in the self-confidence department, do you?"

"It's not bragging if you can do it, Herr Dustmiester."

"Yes, but... can you?"

"What do you think?"

Bobby thought for a moment.

"Yes, I believe you can. I don't quite know why, but I do. I've seen the way you are with the others, and there's definitely something there."

"Then you'll go with me to get the records?"

Bobby stood up and walked across the room.

"Damn it, John. Why do you have to be such a hard head? What's wrong with waiting a bit and then sneaking back in when I'm healed?"

"That's not the way I operate," John said.

"Well, sod it, then."

"Do it for the Beatles."

Bobby sighed.

"All right, you win. I'll go with you. Jesus, John... I couldn't let you go alone, now could I?"

*   *   *

The shop was dark, the street quiet. On the bus ride into Liverpool, Bobby explained the plan to John. He'd open the back door, creep through the shop, check to see if the coast was clear then John would sprint up the stairs and grab the record collection. Bobby explained the boxes were under his bed. It seemed simple.

John waited while Bobby silently opened the door and slipped inside. A few minutes later, he stuck his head out the door and motioned for John to follow. They came to the foot of the stairs.

"I'd go up but my side is killing me," Bobby whispered.

"What are the odds that they're up in your room, asleep?"

Bobby shrugged. "They almost never do that. By this time of day, they're out hustling. Unless one of them is sick which is also rare."

John looked up at the top of the stairs with the trepidation of a mountain climber viewing Everest.

"I guess it's now or never."

John took the stairs two at a time as stealthy as a cat. His ears twitched, straining to hear every sound. He stepped into Bobby's room. The floor creaked. Even though it was afternoon, the room was dark. The lone window had been covered.

John paused to let his eyes adjust to the light and listened. Glancing around the room, he saw that it had been sacked. Clothes and books were everywhere, including a big pile on Bobby's bed. John tiptoed toward the bed, but the old floorboards creaked with every step. He crouched down and thrust his hands under the bed. He could feel the boxes. He had to slide partially under the bed to retrieve them. Just as he was about to push himself up, he heard a snort. It sounded like a water buffalo. John froze.

Another snort. John watched in horror as the great mound of clothes on Bobby's bed shifted. A muscular arm snaked out from beneath the pile and pulled away some shirts. Mick's head poked out, facing John.

John Lennon held his breath. The face loomed, eyes still closed, just inches in front of him. John studied the bulldog features. Mick was still asleep.

John said a short, silent prayer and began to inch away from the bed while keeping his attention focused on Mick's eyes. If they should open, he would be the first thing Mick saw. This time Mick would be out for more than a few broken ribs. John's heart pounded.

The records.

Without thinking John squatted, leaned forward, and reached for the two boxes. The move brought him face to face with Mick, kissing close. John held his breath again and forced himself to grab the boxes. John's will to get the records was greater than his fear. Now he just had to get out of the room.

Every muscle in John's body tensed. He moved stiffly, quietly, trying not to breathe. Inch by inch he withdrew from the bed, the floor creaking each time he shifted his weight. All the while he was fixated on Mick's face. Yet Mick slept.

It seemed like hours before John reached the door. Just as he turned to go, one of Mick's eyes opened. It blinked, looked directly at him, and then closed again.

*　*　*

"You risked your neck to get those records, you maniac," Bobby said. "You're a sick, sick man, John Lennon."

John grinned dementedly. "Yes! But now the band has enough songs to survive."

Bobby shook his head.

"And that makes you a hero?"

"To the Beatles, it does. We'll go to Hamburg with enough music now. Allan Williams says that in the Reeperbahn bands have to play all night long. That's a lot of music."

"Who's Allan Williams?"

"He's the one who booked the gig. He's not really our manager, but he's the closest thing we've got right now."

John removed a record from its paper sleeve and placed it carefully on the turntable.

"A fresh Chuck Berry number. George can play Chuck better than anyone in Merseyside. You should hear him play *Raunchy*. It's inspirational."

Bobby listened as the song started. He watched John play around on his guitar until he found the proper key. Bobby had already seen that John could assimilate a song in a single listening. It was as if the notes were simply a reminder of something he already knew. When the song ended, John put the guitar down and lit a ciggy.

"What about you, Dusty? What will you do next?"

Bobby shrugged. "I've always wanted to go to sea."

John snapped his fingers.

"Great idea! I have this friend, Nigel Whalley, who knows someone down at the Pier Head."

"What's that?"

"The Seaman's Employment Agency. Maybe he can get you a job as a steward on a ship bound for America."

Bobby stared out the window at Menlove Avenue and wondered what life would be like in America. The possibilities excited him. If these records were a glimpse of that world, Bobby wanted to experience it first-hand.

"I'll do it. I'll sign on as a steward."

"Bloody great."

John picked up the guitar again, crushed out his ciggy and started to play. Bobby marveled at John's ability to pick up exactly where he left off. Bobby couldn't do that.

The song John was listening to was *Jaguar and the Thunderbird*, a car song by Chuck Berry. He'd already learned *Little Queenie* and *Almost Grown*. The man's appetite for rock and roll seemed insatiable. He played the records over and over, memorizing every shout and nuance.

George and Paul appeared on occasion and rehearsed when Mimi wasn't home.

Together they were magic. Bobby listened in awe while the three friends dissected the songs, worked on harmonies and guitar parts and didn't seem to have a care in the world outside the music. *Closer than brothers.*

There was much talk of their upcoming trip to Hamburg. The boys were excited about going though conditions would be a bit rough. Their number one problem had always been finding a drummer. Now they had Pete Best, and they were a true working rock band ready for the big time.

The Beatles were just happy to be working. They needed the money and the stage time. They seemed to intuitively sense that the hundreds of hours they would be spending playing to the tough Hamburg audiences would strengthen them, mold their sound, and forge their musical identities. Bobby was impressed by their ability to make everything look easy. Even though they were deadly serious about their music, they went about it in such a lighthearted way that the casual observer might think they were just fooling around. Until they sang. The uncanny blend of John's nasal midrange and

Paul's reedy tenor with George on the lower third fit every kind of material. They tackled ballads and blues, rockabilly, R&B, skiffle and pop, all with the same reckless enthusiasm. They were fearless.

At times it seemed like John was the leader, but there were other times when Paul had his way. George seldom spoke.

John proudly informed Bobby that there would be one last Liverpool gig where he could see the Beatles before they left for Hamburg. The thought of seeing the band actually perform on stage, playing some of the music he'd watched them rehearse, excited him. The energy around the Beatles hummed. Within their gravitational pull Bobby could feel it too; a feeling that something was about to happen.

"We're playing Saturday at Lathom Hall in Seaforth. I gotta warn ya, it's a very rough crowd. I've seen some real cock-ups in the audience, people just pounding each other senseless. We just keep on playing. If we stopped every time there was a fight, we'd never finish a song."

"I'll just stay to the side of the stage."

"You can help me set up the amplifiers. Then, technically, you'd be with the band."

"Great!"

John wagged a finger.

"But there's no safety on the stage, not at Lathom. It's a wicked place. Three Saturdays ago, Tommy Moore our drummer for the gig didn't show up. So we just set up his drums although nobody could play 'em. So, for a joke, I asked if there was a drummer in the house who could sit in. Well, the leader of the local gang, this huge geezer named Ronnie steps up on the stage and says he's joining the band. And he's serious. The guy is ugly, mean and drunk and he's never touched a drum in his life. He gets up there and starts pounding away on Tommy's poor drum kit, beatin' the shit out of it. It made me wince. He wouldn't stop. We couldn't play a proper show with that lout up there, but none of us wanted to tell him 'cause he woulda kicked our arses. Paul stole off and called Allan Williams who drove out there with a couple of bouncers from another gig and removed the guy from the stage after an hour. There was a lot of bad blood that night."

Bobby looked shocked.

"You think he'll be back again?"

John's eyes sparkled.

"Just let him try. This time we'll have bouncers ready."

"You love it, don't you?" Bobby asked. "All the action and adventure, the insanity, the fights, the chaos..."

John looked at Bobby as if he were talking sheer nonsense.

"What I love is the music. Fuck the rest of it."

CHAPTER THREE

LATHOM HALL

The pleasant atmosphere at Mendips made healing easy. Bobby sent word through an uncle to explain the situation to his father. He wanted to make sure his father knew that he was all right but laying low. He also wanted his father to know what Clive and Mick had done. He knew that there was nothing his father could do, but he wanted the old man to know.

Once he was able to get around, he went down to the Seaman's Employment Agency and signed on as an apprentice steward. As soon as he was fully recovered, he would ship out.

One day, Bobby saw a lorry in front of one of the nice duplexes just down Menlove Avenue from Aunt Mimi. He walked up and inquired if someone was moving out. The lorry's driver pointed.

"Yeah, some old lady died. The kids are sellin' the house and everything in it."

"Really? Is there an agent?"

The driver shrugged.

"I dunno. You'd have to ask the missus. She's inside."

Bobby walked through the open door.

"Hello? Anybody home?"

A thin, pale-faced woman in her forties wearing a conservative navy blue dress and clunky footwear stepped into the parlor. An understated string of miniature pearls hung around her Audrey Hepburn-like neck.

"Can I help you?"

"I heard from the lorry driver that you're about to liquidate this estate. And I was wondering if you had procured an agent to handle the sale items?"

The woman looked Bobby over.

"Well, actually... I haven't given it much thought."

Bobby nodded.

"I see. Well, in that case, allow me to give you my card."

Bobby pulled one of his father's business cards from his jacket pocket and handed it to her with a flourish.

She squinted at the card and read aloud.

"Robert Dingle, licensed retailer of antiques, curios, and previously-owned merchandise. Is that you?"

"Yes, ma'am," Bobby lied. "That's me. If you've given any thought to having someone act as an agent for this estate, to sell all the various items for a good price, then I'm your man. I've got experience appraising merchandise like this, and I'm positive I could get you the top price."

The woman put Bobby's card in a tiny pocket in the front of her dress. She looked around the room.

"There's a lot here."

"Normally, in cases like this, people would ring up the local second-hand shop, and the man would come out and give you a bid on the whole lot and cart it away. But you'd be losing out. Imagine selling the individual pieces for maximum value. That lamp, for instance; I know a lamp vendor who'll give me five bob for it. And that clock; there's a bloke on Vauxhall Street who collects clocks. There's no telling what he might pay."

"You don't say?"

"Yes, and for the customary 15 percent commission, I can handle all the arrangements and you won't have to do a thing."

The woman nodded. "I'm Nancy Garlton."

She held out a hand and Bobby gently shook it. She waved at the room.

"My mother's house."

"Oh..."

"She passed away recently."

"I'm so sorry."

She sighed, and suddenly her eyes seemed to focus on something miles away.

"I'm anxious to close this chapter of my life."

Bobby eyed Nancy Garlton. He saw the way her eyes glazed as if she were deep in thought. She might have been pretty once, and the ghost of it still haunted her face.

As Nancy walked toward the door, the weight of the conversation seemed to shrink her delicate shoulders.

"How soon can you start?"

*   *   *

Bobby had the lorry driver take several of the big pieces of furniture to a shop he knew. They were ordinary pieces but in good shape. He negotiated a fair price and realized his first commission. Then he returned with the workman and moved a heavy bookshelf with a wooden bust of William Shakespeare carved into the top. He suspected the bookshelf was worth something more than the other pieces. His suspicions were confirmed when an antique dealer offered him one hundred pounds for it. Bobby realized he could probably get more somewhere else, but the offer was good and it was late in the day. He took the money and arranged to meet Nancy Garlton at the house on Menlove Avenue.

"You've earned this much?" she said. "In just a few hours? Mr. Dingle, I am impressed."

"Why don't you call me Robert? Mr. Dingle is my father."

"Very well, Robert. Well at this rate you'll be done in no time."

"I plan to make quick work of it if that's all right."

"Yes, of course."

"I'll report to you every day at six o'clock."

*   *   *

Once Bobby shared his record collection with John Lennon, Bobby came to realize how important it was to John. It became his only interest. He listened to the records constantly. They talked about the songs and the artists. Bobby knew a lot about American R&B singers and shared his knowledge. He promised to stay in touch once he reached America and keep John up to date with the latest music.

Aunt Mimi treated Bobby like a royal guest plying him with ham butties and butter scones. She saw him as a healthy influence on John. John seemed a bit more polite, a bit less wild with Bobby around. And she was aware of the records.

"Why is John so keen on them?"

Bobby said, "He's excited to learn some new songs."

Bobby continued to work with Nancy Garlton until he'd almost emptied her mother's house. He earned a hefty commission and opened a bank account in Woolton. It would be enough money to make a new start when he returned from America. On the last night, he rang the doorbell and waited for her footsteps as he had done for the past couple of days. When they didn't come, he turned the doorknob and found the door open. He stepped inside where late afternoon shadows painted the walls.

A large orange cat slipped in the door with Bobby. It had been waiting behind a bush, ready to run. Bobby reached down and petted it and it began to purr. Bobby scooped it up and put it out. The cat tried to get back in but Bobby blocked it with his foot.

"Hello? Mrs. Garlton?"

He heard sobbing coming from one of the upstairs bedrooms. He went to investigate and found her sitting on the floor before an open steamer trunk, crying.

"Mrs. Garlton? Are you all right?"

She looked up at him, her mascara smudged.

"I... I..."

Bobby instinctively sat down next to her and put his arm around her shoulders.

"There, there..."

She slumped against him.

"I was just looking through this trunk and I got so... so..."

Bobby said, "Why don't you let me fold everything up and put it back in the trunk for you. I'll take it wherever you want. You can look at it later when you're up to it."

"Thank you. That's nice of you."

"No problem. By the way, there was a big orange cat that came in the front door. I put it out, but it was dead set on getting back in here again."

"Oh, that's Riki-tiki, my mother's cat. God, I'd forgotten about her. She must be eighteen years old by now. Poor thing, I haven't fed her in days."

Bobby said, "I'll go down and open up a tin of cat food for her. She seemed a bit upset."

"I suppose I'll have to put her down. I can't care for her, and mother's gone..."

"I'll ask the neighbors. Under the circumstances, I'm sure somebody will take her in."

Nancy Garlton raised her face to his.

"Do you think I'm old?"

Bobby held his breath.

"Old? Ahh... No. I don't think you're old."

"Today, at the bank, a man said..."

"I wouldn't put much stock into what people say. It's usually just hurtful tripe."

"Will you help me?"

Bobby didn't answer right away. Something about Nancy Garlton was beginning to scare him.

"Sure."

"Will you, really?"

"What kind of help do you mean?"

Nancy Garlton dabbed at her tears with the cuff of her dress.

"I don't know."

"There's no one else you can turn to?"

She shook her head slowly.

"My husband is dead, my mother's dead, my sister is off in America... I'm the last one."

"You're beginning to feel a bit like Riki-tiki, I'll bet."

"Yes... Just like the cat."

"Except in your case, we just can't ask one of the neighbors take you in, can we? The cat seems to be getting on fine, and so will you in time. I'm sure of it."

Bobby became aware of the weight of her body as she leaned against him. He could also smell her overly sweet floral perfume.

"You're a good man, Robert. I can tell. You treat people with respect. There are so few men who are true of heart."

Something clicked in Bobby's head. Conflicting emotions roiled. He suddenly felt uncomfortable.

"Well... uh, thank you. But I don't consider myself any different from anybody else."

"But you are. You're kind and considerate, and you actually care. You cared about the cat, you cared about Mum's estate, and you cared about me..."

Bobby decided to guide the conversation back to business.

"I have the receipts. You'll be pleased that I was able to get more than my original estimates on several items."

Nancy sighed. "I don't want to talk about receipts right now."

Bobby tried to ease himself out of the hug, but the more he withdrew, the more she pressed against him.

"It feels so good to be held," she whispered.

Bobby cleared his throat.

"Uh... Mrs. Garlton?"

"Call me Nancy."

"OK, Nancy. I'm feeling a bit nervous."

Nancy looked into Bobby's eyes. He gazed back at her with clinical interest. Her face was a mess. The age lines, normally expertly masked with paste and powder were now revealed in all their glory. She had raccoon eyes from crying. But still, the more he studied her, the more he could see the beauty that was just below the surface.

Now he found himself in an awkward moment, unable to retreat. *Could this be what I think it is?*

Nancy Garlton touched his chin.

"Robert?"

"Yes, Mrs. Garlton?"

"You needn't be nervous. I won't bite."

She giggled, and Bobby thought of the girls at the flea market who giggled whenever he tried to talk to them.

"I must look a mess. Give me just a few minutes to tidy up then we can talk."

Before Bobby could respond, Nancy Garlton boosted herself up off the floor and walked into the bathroom.

Bloody hell. What do I do now?

For some reason, Bobby thought of John. *What would John do?* Then he knew what John would do. He imagined telling him about it; no doubt he would get a good laugh. But right now, it didn't seem funny.

Bobby stood and stretched his legs. His heart pounded and his mouth felt like sand. Nancy Garlton stayed in the bathroom for a long time. Finally she emerged with new make-up and fresh lipstick.

She looked coyly at Bobby but kept her distance.

"I have to leave now. I have to catch a train. Might we settle the estate on Sunday? Say, three o'clock?"

Bobby exhaled, and a great feeling of relief washed over him.

"Yes, Sunday would be fine."

"Good. We'll meet here."

"Yes, Mrs. Garlton. I mean, Nancy."

"I'll leave some money in the kitchen for cat food."

*　　*　　*

Lathom Hall was a large echo chamber of a room with high ceilings and hardwood floor. It smelled of antiseptic cleaning solution and cigarette smoke. Lathom Hall's Saturday night jive sessions were well attended by the local rabble. The Beatles set up their equipment and tuned their guitars. But there was trouble right from the start.

Ronnie, the non-drummer, had returned determined to ruin another Beatles show. The bouncers hadn't arrived yet, and Ronnie brought a small army of thugs with him.

John cast a nervous glance to the door.

"I hope Allan gets here soon. These punters don't look too friendly."

Bobby could feel the negativity as showtime neared. He kept an eye on Ronnie's gang noticing they were close to the stage, determined to cause some mischief once the music started. Local girls were already in front of the stage, flirting with the band. Paul smiled and eyed the birds while Ronnie glared at him.

John turned around and noticed the girls. He smiled and waved at one of them who waved back. That set Ronnie off.

"Ay! Wot's all this? You flirtin' wif me girl?"

Even though it was barely eight, Ronnie was already drunk and looking for trouble. He screwed up his face and scowled at John.

Ronnie shoved the girl forward toward the stage.

John seemed incredibly calm.

"She's not my type, mate."

"Not yer type? Wots wrong wif 'er? Ya think yer too good for the likes of 'er?

John remained cool.

"I didn't say that. I said she wasn't my type."

"What is yer type?"

John looked at Ronnie's girlfriend as Ronnie clenched his fists and scowled. The rest of the band noticed the confrontation and stopped what they were doing. Bobby waited to see what would happen.

At that moment, Allan Williams and five professional bouncers walked through the door. From the stage John could see them clearly.

"Come on, ya fruit. Ya said she wasn't yer type. Wot is yer type?

John eyed the girl again. Her teased hair and garish make-up exaggerated all her worst traits.

"Human," John said.

The next few minutes were lost in a scuffle of shoving bodies and swinging fists. The bouncers made quick work of Ronnie's boys, and they were escorted off the premises amid shouts of revenge.

"We'll fix it so the bloody Beatles don't come round 'ere again!"

Bobby watched as the band composed themselves and started the show. They wore black leather jackets and tight jeans. They smoked and joked around on stage. Stu didn't even face the audience. He seemed oblivious.

The first song was *Hippy Hippy Shake* followed by *Dizzy Miss Lizzy.* Then came *Rock and Roll Music* and *Memphis,* two Chuck Berry numbers that showcased George's guitar work. John was right, George played Chuck well. The band, though a bit ragged and lacking any sort of professional presentation, were tight in a way that transcended the moment. They simply became the music. Like the impressionists, the Beatles worked in colors and emotion. They were raw and unspoiled. Everything about them was likable.

Bobby was thrilled to hear the songs they had learned from his records. He sat spellbound. Finally, they closed with *Money,* and John dedicated it "to Dust Bin Bob, a man with a great record collection."

Bobby drank in the Barrett Strong number like it was a smooth pint. Under John's direction, it bore scant resemblance to the original. He'd made it a Beatles song. Gone were the keyboards, and in their place, guitars. The music exploded from the amplifiers and blasted the senses. John's frantic vocal galvanized the hall.

"The best things in life are free! But you can give 'em to the birds and bees..."

When John sang it, he meant it. His legs splayed wide in a defiant stance, he belted out the vocal until the veins on his neck stood out. Bobby got goose bumps. He could see John with all the money in the world. The man was a star. Only nobody knew it yet.

The song seemed to last forever. The crowd was glued to the stage. The Beatles wove their magic spell.

As soon as they finished, Bobby was at John's side.

"Absolutely fantastic! I don't believe it! You're the best band in Liverpool!"

Paul lit a ciggy.

"Ha! Not bloody likely. Have you seen Rory Storm and the Hurricanes?"

"No."

"Or Gerry and the Pacemakers?"

"No."

"Or Derry and the Seniors? Or Kingsize Taylor?"

"No and no. I haven't seen anything. Just the Beatles."

John looped an arm around Bobby.

"Well, that's all you really need, isn't it?"

*　　*　　*

Bobby helped carry the amplifiers to the van. Stu and John were talking to some girls near the door.

"Come on, boys. Just a few more trips and we'll have it."

"I'll go with you. Stuart can stay and guard the equipment."

They reentered the hall as Stu stood next to the van. The girls split, and he was alone.

He heard footsteps behind him. Turning, he saw a group of Teds coming toward him.

"Oh, shit," he muttered.

"Well, well, looks like a bloody fairy musician. Hey, fairy!"

Ronnie stepped out of the shadows. Behind him stood Clive and Mick. Stu ran for the door but Ronnie tackled him. Clive and Mick stood him up and punched him repeatedly. Stu crumpled to the street. Clive kicked him in the head.

John walked out the door with Bobby and saw Clive kick Stu as he lay on the ground.

"Hey! Stop that!"

Clive looked up and saw John.

"Him! He's the one I want!"

Bobby ran inside to call the police and summon the bouncers. John bravely faced Clive and Mick.

"Kicking a man when he's down, eh? Right fair, that is. Ya bastard."

"Why don't you do something about it?"

"Hold on, John. I'm with ya," a voice from behind said.

Pete Best, the newest Beatle, stepped up beside John.

"The others are coming."

Clive laughed and kicked Stu again.

John took several running steps and launched himself at Clive. They went down, kicking, punching, and scratching. John fought furiously for a minute.

Pete, who was quick with his fists, held off the other two. Before Clive could seriously hurt John, three bouncers arrived simultaneously with the cops.

As they were separated, Clive hissed, "I knew I'd find you, ya wankin' fairy. Liverpool is a small place. It's only a matter of time until I get my revenge."

The police searched the trio and found illegal flick knives. They called for a paddy wagon and arrested the whole lot.

Bobby helped a groggy Stu back to the van, and the Beatles got out of there quickly.

CHAPTER FOUR

THE DANGLY BITS

"How did they know?"

Bobby shook his head.

"I don't know, but I think we should take Stuart to the hospital."

In the van there had been little talk. Stu sat, dazed and unmoving while John mumbled to himself.

"They had fuckin' knives. They were gonna use 'em on us first chance they got."

"I don't need to go to the hospital," Stu said.

"What do you know? You've been kicked in the bloody head."

"Look, I'm fine. Just a few bruises. I'll be OK."

Bobby blinked. "You could have cracked your cranium. Let the doctors suss it out."

"No, really. I'm not hurt."

John looked at the bruise on the side of Stu's face.

"I don't know, mate. Looks like you got kicked by a horse."

"I'm fine. Just take me home. All I want is to go home. If I feel bad tomorrow, I'll ring up the doctor. Okay?"

John looked around the van.

"Paul? George? What do you think?"

"If he wants to go home," Paul said, "let him go home."

George shrugged.

The Beatles stared out the windows. It had started to rain.

"I still don't know how they found us."

Bobby said, "It could have been a coincidence. They've been known to go out and have a rave now and then."

"They must have known Ronnie and his louts."

"That's possible too. They have friends, criminal friends, all over Liverpool. Maybe they thought they could take on the bouncers. Who knows? Then they saw Stu alone and decided to have some fun and games."

"They know the name of the band now," John muttered.

"Not necessarily. They're both as thick as bricks."

Paul said, "Shit. Is this what we have to worry about for the rest of our days? Every time we play a gig do we have to worry about getting our heads kicked in?"

John watched raindrops, driven by wind, trailing down the window.

"Thank God for Hamburg."

* * *

Nancy Garlton looked different. She'd had her hair done in a modern style with a slightly different shade. Her conservative navy blue dress was gone in favor of a shorter, tighter, black skirt and sweater. On her feet, black high heels.

"Hello, Mrs. Garlton."

"Hello, Robert. Call me Nancy. Please come in."

Bobby saw the wine glasses and candles before he'd even cleared the door.

"What's all this, then?"

Nancy smiled. "It's my way of saying thank you for a good job, but most of all for being a friend."

A look of confusion crossed Bobby's face.

"It was nothing, really."

"Suffice it to say, I thought after we complete our business, a little toast would be in order."

Bobby raised an eyebrow.

"A toast?"

"Why not?"

"Why not, indeed."

Bobby opened his file and put the receipts on the table. He perused his ledger.

"I've listed the amount of sale, the client, the date, and I've computed my commission on the last column."

He handed her the ledger, and she read it carefully, nodding from time to time.

"This is most professional. Very thorough. I'm shocked at how much money you were able to get. Most of those things were pretty shopworn."

"Depends on who you're selling it to."

"You've earned a tidy commission. Will a personal check do?"

"Yes, that would be fine."

She put down the ledger and got out her checkbook. She wrote out Bobby's check in a tiny, perfectly straight hand as dainty as it was strong. She tore it from the book carefully and handed it to him.

"Now, let's have that toast."

Bobby folded the check and put it in his pocket. He watched as she opened a bottle of red wine and poured two glasses. He didn't know much about wine, but he assumed by the look of the label that it was first rate. She handed him a glass.

"Here's to Robert Dingle."

Bobby blushed.

"And here's to Nancy Garlton."

They clinked their glasses together and drank. Bobby watched Nancy's throat as she swallowed, noticing the curve of her neck as it met her shoulder, the smooth planes of her upper back beneath the sweater, and the modest valley between her breasts. She smiled at him through her glass.

Inside Bobby's head, alarms were going off. *This is barmy. I'll go to hell and fry like a chicken for this.*

"Go on, drink," she said.

Bobby took a tentative sip.

"It's good."

He continued to sip until he'd drained a third of his glass. Nancy refilled it before he could object.

"I'm not used to wine, especially at this hour."

"You should cultivate a taste for it. It could serve you well in the coming years. A cultured man can go far, Robert. As far as his imagination can take him."

Nancy proposed a toast.

"Impropriety is the soul of wit. Somerset Maugham, *The Moon and Sixpence*."

"To the toppermost of the poppermost. John Lennon, Beatles."

"I'm afraid I don't quite understand."

"John Lennon is a musician friend of mine. He said that."

Nancy drank her second glass of wine quickly urging Bobby along, sip by sip, until he felt a bit warm around the ears. A rosy glow came to Nancy's cheeks and Bobby's eyes sparkled.

"Tell me about this musician friend of yours. What's he like?"

"Oh, he's a real card. Always the crack-up. He runs a tight little beat group and they're really quite good. There's something special about these boys. I can't put my finger on it, but I get this great sense of destiny when I see them."

"Destiny?"

"Yeah, I can't explain it. These guys have such passion, and so much spirit, it's amazing. I've never seen anything like it."

"Nothing great was ever achieved without passion."

"They're called the Beatles."

"What a dreadful name! Like the crawly insects in my roses?"

"They spell it with an A. Beatles, as in beat."

"Clever."

Nancy refilled their glasses yet again. Bobby took a longer drink. He felt very relaxed.

"My late husband played the bagpipes."

Bobby looked at Nancy and they both exploded into hysterical laughter. The harder Bobby laughed, the harder Nancy laughed. A knot of tension burst, releasing something inside. Their laughing jag continued for several minutes until it trailed off into a cough and a sniff. Bobby's eyes watered.

"That's hilarious."

"What? My late husband played the bagpipes?"

That initiated a second burst of laughter.

"Please... No more. You're killing me."

The laughter sputtered and died as Nancy straightened herself.

"Would you like a cigarette?"

"Sure..."

Nancy took two cigarettes out of a silver case and handed one to Bobby. He lit hers first like he'd seen Charles Boyer do in a movie.

Nancy's personality changed with the cigarette. She took a long drag and exhaled slowly. Bobby watched the smoke curl away from her lips.

"Do you have any girlfriends?" she asked.

"Girlfriends? Well, not really. I mean, I know some girls, and we go out, but... I don't have what you'd call a real girlfriend."

"Have you ever made love to a girl?"

Bobby blushed and almost dropped his cigarette.

"I don't think that's a very good question."

Suddenly Nancy was right in front of him.

"I think it's a very good question."

She slipped her arms around his neck and pulled his astonished face to hers. She led him into the kiss, and he followed, not knowing where it would go. As she kissed him, she pressed her body against his.

Once the kiss broke, she whispered in his ear.

"I can tell everything about you, Robert. Everything. I can tell, for instance, that you're a virgin. My first experience was somewhat less desirable than yours will be. I was taken against my will."

"Jesus H. Christ."

Her finger traced a circle on his shoulder.

"I will teach you, Robert Dingle, everything a young man should know about the art of making love."

Bobby stammered, dumbfounded. "Ah, uhm. Well, ah. It's just that... Should we be doing this? It doesn't seem right."

Nancy cut him off. Her voice trembled slightly.

"I don't care. Do you hear me? I don't care what's right. If what I'm feeling is wrong, then damn being right. Life is so fleeting. You haven't been around long enough to understand the transitory nature of our lives. Experiences, memories, feelings, that's all that we have left after you strip everything away. Don't you see, Robert? In the end, that's all you're left with."

Bobby noticed a microscopic tear form in the corner of her eye. Her voice modulated down a bit.

"Perhaps I'm just being selfish. Perhaps I still want a few more memories, a few more pleasant experiences to take away with me. Someday you'll understand this moment."

"But, Nancy..."

"You find me attractive, don't you, Robert?"

He knew this question had great consequence to her.

"Yes, of course," he said.

"Then make me happy, Robert. For God's sake! Can't you see I'm dying?"

When John Lennon heard the story he laughed until he ran out of breath.
"You boffed 'er? The old bird went barmy on yer?"

"Please, John. I only told you because I thought you'd understand."

John had resorted to his scouse accent, something Bobby loathed because
it sounded so much like his brothers.

"Oh, I understand all right. You got in a little bayonet practice. Your
dangly bits needed a good workout. Tell me, el Dustino, what was it like?
Were her tits all wrinkly?"

Bobby hadn't seen the cruel side of John, and it surprised him.

"For God's sake, John I don't like being the butt of your jokes. If I'd known
you were going to be like that, I never would have confided in you. I won't say
another word about it. Had you been in my shoes, you'd have done exactly
the same. And don't tell me you wouldn't! I know you, John Lennon."

"Nobody knows me, Dustman."

Bobby felt wounded.

"I'll never tell you anything again."

John shook his head. "Look, I'm sorry. I didn't mean to ruffle your
feathers. I just thought it was funny. How old did you say she was?"

"I don't know. Forties, maybe. It's tough to tell."

"You dog, you."

"I still can't believe it happened."

John picked up his guitar and started to improvise *The Adventures of
Dust Bin Bob and His Dangly Bits.*

*Oh, Dust Bin Bob got a silly old fobAnd he humped to a high degreeTill
Dust Bin Bob got a blister on his knobAnd a bruise upon his knee...*

"All right! That's about enough!" Bobby shouted. "You can be quite the
cutthroat, Lennon."

John laughed. "Ha! Feeling the heat of the old Lennon psychological
meat grinder. Don't be too alarmed, Dr. Dustenstein. Many a man has fallen
victim to my rapier wit. I'm known for my sharp put-downs and scathing
send-ups."

"I'll remember you for your ego and for being an absolute asshole."

John ignored the remark and turned on his phonograph. A Clovers'
record was already on the turntable. John carefully lifted the stylus onto the
outer groove of the vinyl and expertly dropped it. *Love Potion Number Nine*
came rumbling out of the speaker.

John began bopping along to the music. Bobby stood in the middle of the room with his hands on his hips, trying to keep his righteous indignation from evaporating.

"Hey! I was talking to you!"

John turned the volume down.

"Excuse me? Did you say something?"

*   *   *

Bobby visited his bank account in Woolton and deposited his commission money. He took a little out to leave with John's Aunt Mimi, and a little more to take with him. His ribs were healed and he no longer felt pain when he moved.

Time to go.

CHAPTER FIVE

ROBBY THE LIMEY

Bobby went back into his room once more during the day when he knew Clive and Mick would be gone. He took what he needed which wasn't much - just some clothes and a few odds and ends. He threw his belongings into a seaman's duffle bag and slung it over his shoulder.

As he crept down the stairs, he heard his father come into the shop below. He made a spontaneous decision to talk to him. He wasn't sure what he'd say even as he turned the doorknob.

"Er... Dad?"

"That you, Bobby?"

"Yes, sir. I wanted to have a word, if that's okay."

Robert Dingle Sr. was a big man with a florid face and a crooked tooth. His newsboy cap covered a bald spot in the middle of a forest of wiry white hair. He eyed Bobby's duffel bag.

"You goin' somewhere, lad?"

Bobby nodded. "Yeah... I'm leaving. I'm goin' to sea."

"What the hell for?"

"Clive and Mick got a bit rough with me, beat me up and broke some ribs. That's why I haven't been around."

"I heard about that. I also heard you were layin' low somewhere in town."

"Yeah, well... I think they mean to do me even more harm, so I've decided to disappear for a while. I filled out the forms and got a job as an apprentice steward. I'm shippin' out."

Bobby could see how tired his father looked, how beaten. Robert Dingle Sr. sighed. His face sagged.

"That's it then? You just walk out and leave and it's as simple as one-two-three? It don't seem right, son."

"It hurts me too, dad. I wish I didn't have to do it, but I just can't live like this anymore. Mick and Clive are just impossible. It's only a matter of time before they do me in."

His father lowered his voice. "I won't tell them where you went."

"There's something wrong with those two. They're just plain mean. It's like they enjoy it, ya know?"

"I don't know what went wrong. They were nice lads when they were little, wouldn't hurt a fly."

Bobby faced his father in the awkward silence. Anxious to begin his new life, suddenly he was reluctant to let the old one go. He wanted to say something profound, something memorable, but his mouth was empty.

"Well, I guess that's it, then."

His father looked worried.

"Take care of yourself, son."

"I will."

His father crossed the floor and held out his arms. Bobby couldn't remember the last time they'd hugged. He stepped into the embrace like a man going through a very small door. His father's sudden tenderness took him by surprise.

"I was hopin' you would take over the shop one day."

"I still can. For God sakes, dad, I'm not goin' away forever. I'll be back in a couple of months."

Robert Dingle Sr. closed his eyes.

"There's a damn good chance I'll never see you again."

"Nonsense. I'll be back before you know it. I'm just goin' to sea, not off to war. I'll miss you, dad."

"I'll miss you too, son. And, if it's any consolation, I'm sorry for what they done, those two. Truly sorry. Damn them. Damn them both."

Bobby felt a lump in his throat.

"Thanks, dad..."

"You're a good boy, Bobby. You've got a good heart and you're smart. I know whatever you do, wherever you go, you'll do well. Stay away from trouble and keep a clean nose. Godspeed."

*   *   *

Bobby got himself a job on the *Pilgrim's Progress*, a Cunard merchant vessel of English registry bound for Baltimore. At first Bobby hated it; the boat seemed like a seagoing prison. The groaning of the hull and the constant rising and falling of the deck took some getting used to. In time he grew to enjoy the predictable life of a seaman. The *Pilgrim's Progress* had a small library, and Bobby began reading everything from detective novels to repair manuals. The quiet, contemplative atmosphere gave Bobby time to think. And, of course, he had his music. Many of the sailors had records, and the phonograph in the galley seemed to go twenty-four hours a day. Jazz, American pop, R&B, blues, rock and roll, and country became the soundtrack for Bobby's apprenticeship.

Assigned as a galley-mate, Bobby was always within earshot of something. He spent hours peeling potatoes to Charlie Parker and Dizzy Gillespie, days washing dishes to Hank Williams, weeks cleaning the stove to Frank Sinatra. Bobby learned about people too. He discovered a whole subculture under the ship's deck; men from all places and backgrounds thrown together for months at time. Some were desperate, some were fools, some were restless wanderers, but none of them seemed happy. To Bobby, those not running away were running to something. A restless energy bubbled behind the monotony of life on the ship.

When the *Pilgrim's Progress* docked at the Patapsco River Docks in Baltimore, Bobby explored the city as if he were the first man walking on Mars. A group of shipmates told him about the infamous stretch of Baltimore Street known as "The Block," a short walk away.

There, he wandered through the dazzle of neon, passing the strip joints as live music blared onto the streets. Saxophones and snare drums reverberated off the concrete. Hucksters shouted at him to come inside. Nervous people ducked in and out of alleys and pornographic magazine shops. He rounded a corner and stepped into Livingston Loans, the largest pawnshop on "The Block." The walls were lined with guitars; the display windows sparkled with cameras, watches, jewelry, saxophones, trumpets, and other musical instruments. Bobby stared at the walls, dazzled by the overwhelming array. The place could have never existed in Liverpool.

"What can I do for you?" asked a gruff man eating a pastrami sandwich.

Bobby tried not to look at the dab of mustard on his chin.

"I wanted to look at some guitars."

The man took a bite of his sandwich and spoke while he chewed.

"You English?"

"Yeah."

A few crumbs fell onto the man's prodigious stomach. He wore a loose tie and an open shirt, and Bobby could see the bulge of a revolver under his waistcoat.

"I could tell by your accent. We get a lot of Limeys in here. It's cause my prices are so fuckin' good. You got any money?"

Bobby nodded.

The man put his sandwich down and wiped his hands on a brown paper bag.

"Well, then. Let me show you the merchandise. Are you interested in an electric or an acoustic? I got both. With the electric, you're gonna need an amp. I can make you a sweet deal on a nice amp too. I got all kinds."

Bobby stared at the gallery of guitars.

"I don't know."

"By the way, I'm Manny. Pleased to meet cha."

Bobby looked down to see a greasy hand extended. Bobby accepted the handshake tentatively.

"Manny Brillstein," the man said. "They call me Manny B, pawn it with me! See? It rhymes."

"I see. Let's look at some acoustic guitars then, Manny."

"You want steel string or nylon? Classical or country?"

Bobby pointed at a guitar hanging on the wall.

"How about that one?"

Manny took it down and placed it on the counter.

"This one's a Kay. Got steel strings, a pick guard, six tuning pegs, reinforced neck, the whole nine yards. I can give it to ya cheap. Seventy-five dollars."

"Seems a bit much."

Manny scratched his head.

"I'm not supposed to do this, but since it's gettin' late and I'm about ready to close up, tell you what I'll do. I'll give you this guitar for sixty dollars."

Bobby's attention was drawn to a young man on the other side of the store sitting on a low stool, holding an electric guitar. He was tall and lean and possessed an amazing, gravity-defying, bleached blond pompadour haircut. Its upswept elegance framed an angular, pleasant face. He chewed gum vigorously. As Bobby watched, he plugged the guitar cord into a nearby amp. As soon as the tubes in the amp warmed up, the guy began to play what sounded to Bobby vaguely like Chuck Berry music.

"Aw, for Christ sake, Clovis. This ain't a fuckin' playground for you deadbeats. Knock it off."

"But I'm lookin' to buy, Manny."

"Buy, my ass. You got no money."

"I been workin'."

"Do you think I'm blind? You been sittin' on yer ass drinkin' all day. Now get outta here."

Clovis unplugged the cord, turned off the amp, and hung the guitar on the wall behind him.

"You in a bad mood or somethin'?"

"Go!"

"Shit, Manny. I'm goin'. Just want to light my cigarette first."

Clovis had a pack of Luckies folded into the short, tight sleeve of his white T-shirt. He popped the pack, tapped out a ciggy, and stuck it in his mouth.

"You got a match, mister?"

Bobby felt in his pockets and found a wooden ship's match. He handed it to Clovis. Clovis struck it on the side of the counter and it exploded into flame.

"You must be off that big boat that just come in."

"Yeah, the *Pilgrim's Progress*. From Liverpool."

Clovis lit his Lucky Strike with the crackling torch then shook it out. The pungent smell of the match lingered in the air in front of Bobby's face.

"You gonna buy that piece of shit?" He nodded at the guitar.

"Clovis!" Manny barked. "I'm makin' a sale here!"

"Then why don't you sell him something good, so he don't hate your guts later."

Bobby said, "Like what?"

Clovis walked across the shop and pulled an old, scratched up Gibson acoustic off the wall.

"Like this."

He handed the guitar to Bobby. It was well scuffed, and the finish on the neck had completely worn off from use, but it did have the look of a well-made instrument.

"Kay guitars are junk. Gibson is what you really want. This here baby will take you anywhere you want to go. I happen to know that Manny's had this one layin' around for awhile, and he'd probably make you a deal on it since it's kinda beat-up. But look at how much better it plays."

Clovis played the opening riff to *That'll Be The Day* by Buddy Holly and the Crickets. The guitar sounded as clear as a bell. Bobby was surprised how professional Clovis sounded. He'd heard John play exactly the same riff, although not as well.

"Are you a professional musician?"

"Used to be until I got fired from The Thunderbirds. Name's Clovis Hicks."

Clovis waved a casual salute like Marlon Brando in *The Wild One*.

"I'm Bobby Dingle. Why did they fire you? Looks like you're pretty good."

"Drinkin'."

Clovis handed the Gibson to Bobby. It smelled of stale cigarette smoke. Bobby held it as if he could play, enjoying the sensation. He remembered how John held his guitar.

"Well, I'll take your advice on this Gibson."

"You can't go wrong. It's a J45. Probably 'bout fifteen years old. Somebody played the shit out of it. I've had my eye on that rascal for weeks, but... Aw, hell, who am I foolin'? It's like Manny says, I ain't got no money. Ain't gonna get none either. How come you're buyin' a guitar? You gonna learn to play that thing?"

Bobby ran his fingers down the fret board. There were hairline cracks in the finish on the headstock. The front was a faded sunburst.

"I've got a lot of time on my hands at sea. It would be nice to have the guitar to mess about."

Manny slapped the glass counter top with the palm of his meaty hand.

"Hey! I'm the salesman here! You want this guitar? It's gonna cost you."

"How much?"

Manny's eyes narrowed.

"One twenty-five, plus the case."

Bobby kept a poker face.

"That's more than I can spend."

Clovis chimed in. "Offer him fifty-five."

"No! One ten. That's it. I can't go any lower."

"Sixty-five."

Manny wrung his hands.

"You're killin' me here. OK, hot shot, ninety, plus the case. That's the best I can do."

"How much is the case?"

"Twenty."

"Throw in the case for eighty-five."

For a moment Bobby thought Manny might cry. His face twitched and he sighed so deeply it sounded like steam escaping from a broken pipe.

"Sold."

"Yee-ha!" Clovis whooped. "You bought yourself a git-box, boy! A nice one too!"

Clovis followed Bobby out onto Baltimore Street. Bobby carried his new guitar in its case, feeling very self-conscious.

"Where ya goin', buddy?"

"I don't know. Back to the ship, I guess."

"I could show you some chords on that thing. All you gotta do is buy me a couple drinks. Deal?"

Bobby contemplated spending time with Clovis and was about to say no when they walked past a strip club where an extremely buxom woman stood at the front door. A neon sign in the shape of a clock over the door at 414 East Baltimore Street said The Two O'Clock Club.

"Hey! Blaze! Blaze Starr! How're ya doin', baby?"

"Clovis, you old swamp rat. They fire you again?"

"Yep. But they'll come a-crawlin' back. You can bet on it. Ain't nobody on The Block plays like Clovis."

Bobby couldn't help but notice Blaze Starr's oversized breasts. They spilled out of her silver bustier like five pounds of cotton bursting from a one-pound sack. Her hair peaked at the crown then cascaded down the small of her back in a voluminous brunette avalanche. Her lips were impossibly pouty and painted the reddest red Bobby had ever seen.

"Who's your cute friend?"

"This boy? He's English."

"What's your name, hon?"

"Robert Dingle, ma'am."

Blaze looked Bobby up and down approvingly.

"Robby, the Limey, eh? What do you have there? Is that a guitar or a machine gun?"

"A guitar."

"Another guitar player, no less. I love musicians. Ain't that right, Clovis?"

"It sure is, Blaze. You love me, and I'm a musician."

Blaze put a bejeweled hand on Clovis' shoulder.

"This guy used to play in the band behind me while I danced."

"I had the best seat in the house. Half an acre of creamy white ass a-twitchin' in front of me. Thought I'd died and gone to heaven."

Bobby tried not to stare, but it seemed as if Blaze Starr was made to stare at.

"Don't be shy, little boy. You want to look at my titties? Go ahead. Take a good look. Guys pay good money for that."

She thrust her breasts toward him. Bobby blushed.

"Aw, look, he's embarrassed. Isn't that sweet? Hey, it's kinda slow right now. Why don't you guys come on in and have a drink on me?"

Clovis grabbed Bobby's hand and pulled him toward the door.

"Come on, pardner. Offers like that don't come everyday."

Blaze called after them. "Don't you go botherin' Erlene, Clovis! She's workin'!"

Bobby's heart raced as he looked at the framed photos that lined the entrance. They were black-and-white glamour studio portraits of famous striptease artists with names that seemed larger than life like Tempest Storm and Blaze Starr.

Bobby had never been in a strip club and didn't really know how to behave. It took his eyes a few minutes to adjust to the dark. The place smelled like cigar smoke. A live band with sax, bass, drums, and guitar ground out a slow blues behind a bored looking stripper. Her routine consisted mostly of bending over; pendulous breasts swinging in the front, bountiful ass swaying in the rear. A spotlight followed her across the stage and down the runway.

There were only a few customers scattered among the tables.

"Hey, pardner! Let's sit right over there next to the stage. I want to talk to Erlene."

"Erlene?"

"Right. She's onstage right now."

Bobby was flabbergasted.

"You actually know her?"

"Damn right I know her. We was datin' steady back when I had a gig."

Clovis led Bobby to the center front table. Bobby felt self-conscious being right down in front, but Clovis didn't seem to care. He plopped down in the first chair and leered at Erlene. She turned around and gave him the rear-end view. As she bent over, Bobby heard her break wind with a robust trumpet salute.

"Hey! What the fuck? She farted on me! Jesus Christ! Hey, Erlene, what's the big deal? Is that how you greet me?"

Erlene looked back over her shoulder at Clovis.

"Hi, hon. Where ya been?"

Clovis waved at the air.

"Phew! That was real lady-like, Erlene."

The music stopped and Erlene straightened. The band stood and shuffled off toward the bar.

"Break time."

Erlene jumped off the stage and sat down next to Clovis and Bobby. She slipped off her high heels and put her feet up on the table.

"My dogs are barkin'," she said with a hoarse southern accent. "Did you find a job yet?"

Clovis hung his head.

"Nah, I can't get no work."

"Well, I ain't havin' no deadbeat boyfriends. You got that? Ain't no use comin' 'round here and tryin' to act all nice. That shit don't work no more. I told ya, no job, no Erlene."

"Aw, honey, don't be like that. How about a little kiss for old times sake?"

"The only thing you can kiss is my ass."

Clovis chuckled. "Well, that would normally be a pleasure but not after the way you greeted me."

Bobby watched their interaction with the enthusiasm of an anthropologist. This was true Americana, the kind he'd always daydreamed about: a striptease artist arguing with her guitar-playing ex-boyfriend. Bobby found their accents compelling. He wanted to hear more. Their southern-fried dialogue might have been written by a drunken Tennessee Williams. *All that was missing was the banjo.*

"Who's he?" Erlene asked, nodding to Bobby.

"Another worthless guitar player?"

"Him? Oh, no. He's Robby, the Limey. Chicks love him."

Bobby smiled at Erlene. He didn't know what to say.

"That true?" Erlene asked.

Bobby shrugged. "I don't know."

Clovis leaned over and whispered something in Erlene's ear. Erlene laughed and looked at Bobby again with wider eyes.

A waitress brought two shots of Jack Daniels and two beers.

"Compliments of the house," she mumbled. "Shot of Jack, beer back."

Clovis waved at Blaze Starr who stood near the entrance.

"Thanks, baby! I'm gonna remember you in my will."

Erlene snorted. "Don't bother."

"At least somebody around here respects me."

Erlene boldly unrolled Clovis's T-shirt sleeve and removed the pack of Luckies. She helped herself to one and lit it with a pack of complimentary matches from the bar. Bobby studied her face while she smoked. He couldn't tell if she hated Clovis or loved him. Her face broadcast mixed messages; hard, yet soft, tough, yet gentle. Part of her didn't belong here and part of her did. Bobby hadn't seen that before, except in John.

And then there was her voice; Bette Davis rough and southern smooth which made everything sound exotic.

"Blaze don't respect you. She feels sorry for you, ya big dope. Look at you. You're a real basket case."

Clovis picked up his glass, the insults sliding off of him like tiny ice cubes.

"Here's mud in yo' eye!"

He drank it in one swallow, letting his throat burn for a moment before washing it down with a cool swig of beer. Bobby tried to do the same but the Jack took several attempts.

"Listen, hon, could you do me a favor? Limey Rob is new in town and I thought maybe you could fix him up."

Bobby looked up.

"What?"

Erlene chuckled. "What kind of fool do you take me for? Jesus Christ, Clovis. You got a lot of nerve comin' around here, tryin' to get dates for your buddies! What do I look like? A whore house?"

"I missed ya, Erlene. I really did."

"Fuck off, Clovis."

Erlene stood up and walked away. Bobby watched her go. She walked like a Cadillac steering through Fords and Chevys.

"She's crazy about me," Clovis said.

"Why on earth would you ask her to get me a date?"

Clovis snapped his fingers.

"Don't mention it, pardner. I always take care of my boys."

Bobby looked horrified.

"I appreciate it, Clovis, I really do. But in the future, don't speak for me. I can take care of myself."

Clovis whistled. "Hey, no offense, but I can tell by the way you act that you ain't never even talked to a professional stripper before. I'm just tryin' to school ya."

The band began to drift back to the shallow orchestra pit in front of the stage. Bobby watched them take up positions.

"Clovis-" Bobby began to say something, then stopped.

The music started and a new stripper tottered out on high heels. Bobby wanted to leave. They'd finished their drinks and Bobby decided not to buy the next one. He knew Clovis didn't have any money.

A few minutes later Clovis said, "How about that drink?"

"I'm going back to the ship."

Clovis pointed at the guitar.

"Don't you want to learn how to play that thing?"

"I'll figure it out."

Clovis thought for a moment.

"Oh, I get it. This is not your scene. You must be more into that beatnik thing. I can dig that. I know some caves."

Bobby didn't understand.

"I'm afraid you lost me there."

"A cave. You know. A coffee house with folk music and cute little chicks in black tights."

"I should be going now."

Clovis put a hand on Bobby's shoulder.

"Hold on, man. I know a place uptown where we can groove, and I'll give you a guitar lesson."

Bobby considered Clovis' offer. He'd surprised himself by sticking with the guy, buying a guitar and going to a strip club. Pushing on seemed like madness. Yet the thought of more adventure intrigued him. And he really wanted to learn some chords.

"Where is it?"

"It ain't far. We could catch a bus or walk."

"I'll think about it."

Bobby stood and picked up his guitar case. Clovis clapped his hands.

"Hot damn! We're a-goin' to Flipsville!"

Bobby exited the Two O'Clock Club and continued down East Baltimore Street toward the dock. Clovis followed, a few paces behind.

Bobby said, "I'm not lending you any money."

Clovis wrung his hands.

"Money? Who said anything about money?"

"Well, you don't have any. The only guy with cash is me which means I'm going to wind up paying for everything."

"Hey, you got me all wrong, man. I don't want any money. That's not my thing. Moneys a drag. I got my heart and my hands. I can take care of myself."

Bobby stopped walking.

"What did you whisper to Erlene back at the club?"

Clovis' grin threatened to split his face.

"I told her you had a giant schlong."

CHAPTER SIX

BEATNIK WOMEN FROM THE MOON

When the bus came Bobby paid Clovis' fare. They got off the bus at the corner of Read Street and Charles and walked half a block to a basement bookstore. A dirty window reflected the lower half of Bobby's body until Clovis led him down a short flight of stairs into the low ceilinged room. It smelled of old paper and tobacco smoke.

They walked through the small bookshop, then through a short hallway. The door at the end had an eyehole in it.

Clovis whispered, "Back during prohibition this place was an honest to God speakeasy. The bookshop was just a front. Peabody Book Shop, man. It's got some history."

They entered a second room with a fireplace and half a dozen tables.

Like the Jacaranda back home in Liverpool, the Peabody was a student hangout. Art students from the Maryland Institute mixed with music students from the Peabody Institute. A scholarly, yet homey, atmosphere permeated the place. Bobby wondered how Clovis fit in here.

"Let's grab a table and open up that git-box."

Bobby threaded his way back to the only open table. He put his guitar case up and eyed a couple of girls sitting nearby. One of the girls, a petite brunette with hair down the middle of her back, smiled at him.

"See? What did I tell ya?" Clovis beamed. "Chicks, baby! Beatnik women from the moon! Ya gotta love 'em!"

Bobby sat down.

"What's with you? Are you some kind of crazy Casanova? All you care about is women."

"No, that's not true. I care about drinkin', hell-raisin', and guitar pickin' too."

Bobby opened the case and removed his precious cargo. The Gibson gleamed. It looked completely different from the instrument he'd bought at Livingston Loans. Now it seemed cooler. Bobby caught the stale smell of it and his nostrils flared. Like the Peabody, Bobby sensed the guitar had some history too.

"Gimme that thing," Clovis said.

As soon as it shifted from Bobby's hands to Clovis', its new personality came into focus. Clovis commanded respect from the guitar. In his hands, it came alive. His strong fingers wrapped around the neck and hammered down on the frets with authority. He adjusted the tuning.

Clovis fingerpicked a folk song. People stopped what they were doing and listened. Clovis played the intricate melody softly, yet evenly, from start to finish. Bobby had once heard a variation of the song played by a skiffle group but had never heard it like this. Clovis' guitar style was honest and direct. He concentrated on the strings with monk-like intensity.

Bobby noticed the girls watching. *So this is what it's like. I think I'm going to like being a musician.*

Clovis ended the song and several people clapped, including the girls. Clovis waved at their table.

"Hey, why dontcha come on over here so you can hear better?"

To Bobby's complete surprise, two of the three girls sitting at the other table rose and walked toward them. Bobby stood up, his mind racing.

Before he could decide on a greeting, Clovis said, "I'm Clovis and this is Robby the Limey. He's English."

"Really?" the petite one said. "What part of England?"

"Liverpool."

She smiled again and Bobby found himself lost in her perfect face. She wore very little make-up; her natural beauty colored her face with a pleasant, easygoing loveliness. Her slightly oversized lips had a Bardot-like quality that Bobby found mesmerizing.

"This is his guitar," Clovis said, pointing at Bobby. "It's a beaut, ain't it? Gibson. The best. He's just in from Europe."

"Hi, I'm Cricket."

It took Bobby a moment to realize she was holding her hand out. Once he'd processed that bit of information, he took her tiny hand. Her skin was soft and smooth to his touch. Her fingers were slender and pale.

"I'm Bobby Dingle. He's Clovis Hicks."

"This is my friend, Bonnie."

Clovis seized the moment and started another song. They all sat down to listen. When he finished Bonnie asked where he'd learned to play so well.

"In jail," Clovis said casually.

"Really? You've been in jail? For what?"

There was a twinkle in Clovis' eye.

"Stealin' cars when I was a kid. No big deal, but I did do some time. There was an old guy in there who taught me the blues. I realized everything was the blues; country, rock and roll, folk, jazz, bluegrass, it's all just the blues."

Bobby could tell that the girls were impressed.

Cricket said to Bobby, "Why don't you play a song?"

"I've never been to jail," Bobby deadpanned. "But I have been to see the Beatles at Lathom Hall."

Cricket laughed. "That's funny. I have no idea what that meant, but I love your accent."

Clovis looked at Bobby oddly.

"What the hell are you talkin' about, man?"

"The Beatles. A couple of Teddy boys jumped Stu and kicked him in the head."

"What the hell? Beetles? Teddy bears?"

"Not Teddy bears, Teddy boys. You know, juvenile delinquents. Rough trade and all that."

Clovis winked at Bonnie.

"Must be an English thing."

Cricket seemed interested.

"What's a beetle?"

The image of John Lennon on stage came to Bobby's mind.

"Not what, who. The Beatles are a beat group back home in Liverpool. They play American rock and roll."

"Well, we've already got American rock and roll, performed by American rock and rollers," Clovis said with a smirk. "Don't make much sense to me."

Bobby nodded. "Yeah, here. But over there, it's pretty exotic."

"Now, if they played bluegrass, then you'd have somethin'."

"What's Liverpool like?" Cricket asked.

Bobby wondered how old she was. Her American accent made ordinary words sound like the names of tropical flowers. She had the scent of sophistication, something he hadn't noticed in other girls.

"Liverpool is a lot like Baltimore except it's about four thousand miles away. It's a port city too. Working-class, honest people, good sense of humor. I think you'd like it."

"Do they have art schools there?"

"Oh, yeah. I know some art schoolers. Some of the Beatles are in art school."

"You keep talking about these beetles. Sounds buggy. What's the fascination?"

"They're a beat group."

Bobby wanted to explain to Cricket, but trying to tell a stranger about something as magical as the Beatles seemed impossible. Instead, he changed the subject.

"Cricket is an interesting name."

"It's a nickname my father gave me when I was a kid. My real name is Bernice which I hate. You can see why I use Cricket. Hey, do you want to pose for me? I've got a project due tomorrow. I'm supposed to do a portrait of somebody I don't know but would like to know."

Bobby blushed. "I'm flattered."

"We'll have to go back to my place. All my supplies are there. It's only a few blocks away. My roomie won't mind. What do you say?"

Bobby was again amazed at his good fortune.

"Of course."

"Maybe we can all go," Clovis said hopefully. "We could get a bottle of wine."

Bonnie shook her head.

"I have to go home. I've got early classes. You two just go along."

"What about me?" Clovis said.

"What about you? Looks like you're the odd man out," Bobby said.

*   *   *

Cricket and Bobby walked down Read Street in the direction of her apartment. Bobby made easy conversation trying to be cool. His heartbeat accelerated at the prospect of being alone with Cricket. She seemed so delicate, so incredibly feminine, and her voice rang like chimes. She clutched a wooden box of watercolor paints under one arm. Bobby offered several times to carry it, but she refused.

Bobby wanted to slip his arm around her waist and pull her close. Once or twice their hands brushed, but Cricket ignored the contact. She seemed aloof.

Bobby willed himself to act casually as if this sort of thing happened to him every day.

Waiting for the traffic to pass on the corner, Cricket looked at him and smiled.

"So is it true what they say about sailors? That they have a girl in every port?"

Bobby's eyes twinkled.

"A loaded question, that one is. Well, it's not true. Most of the crewmen are married."

From the corner of his eye, Bobby saw two men behind them. Something about the way they moved struck Bobby as vaguely menacing. Feeling protective, he stepped closer to Cricket.

Bobby and Cricket started to cross the street and the two men stayed behind them. When they got to the corner and started down the next block, the men hurried past them. Bobby slipped his arm around Cricket and she leaned against him. Whatever inhibitions prevented him before had evaporated.

The men were at least ten years older than Bobby, dressed in dirty jeans and leather jackets like Teddy boys only more sinister. Bobby recognized the look in their eyes. He'd seen it before in his brothers. Both were bigger than Bobby, and one had a scar on his cheek. The other wore a knit cap.

The one with the scar said, "What's yer rush? Where you goin', little lady?"

"Home," Cricket said.

"Is that where the party is?"

Bobby could smell liquor.

Cricket's answer came quickly. "No."

The man talking turned towards Bobby.

"What about you, sweetheart? Why don't you get a haircut? Don't you know you look like a girl?"

"I'm getting one tomorrow. I've been at sea."

The two adult delinquents exchanged a glance.

"What do I hear? Is that what I think it is?"

Bobby shrugged. "What?"

"An English accent. Well, fuck my old boots! A limey! You wanna know something? I hate limeys. They're all a bunch of faggots. And you're a musician too. That's even worse."

Bobby considered a reply but held his tongue.

"I'm right, right? You're a ball-kissin', ass-slappin', guitar playin', little girlie-boy Englishman, ain't cha?"

"Well, if you put it that way..."

Scarface stepped close to Bobby, until their noses were only inches apart. "Gimme the guitar."

Cricket put her arm between them.

"Hey, back off, creep."

The one with the knit cap grabbed her wrist and twisted it.

"Let go of me! I'm warning you!"

He laughed. "You're warnin' me."

"Leave her out of this," Bobby said forcefully.

Scarface wrapped his hand around Bobby's collar and stood him up until Bobby was on his tiptoes. Bobby held onto the handle of the guitar case, his knuckles turning white.

"What are you gonna do about it, punk?"

Bobby looked at Cricket and saw that the other guy still had a grip on her wrist. He looked back into Scarface's eyes and saw Clive. For a moment Bobby felt outside his body. His fear vanished and a Zen-like calm vibrated in his chest.

Bobby spoke calmly. "I guess I'll do whatever I have to do to convince you two gentlemen to leave us alone and go away."

"Christ, don't you sound like a lawyer! He called us gentlemen. Damn, that's a pisser! Ain't gonna happen though. Your ass is grass."

Cricket wrenched her hand free.

"That's enough! You two assholes want to fight? Right here on Read Street? Then come on, let's go!"

Cricket's tiny frame shook with the power of her words. She stood defiantly, shoulders square and chin thrust courageously forward. Her nostrils flared.

Bobby's jaw dropped.

The look of surprise on their faces, elongated by the harsh shadows created by the streetlight, had a surreal edge. Scarface relaxed his grip on Bobby's collar. Bobby's weight sunk back onto his heels.

For a moment time seemed suspended. The man with the knit cap put his hands on Cricket's shoulders and shook her.

"You're gonna fight us? I'd like to see youse try! You talk big for a..."

The last word was cut off with a sharp grunt. Cricket moved like a fire dancer. Turning clockwise, she stepped into the man, tucked his wrist under her arm, pivoted, dropped to one knee, and threw him over her shoulder.

The man with the knit cap flew head over heels onto the pavement.

It happened so fast that neither Bobby nor Scarface had time to react.

"Jesus Christ!"

The man with the knit cap didn't move. Scarface released Bobby and squatted next to his fallen comrade.

"What the fuck? He's out cold."

Scarface stood and turned to Bobby.

"It's all your fault."

He clenched his fists and stepped toward Bobby. Bobby braced himself.

Before Scarface could take a second step, Cricket came from behind and smashed him on the head with her heavy wooden paintbox. Scarface crumbled. The top of the paintbox broke and dozens of metallic tubes of paint spilled onto the ground, scattering in every direction.

Bobby gaped at Cricket. He'd never seen anything like it. Cricket was nothing short of wonder woman. Bobby saw a prideful gleam in her eyes. She stood with her hands on her hips.

"Judo," she said. "My father was on the national team. I grew up on the mats. It's nothing really."

"That was incredible!"

"Dad's strategy was always strike first then finish the opponent before he can retaliate. He won a national championship with that philosophy. It works."

Bobby eyed the two downed bullies.

"I don't believe it."

"What? That someone as small as me can defeat two big lugs? In Judo it's actually easier if they're big and slow. They land like a load of bricks. It's all a matter of leverage."

"Next time they try to rough up some innocent pedestrians maybe they'll think twice."

Bobby got down and began to collect the tubes of paint strewn across the sidewalk. Cricket knelt next to him. He felt embarrassed that she'd acted so decisively while he'd wondered what to do.

"You broke your box."

"I can fix it. Don't worry."

"You are an amazing woman. I thought I was about to go toe to toe with King Kong there, and you flipped him like a rag doll."

"That's about all the shit I could take from those two. I just did what I was taught to do.

"Are you OK?"

"I'm fine, but these two won't be feeling too chipper when they come to."

"You think they'll tell all their friends that a girl did this to them?"

Cricket laughed. "I don't think so."

"Can you teach me to do that?"

"Sure. It's really a lot of fun. You'll like it."

"It might come in handy someday."

"Like today."

Bobby found the last of the paint tubes and threw them into the broken box. Cradling it, he got to his feet. Cricket stood close to him. She looked at his face, closed her eyes, and leaned forward to kiss him. Bobby kissed her tiny mouth gently.

She hugged him, suddenly shivering. They walked to her place arm in arm without saying a word. Bobby had never felt more alive.

*   *   *

Cricket's apartment was up three flights of stairs in a Baltimore row house. It consisted of two rooms and a kitchen with a closet-sized bathroom wedged in the corner. The apartment was decorated with colorful Indian bedspreads hanging from the ceiling, beaded curtains, and a Persian rug.

The linoleum floor, a vomit-like green, clashed violently with the Eastern motif of the room.

"It's like another world in here," Bobby said.

"It is another world. My world. Let's set up over there."

Cricket pointed to the window which had a bench seat built into it.

"You can sit in the window. It will frame you nicely, I think."

Bobby felt nervous. He tried to suppress his awkwardness around her. She acted as if she didn't have a care in the world which seemed especially odd considering she'd just been in a street fight. Bobby was strongly attracted to Cricket, and it made him feel weird. He put his guitar case down and took a breath.

"Take off your coat and stay awhile," Cricket said. "Relax, this is a creative place."

Bobby wordlessly took off his coat and slung it on a low couch covered with a multi-colored paisley bedspread. He ran a hand through his hair and realized he must look a little rough. His hair hadn't been cut lately, and it peeked over his collar in the back. Also because of the casual life on board the ship, he'd stopped using hair tonic. He felt a bit scruffy, but his hands and face were clean. He caught a glimpse of himself in her mirror and barely recognized the reflection. The guy who stared back at him looked harder, cooler, with a lean and hungry look.

Who's that guy? And why is he wearing my clothes?

"I want to draw you with the guitar."

Bobby blinked. "Guitar? I don't know how to play it yet. I just bought it today."

"I thought..."

"I'm sorry if I gave you the wrong impression. Do you want me to leave?"

Cricket laughed like a English schoolgirl.

"Of course not! That's silly!"

Cricket motioned for him to take out the guitar.

"You don't have to play it. Just hold it while I draw. It's interesting."

Bobby did as he was told. He sat in the window seat and held the guitar the way he'd seen John do it. John held his guitar high, proud and defiant. Clovis, on the other hand, held his slung low. Bobby liked John's style better and decided when he learned to play that's the way he'd hold it.

He caressed the strings, daring to gently pluck one. The warm tone of the open E string resonated through the body of the guitar and into his torso. He'd never considered the physical aspect of playing music.

"That's it! Don't move!"

Bobby froze.

She began to draw, her small hands moving quickly across the page of the sketchpad. She sat Indian-style on the floor with the pad in her lap. Working with pencils, her face pinched with concentration. She lost herself to her task. Five minutes went by, and she said nothing.

Bobby watched her as she drew.

He noticed a world of tiny details about her - like the way she brushed her hair away from her face, and the way her lips seemed to radiate soft pink light.

Cricket seemed too absorbed in her drawing to notice him noticing her.

She seems so happy. I can't believe she stood up to those guys.

Another five minutes passed and she paused.

"It's starting to look like something."

Bobby relaxed.

"Can I see?"

She clutched the sketchbook to her breasts.

"No. Not yet. Not until it's more finished. What about you? Are you thirsty? Can I get you something?"

"What do you have?"

Cricket thought for a moment.

"Water."

"No thanks."

She chewed the end of her pencil.

"I want to know more about you. Why don't you tell me your story while I draw?"

"My story?"

"Yeah, everybody's got a story. What's yours?"

Bobby looked down at his guitar wondering what to say. *I've got a story, all right, but do I really want to tell it?*

"I don't want to bore you," Bobby muttered.

Cricket's head bobbed when she talked.

"I got nothin' better to do. Besides, you're interesting. I love your accent and could listen to you talk for hours. You come from a faraway place, you have exotic friends, you've traveled the world, and you have great hair."

"Hold on. Great hair?"

"Yeah, it's very beat. Very bohemian. It's arty. A little long but not combed back like most guys. I like it."

Bobby smiled. "I love your hair too."

"I used this new coconut oil shampoo. It smells like the tropics."

Bobby told Cricket his story starting with the American R&B records and meeting John. He left out the part about Mrs. Garlton. When he finished talking the portrait was done.

She showed it to him without a hint of self-doubt.

"What do you think?"

Bobby's jaw dropped when he saw his face on the paper. She had somehow taken all the information he'd been feeding her and channeled it into the drawing.

"My God. It's great. I don't believe it. You are very, very good."

"Thank you." Her smile lit the room.

In the picture it looked like he could really play the guitar. His eyes had a brooding energy, his lips pressed tightly together, his face half bathed in shadow. The portrait burned with just below the surface intensity. He felt like James Dean.

"I think I captured you pretty well. Do you like it?"

"Yes, of course. I love it. I've never had my portrait done. Can I have it, once you've been graded?"

Cricket stared at her work.

"Well I have to turn it in tomorrow. I'll probably get it back next week."

Bobby looked away.

"I'll be gone by then."

"Maybe I can send it to you."

"I'll give you my mailing address."

She handed him her sketchbook and a pen. He paused, not sure which address to give her. Then, in careful box letters, he wrote, "251 Menlove Avenue, Woolton, U.K., care of John Lennon."

"Who's John Lennon?"

"He's that guy I told you about, a friend of mine."

"Oh..."

She closed her book and swung a mass of dark hair over her shoulder.

"Well, what's next?"

Bobby decided to do something bold.

He pulled Cricket close and kissed her. She melted into his arms and returned his kiss the way he'd hoped. Something about kissing her filled him with a strange sadness. He couldn't help but think of Nancy Garlton. Though Cricket was the exact opposite of Nancy, he realized that it was he who had changed.

*　　*　　*

Bobby stayed the night, but he didn't make love to Cricket. He could have, and he wanted to, but he didn't. Wondering about it the next day, he supposed that some vestige of English reserve had surfaced in the tidal pool of his libido. Or maybe it was Nancy Garlton or the alien surroundings or a twinge of homesickness, but something had adjusted his valves.

Side by side all night in her single bed, hugging and talking, Bobby wondered about it.

She's a great girl. I don't want to ruin this.

They were still talking when the sun came up.

Bobby went back to the ship and stowed his guitar in the crew's quarters. Most of his shipmates were ashore, so no one saw him put the guitar case behind his footlocker. He couldn't get Cricket out of his mind.

She still has her innocence. Mine is gone.

CHAPTER SEVEN

THE HIGH-DEE-HO MAN

Bobby knew his time in Baltimore would soon come to an end, but he still had one task to accomplish. He wanted to buy some records. He asked some of his shipmates where he could find a good record store. There were many suggestions but the name of one store intrigued him: The Hi-Dee-Ho Soul Shack. He decided to make a pilgrimage. Cricket acted as his guide through a distressed East Baltimore neighborhood. When they reached the Hi-Dee-Ho Soul Shack, they stood staring at the grimy storefront window.

"My God, look at this place," Bobby said.

"Are you sure you want to go in there?"

Bobby shot a sidelong glance at Cricket.

"Of course. I've traveled halfway around the world to come here."

"Just for some R&B records?"

Bobby adopted an imperious tone. "It's not just R&B records. It's the very soul of the American Negro."

Cricket rolled her eyes.

"Right. Come on then, let's go inside."

She took Bobby's hand and led him into the shop.

Bobby stopped just inside the door.

"Holy shit. Look at all this."

Thousands of records hung from the walls and ceiling. Album racks were stuffed into every available crevice. Stacks of singles lined the shelves. Colorful posters and album covers were everywhere. Not one inch of original wall or ceiling remained visible beneath the riotous colorations. Bobby was dumbfounded by the choices.

"Where do I start?"

"Can I help you?" A deep, resonant voice boomed from behind them.

Bobby turned to see a huge black man, well over six feet and weighing at least three hundred pounds. He wore a brown silk shirt, a black vest, and a pair of shiny mustard-colored pants.

"You white folks need some help?"

Bobby faced the black man.

"Yes, sir. I would like to buy some records."

"Well, you come to the right place. What artist were you looking for?"

Bobby repeated the names he'd learned. "Solomon Burke, James Brown, Little Richard, Ray Charles, Hank Ballard, the Coasters, the Clovers, Bo Diddley, The Drifters..."

"Hold on there, young man. Let's just go one at a time."

Bobby noticed some fliers on the counter. They were the top forty lists of record sales in Baltimore that week, published by several radio stations. He picked one up from WSID and read it. *Fat Daddy's Hot Hits.*

"I'll have all these," Bobby said.

"All of 'em?"

"One of each."

He picked up another flier from WWIN. *Commander Hot Rod's Top Tracks.*

"And all of these as well, unless some are repeated from the other list. Tell me, of these two disk jockeys, who's better? Fat Daddy or Commander Hot Rod?"

The black man grinned. "You're from a radio station, right? This is a gag, right?"

Bobby pulled out his wallet and flashed a wad of bills.

"I'm completely serious."

The black man stuck out his hand to shake.

"Glad to meet you. I'm Preston Washington. They call me the Hi-Dee-Ho Man. I own this place. I'm the vinyl expert."

Bobby shook the hand and put his wallet away.

"Pleased to meet you, Mr. Washington. I'm interested in buying a lot of records here today as long as you can give me a good price."

"Oh, yeah. I got discounts up the ass."

"Good. Now, what I need is some guidance. I want you to pick out the cream of the crop for me since I don't have time to listen to all these right now."

Preston put a few cardboard boxes on the counter.

"I gotcha covered. You know, Paul Johnson comes in here all the time. He's Fat Daddy. He trusts my taste one hundred percent. He says, 'Good cooga-mooga, straight shooter, right here in oompapa diddy, Bal-ti-mo City!' That's my man, Fat Daddy. If I find a record I really like, I recommend it to him and he plays it on the air. He's got the smoothest jive this side of shit. I'm tight with the fat man. Yep. I'm a real influential man around here."

Bobby nodded. "Well then, you're just the man I need. You see, I'm from England, and they don't have any records like these over there. Can you help me?"

"You're gonna take 'em back there with you?"

"Yep. I'm gonna play 'em for all the musicians back home."

Preston Washington slapped the countertop.

"Damn! That sounds like a noble cause. Well, in that case, I'll give you the Presidential service. We can start with top forty. Then you got your new releases, your oldies, your overlooked gems. Hey, this is gonna be fun. How much you want to spend?"

Bobby told him and he whistled.

"Shit, man. I can just close up for the day after this."

Preston gleefully filled Bobby's order. When Bobby left the Hi-Dee-Ho Soul Shack, he had four boxes of fifty records each. They represented the finest soul music money could buy and handpicked by Preston Washington. Preston gave Bobby his business card and urged him to call whenever he was in town. Bobby felt ten feet tall.

The records would make Bobby the ruler of the universe in the Merseyside scene. In those boxes were tunes Liverpudlians would never ever hear unless the music was performed by their local beat groups like the Beatles.

Preston had gone out of his way to include some regional hits from unknown artists he insisted would be huge one day. And every single one, he insisted, was great. Bobby believed him.

Preston Washington personified everything that was noble and great about American rhythm and blues. To Bobby, the visit to the Hi-Dee-Ho-Soul-Shack had been a religious experience. He never once thought to ask what Hi-Dee-Ho meant.

Bobby's time ashore ended the next day. The *Pilgrim's Progress* was bound for Hamburg. When he told Cricket, she cried.

"I never thought about you leaving," she said. "I guess I've been denying it since that first night. I just assumed that you would stay longer. But, the truth is... I'm really fond of you, Bobby. I don't want you to go."

Bobby held her close.

"I don't want to go either, but I have to. I signed a contract. The good news is I'll be back again next month."

She managed a hopeful, petite smile.

"I'll miss you."

"I'll miss you too."

"Bobby?"

"Yes?"

"How come you never made love to me? A lot of guys would've jumped at the chance."

The question surprised Bobby. Cricket seemed incapable of anything except complete, utter, gut wrenching honesty. She was almost too open. To Bobby she represented freedom of a sort he had never known. Freewheeling American freedom. Big sky, lots of elbow room, ass-kickin' freedom.

Bobby looked at her and realized the depth of his affection. He spoke quietly.

"I don't know. I guess I didn't want to sully our relationship. I didn't want it to end."

"You mean, you thought it would end if we had sex? That's ridiculous."

"I didn't want anything to change between us. I thought if we did it, then we'd change, and it wouldn't be the same."

Cricket touched his cheek with her delicate finger. Her eyes filled with tears.

"Oh, God. That's so sweet. And so wrong. I love you, Bobby Dingle."

Bobby looked back at her. His mouth hung open as if the words were caught there and could not come out. He felt a flush of heat on his face. His saliva dried. He cleared his throat. He had never used the word 'love' that way before: full strength, all-in, without limitation. This time he wanted to say it the same way she had, the dangerous way.

"La?" he managed to say.

She kissed him.

74

"Yeah, as in I la-la you."

An awkward silence, then Bobby asked, "And now you want to know if I love you?"

"Exactly."

To Bobby it all seemed like a dream. Standing on foreign soil with a beautiful woman in his arms, far away from Clive and Mick and Mrs. Garlton and his old life. Time slowed down, became distorted, and finally stopped.

Free-falling, he said, "Yes, I love you. This is insane. I love you, and I don't even know your last name."

"Samansky."

"I love you Bernice Samansky."

*　　*　　*

Bobby said good-bye to Cricket and walked back to the *Pilgrim's Progress*. As he neared the dock he recognized Clovis lounging against a pallet, smoking a cigarette. As soon as Clovis saw Bobby, he flicked the butt and whistled.

"Hey! Robby, the Limey! What's up, pardner?"

Bobby smiled at Clovis' pink shirt and skin-tight pants. "That's quite an outfit. You'd make a fine Teddy Boy, Clovis. You've got the taste for it."

"Hey, I ain't no Teddy Bear and stop makin' fun of my clothes. I asked around and found out what ship you were on and came around to give you that damn guitar lesson."

Bobby stopped. "Are you serious?"

"Yep, I figured you were shackin' up with that beatnik babe, and that's why you weren't around. I knew you were shippin' out today. I talked to some of your shipmates at the bar last night and decided to come down and see if I could catch you."

"And you want to give me a guitar lesson?"

Clovis winked at him. "Sho'nuf. What do you say?"

"But why?"

Clovis laughed. "Because every stripper on East Baltimore Street thinks you have a giant schlong. Good news travels fast. Looks like you're covered when you come back to town, buddy. You don't have to thank me. I do this for all my friends."

*　　*　　*

Bobby led Clovis onboard and for the next hour-and-a-half he showed Bobby the basic chords. A few of his shipmates joined in, grateful for the lesson. It surprised Bobby to learn that three guys on board played guitar. One was pretty good, and the other two were beginners like Bobby. When Clovis left the ship, he'd made a few more friends.

Bobby absorbed the records, savoring them like the best bottles of a well-stocked wine cellar. One by one he played them, keeping a diary of his impressions. His notes filled the pages, describing the songs, the arrangements, and the vocals. He had time enough to focus on each record. The music filled his mind.

He began to practice the guitar in earnest, suffering the blisters that came before the calluses. He found the basic chords nearly impossible for his fingers. Stuff that looked effortless when Clovis did it seemed to require super powers. He knew that making an "A" chord was possible, but crowding his fingers together in the center of the neck then pressing down behind the fret hard enough to strike a note proved as difficult as anything he'd ever done. *Maybe my fingers are too fat*, he thought. *Maybe I don't have the manual dexterity.*

When he pulled his fingertips away from the strings, deep grooves remained. They lasted for hours, marking his tender digits as the sight of future blisters. When his fingertips throbbed, the hope of actually playing songs from the records spurred him on.

With the memory of Cricket still fresh in his mind, he wrote her letters describing life on board the *Pilgrim's Progress*. He wondered if what he could remember of their brief time together had actually happened, or if it had been a dream. *She had used the word 'love,' hadn't she?* He also wrote to his father and Nancy Garlton. These letters were short and upbeat, designed to mollify the reader not the heartfelt journal-like pages he wrote for Cricket.

As the ship plowed across the Atlantic, and the summer faded, Bobby looked forward to seeing the Beatles again. His next port of call, Hamburg, promised even greater adventures.

CHAPTER EIGHT

THE REEPERBAHN

The Reeperbahn, his shipmates said, made The Block on East Baltimore Street look like a Holiday Camp. Bobby could only imagine the lascivious delights a man away from home might find there. *And the Beatles are right in the middle of it, I'll bet. God, what fun it must be for them.* Everything, it seemed, was legal. Along the Grosse Freiheit, the Reeperbahn's main drag, anything could be had for a price, or so nearly every man on board had told him.

Three hours after the *Pilgrim's Progress* docked, Bobby went ashore. Anxious to sleep on dry land, he had the address of the British Sailor's Society, a mission that offered beds and meals to English seamen in foreign ports. He was told to ask for the resident manager, Jim Hawke.

The mission was a large four-story building that resembled a library more than a place for weary seadogs. Jim Hawke, a barrel-chested, ex-military man, greeted Bobby as he crossed the threshold.

"Hello, mate, I'm Jim Hawke. What's your vessel?"

"It's the *Pilgrim's Progress*, sir."

Jim's broad Londoner accent made toast of the words, drying the vowels and browning the edges.

"Right. Know it well. Served with your captain during the war. Chester Blodwyn, he's a good man. A damn good man. You're new, aren't you?

I haven't seen you here before."

Bobby nodded. He was about to point out that the captain of the *Pilgrim's Progress* was a dwarfish South African named Zanker then thought better of it. Something about being at sea had changed Bobby, made him more cautious. Now Bobby felt quite comfortable saying nothing. Saying nothing had served him well of late. Who cared who the captain was anyway?

Bobby added a chipper ring to his voice.

"It's my first tour of duty, sir."

Jim Hawke smoked a pipe, and sucked on it thoughtfully as he spoke.

"Right. How long in port?"

"Three days, sir."

Jim Hawke pointed out the door to the streets of Hamburg.

"There's a lot of trouble a young lad can get into out there. It's a bloody den of iniquity, if you ask me. I've seen many good English lads fall prey to temptation."

He raised an eyebrow, changing the geography of his face just enough to make Bobby uneasy.

"And I've seen many a poor soul ruined because of it. If you know what's good for you you'll keep away from the Reeperbahn."

Bobby did not reply.

Jim cleared his throat and continued.

"Right. That being said... a young buck like yourself in port for the first time, I know how it is. I give this speech to every man who comes in here and you know how many it dissuades? None. Here's a list of places to avoid."

He handed Bobby a typed sheet with fifty or sixty names on it.

"Of course, if you see a place and it's not on the list, it doesn't mean it's safe. Remember anything can happen in the Reeperbahn."

Bobby scanned the list. None of the names meant anything to him. He folded the paper and put it in his pocket.

"That's good to know, Mr. Hawke. Thank you."

Jim handed Bobby a clipboard.

"Just sign right there. Put the date and time, the name of your ship, line and registry."

He took a worn key off a pegboard.

"You'll bunk in 106. Shower's down the hall. Breakfast served until noon, dinner's at six. One bit of trouble and you're out. Agreed?"

"Agreed."

They shook hands and Bobby accepted the key.

"Thank you, Mr. Hawke, sir."

"Just call me Jim. Everybody else does."

"OK, Jim. I have one more question. Do you, by any chance, have a record player here?"

"A phonograph? Yes, actually, we have two. There's one in the recreation room and one in my quarters. Do you have an interest in music?"

"Yes, sir."

Jim grinned. "Then I'm sure you'll find your stay here enjoyable. Welcome aboard."

* * *

Bobby slept most of the first day. Exhausted from his travels, he collapsed into his bunk and slumbered until the smell of bacon woke him and drew him to the dining hall at noon. He gorged on an excellent English breakfast; eggs, bacon, and chips. The old German woman who cooked the meal knew the secret of frying potatoes into proper chips. Bobby liked his a bit soggy, and these were perfect. He showered and returned to his room, surprised to find two other sailors there.

"Thought you had a private suite, eh?" the taller one said.

His laugh sounded like a shaking a can of marbles.

"Welcome to *das boot*. I'm Donovan and this is my partner, Archie. Just came in on the *Manila Prince*."

"I've heard of the *Prince* line. It's a passenger ship, right?"

Donovan winked. "Just between you and me, I'd rather haul freight. Those people look down their noses at us and treat us like dirt. At least on a cargo ship except for the officers, everybody's more or less equal. What do you do?"

"Steward's apprentice on the *Pilgrim's Progress*."

"Are you union?"

Bobby nodded, wondering what Donovan meant by that. Archie had a sinister look not unlike Bobby's brother Clive only shorter and more compact. His eyebrows arched ominously upward, away from a cheap glass eye that didn't match the real one. Donovan was tall and thin; middle thirties, drab and angular. His clothes were faded and his face seemed longer than it should be. When he smiled, he showed an improbable jumble of crooked teeth.

Bobby wondered if his stuff was safe in the same room with these two.

"What's your name, mate?"

"Bobby Dingle from Liverpool."

Donovan shook his hand vigorously. Archie didn't move.

"Look, young master Bob, me and good old Archie here were just about to go out and find some fancy whores. Care to join us?"

Bobby thought for a moment and shook his head.

"No thanks, I have plans of my own. But good luck."

Donovan sniggered. "Luck's got nothin' to do with it as long as you got the cash. Sure you won't come?"

"No, I've got something I need to do."

"Suit yourself."

Donovan and Archie strolled out of the room and disappeared down the hall. Bobby decided to buy a lock for his footlocker.

Bobby took a few records from his box and headed to the recreation room. When he found the room he smiled. The booming sound of the record player in the echo filled, high ceilinged room would be exciting. It would add to the driving beat of the drums and bass. No sooner had he started playing *Stay* by Maurice Williams and the Zodiacs, he heard a commotion in the hall. A group of black-leather-clad guys were pushing and shoving like schoolboys to get through the recreation room door.

"My God, it's the sacred sound!" someone with a thick scouse accent shouted.

Bobby took a step toward the door, squinting at the newcomers.

"Bloody amazing! Heaven in Hamburg!" the same voice shouted.

Bobby took another step. The leather boys were through the door now and hurrying toward the record player. Bobby could see their faces.

"I don't believe it! John!"

Three Beatles all looked at once and shouted in semi-unison.

"Dust Bin Bob!"

John was the first to hug him.

"Man! What are you doing here?"

"I'm in port for a few days. When I heard we were docking in Hamburg, I remembered what you said. I was going to look you up. Why are you hanging out at the British Sailor's Society of all places?"

The song ended and John looked at the record spinning on the turntable.

"They make the best breakfast in town. Eggs and chippies with a spot of bacon."

"And it's cheap," Paul said.

"Still poor as a church mouse, eh?"

John held up his hand.

"Stop. I'll not have any of that talk in my universe. In my universe the Beatles rule the world. Where are we going, lads?"

There was an awkward pause.

"To the toppermost of the poppermost," George and Paul chanted mockingly.

Clearly they had grown a bit tired of the official Beatles rallying cry.

"Still harboring those visions of grandeur," Bobby said. "So tell me, how has Hamburg treated you so far?"

John chuckled. "Bloody fantastic! This place is like a wonderland. We play to packed houses every night."

"The accommodations leave a little to be desired," Paul admitted. "But we get by."

"We live in the ladies' toilet at the Bambi Kino," George said, his voice a scouse deadpan. "Lovely spot, that."

Bobby pointed to John's pants.

"What about the leathers? Are you a bunch of kinks now?"

John modeled his black leather trousers and matching jacket, prancing comically in front of them.

"Like it? It's the spring collection. Hamburg has everything, Dusty. I could set you up."

"I don't think so."

"Don't be shy, oh man of La Dusta. Tell us what you think."

"I think you've lost your fuckin' mind, John Lennon. Hamburg has obviously got the better of you."

John leaned over the turntable and studied the still-spinning record.

"You're just jealous."

Bobby laughed. "Of you? You've got to be kidding. You don't have two *pfennigs* to rub together."

"There's more to success than money," John replied quickly.

"The last time I checked money was still the legal tender."

Paul, always the diplomatic voice, said, "I think he means the respect of his peers."

"I didn't think guys like you had peers."

John's voice dripped sarcasm. "Come down to the Kaiserkeller tonight and see for yourself. It's just down from the brothels. But we can talk about all that later. What wondrous records did you bring back from the hinterlands? Can we give that last one another play?"

"Maurice Williams and the Zodiacs. It's a big hit in the States right now.

The guy has an incredible voice."

"That's called falsetto when he sings high like a girl. I can do that. You just constrict your voice. It's easy."

Bobby clapped his hands.

"Listen to you. The old show business veteran. How long have you been an expert, Mr. Lennon?"

John and Paul exchanged glances.

"Actually, we've gotten quite a bit of experience here in Hamburg. You'd be surprised," Paul said.

"We've grown up," George said, looking impossibly baby-faced and serious. "Six sets a night from eight to two, seven days a week with extras on the weekend. Basically, it's get tight or die."

John had the same smirk on his face that he'd had the day he'd given Bobby a hard time about Nancy Garlton.

"You better start taking me and the Beatles seriously, Dusty, or you'll get left behind."

Bobby busied himself with the record player and said nothing. Memories of John's dark side bubbled to the surface. He remembered how quickly John could turn. Kept in check at Aunt Mimi's house, John's cruel streak had nothing to restrain it here in Hamburg. Bobby wondered how much his friend had changed in the past months.

Bobby started the song again. Maurice Williams's voice soared over their heads.

John reached over and lifted the needle ending the song abruptly. The snap of silence echoed like a whip-crack. John sneered.

"Tell us, Dust Bin Bob, were her tits all wrinkled and saggy?"

Bobby wanted to hit John. But he didn't. Instead he answered like a politician in a nasal, upper-crust accent.

"No, actually, my recollection was that they were quite firm and smooth."

John burst out with a laugh that broke the tension.

"Quite firm, he says! And smooth, he says!"

Bobby didn't know what to say and started the record for the third time. This time it played through.

John looked through the twenty-five singles Bobby had brought from the ship. He studied the labels like a bookkeeper reading each credit, noting the writer, producer, record label as well as the artist. He pulled one record out of the stack and placed it on top.

"Let's play this one next."

Bobby picked it up. *Will You Still Love Me Tomorrow*, by the *Shirelles*. On Scepter Records.

"Why this one?"

"Look at the writers; Goffin and King. I know those names from other records. I know they do some pretty good stuff."

Bobby played the Shirelles for John. The song interested him as soon as the needle touched the vinyl.

"Listen to that groove," John said. "And the vocals. Damn, that's sexy. It's givin' me a tingle down in me old kilts."

The Shirelles were a girl group, and the blend their voices achieved was earthy and lush. The background vocals seduced John's ear. "Is this some lasting treasure, or just a moment's pleasure?" they sang.

The way the drums and guitars syncopated the beat reminded Bobby of some Everly Brothers records he'd heard. John was obviously infatuated with the texture of the vocals. Nearly impossible to describe, the sound of the Shirelles could be characterized by the words 'hard' and 'soft' at the same time. The quality of the lead vocal at times tender, at times Pentecostal, at times earthy, but always honest. Combined with the background vocals in beautiful three-part harmony, it achieved a kind of siren's song. Hard and soft, yin and yang, in and out. It was also something Bobby saw in John. *No wonder he's so keen on it.*

When it was over, Paul said, "Let's use the piano upstairs to work out the chords."

*　　*　　*

The Kaiserkeller throbbed with a kind of energy that produced dangerous situations. Drunken sailors jostled working-class Germans and collided with foreign businessmen. Students danced next to prostitutes. Gangsters watched from their private tables. The Beatles roared from the stage.

As Bobby entered the club, he heard them performing *Will You Still Love Me Tomorrow*, the song they had heard for the first time that morning. Bobby stopped and listened. John's voice handled the melody surprisingly well, transposing it from female to male. He'd grown considerably as a vocalist. He was supremely confident now and completely unafraid as if it were all a great experiment. That venturesome spirit shone as he belted out the verses.

Paul and George did the backgrounds not as smooth as the Shirelles but serviceable. They sounded amazingly tight. Bobby edged closer to the stage, making his way through the crowded room. *Will You Still Love Me Tomorrow* ended and the Kaiserkeller patrons applauded sporadically. The din of the crowd filled the sonic gap left by the song. The Beatles lit cigarettes and drank some beer. John shouted something incomprehensible, and the band lurched into another song. Bobby recognized it. Chuck Berry's *Roll Over Beethoven*, an up-tempo rocker with a killer guitar riff. George handled the part skillfully. John's voice cut through the smoky air like a switchblade.

The long hours on the Kaiserkeller stage had matured them in a profound way. The group had become more like a single entity. What had been a collection of guys on stage at Lathom Hall, now seemed to be extensions of one group mind. All the band members watched each other, sensitive to every chord change, every snare beat and every vocal line. While they obviously played to the crowd, they also played for themselves. John and Paul sang uncanny harmonies to each other.

A short, round, stylishly-dressed gray-haired man with a pronounced limp ambled in front of the stage and shouted at the band. Bobby moved closer to hear.

"Mak shau! Mak shau, Beatles!"

John Lennon shouted into the microphone.

"You fuckin' Nazi! Back to your tank!"

The man shook his fist at them.

"Mak shau! Beatles mak shau now!"

Paul shrugged and crushed out his ciggy on the floor of the stage.

"Right. Long Tall Sally! One-two-three-fah!"

The band launched into the Little Richard song with Paul doing a screeching vocal. Bobby noticed the cheesy echo effect on the club's P.A. system, which gave everything a crazy rockabilly sound. Paul's vocal reverberated off the walls like sonic shrapnel.

"Long Tall Sally! She's built for speed! She got everything that Uncle John needs! Oh, baby! Whoooooooooo, oh, baby! Have some fun tonight!"

Bobby realized he was standing right next to the sound system speaker so he moved more toward the middle of the room. His ears rang for a few moments then adjusted to the volume. The Beatles were loud, brash and juiced with echo.

The short man who had shouted at the band went back to the bar. The Beatles continued to "mak shau" for another thirty minutes. When the break came, Bobby approached the stage.

"Hey, Dusty!" John shouted. "Come over and meet our friends."

The Beatles had commandeered a table next to the stage. They held court there with several young Germans who looked like students. Bobby's eye was drawn to a beautiful blond girl with an angelic face and short-cropped hair. She was dressed in a black turtleneck sweater and tight black leather pants. Bobby couldn't take his eyes off her.

"Hey, man," John shouted over the din, "I see you already noticed Astrid."

Bobby looked away and blushed.

"Oh, ah, terribly sorry. Didn't mean to stare."

Bobby looked at the others seated at the table.

"Meet the exis," John said.

Bobby looked around the table. All the boys had their hair combed forward, dry and slightly longish. The entire group was androgynous because the girls shared the same haircut. They all wore black.

"You know, existentialists. They believe everything's just a big load of bollocks not unlike yourself."

"Hello," Bobby mumbled.

"Only Klaus and Astrid speak English. I should tell you straight away that Stu has beat us all to the punch with Astrid. They're thick as thieves."

Bobby said, "I just wanted to say how great the group sounds. Man, it's amazing how you've grown."

Stu sat down next to Astrid and held her hand. Bobby noticed that Stu had changed his hairstyle, adopting the exis' look, but the other Beatles hadn't.

"Thanks. We're gettin' better all the time."

"Nothin' like playing non-stop seven nights a week to get the band tight," Paul said.

Bobby looked at Paul's fingers.

"You must have calluses on top of calluses."

Paul held up a hand. The strings had impressed deep grooves into his fingertips.

"I'm beyond that now. Meet the fingers of steel."

Bobby whistled low. "They look like screw heads."

"On the plus side, they'll never be able to fingerprint me. I'll be known as Doctor X."

"Paul Ramon, Doctor X," Bobby said. "You're collecting aliases like some people collect ceramic toads."

John interrupted with a loud belch. He wiped his mouth with the back of his hand.

"Since when did you become one of the exis?"

"What are you talking about?"

"Your hair, man. It's exi."

Bobby unconsciously ran a hand through his hair.

"Oh, this? Christ, John, I've been at sea. I had this same problem back in the States. Sorry I haven't seen a proper barber lately."

"It's even longer than Klaus'. And he's got the longest hair in town."

"I see Stu's already changed over."

John frowned. "It's not rock and roll, man. What Stu does is his own business, but I think it looks queer."

Paul lit another ciggy.

"I think it looks cool. I'm going to ask Astrid to cut mine like that."

"Astrid cuts hair?" Bobby asked.

"Astrid does a lot more than that," John said snidely. "She designs things, like clothes, and she's a photographer."

Astrid spoke for the first time. Her German accent reminded Bobby of Marlene Deitrich.

"Who does your hair?"

Bobby shrugged. "God."

"God does your hair? How wonderful. I would like to style it sometime, providing God allows."

"I'll do it if you do it," George said. "I'm ready for a change."

"Me too," said Paul.

"Don't look at me," John said. "I don't want to look like a bloody fairy."

Astrid leaned into the table, scanning all their faces.

"Then it's settled. Tomorrow you will all come 'round to my mother's house and I will style your hair. All except John, of course."

"And Pete," John said. "He's with me."

Astrid's charm and influence at the Beatles table impressed Bobby. She seemed to hold sway over the wild Liverpool boys.

"Those who choose to join the new look will be rewarded with a fabulous dinner of my mother's making."

"That's a hard offer to refuse," Paul said. "Count me in."

Astrid ran her slender fingers through Stu's hair.

"I love the way it feels. No boyfriend of mine is going to have greasy, slicked-back hair. It's uncivilized."

John sneered. "It was good enough for Elvis."

Klaus spoke in a thick German accent. Bobby had to listen carefully to understand.

"John, you said yourself that Elvis is dead. He died when he went into the army. You are the new guard. You can't cling to the old haircuts. It's time to move beyond the Teddy Boy look."

John lit a ciggy.

"I don't tell you how to comb your sodden' hair! So shirrup! I'm a musician! That's all I do, I play music. I hate style! Style is shit!" John stood up and left the table.

"What's wrong with him?" Bobby asked.

"He's a bit cheeky tonight," Paul said. "He says a lot of things he doesn't mean when he gets like that. Sometimes it's like he can't control himself."

They watched John weave through the crowd to the bar.

"I worry about that boy. He's a genius and a madman. It's the old Jekyll and Hyde bit."

Bobby shook his head.

"How do you do it? I mean, how do you keep this up all night, night after night, with this insane intensity? It must wear you down."

Paul grinned. George nudged him and winked. Their smiles looked devious in the flickering half-light of the darkened nightclub.

"Go ahead, tell him. He's one of us."

George reached into his pocket and withdrew a handful of pills.

"These are Prellys. Preludins. It's a German slimming pill."

Bobby gawked at the pills.

"What are they for?"

"They're stay-up-all-night-and-play-music pills. They give you a burst of energy."

Bobby looked askance at the handful of little white pills. He disliked pills in general, and these seemed particularly evil.

"You're not hooked on these are you?"

"No, of course not, but it's the only way we can last the night."

Astrid said, "I get them from my mother's chemist. We usually take one and a half. It's a mild dose. If you drink beer you get a little higher."

"I got mine from Mutti," George said. "The ladies washroom attendant at the Bambi Kino. She's got a big jar."

"Fact is, you can get 'em anywhere around here. Most of the waitresses and bouncers have their sources."

Bobby shook his head.

"Does everybody take them?"

Paul nodded. "Yeah, pretty much. Except Pete, the drummer. He doesn't care for 'em.'"

Bobby watched John argue with someone across the room. A patron nearly came to blows with John. As soon as he physically made contact with John, a group of bouncers appeared magically and whisked the offensive man away. John shouted after him as they carried him out the door.

Paul watched too.

"You think the pills might have something to do with his mean behavior?"

Paul nodded. "That's why it's so important to keep together; me, George, Pete, Stu, and John. That way, there's always somebody around to keep him in check. Otherwise, there's no telling what he'll do. Besides, we've got four more sets to do tonight."

"I meant to ask you, who was that old guy who was shouting at the band in the middle of the set?"

"That was Bruno Koschmider, the owner of this place. He's a local big shot. One night Allan Williams was shouting at us when we were at Bruno's other club, the Indra. He was shouting, 'Make it a show, boys! Make it a show!' Only Bruno heard 'mak shau' and that's what he's trying to say. Mak shau! Beatles! Mak shau!"

"Bruno was with the Panzer division during the war. He's a heavyweight. He's got an army of bouncers, some of the toughest guys in the Saint Paulie district."

Paul pointed to a smallish, athletic young man across the room.

"See that guy over there? That's Horst Fascher. He boxed on the German National Team, accidentally killed a guy and was in prison for manslaughter. Bruno got him out so he could work here. He's the head of the bouncers. They're known as Hoddel's gang. Don't mess with any of them. They protect us, though, so I'm all for 'em."

CHAPTER NINE

BRUNO KOSCHMIDER

Bobby watched the Beatles play three more sets. He sat with the exis, between Klaus and Astrid, nursing a beer and listening to what they said. Bobby spoke no German and found their accents difficult to understand when they tried to speak to him in English. He was surprised to find Astrid the most talkative.

Maybe it's because of the pills, he thought.

She talked mostly about the Beatles.

"They are part of my life now. It's because I am in love with Stu. He's the most delicate, the most introspective of the band. Did you know he's not really a musician? He only bought the bass and joined the group because John talked him into it. He has a career in art ahead of him. He's a brilliant artist. You must see his work."

Bobby watched Stu. He didn't seem to be playing most of the time. He kept his back to the audience, hunched over his big Hofner "President" bass. He only hit one out of every four notes. The rest of the band made enough noise to cover it up.

Astrid continued. "See how he's so shy? The others give him a hard time about his playing except John. Paul can be very cruel about it. He hates it when Stu makes a mistake which is in every song. Paul is a perfectionist. He wants the band to sound its best all the time."

Bobby yawned and stretched.

"I don't know how late I can stay. I'm a bit fagged out."

Astrid offered him a Prelly.

"Here. If you just take one it will keep you up for a few hours."

Bobby looked at the tiny pills in the cup of her petite, white hand, pale and fragile. He considered the offer.

"I don't know. I'm not a pill taker."

Astrid nodded. "It was like that for me the first time. But it's really nothing."

Bobby hesitated and Astrid placed one of the pills in his hand.

"Take it for later."

"OK. Thank you."

The Beatles finished their set and joined Bobby. A commotion at one the nearby tables caused them all to look across the room. Bobby saw Donovan and Archie in the middle of a group of women. They were making a show of paying for everyone's drinks with a big wad of German money. They were drunk and acting crazy. The women, prostitutes drawn by the money, tried to grab it out of their hands. Archie, laughing maniacally, put a fistful of bills down his pants imploring the girls to retrieve it. They did and with great gusto. Archie, acting as if the money meant nothing, tried to wrap a bill around his penis, but it was snatched away by one of the girls before he could wave it around.

Archie shouted, "That's it, mate! That's it! Take me home, I'm done!"

Donovan said nothing.

Bobby watched from across the room.

Astrid said, "In the Saint Paulie District things like that happen all the time. It's usually foreigners. They spend three months pay in one night then wind up in jail."

"I saw those two today at the British Sailor's Society."

"They look rough."

George tapped Bobby on the shoulder.

"Excuse me, but I've seen those two before. They're friends of Bruno. I've seen them go into his office."

Bobby looked at George.

"Are you sure?"

"Quite sure," George said. "I've seen them talking on several occasions. They were in here last month. The tall one really likes the band."

Bobby ran a hand through his exis hair.

"That's odd."

"Not really. Everybody knows Bruno. He owns a bunch of businesses in the district. People come and go all the time."

"You think they could have some type of business dealings with him?"

"It's entirely possible."

Bobby watched Archie drink a pint of beer in one mammoth swig. Even from across the crowded nightclub, he could see the man's Adam's apple bob with the intake.

"What kind of business could those two possibly have with the owner of this place?"

George looked around the place and laughed. "Here? Anything. Absolutely anything."

*   *   *

Bobby began to fade around three o'clock in the morning. He resisted the urge to take the Prelly he had in his pocket. Bobby wondered how much of the Beatles behavior could be attributed to their use of the Prellys. Now that he noticed, the whole scene seemed to run on artificial energy.

Astrid and the exis didn't seem to show any ill effects other than excitedly talking and smoking for hours on end. The Beatles themselves seemed more drunk than stoned. Watching them on stage, Bobby marveled at their complete lack of inhibition. John never missed an opportunity to do something outrageous in his unending endeavor to "mak shau". Already tonight Bobby had seen him hang a toilet seat around his neck, try to set fire to the curtains, pick a fight with a German sailor, and shout incredibly insulting things at the audience through the P.A. system.

Early in the morning an exhausted Bobby followed the Beatles out of the Kaiserkeller and back to their room behind the Bambi Kino. They strode up the weary stairs to the tiny backstage area of the cinema. Bobby looked around and whistled.

"This is where you live? My God, it's utter squalor."

John raised an eyebrow.

"Squalor, you say? Our suite at the Ritz wasn't ready. We don't spend much time here anyway."

"I can see why."

George said, "It's not too bad. We get to see all the movies for free from behind the screen."

Bobby shrugged. "The things you boys do for music."

"Hey," John said, "I got an idea! Let's show Dusty the sights of the Reeperbahn!"

Bobby shook his head.

"No, I'm too tired for that. Why don't we do it tomorrow night?"

John held up his hand.

"Nonsense! No time like the present, I always say. Come on, Dusty. Where's that old Liverpool spirit?"

Bobby hesitated. "I think I left it back in Baltimore."

John ignored Bobby's answer.

"Who's with me? Let's go to the Roxy for a nightcap."

Pete declined. Stu had gone with Astrid, but George and Paul still fueled by the Prellys agreed readily. Paul looked at his wrist as if he had a wristwatch which he did not.

"God knows we can't sit around in this shit hole with nothing to do. Besides, the idea of showing Dust Bin Bob the sights appeals to me. I say off into the night with him!"

"Oh, shit," Bobby uttered, as three Beatles hefted him to his feet and started marching him toward the door.

"My God, have you all gone mad?"

John said, "Mad as hatters from the first night."

Bobby went along with them; he had no choice.

The Roxy was busy after hours. Aggressive hostesses hustled the tables, and one found her way onto Bobby's lap. Bobby shifted uncomfortably under her weight.

"Vat do you leetle boys vant to drink?" she purred in a smoky, German-accented voice. "I can get you anything you vont. Anything..."

Bobby looked at her face and frowned.

"I'll have a beer."

"Beers all around," said Paul. "Thanks, love."

John and George were snickering.

"What's with you two?"

Unable to contain himself, John burst out laughing. The hostess removed herself from Bobby's lap and made a great show of walking away, hips swaying like saddlebags.

"What's the joke?" Bobby demanded.

John and George could not stop laughing long enough to answer. Paul averted his eyes. Bobby knew something was afoot. Another hostess, this one small and dark, pranced to their table and stood behind Bobby's chair. She caressed his cheek with a velvet-gloved hand. Bobby looked over his shoulder into her steamy pink lips.

"Can I help you?"

George and John nearly fell off their chairs. They laughed so hard their eyes watered. The hostess hoisted her leg up and put a stiletto high-heeled shoe on Bobby's chair right between his legs. She let her dress slide up her leg to reveal the tops of her fishnet stockings. While they all watched, she adjusted her stockings.

"Excuse me, Miss." Bobby started to say. "But, I think there's been a misunderstanding. You see, I-"

"Don't talk," she said.

"But-"

"Don't talk!"

Bobby shut his mouth with a wet click. The hostess's leg started to flex. She began to writhe like a stripper. Bobby felt sweat collect on his forehead. His discomfort peaked when she thrust her pelvis forward.

"What's goin' on here?" he shouted at John.

"Go on, tell him," Paul said. "You're making the boy nervous."

John's laughter sputtered. George wiped a tear from his eye. The hostess not to be denied leaned over and kissed Bobby's cheek.

"Damn you, stop it!"

Bobby stood up and pushed the table away, knocking over some of the beer glasses. Paul and George jumped up to not get doused. Only John sat, grinning and defiant. Bobby glowered at him.

"OK, Lennon! That's it! What's going on here?"

"They're transvestites," Paul said sheepishly. "All the chicks here are guys."

Bobby's fists clenched. He stepped toward John and sucker-punched him on the jaw. John fell back, legs and arms flying.

"You arsehole!" Bobby shouted. "That's the bloody end! No more records for the likes of you again. Ever!"

Paul and George stood aside while Bobby strode from the club. Only a few people noticed.

* * *

Bobby walked quickly through the Saint Paulie streets, down the Gross

Frieheit and out of the Reeperbahn. He ran the gauntlet of prostitutes and drug dealers, keeping his eyes downcast and never stopped putting one foot in front of the other until he arrived at the British Sailors Society Mission.

The lights were on but nobody greeted him as he passed through the oversized door into the main hall. Bobby went to room 106 and collapsed on his bunk. He closed his eyes and tried to release some of the anger he felt. He hated being played for a fool. Here in Hamburg, it seemed that John had let his dark side take over.

What happened? Was it the result of taking a restless soul out of a safe, familiar environment, and thrusting him into a world of unrestricted personal freedoms? Bobby tried to find a parallel in his own experience but nothing came close. He'd felt the exhilaration of being completely footloose in Baltimore but never let it change his overall character.

Bobby drifted off to sleep wondering if John would ever be the same. He hadn't been asleep for half an hour before the door kicked open and Donovan and Archie stumbled in. The light came on. Something fell over. Bobby pulled back the covers and squinted.

Archie fell against the wall, slid down, and rolled forward onto the floor. Donovan sat on his bunk and took his boots off, letting Archie gurgle incoherently with his face pressed into the filthy carpet.

Donovan nudged Archie with his toe.

"Look at that. Pissed as a goat, he is. Dead nuts and brain gone blotto. Sleep where ya fall, ya sacka shit."

Bobby slunk back under the blanket and said nothing. He pretended to sleep.

When the first shafts of sunlight filtered through the curtains he rose and took a shower, leaving a comatose Archie on the floor and Donovan snoring in his bunk.

*   *   *

Paul found Bobby reading in the library area of the recreation room.

"Come on, mate. It's time for our haircuts."

Bobby closed the book.

"Where's John?"

Paul coughed up a laugh and smiled. "He's sleeping off the hangover of the century."

"Serves him right. I've never been so embarrassed in my life."

"You know... With John, sometimes you don't know if he's serious or not. But I'm pretty good at figuring out the difference. You must realize he meant no harm. He's a bulldog when it comes to taking the piss out of someone. He's even done it to me. But the fact remains, John has a good heart underneath it all. I've known him longer than anybody and I've seen everything he has to offer. The man is complex, but then aren't all geniuses like that?"

Bobby paused, put the book aside, and looked Paul in the eyes.

"You really think John Lennon is a genius?"

Paul waited to answer.

"A twisted genius. Yes, I believe he is. Of course here in Hamburg everything is multiplied by ten. All your wrong bits and right bits are magnified, see? The good is gooder and the bad is badder. And the music is music-er. John's all right. Don't worry about him. He'll wake up apologetic and philosophical, you'll see. He doesn't mean half of what he says, especially when he's drunk and cranked up on Prellys. I wouldn't worry about it."

"I hope your right."

"I know I'm right. Now let's go make some rock and roll hair history."

CHAPTER TEN

HAIR

Astrid Kirchherr's house was a short bus ride from the Reeperbahn to the Altoona suburbs of Hamburg. As they stepped off the bus, the quiet, tree-lined neighborhood seemed like another world. Paul, George and Bobby walked through it like invaders from some parallel universe. The few people who were out stared at them, mouths agape. Paul led them to Astrid's door.

"Look at this place," Bobby whispered. "And this is the country that *lost* the war?"

"The Kirchherrs are a solid middle-class family," George said. "Well educated, intellectual, somewhat artsy-fartsy. Hope that doesn't put you off."

"Not at all. I'm looking forward to it."

"They are some of the nicest people I have ever met."

Mrs. Kirchherr opened the front door and let them in. She spoke to them in German which none of them understood too well. Astrid had converted the living room into a makeshift hair salon with sheets covering the floor and a chair in the middle.

Klaus and Jürgen were there both just having had their hair trimmed. Stu sat alone in a corner, drawing on a sketchpad. Bobby noticed that even in the well-lit, cheery atmosphere of the Kirchherr living room, Stu still seemed swathed in shadow. Forever brooding and intense, he never really fit in with the rest of the Beatles. Noticing his hair, Bobby could see the artistic way Astrid had styled it.

Astrid looked magnificent in a short, black leather skirt and a black silk blouse with a white collar. She motioned for someone to sit in the chair.

"Who's first?"

Bobby looked at Paul.

"I'll go," they said in unison.

Astrid made a face.

"First you'll have to wash your hair so it is completely clean. There's a small sink under the stairs. Shampoo and towels are there."

* * *

"Bobby first, since his hair is the longest."

Bobby sat in the chair while Astrid draped a sheet around him.

"I love your hair," she said. "It's so nice and thick. You must have some blood in you."

"Blood?"

"She means non-English blood," said George.

"My mother was Greek. I'm half-Greek."

George said, "I'm one-third Scottish, one-eighth Irish, two-quarters Welsh, cuppa French, and one hundred percent rock and roll."

Astrid approached Bobby, scissors ready, and studied the way his hair grew. She gingerly took a few small snips off the back.

George watched, spellbound.

"Hair is important. It's the top of your head."

Astrid began to cut more of Bobby's hair, combing it in different directions and playing with the part.

"It looks so modern," George said. "It goes the opposite way, against the grain."

Astrid spoke as she worked. "Actually, when you comb it back like a Teddy Boy, that's when you're going against the grain. That's why you need all that greasy stuff to make it stay up. What we're doing now is going with the grain. It's much more natural. Your hair wants to go this way. It wants to be liberated. Your whole head will be lighter and more in tune."

George looked worried.

"What will John say?"

Astrid smiled but only Bobby could see.

Paul answered George's question with another. "What are we gonna do? Wait for John Lennon every time there's a decision to be made? It's my hair, man."

George wrung his hands.

"Right. But when he sees us all with new snippets, he's gonna feel like we went behind his back. We Beatles have to be tight. We gotta stick together."

"Well, what about Stu? He didn't ask anybody. He just did it."

"Stu's different. John worships Stu."

Klaus raised his hand as if he were in class. Everyone in the room looked at him.

"I can get the car, get John and be back in half an hour."

Paul shrugged

Paul shrugged.

"Problem solved," Bobby said.

Astrid pointed at Klaus and said something in German. He nodded and left the room.

"What did you tell him?"

"I told him to warn John to be on his best behavior in front of my mother; not make a scene."

*   *   *

"What's all this, then?" John croaked through vocal chords so raw it hurt to listen. He squinted at the rest of the Beatles.

Paul raised his hand.

"Just your neighborhood hair parlor."

Bobby waited for George, Paul or Stu to say something by way of explanation but none spoke. Bobby looked at Astrid hopeful her Bardot presence would calm troubled waters, but nothing happened. Klaus and Jürgen shifted uneasily in their seats. The uncomfortable silence hung over their heads. Bobby cleared his throat.

"I think I deserve an apology from you for your disgraceful behavior last night."

"What did I do?"

"You made a fool out of me!"

"Just for taking you to the Roxy? Everyone knows about the Roxy. It's no big deal. Derry and the Seniors did the same thing to us."

"That's not the way I treat my friends."

John's face was puffy, his complexion sour. He looked like he might be sick at any moment. He rubbed his eyes and blinked.

"What time is it?"

"It's after two."

John coughed making a dry chest-rattling vibration. He still had the mark on his jaw left by Bobby's fist.

John said, "Dust Bin Bob, you are one hundred percent right. I was a proper arse last night. For that, I apologize. I didn't mean anything by it, just havin' some dirty fun. The Reeperbahn brings out the beast in me."

Bobby stood up, legs slightly spread, hands on hips. It was challenging body language much like John's own onstage stance.

"Now there's the matter of some haircuts. Astrid has already cut my hair and styled it. How does it look?"

"I think it looks great," said Paul.

The others nodded their approval.

Bobby pointed at his head.

"See this? This is the way the Beatles should look. John, they want to do it. They want to make a change. I would think a guy like you would welcome a new look. After all, you're the resident rebel of the group. The old Elvis image is dead, over. It's time to do something radical, something new; something nobody else is doing. Personally, I don't give a shit what you do, but it doesn't seem right to hold the others back."

Astrid's mother wordlessly glided into the room and handed John a cold bottle of Orangina. He took a swig then looked around the room.

"Your words are strangely moving, Dust Bin Bob. I don't know what to say. A few minutes ago I was ready to break up the band because of some stupid haircuts. Now it all seems silly."

Paul said, "But, you must agree. It looks cool and different."

"It does look good."

Paul looked hopefully at John.

"Then you'll do it?"

John waited. His lips were pressed together like two white worms. The bags beneath his eyes seemed to quiver.

"I don't know, man..."

"Look, John. We either all do this together or we don't do it at all."

"What about Pete?"

"Forget about Pete. I'm talkin' about you, me and George."

"Do I get pork chops?"

"Yes," Astrid said. "But first you must wash your hair and sit in the chair."

John took another swig of the Orangina.

"All right then. I'll do it for the pork chops. The pork chops and the Beatles."

Klaus and Jürgen threw their arms up and cheered. Astrid rolled her eyes.

"Thank God that's over," George said. "I was gettin' a pimple worryin' about it. We can't let stuff like this come between us, man. It's not right. It's got to be Beatles first, last, and forever."

"George is right," Paul said. "We have to stick together. Toppermost of the poppermost and all that crap."

John bowed to George as if he were greeting royalty.

"No flies on Frank. My thickheaded pettiness will never hurt the band again. Bloody hell. I'm sorry. And now I hope you'll all join me in a rousing chorus of 'God Save The Queen.'"

Paul patted John on the back.

"So then all is forgiven?"

John nodded.

And it came to pass that the Beatles got new hair. Now we can go back to our luxury cubbyhole behind the Bambi Kino and not have to worry if we look cool.

*　*　*

George went first, watching every snip of the scissors in a mirror Astrid had set up in front of the makeshift barber chair. He winced when she pulled the top hair between her fingers and cut an inch away.

"There it goes."

A skilled hairstylist bent on perfection, Astrid concentrated on doing a good job. George tried to remain motionless, but Astrid still found reason to scold him for shifting in his seat.

"It won't be even unless you hold still."

"I am holding still. The chair is moving."

"Think about the pork chops," John said.

Astrid spent about thirty minutes carefully working on George's head as if it were a piece of sculpture. When she finished, she held up a mirror so he could view his new hair from every angle.

George said, "There's a revolution going on in me head. I can feel the strands of hair relaxing. I can feel the roots wiggling around in my scalp. This is amazing."

Paul jumped up and nearly leapt into the chair.

"I'm next!"

John sipped on his Orangina and studied George's hair. He said nothing. Bobby shook George's hand.

"Welcome, my friend."

He reached into his pocket and pulled out a small, foldable hairbrush. The type that sailors kept in their pea coats while at sea. George stared at it like a child staring at a sparkler.

"Take this, brother. May it serve you well."

George accepted the artifact. He grinned and flipped it up in the air.

As he caught it, he shouted, "Beatles new hair, a bloody smash!"

Astrid went to work on Paul's hair. When she finished, Paul stood before the others.

"My head has been liberated."

John, quiet for forty-five minutes, finally spoke in a hoarse whisper.

"I suppose it's my turn now. Just let me take one last look at my beautiful locks. My handsome sideboards. Ahh, Elvis, how I'm gonna miss ya."

John stepped reluctantly up to the chair. Astrid pointed to the washroom.

"Go and wash your hair and be quick about it."

"Achtung!"

John goose-stepped out of the room. Astrid folded her arms and shook her head.

"He's terrible. It's a wonder he's not in jail."

Astrid spent longer styling John's hair than she had on the others. She seemed to rise to an unspoken challenge between them. At one point John mentioned that he could always comb it back if he didn't like it. Astrid stopped cutting and put her hands on her hips.

"How dare you say that after I spent all this time cutting and styling your hair!"

"Sorry, Astrid. I didn't mean it like that."

"How did you mean it?"

"I just meant... Well, I just meant I could always go back... if I had to."

Astrid exhaled sharply with a loud, derisive huff.

"John Lennon, you should know more than anybody you can never go back."

"Never? Come on now."

"Never. Once the corner is turned, it is behind you. You want to comb your hair back the old way, then I stop wasting my time with you right now."

She put the scissors and comb down.

"Aw, Astrid, something got lost in the translation there. I really appreciate what you're doing for me. For us. It's just that I say the wrong thing sometimes. I'm not quite myself today. This bloody hangover is makin' me barmy. Please continue, if you will."

Astrid retrieved scissors and comb and resumed styling John's hair.

"The way I've cut it, it won't go back. The top and sides are too short. You'll have to live with it."

"Bloody hell..."

Stu who hadn't said much since Bobby arrived in Hamburg suddenly stood and pointed at John.

"You keep a civil tongue with Astrid. She's only trying to help."

"Are you two ganging up on me?" John mumbled.

"Yes, we are."

"OK, fuck it. It's not worth fightin' about."

Astrid finished John's hair and lined all the band members up against the wall. The smell of frying pork chops wafted from the kitchen making their mouths water. Astrid admired her work.

"I think it looks good, all four with the same haircut," she said. "From now on you have your own style."

George said, "Now we just have to get Pete in on it."

John laughed. "Good luck. Pete's tougher than me. He'll never go for it. He loves his hair. Besides, Pete marches to a different drummer. He's not one to go with the crowd. He likes to keep to himself."

*   *   *

The effect of the Beatles new hair at the Kaiserkeller was immediate. Bruno Koschmider didn't like it.

"Why do you do that? You look like students. I don't need more students coming in here. They don't have any money. They just take up space. You Beatles, you do everything wrong. Be careful or I'll throw you out of here on your asses. Then we'll see who's boss."

John just shrugged.

"Hey, Bruno. Why don't you just fuck yourself?"

Bruno's face trembled for one uncomfortable moment. An eye twitched, a nostril flared. Tension seemed to gather across his forehead. Then he laughed.

"Fuck myself? Ha! How is that possible? You Beatles, always clowning."

He looked at his watch. "Enough talk. Time to go on and mak shau!"

"Mak shau!" they shouted. "Mak shau! Mak shau!"

So the Beatles with their new hair took the stage at the Kaiserkeller.

Above the din, John shouted, "Here's one we wrote ourselves without any help from the army. One, two, three, fah!"

George struck up a rhythmic guitar riff with just the type of infectious, driving cadence he gave to the Chuck Berry songs. The groove expanded from the bandstand across the room.

John and Paul began to sing in unison, giving their combined voices a big boost. The effect was different, one Bobby hadn't heard before. The song was new too.

"Well, she was just seventeen, you know what I mean!" they sang defiantly. "And the way she looked was way beyond compare!"

Bobby listened to the lyrics clearly defined by the double vocal.

"Now, I'll never dance with another! Whoooo! Since I saw her standing there!"

They broke into harmony on the last two lines. Bobby tapped his foot and smiled. Did John say that they had written it?

Damn catchy.

Watching the band through the smoky gloom of the Kaiserkeller dance floor, Bobby felt a chill. Lit by a harsh spotlight in stark shadow, they appeared to be in a black and white movie. The song, the band, the haircuts, the attitude, it all seemed perfect.

Later when the set ended, the band rallied around Astrid's table.

"Did I hear you say you wrote that?" Bobby asked.

"That's right, yeah."

"We wrote it together," Paul said. "Back at me mum's house. It's a McCartney-Lennon original."

"That's Lennon-McCartney," John sniffed. "All our stuff is Lennon-McCartney."

Bobby felt a tap on the shoulder. George's voice whispered in his ear.

"Take a look over there." He pointed at the door to Bruno's office, a red "verboten" sign screwed permanently to the wood.

"It's your gruesome twosome, back again."

Donovan and Archie came out of the office with a huge Polynesian looking guy in a semi-transparent white shirt followed by Bruno. Standing next to the big guy, Bruno appeared to be about three feet tall. Bobby estimated the Polynesian's height at well over six feet. He was thick and bearish with slicked-back black hair and a flashing diamond ring that caught light from across the room. He loomed over the others like a Sumo wrestler.

"A very large person, that one is," George said. "Haven't seen him around. I'd remember."

"A brute like that could crush your windpipe with his thumb and forefinger," Bobby said.

"There's a happy thought."

George raised his left eyebrow.

"Do you suspect those two of doing something nefarious, perhaps even dastardly?"

"They do seem unsavory."

George laughed. "That describes half the people in here, including us."

The Beatles enjoyed their break, smoking and drinking and flirting with some of the female patrons. Just before they went on stage again, Bobby asked John for a minute.

"I ship out of here tomorrow. Won't be back for a couple of months."

John's face sank.

"Hope I didn't hurt your feelings what with all the crazy shit here. I can be a right arse at times. But I'm gonna miss you, Dusty. I really am. You have the best records of anyone I've ever known."

"Well, thank you, Mr. Lennon. I'll take that as a compliment."

"Plus, you're a good man."

The other Beatles were already on stage, plugged in, waiting for John. John stood awkwardly next to Bobby for a moment, then hugged him. Bobby patted John on the back.

Bobby said, "I'll see ya soon, mate. And I'll have a whole new batch of American 45s to hear."

"Dust Bin Bob, you are a man amongst men."

"I'll stay for one more set."

John Lennon took the stage with all the piss and swagger of a rock and roll thoroughbred. He approached the microphone defiantly and let go of a war whoop that got the attention of the whole room.

"This set is dedicated to Dust Bin Bob!"

"Long may he wave!" shouted Paul.

"Here! Here!"

They lurched into the Ray Charles hit, *What'd I Say?* and milked it for fifteen minutes. The electric piano riff worked like magic.

"Tell your momma, tell your paw, I'm gonna send ya back to Arkansas!"

Bobby watched his last Beatles set with a measure of sadness. What would happen to John without Bobby to keep the faith? Would these special guys dissipate into English mediocrity when the gig was over and they returned to Liverpool? Bobby didn't think so.

On stage the Beatles followed the Ray Charles rocker with a show tune. *Till There Was You* sounded familiar and different at the same time. Paul's vocal teetered on cute yet he pulled it off with an honest delivery completely devoid of pretension. Paul sang the song straight, and let the lyrics and melody create the mood.

The next song was sheer Chuck Berry passion. *Roll Over Beethoven* gave John a chance to scream his lungs out. Bobby watched the way John stood, guitar high on his chest, belting out the corrosive teenage poetry to a captivated audience.

The band made their way through a diverse set of cover tunes mixed with the occasional original composition. Chuck Berry's *Memphis,* Barrett Strong's *Money,* Little Richard's *Dizzy Miss Lizzie,* Buddy Holly's *Words Of Love.* More show tunes and standards like *Besame Mucho, The Sheik of Araby,* and *When The Saints Come Marchin' In* effortlessly flowed out of them. The group's repertoire seemed limitless.

When the set ended Bobby said his good-byes. With hugs all around from the Beatles and the exis, Bobby was about to leave when Horst Fascher, the head bouncer, approached.

"Bruno wants to introduce the band to his friend."

"Who's his friend?" John asked.

"The big man. Ragasa. He's a hot shot from the Philippines. He comes in when he's in town to pay his respects to Bruno. Come on, he wants to meet you."

John, Paul, and George went with Horst. Bobby walked a few feet behind curious about the meeting. He caught Donovan's eye and nodded.

"Well, well, young shipmate. You know these boys?"

"They're fellow Liverpudlians."

Bruno introduced "der Beatles" to Ragasa like a farmer showing off choice livestock. The big man complimented them on their version of *What'd I Say.*

"Ray Charles! Very good! Ray Charles! Very good!"

Paul strayed too close to Ragasa who grabbed a handful of leather-clad ass. Paul jumped.

"Hey!"

"Leather pants! Very good! Very good!"

"Hey, Bruno, tell your friend to not handle the musicians."

Bruno laughed.

Ragasa jabbed a meaty finger at Paul's black and silver cowboy boots. The pointy toes and high Cuban heels seemed to intrigue him.

"Boots?"

Paul kept his distance.

"Yeah, cowboy boots."

"Cowboy boots! Very good! Very good!"

John who'd been watching mumbled thanks and went back to his table. Donovan seemed interested in Bobby's plans.

"When do you ship out?"

"Tomorrow."

"Next port of call?"

"Baltimore."

Donovan's eyes gleamed.

"Back to the open sea, lad. Back where a man is free from oppression."

Bobby cocked his head.

"Oppression? There's no oppression."

"All working-class people are oppressed."

"I do all right for myself."

"I'm sure you do, laddie. I'm sure you do."

Baffled by his short conversation with Donovan, Bobby walked away from the table and found Horst Fascher standing near the door. He greeted Bobby with a nod.

"Couple of strange birds, eh?"

Bobby said, "What do you know about Donovan?"

Horst shrugged. "Not much. Him and the other guy pop up every few months, go into Bruno's office, come out, and get drunk. That's it."

"They must have some business with Bruno then."

Horst laid a hand on Bobby's shoulder.

"Everybody here has business. Don't talk about it and you'll live a lot longer, friend."

Bobby left the Kaiserkeller and walked along the Gross Freiheit. Hookers made sucking sounds when he past them, drunks leaned against walls, angry voices shouted in German behind glass doors. The Reeperbahn seethed with manic energy. On the edge of the Saint Paulie district where the nightclub area ends, he found a quiet cafe. He wanted to sort things out and spend some time alone. He stayed for an hour, drank two pints, then walked slowly back to the mission.

Along the way a dark figure came out of an alley. It darted toward him and Bobby jumped aside. The figure turned, bent over, and vomited all over Bobby's legs. Bobby jumped back.

"Jesus! What are you doing? Get back, damn it!"

The figure hunched over and continued to spew vomit all over the ground. Bobby turned and walked away as quickly as he could.

Once inside the mission, Bobby went to his room and changed his pants. He threw his trousers and socks in the garbage. He cleaned his shoes.

As he walked down the hall to the shower, Archie and Donovan came up the stairs. He caught a glimpse of them as they rounded the corner and entered the room. Archie looked up, made eye contact with Bobby but didn't change his facial expression. They entered room 106 and closed the door.

Bobby washed himself thoroughly. The thought of the vomit made him nauseous. When he was convinced he was clean, he put on a white cotton robe and went back to the room. Loathing the idea of further conversation with Donovan, he decided to go to sleep.

He opened the door and the light was out. As he reached for the light switch, he slipped on something wet and fell. The light from the hall spilled into the room, illuminating a dim triangle of floor. Bobby looked down and gasped.

"Blood!"

He tried to stand but slipped again. Blood was everywhere. His elbows, knees, hands, and feet were slick with it. His white bathrobe was splattered and soaked with rich red swatches. He crawled backward to the door and felt the jam with his shoulder. Steadying himself, his heart pounding out of control, he slowly rose and flicked on the light.

Archie was in his cot, his throat slit from ear to ear bathed in blood. Donovan was gone.

Bobby opened his mouth to scream but managed only a dry squawk. He tried to swallow, but every molecule of moisture in his mouth had suddenly evaporated. He pounded the wall with his fist.

"Hey! Somebody's been knifed in here!"

He ran down the hall leaving bloody footprints on the hardwood floor. Jim Hawke lived with his family upstairs. Bobby pounded on the door until Hawke answered. He took one look at Bobby covered with blood, and shrieked.

"Oh, God! What's happened, boy?"

"There's been a stabbing. I came back to my room after using the bath, and I slipped on something. Archie was on the bed with blood all over."

Jim saw Bobby's trembling hands, and the path of bloody footprints leading down the hall.

"Then what?"

"Then I came here."

Jim closed the door behind him.

"Let's have a look."

Bobby led him back to room 106 and pointed inside.

"In there."

Jim looked, then backed out shaking his head.

"It looks like the work of Jack the Ripper. You saw nothing?"

Bobby nodded. "I saw Donovan and Archie come in as I was going to the shower. I saw them go in and close the door. When I came back I found it like this."

"Where's Donovan?"

I don't know."

"We'll have to call the police. Close the door and come back to my apartment. We can phone them from there."

They hastened down the hall.

"I have to ask you, son. Did you have anything to do with this? Anything at all?"

Bobby's shock registered on his face.

"No! Of course not!"

"I had to ask, you understand. I want to protect you. The German cops can be hard to deal with. But you came to me as soon as you saw it. That was the right thing to do so you should be cleared."

"Mr. Hawke, I'm scheduled to ship out tomorrow."

Jim shook his head.

"Oh. That's bad. The investigation could take a while."

"I can't miss the boat, sir. I'll lose my place."

Jim looked at Bobby's bloody robe and the look of panic on his face.

"I'll see what I can do, son."

CHAPTER ELEVEN

ARCHIBALD STILLMAN

Hamburg Police Detective Rolf Schmidt spoke excellent English. His even, professional line of questioning gave Bobby confidence. He'd expected the worst. Again and again, they went over the facts.

"You say you saw both Donovan and Archie at the Kaiserkeller earlier in the evening?"

"Yes. They were talking to Bruno Koschmider, the owner of the club. They were with a big Filipino guy; I think his name was Ragasa. They all seemed friendly. I left and walked back here, stopping for a few beers at the little cafe I told you about. A drunk vomited on me so I was in a hurry to wash up. I came here, saw the two of them enter the room and close the door. I don't know if Donovan saw me, but I'm pretty sure Archie did. I took a shower and when I came back to the room I found Archie dead and Donovan gone. That's it. I've left nothing out."

The Detective took notes and nodded.

"What do you know about them?"

Bobby sighed. "Very little. I don't even know their last names. I know that they were from the *Manila Prince* and that they frequented brothels. I know that they knew Bruno Koschmider and Ragasa, and they liked to drink."

Rolf snapped his leather bound notebook shut. He studied Bobby's face.

Bobby, though frightened, kept his cool. *Let him see I have nothing to hide,* he thought.

Rolf's blond crew cut showed his scalp pink and clean. He was immaculately dressed. With his hands folded he seemed almost robotic.

"I understand that your ship is scheduled to sail today. Mr. Hawke has informed me of your situation. I'll need to corroborate the details of your story, but I am not naming you a suspect, just a witness. This could change later. You'll need to make yourself available for future testimony in a German court. Your shipping line will be notified, as will your captain. I may allow you to return to your ship before it leaves."

Bobby shivered. "Thank you. Thank you, so much."

"Clean up and change your clothes. The officers will remove your duffel bag from the crime scene. I've already searched it and found nothing incriminating. Mr. Hawke will assign you a temporary new room. You will not leave this place until you hear from me. Understood?"

"Yes."

"Good."

Bobby took another shower, got his duffel bag, and changed his clothes. Jim Hawke gave him a private room. Bobby sat on the bed and worried.

A few hours later another group of detectives arrived to question him. They identified themselves as Interpol Agents. The senior agent, Hans Kruger, went over every detail of Bobby's story yet again.

"Why would Interpol be interested in a couple of dockside lowlifes?"

Hans Kruger smiled politely. He was a smallish man with pale skin and a mustache. He wore a gray suit and sat straight. His piercing owlish eyes saw everything.

"The man that was killed, Archibald Stillman, was someone of interest to us. We've been looking for Mr. Stillman for a long time."

"Are you serious? Interpol was interested in Archie?"

"Did you have any conversations with him?"

"No. Donovan did most of the talking."

"About what?"

"The first conversation I had he invited me to go whoring with them. I declined. Then he asked me about my ship, where I was going, stuff like that. He seemed to be more interested in me than I was in him. I thought they were unsavory types and wanted nothing to do with them."

"Did he say anything unusual?"

"Now that you mention it, he said something odd tonight at the

Kaiserkeller. He said all working people are oppressed."

"Why did he say that?"

"I don't know. When we first met he asked me if I was in the union. I thought that was a bit odd."

"Interesting. What about Ragasa? Did he say anything?"

"No. He just wanted to meet the band."

"The band?"

"Yes, the Beatles. They're a beat group. They play at the Kaiserkeller. Friends of mine."

"You've told me everything?"

Bobby nodded. "Absolutely."

"Detective Schmidt of the Hamburg Police is very thorough so I'll wait and read his report. You seem to be telling the truth, and I expect they'll let you board your vessel. You will be required to return to testify, you understand. Failure to do so would be a crime punishable by prison."

"Yes, of course. Are you gonna let me go now?"

"For now, Mr. Dingle. One more thing, if any of these gentlemen try to contact you, I want you to call me immediately. My office will accept the charges from anywhere in the world."

Hans handed Bobby a business card with a handwritten phone number on the back.

Bobby frowned. "Why would they try to contact me?"

Hans shrugged. "You were one of the last people to see Archibald Stillman alive."

*　　*　　*

Detective Schmidt drove Bobby to the Hamburg docks and escorted him onto the *Pilgrim's Progress*. They met briefly with the Captain and paperwork was signed. All non-crew members left the ship, the lines were cast, and Bobby watched the Hamburg docks recede as the aging cargo vessel pulled away. The lights of the city soon became distant points on the horizon.

Bobby resumed life at sea. Tedium returned, giving him too much time to ponder the events of Hamburg. Had Donovan killed Archie?

Bobby couldn't stop thinking about Archie. The mental image of his murdered body haunted Bobby. Archie seemed little more than a grunting pig; Donovan's sidekick, a thug. To think of him as Archibald Stillman, an Interpol fugitive, was unsettling.

Another life lesson that *things were not always what they seemed* imprinted itself on Bobby's psyche.

After a stop in Liverpool, the *Pilgrim's Progress* would once again make passage for Baltimore. Bobby took a bus to Woolton where he visited John's Aunt Mimi. They pumped him for information about John. How was he getting on in Germany? Was he making enough money to live?

He answered, assuring them that everything was just fine and at the end of the Beatles' engagement, John would be back home. Aunt Mimi expressed her doubts.

"He'll come back as broke as ever, a year behind in his studies and further from a real job than before. I fear for that boy's future."

"He has his music," Bobby said.

"Music? Ha! It'll be the ruin of him."

Aunt Mimi insisted Bobby stay for dinner. After a wonderful meal, Bobby excused himself and walked to Nancy Garlton's house.

He knocked on the door for several minutes before a small, nervous-looking woman dressed in a nurse's uniform peered through the window.

"Yes?"

"I've come to see Mrs. Garlton."

"Mrs. Garlton isn't feeling well. I'm afraid you'll have to come back some other time."

"I've only got one day ashore. I'm off for the States aboard the *Pilgrim's Progress* tonight. Could you just tell her that Robert Dingle has come to visit?"

"Wait here."

A few minutes later she returned and led Bobby through the house. As they ascended the stairs to the second floor, Bobby remembered the last time he'd been there. He remembered the expert way Nancy Garlton's fingers led Bobby through the awkward stages of lovemaking; the infinite patience she showed, the care and sensitivity. Bobby's life had changed profoundly that day.

Bobby approached the door to her room with trepidation. The nurse knocked discretely and opened the door. Bobby followed her into the room.

Nancy Garlton looked up from her bed.

"Robert? Is that you?"

Bobby stood next to the bed and held her hand.

"Yes, Mrs. Garlton."

"Nancy."

"Yes, Nancy. I've been at sea as a steward's apprentice on the *Pilgrim's Progress*. It's been quite an adventure. But what's all this?"

Nancy turned to the nurse.

"Please leave us for a few minutes, dear. I'd like to talk to Mr. Dingle privately."

The nurse left. Bobby pulled up a chair and looked at Nancy Garlton. His heart sank as he gazed into her gaunt face. She had aged twenty years.

"Oh, Robert. Where do I begin? Things have taken a turn for the worse, I fear. I have cancer. I don't have much time left."

"Oh, God. I'm so sorry."

"Why should you be sorry? It's not your fault. People always say that but they never mean it. I'm the one who's sorry. Of all people you shouldn't be sorry, Robert. You're the only one who brought a little happiness into my life."

Bobby swallowed hard. Seeing her like this made him uncomfortable. He shifted in his chair.

Nancy continued. "You were the only ray of sunshine in a very dark time, and I treasure that memory."

"Thank you. But I don't know what to say."

Nancy managed a knowing smile.

"That's a good trait. If you don't know what to say, say nothing."

Bobby nodded. "I've learned a lot about life since we last spoke. I think I'm beginning to catch on."

"I'm so glad you came, dear. I can't tell you how happy it makes me. How's your antique business?"

"I'm going to my father's place on my way back to the ship. I've gotten a few letters from him. Things are the same as when I left."

"Why did you come all the way to Woolton before you went home to visit your father?"

"I'm going there next. I promise."

"See that you do."

The sun's rays filtered through the lace curtains, sprinkling the room with dappled shadows. Nancy's hair looked dry. Bobby noticed some tubes snaking under the sheets.

"Robert, would you go over to the bookcase and take out the last book on the top shelf?"

Bobby found the book and handed it to Nancy. She opened it with thin fingers and started to read.

"Nothing is real in Strawberry Fields. In fact, the fields are clover."

She snapped the book shut and closed her eyes.

"It's the duality of life."

"It is?"

"Yes. I want you to have this."

She handed the book to Robert and he read the cover.

"*Strawberry Fields* by Nancy Garlton. A book of Liverpool poems."

"My last published work."

"I always suspected you were a poet."

Bobby examined the book. It was a thin volume, light in his hand. He opened it to find an inscription. "To Robert Dingle, a truly beautiful man."

Bobby blushed. "Thanks."

Bobby thumbed through the pages filled with Nancy's poetry.

"How many volumes have you published?"

"Six. The poetry market has fallen off a bit lately. Thank God it isn't my primary source of income. After my husband died, I didn't have to work, but I wanted to. I got a job writing greeting cards. From there I wrote my own poetry, found a small publishing house and convinced them to publish me."

He gently closed the book and smiled.

"I'm very flattered. Thank you. I'll treasure this."

"And I'll treasure the memory we had together. After I'm gone, you'll be the only one with that memory. Promise me you won't forget."

Bobby felt a lump in his throat.

"I won't forget, Nancy."

She reached out and squeezed his hand. Bobby leaned over the bed and hugged her.

"Oh, God, Robert. That feels so good. I haven't been hugged in so long."

He hugged her tighter and she moaned. Bobby could feel the frailness of her body. He felt like crying as he she pressed against him desperately.

The nurse cleared her throat behind him, and Bobby released Nancy. She fell back against her pillow, exhausted.

"It's time for Mrs. Garlton to rest," the nurse said.

The sharpness in her voice made Bobby turn around, and he saw her frowning.

Nancy was smiling.

"I better be going. I've still got to see my dad before I leave."

"Godspeed, Robert. Come back again soon."

Bobby walked past the disagreeable nurse and out the door.

*   *   *

Dingle's Second Hand Shop was closed, the storefront dark. Bobby looked up at the second floor window. The lights were off. He went around to the back entrance and let himself in. The place seemed deserted.

He walked up the stairs to his room and saw several cardboard boxes piled in the corner. He peered inside and wanted to shout out with joy. *Records! American rock and roll records! God bless Mrs. Swithins!*

Bobby took the boxes with him. He took a letter he had written at sea and placed it in his father's room. As he was leaving, he heard the shop door being unlocked.

Bobby waited.

Somebody walked inside and turned on the light switch.

"Dad?"

"Bobby?"

"Yes, Dad. I just have a short time in town and wanted you to see you."

Bobby hugged his father.

"You know, son, it's strange. You never know how much you'll miss someone until they're gone. I found myself looking for you around the house."

"I'll be back again next month."

"Let's go down to the pub and have a pint before you go."

Bobby said, "What if we run into Mick and Clive?"

Robert Dingle, Sr. smiled. His voice was warm.

"We can't let those two run our lives, can we?"

They walked to a corner pub. His father ordered two pints and they took a booth away from the door. They drank silently for a few minutes.

"How's life at sea?"

"Not too bad once you get used to it. I've seen America."

"Is it like in the movies?"

Bobby chuckled. "Not at all."

"You know, Bobby, I've always had high hopes for you. The other two are doomed to fail, but you got your mother's brain and your mother's heart. You're smarter. You speak better. You have a nose for business. It's like old Mrs. Swithins said. You're gonna go far in this world."

Bobby sipped his beer.

"Thanks, Dad."

"It's true. I'm proud of you, son. You're gonna do all right."

Bobby's father glanced in the direction of the door.

Bobby said, "You don't have to be afraid, Dad. Chances are those two are out causing trouble somewhere. Besides, they don't drink here. It's too boring."

"I'm not afraid of them, but I do worry about what they might do to you if they found you here. Since you've been gone, they've been happy as a pair of buggers. They might not like it if you came back."

Bobby looked at the door.

"I'm not afraid of them anymore."

"You should be. There's something wrong with those two. They feed off each other. I don't like it. God knows I wasn't the best father in the world, but I never dreamed they'd be this bad."

Bobby watched a man playing darts on the other side of the room.

"They never forgave you for marrying mom after their mother died. When I came along that made it worse."

His father smiled. "Ahh, your mother was such a joy. She was truly something special. Prettier than the others, she was. Cultured, always cheerful and neat as a pin. God, I miss that woman. I always wondered what she saw in me."

Bobby had never heard his father speak like this.

"You thought she was too good for you, Dad?"

His father nodded. "Your mother was a princess. I was a pauper."

"Then why do you think she married you?"

His father paused. A satisfied grin spread across his face.

"Well, you know, son, back in the day, I was quite the ladies' man."

"You?"

His father nodded. "Oh, yeah. Women came from near and far to taste the Dingle treatment."

"G'wan!"

"It's true."

"Come on, Dad."

His father laughed. "I might've caught that little hummingbird with honey, but the reason she stayed was because I treated her like a queen. Women love to be wined and dined in the beginning, but once you get married and the drudgery of housework sinks in, they become miserable. That never happened with your mother. I made sure she was always happy every day of her life, and I never stopped loving her and treating her like a lady."

Bobby thought he might cry. Instead he drank beer.

His father raised a toast.

"Here's to you, Bobby! Do right, son, and you'll never be wrong!"

CHAPTER TWELVE

THE BIG B

While at sea, Bobby received three letters from his father addressed to the *Pilgrim's Progress*, Albert Dock, Liverpool. The first two, dated weeks before, contained friendly greetings from home, a bit of news, and some advice. The third was shorter. The handwriting looked rushed, nearly scribbled. The sentences were short and direct.

Bobby read: "Dear Son, I hope this letter finds you in good health. There is bad news about your brothers. They got into a fight with some foreigners. Mick's been shot and is in the hospital. The doctors don't know if he'll live. Clive is in jail. I am disgusted with them."

Bobby folded the letter. "Jesus."

He decided to send his father a ship-to-shore telegram. As despicable as Mick was, he was still family, and Bobby still wanted to know his fate. The last letter was dated three days ago so anything could have happened.

Bobby urged his father to wire back as soon as possible.

Days passed. Bobby waited for a reply but none came. Bobby became preoccupied and spent many hours staring at the horizon. Time that he used to spend in blissful rapture listening to rock and roll was filled with dark thoughts about his father, Mick, Clive, Archie, Donovan, and Nancy Garlton. He hardly played the old Gibson guitar anymore.

He stared at the records Mrs. Swithins had collected for him but could barely work up enough enthusiasm to play them. The titles were intriguing: *Kansas City* by Wilbert Harrison, *Sea Cruise* by Frankie Ford, but he found it difficult to focus on the music. Only one record spoke to him now: *Since I Don't Have You* by the Skyliners. Haunted by the melody he played it over and over again and thought of Cricket.

Cricket's letters had been few but sweet. Bobby longed for her during the lonely nights at sea. He'd never been in a strong romantic relationship. Now he realized the downside of it. The longing, the jealousy, the anxiety hit him hard. She might not feel the same about him. At times he convinced himself that the whole thing had been a fantasy blown way out of proportion. A few days with a beautiful girl in a foreign port; it happened all the time.

But Bobby felt sure he was in love. Standing on the heaving deck of the *Pilgrim's Progress*, a thousand miles from anywhere, he tried to find perspective. Out here in the middle of the ocean, one person's problems seemed less significant. Yet, Bobby's heart roiled with conflicting emotions. His dreams became fitful, full of Nancy Garlton, Archie's bloody corpse, and Mick and Clive.

The journey from Liverpool to Baltimore passed uneventfully. When the *Pilgrim's Progress* arrived at Patapsco River Dock, Bobby couldn't wait to get off the ship. He went to the company office to send a telegram and found one waiting for him.

It was from his father; the words short and final.

"Mick dead. Clive in jail."

That was it. Five words. Bobby folded it and put it in his pocket. He didn't know how to feel. He went over to the counter and wrote his reply.

"Sorry about Mick. It's terrible."

Five words of his own. He handed the paper to the agent and paid the fee. His hands began to shake. He felt weak as he caught a cab.

He had the driver wait while he went to the door and rang Cricket's buzzer. He rang several times until he was convinced she wasn't home. He went back to the cab and sat in the back seat.

"Where to now, Mac?"

Bobby shrugged. "Peabody Book Shop."

"The Peabody. Got it. Hey, you from overseas?"

"Yeah, Liverpool."

"I got an uncle in Liverpool. He says it's a lot like the good old Big B."

"Big B?"

"Yeah, Baltimore. Big B. That's our nickname. You wanna know something?"

Bobby was about to answer when the cabby continued. "That place you're goin'used to be notorious. H.L. Mencken was a regular."

The cab turned on Charles Street. Bobby watched the neighborhood change. Block after block of row houses with white marble steps gave way to bigger, older buildings. The Peabody looked closed from the street. Its dusty front window, piled high with used volumes, barely let light escape.

"Is it open?"

"Oh, yeah. Rose don't close as long as she knows."

"Knows what?"

"Knows there's somebody spendin' money. That would be you, right?"

"Maybe. I'm looking for somebody I met last time I was in town."

The cabby nodded knowingly.

"A girl?"

"Yeah."

"Student?"

"Yeah."

"This place is crawlin' with 'em. Good luck."

Bobby paid the cabby and entered the dimly lit bookshop. He made his way to the back. He scanned the room for Cricket and felt his heart sink. She wasn't there. Bobby fell into a chair and rubbed his eyes.

"Long day, hon?"

Bobby looked up at large Armenian woman wearing a brightly colored gypsy blouse with a dozen bracelets that jangled on her wrist.

"Pardon me?"

"Oh, an Englishman. Say something."

"What do you mean, say something? What should I say?"

"Liverpool."

Bobby smiled. "Very good."

"I'm Rose. I pride myself on accents. What can I get you to drink?"

"Oh, I don't know... A beer, I guess. Might you have any English beer?"

"Can't help you there, but I got Rolling Rock."

"I'm not familiar with that."

"From the glass-lined tanks of Latrobe, Pennsylvania," Rose quoted the bottle. "Try one. It'll cheer you up."

Rose left to get the Rolling Rock and Bobby looked around the room. Candles burned in Chianti bottles, soft conversation filtered through the atmosphere of dark wood and cigarette smoke. There was something universally familiar and soothing about the place.

It must have been a great speakeasy.

Rose returned with the Rolling Rock.

"You lookin' for somebody?"

"How did you know?"

"You have that look. I can tell 'cause I see it here all the time. Who are you lookin' for? Maybe I know 'em."

"She's a Maryland Institute student. Long dark hair, slim, kinda arty-looking."

"You just described most of the girls who come in here."

"They call her Cricket."

"Doesn't ring a bell."

"Well, thanks anyway."

"Suit yourself," Rose said.

Bobby nursed his beer for an hour. Cricket never showed.

Bobby walked up the steps to Charles Street and watched the traffic flow past. He tried to catch a cab but had no luck so he walked south toward the Washington Monument. At Mount Vernon he stopped and listened to some folk singers sitting on the steps. Their sound reminded Bobby of skiffle music.

He wandered into the central branch of the Enoch Pratt Public Library. Around the corner he found a bustling newsstand and bought a week-old London Times. He saw a cab parked nearby and got in.

"Where to?"

The cab pulled away from the curb and Bobby thought about Cricket. It was too late to go back to her place; he'd try again tomorrow. He told the cabby to take him to the only other place he knew in Baltimore.

"The Block."

"Baltimore Street?"

"Yeah. The place with all the strip clubs."

After the Reeperbahn, The Block no longer intimidated Bobby. In fact, it seemed downright tame to him now. When the taxi dropped him off in front of the Two O'Clock Club, he was almost looking forward to the tacky pleasures of Baltimore nightlife. A cold beer and a sleazy strip show seemed right somehow.

Erlene was onstage and Blaze Starr was at the bar, exactly as it had been when Bobby left. He took a seat near the stage and ordered a drink. Erlene noticed him immediately and danced in front of him until he began to sweat and squirm. When the song was over, she came and sat at his table.

"Ain't you the Englishman with the big cock?"

She lit a cigarette and blew the smoke in Bobby's direction.

"Big cock? Clovis told you that, right?"

"That no-goodnik still owes me money. You seen him?"

"No. I just got here."

"Well, if you see him, tell him I want my money or I'm sending Big Marv over to collect it for me."

Bobby shrugged. "I haven't seen him in months. I've been at sea."

"You really got a big salami?"

Bobby laughed. "Well... It's been reported in the press, but I..."

"Lemme see it."

"I beg your pardon?"

"Lemme see that thing."

"No."

"Come on, mister, whip it out and let's get a good look."

Bobby blushed. "Here?"

"Not here. In the dressing room. All the girls will want to see. It's something we do to break the monotony. We had a Nigerian guy in here last week with a fuckin' baseball bat. A regular Louisville Slugger."

Bobby's mouth hung open as he tried to find words.

"I think I'll keep the dangly bits in my pants for now."

"You're missin' the boat, fellah. Half the guys in Baltimore would kill to be in your shoes but suit yourself."

Bobby finished his drink quickly and stood.

"I gotta go. See you soon, Erlene."

"Come back any time."

"I will. Thanks."

Bobby hurried out into the Baltimore night and walked in the direction of Livingston Loans. He passed the entrance to a small, seedy, bar in the middle of the block. A live band was belting out *Sweet Little Sixteen* by Chuck Berry. Bobby was drawn by the crisp guitar work. He went inside and found a long, dark room with a bar along one side. In the back was a tiny bandstand. A five-piece band furiously ripped through the instrumental break in the song, driving home the beat.

Bobby looked closer at the band and recognized Clovis as the lead guitar player. Bobby was surprised at how professional Clovis sounded. If he closed his eyes, he wouldn't be able to tell the difference between Clovis' lead and Chuck's.

Bobby watched the band until their break and then approached Clovis at the bar.

"That you? Robby, the Limey?"

"It's me. How are you, Clovis?"

"I ain't got a pot to piss in, but I guess I'm doin' all right."

"I saw Erlene a few minutes ago and she said she wants her money or somebody named Big Marv will pay you a visit."

Clovis took a long drink on a glass of whiskey.

"Yeah, yeah. So what else is new?"

"Are you and Erlene having problems?"

"You might say that. She took a shot at me with a twenty-two pistol, had her new boyfriend beat me up, then called the cops on me and had me arrested."

"Ouch."

"She said I owed her five hundred bucks."

Bobby noticed how threadbare and shabby Clovis' burgundy show jacket was.

"Are you in this band?"

"Nah, I'm just fillin' in tonight to make a few bucks. I'm reforming my own group, the Thunderbirds, and gettin' ready to make my move. I know a cat down in Nashville that'll get me an audition with Decca Records."

"You sounded great on the guitar tonight. Chuck Berry would've been proud."

"That's my old Telecaster. Just about the only thing I ain't hocked yet. Hey, whatever happened to that girl you met? Chicklet?"

"Cricket."

Clovis rolled his eyes.

"Cricket, mosquito, who cares? The main thing is she's cute. Have you looked her up yet?"

"I went straight over to her place but she wasn't home.

Clovis nodded. "Yeah, man. That's the story of my life. They're never home."

Bobby noticed three big guys moving through the tables toward them. Clovis, with his back to them, couldn't see. Bobby nodded at the intruders.

"You know those guys?"

It was too late. Clovis turned around and faced the biggest of the three.

"Shit."

"Thought you could skip out on me?"

"No, Big Marv. I swear I didn't."

"You owe me and Erlene five hundred bucks. You got it?"

Clovis shook his head.

"You know I ain't got that kinda money, Marv. I'm broke. Honest."

"Then I'm gonna have to bust your head."

"Well, go ahead and bust it, but it ain't gonna get you any money."

Big Marv loomed over Clovis, menacing and belligerent. Bobby could feel his knees weaken. The two guys with Big Marv looked like professional wrestlers. Bobby watched Clovis closely. When Big Marv's hand wrapped around Clovis' collar and drew him to his feet, Clovis showed no fear. Bobby had seen that before when John defended Stu in the parking lot of Lathom Hall and when Cricket used her Judo on the two muggers. Here in a sleazy bar, Bobby sensed the same noble lack of fear. A down and out guitar player in a threadbare sports jacket stood up to a professional goon.

Clovis said, "She's got you on a string, Marv. You're dancing to her tune now, man. You can kick my ass all you want but it ain't gonna change nothin'."

Big Marv's eyes widened.

"That's it, you asshole!"

Big Marv's fist came back ready to knock Clovis' head off. For Bobby, time slowed down.

"Wait a second," Bobby said.

Big Marv looked at Bobby with contempt.

"Who the fuck are you?"

Bobby said the only thing that made sense.

"I'm from England."

Big Marv relaxed for a second. Bobby could almost see Marv's mind processing the information.

"So?"

"In England we have a way to settle disputes like this so that all the parties come away happy."

Big Marv loosened his grip around Clovis' collar. He seemed amused.

"Well, kiss my ass, Percy. What are you, some kinda lawyer?"

"I'm just an innocent bystander who may have a solution to your dilemma."

Big Marv grunted at the other two thugs and they all grunted together.

"My dilemma, he says! Ha! That's a good one! All right, Little Lord Fauntleroy, I'm listenin'. It better be good 'cause now I'm gonna kick your ass too."

Bobby motioned to the table.

"Why don't we all sit down and have a beer while we discuss this."

Big Marv squinted at Bobby.

"You got big balls, I'll say that. All right, Englishman, I'll let you buy us a beer before we break your legs."

They all sat down. Clovis ran a comb through his pompadour and broke out a pack of Beemans chewing gum.

"Want a piece?"

Clovis popped a stick into his mouth and started chewing earnestly.

Bobby signaled to the bartender for a round of beers.

"OK, now, what's your complaint with this man?"

"He owes me money."

"I thought you said it was Erlene's money."

"It's both our money."

"How did you arrive at that dollar amount?"

"Erlene did."

Clovis shook his head.

"You got it all wrong, hoss. She's just sayin' that so you'll come over here and kick my ass. She's usin' you to get to me, playin' us both for chumps. I ain't got no money, everybody knows that, so the only possible thing that could happen is you'd whup me. And that would make her happy, see?"

Big Marv said nothing. The beer arrived. He drank quietly for a few moments.

"Erlene says you owe her money for rent while you stayed at her place and freeloaded off her."

Bobby leaned forward.

"What's the monetary value?"

"What do you mean?"

"How much is her rent?"

Big Marv sputtered. "I think it's... shit, I don't know."

"She ain't livin' at the Ritz," Clovis said. "I think it's pretty cheap."

"How long were you there?"

"It's hard to say. I guess two months or so, but you gotta figure I was kicked out half the time."

"So the time you actually spent with her in the apartment was a month. I don't know about this town but in Liverpool, the rents are low in neighborhoods like this. Allowing for the difference in currency, and taking into consideration that Clovis only owes half the rent... It's maybe forty dollars at the most. Does that sound right? Then there's food. I don't suppose you were eating T-bone steaks every night."

"Hot dogs, man."

Bobby nodded. "Let's say fifteen dollars."

"How about booze? They both like to drink," Big Marv said.

"Twenty dollars in booze then. That's seventy-five dollars total."

Big Marv looked sheepishly at his cohorts. They pulled on their beer bottles and said nothing.

"So we've figured the amount to be seventy-five dollars. What would you be willing to settle for?"

Big Marv looked confused. "Settle?"

"Yeah, Clovis is broke. What would you settle for?"

Big Marv shook his head.

"I ain't about to settle. He owes seventy-five, I want seventy-five."

Bobby pushed himself away from the table and stood up.

"In that case go ahead and start your beating."

Big Marv stood.

"OK, if that's the way you want it."

Bobby held up his hand.

"Allow me to make a counter offer. How about fifty bucks to just forget about the whole thing?"

Big Marv scratched his head.

"Fifty? Cash? Right now?"

Bobby nodded.

"Deal."

Bobby pulled two twenties and a ten out of his wallet.

Clovis looked at the money in disbelief.

"Are you sure? That's a lot of jingo for a guy you hardly know."

"You can owe it to me."

After Big Marv left with the fifty dollars, Clovis hugged Bobby.

"Man! You saved me a big whuppin'. Why did you do that?"

"Seeing you face down Big Marv like that, showing no fear, it inspired me."

Clovis laughed. "No fear? Man, I was petrified! I learned to stay cool in prison. If you show any fear at all, those cats will be up your ass quicker than you can whistle *Dixie*."

"Why does Erlene hate you so much?"

"She don't hate me, hoss. She loves me."

"She's got a strange way of showing it. What about Big Marv? Is she makin' time with him?"

Clovis winked. "Marv ain't no Marlon Brando. What I said was true, man. She's just usin' the big ugly sumbitch. He thinks he's got a shot at those bodacious ta-ta's of hers, but she's playin' him like a fiddle. She'll get you all hot and bothered, then she'll throw cold water on your boner and leave you climbin' the walls. She's been leadin' men around by the pecker her whole life. Marv thinks he can take it, believe me, he can't. In Erlene's hands, he's just a little bitty puppy."

Bobby sipped his beer fascinated by Clovis' monologue.

Clovis said, "I'm the only one who can tame that wild filly, and she knows it. She's just playin' hard to get."

He let out a rebel yell that caused everyone in the bar to look.

"That woman is one hot firecracker!"

CHAPTER THIRTEEN

SHE LOVES YOU

Bobby emerged from a deep sleep, his mind categorizing all the sounds on board the ship. Then he heard a peculiar chewing sound which wasn't one of them. He opened an eye and saw Clovis eating an apple.

"Jesus Christ, Clovis! How did you get in here?"

Clovis grinned. "Told 'em I was your rumba teacher."

Bobby blinked.

"It's too early. Go away and come back later."

He pulled the blanket over his head. Clovis addressed the lump in the blanket.

"Rock and roll has been goin' downhill since Chuck Berry was convicted of the Mann Act."

Clovis finished the apple, tossed the core, and lit a cigarette. The smoke from it made Bobby nauseous.

"Once they busted old Chuck, man, that was it. That was all she wrote."

Bobby spoke from beneath the covers.

"Clovis, you can't come in here like this and wake me up. It's not right."

"No charge for the personalized service, pardner. I do this for all my friends."

Exasperated, Bobby pulled back the covers and sat up.

"I want to sleep!"

Clovis shook his head.

"Not today, pardner. We got us a little chickie to find."

Bobby rubbed his eyes and looked at the clock.

"You came all the way down here at this hour to help me find Cricket?"

Clovis nodded.

"Go away!"

Clovis shook his head.

Bobby sighed. "Shit."

*   *   *

Clovis hustled Bobby off the ship and onto the streets of Baltimore.

"We're goin' for crab cakes. You ever had a crab cake?"

"I've never even heard of a crab cake. How is it possible to make a cake out of crabs?"

Clovis led Bobby to the Broadway Market. They sat on round, padded stools at the black and white tiled counter of Previs Brothers Luncheonette.

"Crab cakes are the specialty of the house and they are heavenly."

Bobby looked confused.

"It's a hamburger-sized patty of spicy crab meat, lightly fried, then served on saltine crackers with a dab of mustard. They are one of God's little miracles, and Baltimore is the only place you can get 'em."

"I saw something like that in Hamburg except I think it had fish in it."

"Were hamburgers invented in Hamburg?" Clovis asked.

"No, I think Chuck Berry invented the hamburger."

Clovis ordered crab cakes and cokes. Bobby slowly spun on his stool, taking in the three hundred and sixty degree panorama of Broadway Market. The air swirled with the smell of the fish market just inside the building.

Bobby said, "I'm gonna catch a cab to Cricket's apartment."

Clovis clapped his hands.

"Excellent plan! You can drop me off at Read Street and I'll hang out while you do your sparkin'."

Bobby didn't want Clovis hanging around but found it impossible to say no to him. He'd never met anyone so quick to insinuate himself into the lives of others. Bobby speculated it was a weird combination of southern hospitality and hard-boiled Yankee aggressiveness. It was very brash, very rock and roll, and very American. Something about Clovis intrigued Bobby. There was a boyish innocence behind his freewheeling philosophy. Beneath it all, Clovis seemed like a good soul.

The crab cakes arrived arranged between two saltines like a strange, flat, brown sandwich. Bobby bit into his and chewed.

"This is pretty good. What's that flavor?"

"That's Old Bay Seasoning, my man. The taste of Baltimore. Made by the McCormick Spice Company right up the street."

"It's wonderful."

"Of course it is. Clovis wouldn't steer you wrong."

Bobby devoured his crab cake and ordered another.

When they were finished eating, Bobby walked out onto Broadway and flagged a cab. He and Clovis jumped in. Sitting in the grimy back seat of the taxi, Clovis pointed out landmarks along the way. Bobby could see the similarities between Baltimore and Liverpool. Some of the narrow streets lined with row houses could have been his old neighborhood.

"How you comin' on that old Gibson guitar? Can you play that thing yet?"

"Not really. I only know three chords."

"That's all there is, hoss. That's all there is."

*   *   *

Clovis got out at Read Street and Bobby continued on to Cricket's apartment. He rang her buzzer for a long time with no response. He decided to write a note and slip it into her mailbox.

"Dear Cricket. Just got in yesterday. Can't wait to see you. I'll come back tonight. Love, Bobby." He included the address of the dock where the *Pilgrim's Progress* was moored.

As he put the note into the slot, he felt as if he would never see Cricket again. *Maybe she's got someone else.*

Bobby walked slowly back to the cab and asked to be dropped off where Clovis got out. He wandered down the street not really caring where he went. He passed an antique shop and something in the window caught his eye.

An antique harmonium. He went into the shop. An elderly man wearing a green celluloid visor greeted him.

"What can I do for you, son?"

"I was passing by and I saw your antique harmonium in the window. My father has one like it back home in Liverpool and I'd like to take a look."

"Be my guest. I'm asking fifteen hundred for it. As is. It needs a little work."

Bobby examined the harmonium. It was smaller than the one in his father's shop and in worse condition. He glanced through the window.

Across the street he saw Cricket come out of a store. He started to move but froze when he saw that she was with somebody.

Another guy.

Bobby's heart sank when he saw her slip her hand into his. Bobby wanted to run out into the street to confront her. He stepped toward the door, contemplating what to do.

She looked even more beautiful than he remembered. Her face, still perfect, radiated even from across the street. Bobby stared at her through the dusty glass, absorbing all the details. He'd never seen jeans so tight or so faded. They hugged her buttocks like plastic wrap accentuating every curve. She wore a thin white peasant blouse open at the throat. Her hair was longer than he remembered.

To Bobby's surprise, Cricket crossed the street and walked directly into the antique store. She saw him immediately.

"Bobby? Is that you?"

Bobby's mouth hung open. He swallowed hard.

"Yeah."

"Oh, my God!" She threw her arms and around him. "I don't believe it."

The other guy watched. Bobby could see the man's eyes boring into Cricket's back as she hugged him. Certain that she could feel his hammering heart, Bobby tried to control his breathing.

"When did you get back?" she asked.

Bobby looked at the other guy. He looked like another art school student, carefully casual with the merest hint of a goatee.

"Oh, this is Dirk. Dirk, Bobby, Bobby, Dirk."

They shook hands gingerly. Dirk said nothing.

"Got in last night, actually."

"How long are you in town?"

"A few days."

Cricket pulled a slip of paper and a pencil out of her purse and jotted down a number.

"I finally got a phone. Here's the number. Call me."

Bobby stood with the slip of paper in his hand, dumbfounded.

"Right," he said, too confused to say anything else.

"We gotta go. Make sure you call. Missed you."

"Yeah, me too."

Cricket kissed Bobby on the cheek and walked out the door, Dirk in tow.

Bobby watched her disappear into the dazzling sunlight.

The shopkeeper stepped in front of Bobby. He spoke with a Baltimore accent, elongating the vowels like a Liverpudlian.

"I don't believe it. It's downright uncanny. That exact same thing happened to me back in 1945. I was in the Navy and got a last minute shore leave. I came home for a surprise visit. I saw my girl with another guy. Damn near broke my heart."

Bobby looked at the shopkeeper.

"How do you know that's what happened to me?"

"It was written all over your face. You, the girl, that other guy, Dirk. A classic. Just like a scene from Shakespeare."

Bobby shook his head.

"What just happened here?"

"You got shafted. That's what happened to me back in '45. Two years later, I'm out of the service and I run into the guy, only now he's no longer with her. I ask him what happened to that girl. You know what he said? He said, 'She loves you.' 'Yeah, yeah, yeah, sure she does,' I said. He says 'No, she really does,' and that's why they broke up."

"What happened to the girl?"

The shopkeeper had a mischievous twinkle in his eye.

"I married her."

Clovis came through the shop door like James Dean, pausing to comb his hair in one of the many antique mirrors. He saw Bobby and the snapped his fingers.

"Hey, Daddy-O. Did you see Chicklet?"

Bobby nodded. "Yeah, I saw her. Did you see the guy she was with?"

Clovis snorted. "A real lady-killer. You want me to kick his ass?"

"Did you talk to them?"

"Yep. I engaged 'em in some conversation."

Bobby became annoyed when Clovis paused.

"Well, come on, man! What did they say?"

Clovis grinned. "I asked Chicklet if she'd seen you, and she said no. Then I asked her if that guy was her boyfriend."

Bobby groaned. "You asked her right in front of him?"

"Yeah, I wanted to know. What the fuck do I care if it's in front of the guy or not?"

"Tell me what she said."

Clovis hooked his thumb out to the street.

"Why don't you go ask her?"

Bobby looked in the direction she had walked.

"She's gone."

"It don't matter 'cause you're gonna see her tonight."

Bobby spun around on his heel the way he'd seen John do it on stage in Hamburg.

"What are you saying?"

"That we're goin' over to her place tonight."

"We?"

"I told her to invite that other chick from the Peabody. The mousy blond? I really dig those intellectual types."

"Like Erlene?"

"Bingo."

"How do you know she'll come?"

Clovis pulled Bobby away from the shopkeeper and whispered.

"'Cause we're havin' a little party with just the four of us. I told her I got some smoke. Real good stuff. Art chicks love to smoke. She went for it. Oh, and I told her to get rid of art boy."

"You're kidding."

"I'm perfectly serious. I just happened to have some fine Jamaican smokin' weed that I got from a friend of mine. You smoke pot, don't you?"

Bobby nodded. Though he'd smoked only hash back in Liverpool, he knew hash was made from pot so this wouldn't be all that different.

"It's settled. We'll have a nice long smoke and get all goofed up. I'll play the guitar, we'll pass around a bottle of wine. Next thing you know, we got their panties off. Bim, bam, boom. What do you say?"

Bobby laughed. "What an amazing chap you are, Clovis."

Clovis stood a little taller.

"Yeah, I know. Sometimes I even amaze myself. I'll teach that Erlene to mess with me."

The shopkeeper cleared his throat.

"Excuse me, but did you ask the young lady about her true feelings for your friend here?"

Clovis looked surprised.

"You mean him?" He pointed at Bobby.

The shopkeeper nodded. "I know what she said. I have a premonition."

"OK, then. You tell me."

"I want you to say it."

Clovis turned to Bobby.

"You got this one in the bag, pardner."

Bobby threw his hands up in frustration.

"Why do you say that?"

"She said she loves you and you know that can't be bad."

The shopkeeper slapped the counter top with his palm.

"She loves you! I knew it. Just like 1945."

*   *   *

Clovis standing behind him, Bobby rang Cricket's doorbell and waited for her to buzz the front door. As Bobby and Clovis stepped into the foyer, Cricket called down from above.

"Come on up."

They climbed the steps to the third floor. Cricket stood on the landing and when Bobby ascended the last stair, she flew into his arms.

"Oh, Bobby. I missed you."

Clovis came up behind.

"If you missed him so much what were you doin' with monkey boy?"

"Dirk? He's just a friend."

"You were holdin' hands with him."

Bobby pointed at Clovis.

"Shut up, Clovis."

Cricket led them into her apartment.

"Sometimes friends hold hands."

Bobby shot Clovis a hostile glance. They walked into a dark room with candles and incense burning. An Odetta record played softly. Folk music filled the air.

Cricket's friend was on the couch reading the album cover liner notes.

"This is Bonnie. She's in my drawing class."

Clovis took her hand and kissed it. "Mmmm. Tastes like chicken."

Bonnie burst out laughing.

"Chicken? My hand tastes like chicken? That's wild."

"I'm Clovis, the chicken plucker."

"I'm Bonnie, the Cornish game hen."

Clovis laughed heartily.

"I like your style, ma'am."

"I'm plucky."

They laughed again.

"Damn, we haven't even smoked yet and already we're gettin' giddy."

Cricket took a seat on an easy chair across from the couch leaving Bobby to sit uncomfortably next to Bonnie and Clovis. Clovis pulled a baggie and some Zig-Zag rolling papers out of his pocket and rolled a joint. Bonnie picked up the bag and sniffed it.

"Smells strong."

"It's Jamaican super weed. Got a real nice kick to it."

Bonnie watched with great interest while Clovis rolled the joint. He took his time and rolled a perfectly shaped torpedo. Bonnie applauded.

"Yay! That's the best looking joint I ever saw."

"I am a master joint roller."

Clovis brought the joint to his lips and flicked his Zippo lighter open. With a practiced motion he torched the end of the joint. Clovis sucked the end and watched the ember glow. He inhaled a mighty lungful of smoke and held it in. With his eyes watering, he handed the joint to Bonnie.

She took a toke and handed it to Bobby. Bobby smelled the pungent aroma and tentatively inhaled.

"Go on. It won't hurt you."

Bobby pulled on the huge joint and coughed instantly.

Clovis laughed. "Easy, Kemo-Sabe. Just take a little and hold it in."

Bobby handed the joint to Cricket who took a dainty toke and let the smoke drift out of her nostrils.

"Hey, you're pretty good at this."

Cricket said, "I've done it before. No big deal."

They smoked until the joint burned down. They sipped wine and made small talk. Clovis was making points with Bonnie and after a few minutes he noticed they were sitting closer together on the couch. Bobby sat on the floor next to Cricket. The Odetta album ended and Clovis put on a record by Sonny Rollins. Bobby's mouth became dry and he lost track of time. Cricket started talking about UFOs and Bobby looked over at the couch, surprised to see Clovis making out with Bonnie.

Fifteen minutes later they walked out of the room holding hands. Bobby heard the door to Bonnie's bedroom close.

"Wow, they sure didn't waste any time," Cricket said.

Bobby gently pulled Cricket to the floor and kissed her.

"I missed you so much."

"So did I."

"Can you stay longer this time?"

Bobby shook his head.

"I can't on this trip, but next month I get a break and can request to stay here until the ship returns."

They spent the night together entwined in each other's arms. When dawn came, they made love.

*   *   *

Bobby spent the next year criss-crossing the ocean. He returned to Baltimore and moved in with Cricket, taking time off like he'd promised.

He hadn't seen the Beatles since Hamburg. He wondered how they were getting along. He sent a box of records to Aunt Mimi's house in Woolton but received no letter in reply.

Bobby visited the antique stores on Read Street, studying the selection of items and the prices asked. He realized that many of the things in his father's shop would be worth much more in Baltimore. The idea of opening a Baltimore shop occurred to him, and he discussed it with Cricket.

"How do I get a business license and a VISA?"

Cricket shrugged. "I don't know, but my brother's a lawyer. Why don't we ask him?"

Cricket's brother, Arthur, met them for dinner and gave Bobby a ton of free advice. During the course of the conversation, Cricket blurted out that she was in love with Bobby.

Bobby dropped his fork.

"You are?"

Cricket nodded.

Arthur laughed. "Why don't you marry him and make him a citizen? It would be easier for him to open a business then."

Cricket and Bobby looked at each other.

Bobby said, "Let's talk about it later."

*   *   *

Bobby examined the antique harmonium in the store on Read Street. This time the owner told him more about it.

"It's German. Maybe a hundred years old. Most of the keys work but some are stuck. Are you interested in buying it?"

Bobby shook his head.

"Actually, I have one back in Liverpool that's quite a bit like it except it's in better condition. I was interested in selling it here in Baltimore."

"I could take it on consignment. You got any other stuff?"

Bobby smiled. "My father has a shop in Liverpool. He's been collecting things for decades. He has an extensive inventory."

The shopkeeper stuck out his hand.

"My name is Herb Snyder. I'd be pleased to do business with you, son, if it's all on the up and up. What's your name?"

"Robert Dingle. I'm a seaman on the *Pilgrim's Progress* currently docked here in Baltimore. I can arrange passage for small quantities of freight on my ship as we go back and forth. It might be beneficial to both of us."

Herb raised his eyebrows.

"Sounds interesting. Let's talk about it in my office."

Herb closed and locked the shop and led Bobby to a tiny office.

"I don't know you, Mr. Dingle, but I'm giving you the benefit of the doubt and assume that you're an honest man."

"Let me assure you, sir, that I am completely trustworthy. I've been in the resale business my whole life and never cheated a soul."

Herb lit a cigarette and blew smoke at the ceiling.

"OK, here's the deal. You bring items, which I have approved in advance, into the shop and I will display them on consignment. If the items sell, I will take the standard commission and pay you the balance. If the items don't sell, you must remove them from the premises at my request. If any of the items are hot, I will turn you over to the police. All transactions must be in cash and approved by me. Fair enough?"

Bobby smiled. "Quite fair. Thank you for the opportunity, Mr. Snyder."

"Call me Herb."

"Right, Herb. I'll be in Liverpool by the end of the month and select the merchandise to ship. I'll arrange for the shipping on the *Pilgrim's Progress*. You can come down to the dock when it arrives for approval. Should be in about thirty days."

"I like your style, young man. You cut to the chase. By the way, how did things work out with the girl?"

Bobby blushed. "She says she loves me."

"You know you should be glad."

Bobby said good-bye to Herb Snyder and took a cab to the Hi-Dee-Ho Soul Shack in East Baltimore. Preston Washington greeted him at the door.

The contrast of Herb Snyder's establishment to the Soul Shack couldn't have been greater. Music blasted from speakers set up out on the street. Posters for R&B shows were plastered on every available surface.

"Hey! It's the Englishman. The Duke of Earl."

"Mr. Washington, my good man, so good to see you again."

"On another buying trip, your Lordship?"

"Yes, my good man. Show me your wares."

Preston Washington laughed. His belly jiggled and his cheeks swayed.

"I've got a bundle of delights for you today. Oh, yes! A big old basket of goodies fit for a king. I think you'll be groovin'. Let me start you out with the latest by Hank Ballard and the Midnighters called *The Twist*. Then we got new platters by Sam Cooke, The Drifters, Ray Charles, Lloyd Price, and James Brown just to name a few."

"Bring me up to date, oh great and wondrous Hi-Dee-Ho man."

Bobby spent the rest of the afternoon listening to records and drinking National Bohemian Beer. He left with several boxes of red hot American R&B 45s.

*   *   *

It's easier to say good-bye to Cricket this time, Bobby thought. The uncertainty was gone now but a new anxiety haunted him. Cricket said she loved him. Her brother had even suggested they get married, but the thought of it made Bobby nervous. He wondered if what he felt for Cricket was love. He had nothing to compare it to except his love for his father and rock and roll. This was nothing like that.

Love was supposed to make you feel good. Why did he feel so twisted up? His involvement with Cricket filled Bobby with a sense of destiny. It was the same feeling he had about the Beatles. He now had it about Cricket. Was she the one he would grow old with? The concept of marriage had never entered his mind until a few days ago and now it scared him.

Bobby made a decision to put any thoughts of marriage on hold and concentrate on the present. He had deals to make.

CHAPTER FOURTEEN

A WALK ALONG THE MERSEY

Liverpool seemed much older and dirtier than Bobby remembered. The narrow streets and crowded buildings were comforting, but now that Bobby had seen something of the world, he knew there were other realities. To people who had never been ten miles outside of town, it was difficult to understand.

Over a year had passed since he'd seen the Beatles. Winter had come and gone, and Bobby had visited his hometown several times without hearing from them. He went to his father's shop and threw his sailor's duffel in his old room. Without the dirty Dingle brothers around, all of Bobby's paranoia had evaporated.

Bobby looked through his mail and a letter from a solicitor jumped out at him. He opened the letter and read that the firm of Jisters, Scheib, and Mulder represented the estate of Nancy Elizabeth Garlton. They wished to inform him of the untimely death of Mrs. Garlton, and that she had named Robert Dingle as the recipient of a special bequeath in her will. Jisters, Scheib and Mulder suggested that Robert Dingle contact them at his earliest convenience.

Bobby let the letter fall out of his hand. It fluttered to the table.

Nancy's dead.

I made love to her and now she's dead.

He stood there for minutes thinking about Nancy not knowing what to do. He read the letter again. With a knot in his stomach he folded the letter and slipped it in his pocket.

Too many things were happening at once.

He locked the door and walked the streets of Liverpool. Near Mathew Street he paused and lit a cigarette. A poster caught his eye: "The Cavern Club."

He looked closer. The Beatles were playing at the Cavern Club. *The Beatles.* They were back in Liverpool. Bobby forgot about Nancy Garlton and smiled. John, Paul, George, Stu, and Pete had returned like prodigal sons. Bobby decided to take the bus to Menlove Avenue to see John.

He rode out to the green lawns and tidy gardens of Woolton. The bus lurched to a stop near the house John called Mendips.

He knocked on the door and met an unsmiling Aunt Mimi.

"Hello, Aunt Mimi. It's me, Robert Dingle. I've just got back to town and I thought I'd pop in and say hello."

"Oh, Robert. How are you?"

"I'm fine. Is John back from Hamburg? I haven't heard from him."

"Yes, he's come crawling back but he hasn't a farthing. All that big talk about him making money in Hamburg was just rubbish. I'm so worried about him, Robert. He's all but given up on his studies. Do you think you could talk to him for me?"

Bobby shrugged. "What would I say?"

"You're his only responsible friend. The rest are all a bunch of cockeyed dreamers. Tell him to give up his silly band before he's too old to learn a respectable trade."

Bobby realized any discussion with John along those lines would be a waste of time but he assured Aunt Mimi he would try. She said John was off rehearsing with George and Paul.

Bobby returned to his father's store buoyed by the idea that he would see his old mates soon. He carefully selected a handful of records to lend to John. He knew the music would be welcomed, and he suspected the band would be hungry for new material.

*   *   *

The Cavern Club on Mathew Street was well-named. Bobby descended slippery steps into the dank, smoky dungeon. It was packed with people, all pressed against each other or the sweaty brick walls. The club was comprised of three arched tunnel sections roughly ten feet wide, joined by six-foot arches. A tiny stage stood at one end of the main barrel-shaped room. In front of the stage was room for seven straight-backed wooden chairs. With no ventilation, the atmosphere was stifling.

The Beatles' equipment stood on the bandstand, leaning against chairs and amplifiers. Pete's drums gleamed in the shadows.

Bobby noticed a small door on one side of the stage. He knocked but received no answer. He could hear voices coming from inside so he cautiously opened the door. John Lennon, dressed entirely in black leather, was standing just inside.

"Well, if it isn't our old friend, Dust Bin Bob! Tell us, where have you been, oh great heavily dusted one?"

One by one, the band members hugged Bobby.

"We missed you, man! Tell us all your adventures and we'll tell you ours."

"Look! He's got records!"

Bobby held the records up.

"Black gold, boys. The very latest from the Hi-Dee-Ho Soul Shack in Baltimore, Maryland, U.S.A. This is the real deal, the cream of the crop, and nobody in this town has heard a single note of it."

John grabbed for the records but Bobby kept them out of reach.

"Aha! The sacred records are not for just anybody. They have been personally hand-carried across the rolling sea by a duly authorized acolyte of Preston Washington."

John lunged again but Bobby parried like a bullfighter.

"Give it up, mate. No one deserves that music more than the Beatles, and you know it. It is our birthright. I say stand and deliver, sir!"

Bobby handed the records to John.

"They're a gift, John."

John gaped at the records and looked as if he might cry.

"This is the most beautiful thing."

He hugged Bobby again.

"Those are the ones I thought you might like. It's all stuff you could cover."

"Thank you, Dust Bin Bob. God bless you."

George took a few of the records from Bobby's hand.

"Bo Diddley, Chuck Berry, Little Richard. Hey, this is really fab."

"You'll rule the scene with these disks. I guarantee it."

"Yes! To the toppermost of the-"

Paul cut him off. "Give it a rest, John."

Bobby looked around the room. "Where's Stu?"

John lit a cigarette.

"He stayed behind with Astrid. They got married."

"You're kidding."

"He was crazy about her and didn't want to stay with the band anymore. He wanted to devote his full time to art."

Paul held up his Hofner violin bass.

"I'm playing bass now, and the group is really startin' to cook."

Bobby shook his head.

"I can't believe he'd leave the band."

Paul tuned his bass.

"He's no longer a Beatle."

"How did the great German adventure turn out?"

John turned on his scouse accent and said, "Hamburg was the all time greatest. We've been and gone several times now. Veterans, we are. We're twice as good now that we know how to mak shau."

George said, "I was deported for being underage and working in a nightclub. Paul and Pete were arrested for pinning a condom to the wall and setting fire to it. Stu quit the band. John had to pack it in and leave the country. It wasn't exactly our finest hour."

"But we did make some truly great music," John said loudly.

"That we did," George replied. "And we wound up going back and doing quite well."

"We got to make a record while we were over there. We're backing a bloke named Tony Sheridan."

Bobby clapped his hands.

"A record? That's great. I must have a copy. What's the name of it?"

"My Bonnie."

"You mean that old chestnut, my Bonnie lies over the ocean, my Bonnie lies over the sea?"

"Bring back my Bonnie to me," George deadpanned.

John puffed his ciggy.

"That's what I always say."

The door opened a crack and a sweaty head leaned in. Bob Wooler, Master of Ceremonies at the Cavern, looked worried.

"Beatles, on stage! The kings of rock and... ahem, dole are wanted. Come on, lads, your public awaits you."

Paul saluted.

"Gentlemen, start your engines!"

John stubbed out his cigarette.

"Gentlemen, mount your burros!"

Paul said, "See you after the gig for a pint?"

"Who's buying?"

John laughed. "You are. You're the famous Dust Bin Bob."

The Beatles walked onto the stage at the Cavern Club looking like a leather-clad motorcycle gang. They were all smoking and acting tough, but the scruffy musicians had no real sinister side and the audience knew it. In fact, there seemed to be a playfulness about them that the audience amplified.

The first song they played was *Hippy Hippy Shake*. From the first note Bobby knew that this was not the same Beatles he had seen at Lathom Hall or in Hamburg. These Beatles were streamlined, tight, and powerful. Their self-confidence propelled them through the song like a V8 engine. Paul's bass playing was dynamic. It locked into Pete's drumming like a piston, driving the band to new musical heights that Stu could never have imagined.

They rocked into each chorus as if their whole world depended on it. *You could power a city with this much energy*, Bobby thought.

Bobby noticed that the audience hung on every note the Beatles played. How different it was from Hamburg where no one paid attention except the exis. The music, brash and exciting, ricocheted off the brick walls like machine gun bullets.

Each time Bobby had seen the Beatles it had been a revelation. But here, in the tiny Cavern Club, with the funky sound system and the cheering audience, they seemed to have improved by light years.

George sang *The Sheik of Araby*. John and Paul mugged a comic vocal on *Three Cool Cats*. Paul screamed like Little Richard on *Good Golly Miss Molly*. John growled like a wounded bear on *Money*. They raved up a medley of Chuck Berry songs and followed with a bizarre version of the classic *Besame Mucho*. They closed with Ray Charles's *What'd I Say*.

Later, John led Bobby and the band to a pub a few doors down on Mathew Street called The Grapes.

They raised a toast to Bobby.

"To Dust Bin Bob! Long may he wave!"

The band seemed excited about the records Bobby had brought. Any new music interjected into the inbred Liverpool music scene hit like a handful of prellys, supercharging everyone it came in contact with. A batch of new records from the states was worth far more than gold.

Bobby knew that. That's why he did it. He liked the Beatles and he wanted to help them get ahead.

John looked up from examining the label of a Chess Record, and said, "You know we have a manager now. We're headed for the big time at last."

"Who is it?"

"Brian Epstein. He owns a record shop called NEMS. He's well connected."

Paul sipped his drink.

"He's going to put us all in suits."

Bobby's surprise was genuine.

"That's great. Maybe he can get you a record contract."

John said, "He better or I'll make him eat these bloody suits."

*　　*　　*

The offices of Jisters, Sheib, and Mulder were stuffy. Bobby sat in a stiff wooden chair and tried to look normal. Samuel Jisters examined his seaman's identification and cast the occasional disapproving glance in Bobby's direction. He had a condescending way that made Bobby uneasy. He had an aristocratic sixty-year-old face and cold blue eyes.

"I've known Nancy Garlton for forty years and I've never heard her speak of you."

Bobby shifted in his chair.

"I only knew her for a short time."

"What was the nature of your relationship with Mrs. Garlton?"

Bobby hesitated. Jisters tapped his finger on the huge mahogany desk.

"Speak up, man."

"I was her friend."

"I see. You do realize that it's highly irregular for a wealthy widow to award such a large sum of money to a friend?"

He peered over his glasses at Bobby.

"I'll not be hoodwinked, young man. If there was anything inappropriate about your relationship with my client, I'll refuse the bequest on the grounds that you coerced her into putting you in her will."

Bobby winced. "Look, Mr. Jisters. I was her friend. I took the time to talk to her. I helped her out, fed her cat, and just did what any decent person would do. As to why she would leave any money to me, I don't know. I certainly never asked for it, nor did I take advantage of her in any way. We never discussed her will. I was just a friend. I got the feeling she didn't have too many at that point in her life."

Jisters tossed Bobby's seaman's card across the desk at him.

"Even though I don't agree with it, the instructions are quite clear. As an officer of the court I am sworn to carry them out. You, Robert Dingle, shall receive the sum of forty thousand pounds in the form of a check from the Garlton estate. You'll need to furnish some more formal identification, but that's the long and short of it. Oh, and then there's the taxes. You'll be hearing from the Tax Authority soon enough."

Bobby's mouth fell open.

"I had no idea she had so much money."

"Were you aware of the late Mr. Garlton's business?"

Bobby shook his head.

"Coal, Mr. Dingle. Vast quantities of coal."

Bobby's mouth became dry, his heart raced. He felt sweat form across his brow. He staggered out of Jister's office and wandered out onto the street in a daze.

*   *   *

Bobby often walked along the Mersey River when he needed time to think. The sounds of the water's edge soothed him. The ship horns, water lapping against the stone embankments, and the call of seagulls pinwheeling in the sky. The familiar smells of seaweed and dead fish brought back pleasant memories. Bobby walked along deep in thought.

His mind swirled with conflicting emotions. He felt shame for having made love to a lonely old woman and then profiting by her death. He'd taken advantage of a fragile creature and now he felt intense guilt.

Later, he felt sadness. Sadness that he hadn't been there with her when she died, that he hadn't comforted her in her final hour.

Then he began to think about the money.

It would change his life. He would be free to pursue his dreams. Having the money, he thought, would probably be as hard as not having the money.

His mind swirled with ideas. He could quit his seaman's job. He could return to Baltimore and open his own antique shop. He could marry Cricket. He could do a thousand things, but he could never tell anyone about Nancy Garlton.

Nancy.

He never said a word. The one person he had told, John Lennon, had made him regret it. He never wanted to tell anybody else. Their memories would be forever private. He never wanted to speak about it again. Like Nancy had said, Bobby alone carried the memory now. He'd promised he would not let it fade, but it pained him to think about it.

After he'd walked for an hour he made up his mind. Bobby decided to put the money in the bank, finish his tour of duty, and tell no one.

He needed time to sort things out. Bobby was far too confused to make life-altering decisions now, but after a few months at sea, he knew he'd see things differently. He needed that perspective.

No matter how far out his thoughts spun, when he returned to earth the facts remained. Nancy was gone, the money was his, and she wanted him to have it. She wanted him to have a fabulous life. She wanted him to have every opportunity. She wanted him to follow his dreams, something she'd never been able to do. *She must have thought it all out while she lay there dying.*

Bobby could hear her voice whispering: *Take it, Robert. It's my gift to you.*

CHAPTER FIFTEEN

DINGLE'S OF READ STREET

Time compressed at sea. Bobby had made several voyages now, some to Baltimore and other ports of call. Only Baltimore held him. Cricket was there with a new apartment on Calvert Street, and Bobby had talked her into letting him pay half the rent. Her name was on the lease, but it was his flat too.

At sea, the endless rocking of the ocean helped Bobby think. Slowly, over the course of months, he dissected his feelings and came to understand that much of his anxiety was rooted in his own ennui. He was itchy. He needed to map his future. While most of his friends had been content to drift through life without much concern for tomorrow, Bobby had always been a dreamer. Now he faced the possibility that his dreams might come true.

When the *Pilgrim's Progress* docked in Baltimore one cool night in the fall, Bobby took his time before going straight home. Returning to his first Baltimore haunts, he walked along East Baltimore Street, lost in thought. He ambled up The Block and stood in front of the Two O'Clock Club, listening to a rockin' band playing for the strippers. They were doing a slow blues, providing a good bump and grind for one of the featured girls. Bobby knew that if Clovis was still alive and in town, he'd be here.

Bobby didn't go inside. He wasn't in the mood for Clovis Hicks at the moment. He meandered past the Two O'Clock Club where he stood looking in the window of Livingston Loans. He wondered about the thousands of stories the instruments would tell if they could. How many Clovis Hicks were there? How many professional musicians, staring at financial ruin, had hocked their axes and tried to carry on?

Bobby realized that a musician without his instrument couldn't make money. In a way the window at Livingston Loans represented a graveyard, a collection of tombstones. Gazing at all the shiny trumpets and gleaming electric guitars made him sad.

Bobby took a cab to Cricket's apartment on Calvert Street. It was an airy first floor suite with high ceilings and hardwood floors. The entrance boasted stained glass windows.

He unlocked the door and called inside. The house was empty. He found a note from Cricket saying she'd be late and go ahead and eat some leftover Chinese food in the refrigerator. "P.S. I love you," she added.

Bobby ate the food and decided to call Herb Snyder. His wife answered to say that Herb was suffering one of his bouts with gout and hadn't been to work in days. Bobby asked if Herb had kept the shop closed during his illness. She said yes. Bobby asked if he could come around to visit Herb the next afternoon. She said yes. Bobby hung the heavy black receiver back in its cradle.

Bobby laid down on the sofa and dozed off. He dreamt of the ocean as seen from the deck of the *Pilgrim's Progress.*

Cricket woke him with a kiss.

"Hi honey, I'm home." Cricket liked silly sitcoms, and often used TV clichés in her day-to-day speech.

"How's the Beav?" Bobby responded, appropriately.

Cricket leapt on him.

"Oh, the Beav is ready! You better believe! The Beav is really ready!"

They entwined, peeling each other's clothes off. Bobby lost himself in her. For a little while all the memories faded.

Later Cricket asked about his travels.

"Dad is older than ever, Clive's still in jail, and the Beatles are still together and playing gigs."

"That's it?"

Bobby thought for a moment.

"Yeah. But let's not talk about that now. That's the past."

"What do you want to talk about?"

"The future. I've been thinking about what to do after my service is up.

I've given it a lot of thought. I want to open an antique store here in Baltimore. I can get the stuff back home and ship it out here where I can sell it for more."

Cricket squealed with delight.

"So that means you'll be staying in Baltimore?"

"I'll go back home to make acquisitions, but I'll basically live here. With you. If you'll have me."

Cricket hugged him tighter.

"Oh, Bobby. That makes me so happy. You know what the worst thing is about loving you? You're always leaving, always saying good-bye."

"Next time I say good-bye, you'll have to come with me."

"Where am I going to get that kind of money?"

Bobby paused. The conversation was at the turning point. He chose his words carefully now.

"We can work it out."

"How are you going to open your own shop? That takes a lot of cash."

Bobby paused again.

"I'm not without resources. I'll find a way."

*   *   *

The last months of Bobby's shipboard service were spent deep in contemplation. He made the run back and forth across the ocean a half a dozen times wrapping up his business. He visited the Beatles several times at the Cavern with a handful of new American records. He got to know Bob Wooler who spun records from the tiny dressing room next to the stage. He met Brian Epstein who seemed almost too shy to manage a beat group. A man with a handful of fresh vinyl from the States opened many doors. Bobby became known as the man with the amazing records.

John deeply appreciated the records and thanked Bobby repeatedly. They both knew how important those records were. They were the very lifeblood of the Liverpool music scene. Bobby arranged to send the occasional packet to Mendips so John and the Beatles would always have a leg up on the other groups. The Beatles were fascinated by stories of the Hi-Dee-Ho Soul Shack. Preston Washington became a mythical hero, and they vowed to meet him someday.

Bobby stayed in his old room when he was in Liverpool. He enjoyed his father's company. They often spoke of Clive and wondered if the time in jail would make him worse.

"I've seen men turn bad from bein' caged."

Bobby thought Clive had been bad a long time before he went to jail. They both agreed that prison time wasn't going to make him any nicer. One day Clive would return and it was bound to cause problems.

*   *   *

Opening a bank account in Baltimore and setting it up to receive an overseas wire transfer proved to be easy. Used to endless British red tape and bureaucracy, Bobby found dealing with Americans refreshing.

Herb Snyder, whose health kept him from running the shop, was very happy to sell the business at what Bobby thought was an excellent price. Cricket's brother, Arthur the lawyer, took care of the paperwork. Bobby bought the shop and everything in it.

He planned to liquidate most of Herb's antiques in favor of more interesting, provocative items from across the Atlantic.

Read Street wasn't part of Baltimore's famous antique row but it was walking distance from it. The prices were reasonable, and the foot traffic brisk. It was in a part of town that had potential. Bobby liked the location. He changed the name of the shop. The new sign over the storefront said, "Dingle's of Read. Exceptional Antiques."

Bobby worked all day every day to build *Dingles of Read* into a highly successful enterprise. He even learned to drive and got a driver's license. Then he bought a pickup truck.

Bobby had a new life.

*   *   *

Baltimore just kept getting better. Bobby ate in corner restaurants where everyone called him "hon." Arthur took him to Memorial Stadium to watch the Orioles play. He insisted Bobby eat a hot dog. Bobby enjoyed himself although he didn't understand the game.

Arthur explained, "Guys come out here, have a couple of beers and forget their troubles for a while. It's very relaxing."

Bobby watched a fat man in front of him stand up and scream at the top of his lungs. He shook his fist and threw peanuts at the field.

"It looks very restful."

"Don't mind him. He's just blowing off steam. If the Os could get some offense going, he'd turn into a pussycat."

The Orioles won and Arthur led Bobby back to his car. They walked across the parking lot where an ice skating rink would be set up in the winter. Now it was just a concrete pad.

"Why did you park so far away?"

Arthur chuckled.

"I love this neighborhood. I grew up here. I thought we might pop in at the Stadium Lounge and have a drink."

"Sure."

They crossed the street.

"That's my elementary school. Good old P.S. 51. That thing has been there forever. We played baseball on this sand lot. There's a mom and pop store on the corner here where we can get some Red Hots. The Stadium Lounge is just down the street on Greenmount Avenue."

The lounge was dark and smelled of cigarettes and beer. Neon beer signs lit in the corners. Three old men sat at the bar. A skinny kid played pinball. Arthur led Bobby to a table in the back. Without asking Bobby what he wanted to drink, he ordered two martinis at the bar.

He placed them on the table and sat down.

"Have a martini."

"I've never had one."

"It's the specialty here. Everybody orders martinis."

"You Yanks can be so bloody pushy."

Arthur laughed. "It's the only way we know to get inside your head."

"Why would you want to do that?"

"Because my sister is in love with you. I thought I could get to know you a little better."

Bobby sipped the drink.

"It's strong."

"Of course it's strong. It's a martini."

With Big B logic like that, what could Bobby say? He sipped some more and got used to the bite. By the time they'd both finished the first round, Bobby's lips were starting to feel numb.

"Let's talk about you and my sister."

Bobby folded his hands.

"Let's."

"First of all, of all her past boyfriends, you're the only one who's worth a shit. She's attracted to artist types, deadbeats who don't work. Man, if there's anything that gets my goat it's guys who don't work. But from what I've seen of you, Robert Dingle, that doesn't seem to be a problem. You're a workin' fool. Then there's the issue of her being crazy. You do know she's crazy, right?"

"What do you mean by crazy?"

"She's had some emotional problems in the past. She went to a shrink for awhile."

Bobby's eyes got big.

"I didn't know that. What were the circumstances?"

"Well, shit, maybe I shouldn't tell you all this."

Bobby put a hand on Arthur's wrist.

"Arthur, you do what you feel is right. You don't want to tell me, that's fine. I'm sure Cricket will do it in time."

"Don't be too sure about that. Cricket's got her own agenda. She sees herself as an artist. She'll do what's best for her art. It may not be the best thing for those around her, but if it serves her artistic vision then she won't hesitate."

Bobby thought of Stu and Astrid. Stu was a brilliant artist, miles beyond the art school types he'd known, and Stu quit the Beatles. He quit the most wonderful beat group in Liverpool to pursue his art. Yet Stu managed to be both an artist and a devoted lover to Astrid.

Arthur kept talking.

"She had this guy named Benjamin. He was a sculptor. This guy was a real piece of work. I have no idea what she saw in him, but she was nuts about him her first year in college. He was always dirty and had a beard. Dad flipped out. He ordered her to not see Benjamin but that only drove her on. He started sculpting her nude. Dad saw one of the pieces in her room and he just about hit the roof.

"They had a terrible fight, and she started acting weird. She lost a whole bunch of weight; she wouldn't eat."

Bobby said, "That seems normal. I mean, you know how girls are."

"Benjamin wound up going to France to study under some big shot. He didn't even say good-bye. Broke her heart six ways from Sunday."

Bobby shook his head.

"She never mentioned it."

"I wouldn't think so."

"Why are you telling me?"

Arthur signaled to the bartender for another round. He brought the drinks to the table.

"I don't want you to break her heart."

"You must know me a little by now. I would never do that."

Arthur took a drink.

"No, I don't think you would."

"So far we've established that I'm a hard worker and I'm not going to break her heart. What else?"

"Where did you get the money to start your own business?"

The question surprised Bobby. Americans could be incredibly blunt. Once again the issue of Nancy Garlton reared its head. Bobby answered quickly.

"I inherited it. It's completely on the up and up. I hope you don't think I did something shady."

"Oh, no. Of course not. Just asking, that's all. I was curious."

Bobby frowned. "I see. What else?"

"Marriage."

"Hold on. Marriage? I don't remember that being brought up except by you and it was when you didn't even know me."

"I was half joking then, but I knew."

"Knew what?"

"That you were the man for Cricket. You're not another artist, you're a businessman. You know the value of hard work. You seem to have some smarts, and you've done right by her so far. Bernice is essentially a good girl."

"I once saw her take down two burly Teddy Boys with Judo and I was amazed."

"Oh, yeah. Dad taught her. Taught all of us. But getting back to Bernice Samansky, my sweet little sister, I want you to consider something."

Bobby sipped his drink. He felt a little flushed. The martinis had loosened Arthur's tongue.

"Bernice or Cricket as Dad calls her, needs somebody stable. Judging from what I've seen, I'd say you are the best bet so far. We're a good Christian family. We want what's best for Cricket. We don't like the fact that she's shacking up with you."

Bobby could feel the conversation slipping away from him.

Arthur went on. "Let's look at this like adults. I think you should marry my sister. You need U.S. citizenship if you expect to flourish as a businessman here. If you stay in Baltimore, you'll make more money, pay less taxes, and be married to a nice girl from a nice family. Plus, we can help you buy a house when the time comes."

"What do you mean?"

"We could help with the down payment."

"Is this a bribe?"

Arthur shrugged.

"In a way. We just want you to know we like you. If you were to help us out by marrying Cricket then we might help you out."

"Did the rest of the family vote you to be the spokesperson?"

"Yep."

"Did they make you say all that?"

"Yep."

"Do you think it'll do any good?"

"Nope."

Bobby grinned. "I'll certainly consider it."

CHAPTER SIXTEEN

LOVE ME DO

Bobby received a letter from John along with a copy of *My Bonnie*. The letter was written as a parody of a BBC newscast, noting events in the lives of the Beatles and thanking Dust Bin Bob for supplying the records. For the first time John mentioned a girl, Cynthia Powell. According to John she has "flips like Brigitte Bardot."

Bobby played the record and was a little disappointed. It was nothing like the raw energy he'd heard at the Cavern. Some bloke named Tony Sheridan sang the lead vocal and Bobby wondered why John hadn't sung lead. His voice was much better than Tony's. Still, it wasn't bad but nothing like you'd find at the Hi-Dee-Ho Soul Shack.

The doorbell rang and when Bobby answered, there stood the new and improved Clovis Hicks.

"Is that you, Clovis?"

The smile was still there, although Clovis now sported a neatly trimmed beard. His blond hair, while still defying gravity, was less greasy, and slightly longer. He wore a black turtleneck sweater and a herringbone jacket.

"That's me, boss. I'm here to tell ya."

"I don't know what to say."

"You haven't seen me for awhile, but it's cool. I got myself a car now. I'm mobile. I'm here on a mission. You're into music, so you'll like this."

"What?"

"Get yourself together 'cause we is goin' out tonight! Get Chicklet too. She's gotta see this."

"What is it?"

"Tonight and tonight only, Josh White is playin' at *The Blue Dog*."

"I don't know him."

"Josh White? Man oh man, he's a real blues legend. Folk blues, you know, like Leadbelly. This guy's a folksinger's folksinger. He's an old black guy, been around forever. Dig this, he lights a cigarette and sticks it behind his ear while he's playin', and you just stare at that sucker wondering if it's gonna burn down before the song ends. He's a fingerpickin' fool and he really thumps those strings. He's playing at *The Blue Dog*, a tiny little coffee house near Poly High School. We have to go. We have to see him before he dies."

"What makes you think he's going to die?"

"Hey, man, everybody dies. These old black dudes, you never know. They've lived a hard life. If you get a chance to see a legend and you don't go, you're blowin' it, man. Because one of these days Muddy Waters and Howlin' Wolf, and all these guys are gonna be dead, and you're gonna wish you'd seen 'em when you had the chance."

"And you're saying that Josh White is in that category?"

"Yes, goddamn it. That's what I'm tryin' to tell ya! Now get your ass in gear, boy! I gotta go get Erlene and I'll be back to pick you up in one hour. Be ready. And bring Chicklet. Erlene wants to meet her. Bye."

Clovis stormed out the door before Bobby could react.

That night, Bobby participated in a great cultural experiment. He sat at a tiny table, shoehorned into the corner of a tiny basement coffee house, with red and white checkered tablecloths and candles stuck in Chianti bottles.

To his left was Erlene looking every bit the off-duty stripper in pink stretch pants and four-inch high heels. Her tight black sweater strained under the pressure of her breasts and her cotton candy hair seemed to scrape the ceiling.

Next to her, Clovis sat like a beatnik choirboy. The new beard and turtleneck sweater didn't seem comfortable on him. Each time Bobby glanced at him he was staring at the cigarette behind Josh White's ear and listening intently.

Cricket hadn't said much all evening, but Bobby could tell she was curious about Erlene. After the show, Clovis ordered espresso and they had a chance to talk.

"Man, was that guy great or what? I love that song, *One Meat Ball*. I really dig it when he sings, 'You don't get no bread with one meat ball.' And did you get a load of that fingerpickin' style? I been workin' on that and let me tell ya, it's a bitch."

Bobby nodded. "You were right. Josh White is a folksinger's god."

"You knew I was right, right? You know I'm always right, right? When it comes to music, old Clovis is your man. Now, I got another one for you. How about James Brown at the Royal Theater next Friday night?"

Bobby clapped his hands.

"James Brown! Fantastic! Count me in!"

Erlene said, "You know, the Royal is as black as the ace of spades. I hope you don't expect me and Cricket to go there. It's a rough place."

Clovis laughed. "Maybe we could start a race riot! How would that be?"

Erlene frowned.

"Very funny, ass wipe. I'm not kiddin'. My cousin and her boyfriend got jumped there last year."

Clovis leaned across the table.

"I walk amongst the negroes freely, bein's how I'm a musician and all. They know I'm cool."

Erlene seemed to enjoy the friction between her and Clovis, and she rose to it. Their peppery exchanges amused Bobby.

"All I'm sayin' is, Bobby might not realize what he's getting' into. He don't know this town the way you do."

"Aw, sugar, you know I wouldn't put the boy at risk. He's my buddy. I wouldn't let anything bad happen to him."

"Clovis, you are so full of shit."

"Hey, if it wasn't James Brown I wouldn't even bring it up but you know the man is Mr. Dynamite. Bobby needs to see this. He needs it bad. Look at him. Christ, he's just dyin' to see James and the Flames rip it up. It'll change his young white life."

"Oh, for God's sake."

Erlene turned from Clovis to Cricket.

"How's about you and me talk, hon. We ain't said shit to each other yet. Tell me a little about yourself. I hear you're an artist. Maybe you can paint my portrait someday."

Cricket smiled. "That would be nice."

"I've had my titties painted on a big poster before, but I ain't never had my face painted."

Cricket's facial expression fluttered with confusion.

"What did you say?"

"Oh, I shoulda told you. I'm in show business."

Clovis said, "She ain't no ballet dancer, honey. She's a stripper down on The Block. She's top billed at the Two O'Clock Club."

"I'm an exotic dancer, hon."

"Oh..."

Erlene whipped out a mirror and checked her makeup.

"As long as there are guys willin' to pay to see my ass, I'll keep peelin' and struttin' it. I'm proud of my body, if you want to know."

Cricket said, "I think you'd be an excellent subject for a painting, Erlene."

"Could you make it a nude?" Clovis asked. "I'd sure like to hang that sucker on my wall."

Bobby loved to listen to Clovis and Erlene talk. Their dialogue reminded him of improvised jazz, shooting off in multiple directions. He felt completely submerged in American culture.

"How's about you do a portrait of her ass?" Clovis added. He seemed completely serious.

Cricket didn't answer.

"Hey, Robby the Limey, you ain't said much. What's the matter?"

"I'm having too good a time listening to you."

"What's new with the beat group you were tellin' us about? The Boll Weevils?"

"The Beatles. They cut a record."

"It any good?"

"Of course it's good."

"They're never gonna make it with a dumb-ass name like that. Tell 'em to try something cool like The Impalas or the Escorts."

Bobby chuckled. "I don't think the exis would like it."

"See? There's another lame name. 'The exis.' Don't these guys know cool?"

"The exis are a group of people in Hamburg. They're existentialists, not musicians."

Clovis' mouth hung open.

"What the hell are you talkin' about?"

"The exis believe that we're here on earth by accident. When you die there's nothing more."

Clovis whistled. "Are they commies?"

Bobby laughed. "No, they're not commies. They're cynics."

"Sounds like they're wastin' a lot of time thinkin' about shit that don't matter. They should worry about shit that means something like music and chicks."

Bobby nodded. "Clovis, you're a true philosopher and you don't even know it."

"Oh, I know it all right. I know there's a lot stuff I don't know, but at least I know that I don't know."

Clovis lit a cigarette and Erlene snatched it out of his mouth and began to smoke it herself. Clovis lit another.

Erlene said, "Clovis is the smartest guitar player on Baltimore Street. All the other musicians say he's way above average."

Bobby chuckled. "I'm sure he is."

Cricket suddenly stood and excused herself.

"I feel sick. I'm going to the restroom."

After she left, Clovis said, "What's wrong with her?"

Erlene looked at Bobby.

"A young healthy girl like that? Gettin' sick on a Friday night? I've seen it before."

"Say what you mean, Erlene."

"I just mean, it might not be what you think."

Cricket returned to the table and sat down in her chair looking pale.

"You OK, honey?" Erlene said.

"I just threw up."

"Are you comin' down with something?"

"I don't think so. I'm just feeling a little sick. I think I want to go home."

Erlene winked at Bobby.

"Better get this little girl home."

*　　*　　*

Bobby tucked Cricket into bed and kissed her on the forehead.

"If you're not feeling well tomorrow, I'll take you to the doctor."

Bobby went to the kitchen and boiled some water for tea. When it was hot enough he poured some in a cup and dropped in a teabag. He held the steaming cup to his nose and inhaled. It felt good. He sat on the couch and took his shoes off.

He looked at his watch. What time would it be in Liverpool? He wondered what the Beatles were doing.

*   *   *

Dr. Haylick peered over her file folder at Cricket. She rescanned the test results and cleared her throat.

"I've been your doctor ever since you were a little girl, Bernice. Is this young man your boyfriend?"

"Yes, ma'am."

"Good, because what I have to say affects both of you."

Bobby sat up straight and paid attention.

Dr. Haylick was sixty-years-old and matronly. The kind of woman who looked comfortable in a white lab coat. She kept her silvery hair wrapped tightly in a bun. She wore her glasses low on the bridge of her nose. Her voice was soft, yet clinically firm.

"Bernice, these tests indicate that you're pregnant."

"What?"

"You're pregnant, dear."

"Are you sure?"

"Yes. Absolutely."

Bobby said, "Can there be a chance of error?"

"No."

Bobby and Cricket looked at each other, shocked. Five seconds passed before they both started talking at once.

"Oh, my God! Oh, Jesus, I'm pregnant! Good Lord! A baby? Me?"

"Oh man, oh man, oh man. I don't believe it. Is it really and truly possible?"

Dr. Haylick held up her hand.

"Now you kids have some serious decisions to make. I want you to know that I will be here for you if you have any questions or you need some counseling."

Cricket stared straight ahead.

"I can't believe it."

Dr. Haylick laughed. "Young girls never think it's actually going to happen to them, it's always somebody else. Then when it does happen to them, they're always surprised. It's the natural consequence of sexual behavior. Babies come from sex. That's how human beings procreate. T'was ever thus, Bernice. You might have considered that before you chose to have intercourse. I suggest you start preparing for a new arrival."

Bobby's mouth went dry. He wanted to ask a million questions, but nothing came out.

Dr. Haylick said, "Cricket, I've known your parents a long time. They're lovely people. Your Uncle Ferd helped me get into medical school at Hopkins. That was back when a woman really needed help getting into medical school. I feel I have an obligation to your family. I expect you to inform them immediately."

"Yes, of course," Cricket said. "Oh, God."

Dr. Haylick patted Cricket on the shoulder.

"It's OK, hon. It happens all the time. The only difference is, this time it's happening to you."

They left the doctor's office in a trance.

Walking together on the way home, Bobby squeezed Cricket's hand. The rest of the world faded away until it was just the two of them. Bobby felt as if he were walking on air.

Cricket said, "This is the biggest thing that's ever happened to me."

"It's the biggest thing that's ever happened to either one of us."

"I mean, am I ready to have a baby? The thought of it scares me."

"It's already been decided by nature."

"I guess you're right. Oh, Jesus, what will my parents say?"

"They'll flip out I'm afraid. There's sure to be a major cock-up about this."

Cricket furrowed her brow.

"I'm scared."

Bobby slipped an arm around Cricket's waist and held her close.

"It's OK, baby. We'll get through this together. I won't let you down."

A tear formed in Cricket's eye. When she spoke it trickled down her face.

"I just want you to know I love you, Bobby Dingle."

"I love you too, Bernice Samansky. You can count on me."

They walked slowly, time dragging along with their footsteps. Bobby couldn't help thinking, *an hour ago we were blissfully unaware of the great forces at work in our lives. How quickly everything changes.* Bobby felt like a leaf floating downstream in the river of natural events.

When they got home, the door to their apartment had a yellow Western Union telegram wedged in the jam. Bobby plucked it out and opened it.

"It's from Mrs. Swithins in Liverpool."

Bobby began to read.

"Robert, come quick. Your father's had a stroke. Contact St. James Hospital immediately."

He looked at Cricket.

"Oh, my God."

Cricket took the telegram and read it again as if the words might change, as if the bad news it contained might reverse itself.

Bobby stood in the vestibule blinking back tears, wondering what to do next. He fell into Cricket's arms, holding back a sob. They shivered against each other, two souls in the night.

"One hour ago I didn't have a care in the world. Jesus..."

CHAPTER SEVENTEEN

RINGO

Bobby had never traveled by jet airliner, and he found the seven-hour flight to London uncomfortable. He'd brought some books to read but nothing captured his imagination. He felt claustrophobic. His legs cramped. He became dehydrated.

He stared down at the ocean he used to cross so tediously on the *Pilgrim's Progress*; it seemed unnatural to be flying. The hours dragged. The dry, smoky atmosphere made him uneasy.

When he arrived in Liverpool, he went directly to the hospital. His father seemed ancient laid out on white sheets. He opened his left eye when Bobby entered the room.

"Dad, I came as soon as I heard. How are you feeling?"

When his father didn't answer, Bobby asked a nurse to call the doctor. She said the doctor would be making his rounds soon and he was too busy to talk to Bobby now. Bobby sat next to his father's bed, numb. The beeping of the monitor sounded like an alien death code.

Bobby wondered what he would do in his father's situation.

Bobby kept the silent vigil next to his father and tried not to cry. A few hours later, he bought a copy of *Melody Maker* at the hospital magazine stand. He opened to the charts page to scan for new records, and his eye was instantly drawn to the Beatles. The Beatles had a record on the British charts!

There it was at number forty-eight, *Love Me Do* by the Beatles. Bobby put the paper down astonished at what he'd read. He wondered what *Love Me Do* sounded like. He hoped it sounded more like the Beatles live show and less like *My Bonnie*.

"I don't believe it," Bobby said to himself.

"Are you his son?" a voice asked. "Robert Dingle?"

Bobby turned to see a doctor in a white coat carrying a clipboard.

"Yes, sir."

"We've been trying to reach you."

"I was out of the country. I came as soon as I could."

"Your father's had a stroke. I'm afraid the news isn't good. He's paralyzed on the right side of his body and can't talk. He's stable now but the another stroke is still a threat."

Bobby tried to swallow, but his mouth had gone dry. When he spoke his voice sounded like a sandpaper whisper.

"Will he ever come back from this?"

"Every stroke is different, and every patient is different. There's really no way of knowing at this point."

"What should I do?"

"You can start looking for a facility to care for your father. After a certain amount of time if he's stable we'll be forced to release him. You'll need to register him into a ward. See the front desk for a list."

Bobby began to sob.

The doctor said, "Some people seem to think praying helps."

Bobby shook his head.

"I don't think God's picking up my calls these days."

The doctor frowned.

"Don't underestimate the positive power of prayer, young man. I've seen it work even for skeptics."

"I'm not exactly a religious man."

The doctor wrote something on his clipboard and turned to leave. He paused at the door.

"What happens next to your father is out of our hands. Medical science can only do so much."

Bobby's voice wavered. "Can he hear us?"

"Yes, as far as I know."

Bobby looked at his father on the hospital bed, tubes and monitors attached to him, and felt completely helpless. The man looked hollow. His chest rose and fell weakly under the white sheets. He looked a hundred years old.

Bobby bent over and whispered into his father's ear.

"Dad. It's me, Bobby. I'm with you. Let's get through this and go home."

* * *

The streets were gray and slick as Bobby walked home. His father's shop was cold. He started the heater and made a cup of tea.

He went up to his room and was surprised to find it full of boxes of records. Mrs. Swithins had been busy collecting 45-rpm singles from the folks around Penny Lane. There were over a hundred records; some used, some new, in every conceivable genre. Mrs. Swithins didn't know what rock and roll was so she just collected everything. He picked up a stack and leafed through it.

His eyes fell on a black *Parlophone* label, and he read the title. *Love Me Do* by the Beatles! The credits listed Lennon-McCartney as the authors. He flipped it over. On the B-side was *P.S. I Love You*, another Lennon-McCartney composition.

"Mrs. Swithins, bless your toad-lovin' heart. I could just kiss you."

Bobby played the record immediately. The first thing to leap out of the speakers at him was a harmonica.

A harmonica! It reminded Bobby of another recent song that featured harmonica, *Hey Baby* by Bruce Channel, an American singer. He also recalled *I Remember You* by Frank Ifield, a yodeling Australian singer. The harmonica was featured the same way, almost like a sax, coming in between the vocal lines. The sound of it changed the texture of the song, made it more compelling. It wasn't a straight blues-style harmonica like Little Walter or Sonny Boy Williamson but rather a pop invention, a hook.

Love Me Do seemed dark and moody compared to everything else he'd heard by the Beatles. The vocals sounded close to the Everly Brothers. He could distinctly hear John and Paul singing, but when the main line of the chorus came in, John dropped out. Bobby surmised that John must be the one playing harmonica otherwise he'd be singing in that spot.

The song ended and Bobby played it a dozen more times before he flipped it over and played the B-side. *P.S. I Love You* sounded like Paul with a sentimental melody that brought to mind some of the show tunes he'd seen them do live in Hamburg.

Bobby decided *Love Me Do* was great. Using the harmonica was a brilliant idea, and it gave the Beatles a leg up on the other groups. They had been incredibly resourceful Bobby thought, using everything in their arsenal.

Bobby's mind jumped back to the hospital. *Don't underestimate the positive power of prayer,* the doctor said.

Then Bobby realized that he hadn't thought about his father for as long as the music played. Listening to the Beatles made Bobby forget about everything else. His body relaxed, his heart stopped pounding, his mind slowed down. *The Beatles,* he thought, *have magic.*

While searching a drawer for some clean socks, Bobby found the *Dust Bin Bob Lifetime Pass* card that John made for him in the hospital waiting room years before.

Bobby read the inscription, *"I, John Lennon, being of stout pine and knotty, do hereby grant a lifetime pass to Robert Dingle, also known as Dust Bin Bob, to all performances by the group known as The Beatles whenever and wherever they may be."*

He smiled and slipped the card into his wallet.

Desperate for more diversion, Bobby picked up a copy of *Mersey Beat* magazine. He saw that the Beatles were performing at the Cavern that very night along with the Zodiacs and Johnny Templer and the Hi-Cats.

Maybe a drink or two with his old mates would ease the weight on his shoulders.

The walk to Mathew Street had never seemed colder. Bobby tried to keep his mind free of thoughts, but the same unwanted images kept popping into his head. His father, the doctor, Cricket, the hospital all seemed to gang up on him whenever he stopped thinking about the Beatles. He whistled the melody of *Love Me Do* as he walked, and it helped a little.

He rounded the corner and stopped dead in his tracks. The line to get into the Cavern stretched down the block. There were twice as many people in line than could fit in the club. Bobby wondered if he should give up and go home when Bob Wooler, the Cavern's master of ceremonies, walked past and said hello.

"When did all this happen?" Bobby asked.

"Since the Beatles became the most popular group in all of Liverpool. Would you like to pop in and see the lads?"

Bobby handed him the lifetime pass card. Bob Wooler read it and laughed.

"That's John all right. Follow me, Dust Bin Bob."

Five minutes later after weaving through the surging crowd, Bobby stood before the backstage door.

Bob Wooler said, "Abandon all hope, ye who enter here."

He opened the door. A guy Bobby didn't recognize stood directly inside. He was dressed in one of the Beatles matching collarless suits. His hair was styled like the others only a little bit shaggier.

"Can I help you? Would you like a table near the door?"

Bobby handed him the card. He read it and passed it to John.

"Dust Bin Bob! You old wanker! Where have you been?"

Bobby said, "I've been in the States soaking up the culture."

"Heard any good records lately?"

"Yeah, *Love Me Do* by some geezers called the Beatles."

John said, "Do you realize your records constitute half the band's repertoire? We wouldn't have made it this far without you, man."

Bobby swelled with pride and blushed deeply.

"Thanks, John. Coming from you, I really appreciate that."

"True, it is. Who else in Liverpool has records like you?"

"Oh, come on. I'm sure somebody does."

John shook his head.

"Nope. Believe me, we checked. Dust Bin Bob, you're the only one, and the Beatles are lucky to have you as a friend."

"I guess that makes me a patron of the arts."

John put a hand on Bobby's shoulder.

"Have you heard about Stu?"

Bobby looked surprised.

"What about Stu?"

John became serious.

"He's dead. He died of a brain hemorrhage back in April."

The words hung in the air. Bobby shook his head.

"Stu? My God, Stu was so young."

"And so brilliant. We saw Astrid and she was devastated. We all were."

The moment of silence that followed seemed like half an hour.

Bobby looked in John's face. "Clive."

John scowled. "That bastard. You saw what he did. Stu was fine before that. I have a good mind to charge him with murder."

Bobby said, "I can't believe it. Stu's dead and my brother probably killed him."

John spat out the words. "Fucker. I hope he rots in hell."

"He's rotting in jail right now and Mick's dead."

"Good."

The atmosphere in the room had darkened considerably.

Paul said, "Hey, it's just about time for us to go on. How's about lightening things up a bit?"

Bobby looked around the room.

"Where's Pete?"

John smirked. "Pete's no longer with the group."

"You're kidding. Pete? He was as loyal as a spaniel."

George and Paul looked away. John was the only one to meet his gaze.

"Pete's out. Ringo's in. That's that."

"But why?"

John heaved a sigh.

"When we went to audition for the record company they said we needed a better drummer if we wanted to make it."

Paul said, "We weren't happy about it, but we had to do it. It's our careers we're talkin' about here. Our new manager, Brian Epstein, was very keen on that."

"But didn't his mother let you rehearse in her basement?"

John picked up his new Rickenbacker guitar.

"If you're tryin' to make me feel bad about it, it won't work. Once we made the decision, we didn't look back. Not once. Paul and George, we all stand together. We're talkin' about our career here, our whole life. Shit, Dusty. Enough about that, eh? Let's not dwell in the past. Life's too short. Dust Bin Bob, meet Ringo Starr, the Beatles new drummer."

Ringo stuck out his hand to shake. His smile was warm and easy. Bobby was struck by the difference in appearance between Ringo and Pete Best. Girls liked Pete, and he was considered quite a good-looking guy on the Merseyside scene. Ringo on the other hand was not blessed with the same matinee idol good looks. His face was somewhat out of proportion with oversized nose and lips and sad, expressive eyes. Ringo seemed more affable, more like the rest of the group in personality and temperament.

Bobby said, "Haven't I seen you somewhere before?"

"Maybe. I was in Rory Storm and the Hurricanes."

"Any relation to Blaze Starr?"

"Who?"

"Blaze Starr. She's a famous stripper in Baltimore."

Ringo nodded gravely.

"My mother's a stripper in Baltimore? I knew she had a secret life!"

John said, "Ringo's the best drummer in Liverpool. When we asked him to join we told him he had to change his hair and shave his beard. And he did."

Ringo pointed to his sideburns.

"But I kept me sidies."

"You quit the Hurricanes for the Beatles?"

Ringo casually examined his fingernails.

"Change is good, Dust Bin Bob. Every time something changes in my life it always gets better. New bird, new suit, new drums, new haircut, new band. See? It's part of life."

John snickered. "The best drummer in Liverpool and the best band in Liverpool. It's only natural."

Ringo said, "Besides they had a recording contract. You don't get that everyday."

George said, "Ringo's got a car. A *Zephyr Zodiac*."

Ringo looked wounded. "Is that all you hired me for? Me car? I feel so dirty and used now."

"When did you doff the leathers for the suits?"

"Eppy says we have to look proper so vast amounts of people will go barmy and buy our records."

"Very chic and collarless jackets to boot."

"Just like the ones Astrid made for Stu."

Bob Wooler announced, "Gentlemen, mount your burros."

The set that Bobby saw that night at the Cavern was inspirational. Ringo was every bit as good as John said. John and Paul sang like brothers and George played flawlessly. The chemistry of the group had changed slightly, and Ringo seemed at the center of it. He smiled and mugged and looked as if he were having the time of his life. The rest of the group picked up on the happy vibe. They looked like they were having fun.

The audience squealed and cheered. They couldn't get enough and neither could Bobby. They played a mix of originals and covers opening with *Hippy Hippy Shake* and ending with *Money*, which had become John's anthem.

Once again the Beatles magic erased all his troubles and cleared his mind. He didn't think about his father or Cricket's pregnancy until he got home.

More than ever Bobby felt pulled along by the tidal forces of life. It seemed to be a recurring theme. Somewhere in the distance a boat whistle wailed and Bobby drifted off to an uneasy sleep.

CHAPTER EIGHTEEN

TWIST AND SHOUT

Clive Dingle's prison cell smelled like disinfectant and cigarettes. He paced back and forth like a caged cat. His huge Filipino cellmate, Ragasa, always seemed to be in his way. They had a lot in common; both in prison for aggravated assault, both big, both mean. They'd become unlikely friends. Clive had adjusted to life behind bars as best he could which is to say his bullying, tough-guy tactics were custom made for the environment. Together they terrorized most of the prison population.

"You've got a visitor," the guard said.

"My lawyer?" Ragasa asked quickly.

"No, not you. The visitor is for Dingle. Come on, Dingle, let's go."

Clive looked surprised. He hadn't had a visitor in months.

"Are you sure?"

"Sure, I'm sure. Quit wasting time."

Five minutes later Clive Dingle sat in the secure room and looked through the thick, plastic window at Bobby.

"My little half-bruvva? What brings you?"

"I have some bad news."

"I'll bet you do. Spit it out then."

Bobby spoke in even, measured words. He hated to be the bearer of bad news, but Clive deserved to know the truth.

"Dad's had a stroke. He's paralyzed on his right side and he can't talk. They don't know if he'll ever come back."

Clive's face sagged. "Not Dad."

"I'm afraid so."

"That's it?"

"Yeah."

Clive stood.

"Well, thanks."

Bobby's mouth hung open.

"Hey, wait. Don't you care?"

"What do you want me to do?"

"He's our dad. We have to do something."

Clive sat back down again.

"In case you hadn't noticed, little bruvva, I'm behind bars. It makes it kinda hard to get involved with the problems of the outside world."

Bobby sighed. "He needs help. We've got to get him into a home, close up the shop, sell everything, and liquidate his assets."

"You do it then. I'll expect my share of his money when he dies."

"You're a real charmer, Clive. A credit to the family."

"Who the fuck do you think you are?"

"I just came down here to tell you about Dad. I thought you deserved that. But it's obvious you don't give a rat's arse."

"Damn brotherly of you."

Bobby cleared his throat. "One other thing."

Clive looked annoyed. "What?"

"You remember Stu Sutcliffe, the bass player for the Beatles?"

"The one I stomped at Lathom Hall? Sure, I remember. That was a sweet moment."

Bobby lowered his voice. "He died of a brain hemorrhage."

Clive raised both eyebrows.

"They can't pin that on me!"

Bobby nodded. "True. Chances are it was your blow that did him in."

Clive's voice lost its civility.

"The little twit was in the wrong place at the wrong time and there were more than me kickin' 'im, a lot more. You can't blame me for any of that."

Bobby stayed focused.

"I was there. I know what happened. The cops arrested you and your playmates for the flick knives, but you were also charged with assault. That assault led to Stu's brain hemorrhage and eventual death. It's a matter of record now. I know it, you know it, and the Beatles know it."

"I don't have to listen to this shit!"

Clive stood again. The guards looked up.

Bobby said, "I wish you'd use this jail time to change your ways, Clive."

Clive frowned. "Fat chance. Just make sure when the old man dies, I get my money. That's all I care about."

"I'll tell Dad you said that."

A laughing grunt burst from Clive's mouth.

"Hey, one other thing. You can tell those little pretty boys, the Beatles, they should forever be lookin' over their shoulders 'cause I won't be in this stinkin' jail forever."

Clive walked out of the Visitors Holding Room without looking back.

Bobby left the building and spent the rest of the afternoon at his father's bedside.

He read newspapers, magazines and music papers and was surprised to see the Beatles everywhere. The Liverpool lads had galvanized this restless seaport town in a way that suggested not only local pride but also a sense that London was no longer the center of the universe. It was audacious to consider that the four working-class musicians from the north might actually change the face of British rock and roll.

It wasn't just the Beatles though. There were a dozen talented Liverpool groups waiting in the wings: Gerry and the Pacemakers, Billy J. Kramer and the Dakotas, Rory Storm and the Hurricanes, the Remo Four, the Undertakers, The Big Three, the Mersey Beats, the Blue Jeans, Lee Curtis and the All Stars, Kingsize Taylor and the Dominoes and The Four Most, to name a few.

It gave Bobby a feeling of pride that his records had made a difference. Some of the songs once preformed by the Beatles became staples for the other bands as well. *Money* and *Hippy Hippy Shake* were nearly Liverpool standards by now.

Bobby recalled the Fats Domino dream he'd had the day before he met the Beatles. Maybe it wasn't so far fetched after all. Maybe Fats was right. Maybe there was something happening here.

He spent hours talking to his father, telling him everything about Baltimore, his antique shop, and Cricket. When he mentioned that Cricket was pregnant, his father opened an eye and looked directly at Bobby. He appeared to be trying to speak but Bobby heard no words. The news had definitely had an impact.

Trans Atlantic phone calls were expensive and nearly inaudible, but Bobby called Cricket several times. The one second delay made intimate conversation difficult. Bobby wanted to pour out his soul but static limited his message.

"Cricket? I'm gonna have to stay here a while longer until I get things sorted out."

"OK, honey. I miss you."

"I miss you too."

"Do what you have to do."

Bobby spent hours in his father's shop wondering what to do with the incredible selection of items the old man had collected. Some of it was junk, some of it was treasure. Mrs. Swithins came round to offer a hand and Bobby had a chance to thank her for the records. She helped liquidate some of the odd lots in exchange for a pair of antique brass lamps in the shape of toads.

"Always a toad with you, isn't it?"

"You can never go wrong with a nice toad, La."

Bobby invited the Beatles to browse through the collection. Paul showed interest in the antique harmonium. John liked some old circus posters. George eyed some Indian musical instruments. Ringo spent an hour trying on rings.

Dad wouldn't mind, Bobby thought. *Helping some local lads would've been right enough with him. We Merseysiders need to stick together.*

Bobby had a chance to catch a few more Beatles shows at the Cavern. Musically they never ceased to amaze growing from week to week. They added new material whenever it suited them. John and Paul wrote songs everywhere: on trains, in cars, on planes, in hotels. Living life on the run supercharged the band's music.

Bobby quickly came to love Ringo's drumming. He created a cheerful, solid backbeat, perfect for the rest of the boys to build on. Paul's superior bass playing fit Ringo's style perfectly. Without consciously trying, the Beatles forged their own sound.

On each occasion he saw the Beatles he brought records. John devoured the music and either covered the songs immediately or used them to inspire new compositions. He and Paul were always working on a new "Roy Orbison-style" song or a new "Everly Brothers-style" song. They borrowed from everyone and still maintained their own uniqueness. Styles merged and mutated with the Beatles. Everything was fair game.

On his last visit to the Cavern, Bobby brought a box of records that he thought were his best. Knowing that he would soon return to Baltimore, Bobby wanted to reduce the inventory of records collecting dust in his room. He remembered the incredible buzz he and John got the first time he played *Money* by Barrett Strong. He wanted to repeat that feeling.

He handed the box of handpicked R&B singles to John. Paul and George looked over his shoulder. John leafed through them excitedly reading the labels out loud. The tiny back room of the Cavern reverberated with John's cries of joy.

"*Twist and Shout* by the Isley Brothers! *He's A Rebel* by the Crystals! *Kansas City* by Wilbert Harrison! *Lover Please* by Clyde McPhatter! *Baby, It's You* by the Shirelles! *Party Lights* by Claudine Clark! *Anna* by Arthur Alexander! *I Sold My Heart To The Junkman* by the Blue-Belles! *Do You Love Me* by the Contours! *Please, Mr. Postman* by the Marvelettes! We've hit the bloody jackpot!"

John Looked up.

"I won't forget this, man. None of us will."

Bobby smiled. "Don't worry about it, mate. It's a kick just to be around."

"God bless you, Dust Bin Bob."

John hugged Bobby, followed by George and Paul. Ringo stood by awkwardly.

"Should we hug?" Ringo said drolly.

"I've been waiting for this moment all my life."

Ringo and John burst out laughing. In a moment the entire room was laughing.

John shouted, "Three cheers Dust Bin Bob!"

"Hurray! Hurray! Hurray!"

"And don't forget the Queen," Ringo said. "She's big."

Bobby left the Cavern Club feeling happy. He'd come to think of the Beatles as brothers. They'd survived their humble beginnings and hardscrabble early days together. Watching the band flourish gave Bobby great satisfaction.

As Bobby rounded the corner to his father's shop, he remembered playing in the street here as a kid. It all seemed so long ago.

He put the key in the lock and looked back over his shoulder. Liverpool was as still as a graveyard at that moment.

There's too much stuff happening to me. I can't keep up with it all.

CHAPTER NINETEEN

WINSTON DINGLE

The lights of Liverpool still reflected off the Mersey River. Dawn at the docks was a special time. Bobby loved the Pier Head at this hour. It was the time adventures began. People had been leaving on ships from this site for centuries. Bobby wondered how many lives had changed forever once they left this dock.

He walked alone. Walking eased the constant anxiety Bobby felt. He had to make life changing decisions in a short amount of time. Bobby knew what he had to do.

Later that morning Mrs. Swithins came to the shop to make Bobby some breakfast.

"Beans and toast, La. Best thing for ya."

While Mrs. Swithins busied herself at the tiny stove in the back of the shop, Bobby looked through the mail. Overdue notices jumped out at him.

"Dad's got quite a bit of debt here."

"Your father is no businessman, La. Not much of a chippie, if ya know what I mean. He was like my Joe. A good soul who suffered life's great indignities with a cheerful quip and a sly smile. Never a cross word. Never had no enemies. Then when they get the short end what happens? The bloody hand of fate reaches in and grabs yer arse. Really annoying, that is."

Bobby snorted. "He may have no enemies, but he certainly has a lot of creditors."

Mrs. Swithins wrestled a huge cast iron frying pan across the tiny gas burners.

"It's all gin and oranges to me. Here, La, come sit down and have a cuppa."

Bobby found Mrs. Swithins' mothering a comfort. He knew she was tough and smart and he admired that. She'd outlived all her friends, relatives, and husbands. *She'll probably outlive us all*, Bobby thought.

Mrs. Swithins patted Bobby's hand.

"Is it bad?"

Bobby nodded.

Mrs. Swithins aged face showed great compassion.

"Gonna have to sell the shop, La? A bloody shame, that is."

"I'm afraid so. Mick's dead and Clive's in prison. Dad's out of it, so I'm gonna have to deal with it."

"You just do what you think is right, La."

Bobby smiled weakly. "OK."

"I suppose it's off to a home for the senior Mr. Dingle, then?"

"A nice home with a garden if possible."

Mrs. Swithins nodded. "I know just the place. My sister Dorothy lives there. It's not far. I'll show you today if you like."

"Mrs. Swithins, you are an angel."

"Oh, please. I done worse than you'll ever know. Eat your beans and toast."

Bobby did as he was told. Later that day he toured the home that Mrs. Swithins had recommended. He found it clean and quiet; perfect for his father. He went to the hospital and filled out paperwork for the rest of the day. Tomorrow his father would have a new home.

He visited his father's room to talk and wished he could get a response. His father never moved, except to occasionally open one eye and stare at him. Bobby patiently explained everything to him. Eventually, the eye closed and Bobby left the room.

Bobby visited a realtor's office in Liverpool and listed the property his father had owned for fifty years. The agent was overly cheerful and optimistic. She assured Bobby the building would sell quickly and fetch a good price. Bobby wasn't so sure. It was little more than a two-up-two-down row house converted into a storefront in a neighborhood with several boarded-up businesses.

John Lennon was right, Liverpool was a bloody poor house.

Mrs. Swithins continued to come to the shop every morning and make Bobby's morning nosh.

"Mrs. Swithins, you've been so kind to me and Dad."

"It's nothing, La."

"I have to return to Baltimore soon. I have some urgent business that I must attend to personally. I was wondering if you could keep an eye on Dad while I'm gone? Check in every once in a while to monitor his condition and drop me a line? I could pay you for your trouble."

"No need to pay me. I'd gladly do it for free. Your dad was a good friend to me and Joe. He done us right on many occasions."

Bobby put his arm around Mrs. Swithins.

"You're a good soul."

The sadness Bobby felt as he left for the airport was profound.

*   *   *

Baltimore hadn't changed. Places like Charles Street had been the same for decades. The building mailbox on Calvert Street still had his name along with Cricket's.

When she saw him Cricket leapt into his arms. He felt displaced, however, as if Baltimore was only a dream and he would wake up and find that he'd never left Liverpool. He wandered through the apartment reassuring himself that he'd already lived in these rooms.

His record collection now in the thousands dominated an entire wall of the living room. He'd lovingly arranged it between planks of wood and cinderblocks grouping the disks by genre. Singles were on the upper shelves, albums across the bottom.

"How's your father?" asked Cricket.

"He's resting comfortably in a nursing home in Liverpool. Mrs. Swithins, God bless her, is keeping an eye on things for me. I've listed his shop with a realty agency but no takers as of yet."

"What about the rest of your family? Can't they help?"

Bobby sighed. "Mum's been dead for years. I've never told you about my stepbrothers and with good reason."

Cricket looked perplexed.

"Clive and Mick were mean growing up. They turned to a life of crime by the time they were thirteen. Mick was killed in a fight with some foreigners last year and Clive is in prison. Not a very nice story, I'm afraid."

"How did you turn out so well?"

"My mother was a great teacher, and she had a heart of gold."

Cricket smiled. "She sounds like a saint."

"She was. She was Greek, but she spoke perfect English. She was better educated than most and she understood the class system. I think that because she was an outsider, she realized how to beat the system. She knew that in England, people judge you by how you speak. She knew the minute someone opens their mouth, you could guess where they were from; their education and social rank. Like Eliza Doolittle, she was able to fool people with her speech. Only someone foreign could truly learn proper, uncontaminated English. She taught me to resist the local inflections. I was not contaminated by the whole scouse culture even though I was surrounded by it. I could sound like a real Liverpool scouser around my friends but in business dealings I could shed the accent and speak proper English. That proved to be the most important thing I ever learned. It's served me well."

"The more I get to know you, the more I want to know you."

Bobby sat Cricket down on the couch and took her hand gently in his.

"When I met you I realized that by some wild quirk of fate, I had stumbled onto my soul mate. I think some people are just destined to meet no matter the odds."

"Maybe we were lovers in a past lifetime," she said.

Bobby shrugged. "Who's to say? All I know is that I love you and I want to spend the rest of my life with you. Will you marry me?"

Cricket burst into tears. Unable to speak, she nodded her head vigorously, indicating an emphatic "yes."

Bobby dropped to one knee.

"Let's do everything right, OK? Let's raise our kid to be a winner."

Cricket spoke through her sobs.

"Oh Bobby, I love you so much. I was so afraid you might slip away."

"I'm sure my mum is looking down from heaven right now and smiling."

Bobby looked up and addressed the ceiling like a gospel singer.

"I did the right thing, Ma! Are you proud of me?"

Cricket wiped her face with her sleeve.

"You're a good man, Mr. Bobby Dingle."

Suddenly Cricket began to laugh through her tears.

"Oh, God! I'll be Mrs. Dingle! I'll be Mrs. Bernice Samansky Dingle! I can't wait."

They laughed together. The sense of relief they felt reinforced Bobby's feeling that he had done the right thing. His child would have a real father, and his wife would have a real husband.

*   *   *

Bobby received a letter from John thanking him for the records. The Beatles had integrated many of the songs into their live show. *Love Me Do* had established them in the English charts but John was convinced that was only the beginning. He and Paul were writing even better songs, he wrote. They had convinced producer George Martin to let them record more of their own material. John made fun of a song George had presented to them called *How Do You Do It* saying it was pop drivel of the worst kind. They had refused to record it.

"We're artists," John said. "We stand on our own. We want to be taken seriously."

Toward the end of the letter, John mentioned he had married Cynthia Powell and that she was pregnant. He jokingly offered to name his first child after Bobby, "Dust Bin Lennon."

Bobby wrote back to John telling him that Cricket was also pregnant. He suggested that if they had sons they name their children after each other's middle names. John's middle name was Winston; Bobby's was Julian. Figuring John would never like a name as fruity as Julian, Bobby felt confident that it would never happen. Besides first they'd both have to have sons, and the odds were against that.

*   *   *

Bobby and Cricket had a simple wedding at her parent's house in the Guilford neighborhood in Baltimore. Clovis and Erlene caused quite a stir among the conservative guests.

Eight and a half months later, Winston Robert Dingle was born. The name was appropriate, Bobby said, because the kid looked exactly like Winston Churchill.

"Our son's name is Winston Dingle," Cricket said. "How can we expect him to make it through life with a name like that?"

"I'm sure he'll do just fine."

Her father loved the name and that carried a lot of weight in the family. Soon the world began to revolve around young master Winston.

Bobby bought a brick row house on Southway a few doors west of Greenmount Avenue and Cricket and Bobby settled into life on the pleasant, tree-lined street. Memorial Stadium was only a few blocks away and Bobby became more interested in baseball. On the Fourth of July they watched fireworks from their second-story balcony.

One day while Bobby and baby Winston were inside Burris and Kemp Pharmacy at 33rd Street, a commotion outside caught his eye. Police cars were lining Greenmount Avenue. Motorcycle cops waved pedestrian traffic aside as they halted cross traffic on 33rd. All the people in the pharmacy went to look.

Somebody said, "I think it's the President."

Bobby joined the crowd gathering on the corner of Thirty-Third Street.

"What's going on?"

"Kennedy's comin' right down Greenmount Avenue! Can you believe that?"

The motorcade rumbled by; shiny black limousines, cop cars, official looking sedans, and from an open-air Cadillac limousine John Kennedy waved to the crowd.

Bobby took baby Winston's hand and waved it at the President of the United States. As he passed, Kennedy glanced at Bobby holding the baby who was no more than thirty feet away. Kennedy smiled and waved at baby Winston. Bobby couldn't believe how close they had been to the President.

When he told Cricket she was delighted that her son had witnessed a tiny piece of history.

CHAPTER TWENTY

PLEASE PLEASE ME

Bobby often spent his evenings watching Cricket playing on the floor with Winston. The baby changed everything. Of all the recent changes in Bobby's life, Winston represented the most significant adjustment. Sleep deprivation, diaper changing, and childhood maladies drained his time and patience, but love sustained him.

Bobby was exhausted, and they hadn't even made it through the first year. How was John doing in the same situation? Bobby wondered. Being a Beatle and a father didn't quite jive in Bobby's mind. He imagined John foisting the burden onto Cynthia and going off to play gigs every night. Bobby knew from his own experience that fatherhood made fundamental life changes. Though John may run fast and far he would always be bound by blood and by law to baby Julian. Bobby couldn't believe John had named him that. He wondered if the two babies would meet someday.

*   *   *

Bobby's subscription to *Mersey Beat* proved invaluable for keeping up with the Beatles. He devoured the weekly music newsletter as soon as it arrived. Bill Harry's articles about the group were exciting and gave Bobby a little taste of home.

The Beatles' star continued to ascend. With a national hit record and a tour with pop singer Helen Shapiro, they seemed to be on top of the world. Their live appearances were generating enthusiastic reactions everywhere they went. Bobby smiled whenever he pictured the Beatles performing songs they'd learned from his records. The thought that audiences all over England were being shaken by music he'd brought to the Beatles made Bobby proud.

When the sale of his father's shop went through Bobby would have an excuse to visit Liverpool again and see the Beatles. So far there had been no word. He got periodic letters from Mrs. Swithins reporting his father's unchanged condition. Bobby said a silent prayer every night asking that his father be comfortable.

Time passed. Bobby watched baby Winston grow. Cricket was a wonderful mother.

A copy of the Beatles latest single arrived in the mail. Bobby tore it open and ran to the turntable. *Please Please Me* was great from the first note. He played it over and over again marveling at how John and Paul's voices blended like the Everly Brothers. Paul's vocal stayed on the high note as John's voice descended down the melody line. Bobby didn't know what the technique was called but he recognized it as a very effective way to present the melody of the verse. Phil and Don would have been proud.

The song featured John's harmonica again. The call and response on the chorus was like something out of the Hi-Dee-Ho Soul Shack. Every time John and Paul sang, "Come on" it ratcheted up the energy. Ringo drove the band with precise, enthusiastic drumming. The Beatles had learned from the records. The Beatles had soul.

Like *Love Me Do*, *Please Please Me* was simple. Spare production gave it an almost Memphis flavor. Like Sam Phillips before him, George Martin knew enough to let the musicians play with excitement. In one of his letters John said that George Martin listened to the first playback of *Please Please Me* and declared, "Boys, you've just recorded your first number one record."

Bobby had to agree. *Please Please Me* was lightning in a bottle. He watched it rocket up the *Mersey Beat* charts. He read the Beatles were featured on TV and radio shows. He read the live reviews. The Beatles were fast approaching headliner status all over England. They'd given Liverpool something to cheer about.

Bobby read John's latest letter with astonishment. He described the Beatles second recording session at Abbey Road Studios in London:

"We realized that the Londoners would look down their noses at us especially the way we talked. The Scouse accents had 'em put off at first. Should we try to talk differently? Shit, Brian took away our leathers and put us in suits. We can't keep giving in like this. But then we thought, sod it. We'll be ourselves and win 'em over honestly with the music. Here's my theory. Elvis who came from the South and had a southern accent hit New York as something new and different. So the Beatles who come from the north and have northern accents would hit London as something new and different. It's working. We take the piss out of 'em and they can't be posh."

Bobby put the letter down. John was right. The Beatles would be viewed as something exotic not only in London but around the world. He wondered what their reception would be in Baltimore.

When he played *Please Please Me* for Clovis he got a cool reaction.

"Sounds like something out of Nashville. Nothing special."

"Nothing special? Are you deaf? This is magic!"

Clovis listened some more then shook his head.

"Nope, I don't hear it, man. You say this is a big hit? They sound like little kids."

"They wrote it themselves. Come on, give it another listen."

Clovis nodded unenthusiastically and Bobby started the record again. The song played until the tone arm came to the end of the grooves. It automatically lifted, rejected, and returned to its original position.

"Well, it's all right, but it ain't no Chuck Berry."

Frustrated Bobby's voice modulated up a half step.

"Of course not. It's the Beatles. The Beatles are not Chuck Berry. Chuck Berry is Chuck Berry. The Beatles are the Beatles."

"You're speaking gibberish, man."

*   *   *

The phone rang and George Harrison asked for Bobby.

"George? Is that you? Where in the world are you?"

"I'm in Benton, Illinois."

Bobby took a moment to distill the information.

"I see. What are you doing in Benton?"

"I'm here with my brother. We're visiting our big sister who lives here. We're having a ball. I bought a new *Rickenbacker* guitar."

"I've been reading about the Beatles. You're really killing them over there."

George laughed. "They're calling it Beatlemania. Girls scream and throw jelly babies acting like fools. It's daft."

"George, can you stop in Baltimore on the way back? You and your brother could stay with us. We'd love to have you. I'll take you to the Hi-Dee-Ho Soul Shack and you can load up on the latest records. Sam Cooke is playing the Royal Theater. Plus you can meet my son, Winston."

"The one with John's middle name?"

"The very one."

"I must say it sounds intriguing. I'll see if we can change our tickets. Did you say Sam Cooke?"

"The one and only."

George promised to call back within the hour and Bobby stayed in the easy chair next to the phone reading *Stranger In A Strange Land* by Robert Heinlein.

Lately Bobby had taken to reading paperback sci-fi novels he bought at the bookrack at Read's Drug Store. The metal bookstand stood near the door and beckoned him with colorful covers and exotic titles. He particularly liked the Ace double novels with two covers and two complete novels. The artwork never failed to titillate. Across the street an open-air newsstand hawked everything from Men's Action magazines to the *London Times*. It became one of Bobby's regular stops. Pete's Grill was catty-corner to the newsstand, and served food Bobby understood like Friday fish and chips.

The Waverly scene suited Bobby who favored British continuity. It didn't seem all that removed from Liverpool; neat row houses, tidy shops, corner bars, and a noisy streetcar that traversed north and south along Greenmount Avenue.

Business had been excellent at Dingle's of Read and Bobby considered expanding. He imagined reopening his father's shop in Liverpool but realized it wouldn't make a profit selling the type of low-end second hand goods it had carried. He thought of upgrading it to antiques but collectors were few and money was tight in Merseyside. Besides his father's debtors were circling like sharks.

The phone rang and jolted Bobby out of his daydream.

"Hello?"

"Hello, Dusty? It's George. It's all set. We have a twenty-four hour layover in Baltimore on the way back. Can you pick us up?"

Bobby wrote George's arrival information down on the back of an envelope. George sounded excited about the visit.

Bobby hurried to tell Cricket. A Beatle was coming.

*   *   *

George Harrison and his brother Peter looked overwhelmed as they wandered out of the Friendship International Airport.

As soon as they saw Bobby they began to grin. George looked different now. He was older, a little more filled out, and his face seemed longer. His hair was longer than Bobby remembered, and the Beatle carried himself with much more confidence. The shy guitarist Bobby had met a few years ago was gone. Somewhere among the countless gigs and hundreds of dingy back rooms, George had grown up.

"How was your trip?"

"Adventurous, it was. You can't believe the things we've seen."

George's accent brought Bobby home with a snap. It felt good to his ears.

"I'm surprised you could get time away from the band. From what I've been reading in Mersey Beat you've been busy as streetwalkers on Lime Street."

George's smile was disarming.

"You wouldn't believe it, Dusty. People are going absolutely barmy every time we play. I've never seen anything like it. Nobody has. It's a bloody circus. *Beatlemania*, they call it. I call it daft."

"Tell him about the jelly babies," Peter said. "You won't believe it."

George blushed. "I recently made this stupid off-hand remark in a *Mersey Beat* interview about how I like jelly babies. I mean we all like jelly babies, don't we? Seemingly harmless, it was. Anyway the next thing you know, they're throwing thousands of jelly babies at me. That can cause an injury. Thrown with great force, they can put out an eye. The stage would literally be covered with jelly babies, squishing underfoot. What a mess."

"That's what it's like for the Beatles in Liverpool these days," Peter added. "Girls even hang around our house."

"It's gettin' so bad we can't go out for chips."

Bobby listened carefully. First-hand news of the Beatles always interested him.

"Over here they call jelly babies jelly beans."

"Jelly beans? That's silly. They're not even related to the bean family."

Bobby hefted George's suitcase and guitar.

"Come on, I'll take these. Let's get you back to my house to grab a bite.

You can wash up, and catch a spot of kip if you like."

George looked at Peter. A conspiratorial smile passed between the two brothers.

"If it's all the same to you, mate, we're in the mood for adventure. We don't have much time and we'd like to squeeze as much as we can into the schedule. We had a twenty-four hour layover in New York and we managed to go to see all the sights even the Statue of Liberty. We don't want to waste a moment. We want to visit that legendary record store you've been talking about all these years. The one with the great name."

"The Hi-Dee-Ho Soul Shack. It's right on the way back into town and probably open."

"Let's go then."

Bobby stashed their luggage and George's guitar in the trunk and drove north. Preston Washington greeted them at the door of the Soul Shack wearing a brown silk shirt and shiny green pants. Two-tone brown-and-white correspondents shoes and tan socks caressed his feet. He lit a menthol cigarette from a pack of Kools and waved. He had a voice like Howlin' Wolf.

"Well, well, my English friend. Good thing you showed up when you did, I was about to close up. It's been kinda slow today, but I got a feelin' all that's gonna change."

"Preston, my good man. This is a friend of mine from England, Mr. George Harrison. He's a musician in a famous rock and roll group back in Liverpool and they've got a hit record right now in England."

"You don't say. Well it's a pleasure to meet you, sir. Come right in and make yourselves at home. It's nothin' ritzy, but just like Mitzy, we aim to please as we make the squeeze. If you say it, I will play it. Here at the Hi-Dee-Ho Soul Shack you'll scream and holler as you spend your dollar."

George shook Preston's giant hand and stepped into the crowded little record shop. He gazed in wonder at the walls which were covered with posters for gigs, adverts for records, autographed pictures of top R&B stars and brilliantly colored record sleeves. The aroma of fresh vinyl was intoxicating.

"Blimey."

Preston beamed. "Yes, blimey it is, my friends. Blimey as hell. Blimey as shit. It's the headquarters of blime. Welcome to the high temple of soul, the spout where the music comes out."

George gazed at the thousands of records neatly arranged alphabetically in bins. He read the names on the dividers. There were at least twenty records in the Chuck Berry section.

"It's the bloody promised land."

Preston grinned and puffed on his cigarette. He put a record on the turntable behind him and music boomed out of speakers in the store and out on the street. *If You Want To Be Happy* by Jimmy Soul filled the room. The good time, slapstick feel of the vocals delighted the Englishmen.

The song's opening lines, "If you want to be happy for the rest of your life, never make a pretty woman your wife, so from my personal point of view, get an ugly girl to marry you!" struck Bobby and George as not only hilarious but strangely true.

The record sounded like it had been recorded at a big party somewhere with people clapping and singing along.

"What is that? That's great!"

"It's Jimmy Soul. Hot record, man. It's my pick to click this week. You're gonna need a copy of that one, I'm sure. I'll just put it aside."

Preston's voice rumbled above the music like a V-8 engine.

"As usual Mr. Dingle, I have my own recommendations, plus there's the radio charts for WSID and WWIN on the wall. If you can't find anything, just ask."

They spent the next hour shopping for sounds. Preston played anything they requested. George collected twenty-one singles and seven albums. He paid for it out of a big wad of money he had in his pocket. When Bobby saw the cash his eyes got big.

"George! You never had money before! What happened?"

George looked up and raised an eyebrow.

"Brian Epstein happened, that's what. I'm making two hundred quid a bloody week, and I don't have time to spend it."

Bobby shook his head.

"That's a far cry from when we first met."

"The funny thing is none of us is quite sure what to do with the money we're making. I think everybody's a bit reluctant to spend it thinking it might be all we get. Paul says he might buy a car. John's still living at Aunt Mimi's, but I hear he's saving for a proper flat. It's a new and wonderful problem we all have now. I think everybody's just waiting to see what happens next. You never know. It could be over next month. Or it could last for years. Nobody has any idea. In the meantime we enjoy the ride and slip a few bob in the old mattress now and then."

"Don't look over your shoulder, the other groups might be gaining on you."

George chuckled. "Look over my shoulder? I don't have time."

Later, George met Clovis who was their guide to the Sam Cooke show at the Royal Theater. There were only a handful of white faces in the audience but none whiter than George. They stood among Baltimore's darkest Sam Cooke fans and cheered. George's elfin appearance and longish hair drew a few curious stares but no one said anything. In fact there seemed to be a bond between the Liverpudlians and the American blacks. Musically, they drank from the same glass.

Sam Cooke worked the crowd. His gospel roots showed in the way he conducted the call and response numbers. An almost religious fervor infused his singing. He sailed through the high notes and growled the low ones.

George had to yell to be heard in the theatre's frenzied Saturday night atmosphere.

"He's much more of a shouter on stage. I'm surprised. I expected more ballads. Most of his big hits are slow songs, you know, pop stuff. But this is fantastic!"

"Sam can rock," Clovis shouted over the din. "All that *Cupid* shit is just for the teenagers. The man's been reachin' down into his soul for a long time since his gospel days with the Soul Stirrers."

"You know about the Soul Stirrers?" George asked.

"Got every record they ever made."

George looked at Bobby.

"Does he really know all this stuff?"

Bobby nodded. "You'll find Clovis Hicks to be a very interesting fellow."

"It's amazing to me that two of the greatest singers in the world were in the same group, the Soul Stirrers. That would be my man Sammy and Rev. Julius Cheeks."

George said, "I'm not familiar with Julius Cheeks."

As Clovis talked music, his voice gained resonance.

"Julius Cheeks is the definitive gospel shouter. Just listen to James Brown or any other R&B singer workin' today and you'll hear Julius Cheeks. He's the greatest singer in the world today, bar none."

Later George and Clovis jammed at Bobby's house. Once George recognized Clovis's passion for music, they got along famously. Clovis' encyclopedic knowledge of songs impressed the young Beatle, and George showed off his new Rickenbacker.

Clovis examined it and whistled low.

"That's a beaut. I do like the Rickys, but I'm a Fender man myself."

"I like the way they ring out. Very jangly, they are."

"Yeah, you need good jangle. But if you're a fan of high-end treble you can't beat a Telecaster through a Super Reverb amp. That's some sweet pickin'. I've been doin' it for years."

George played a bit of Carl Perkins's *Everybody's Tryin' To Be My Baby*. Clovis stopped and corrected him.

"It goes like this, man," Clovis said through cigarette smoke. He played it exactly as Perkins played it on the record.

George slapped Peter's shoulder.

"I knew I was playin' it wrong."

"You know any other Carl Perkins songs?"

"I know every song he ever did."

"Can you show me *Dixie Fried*? I could never get that one right."

"Sure, pardner, whatever you want. Same three chords in all of 'em. It's just how you play it."

Bobby knew *Dixie Fried* only because he was a diehard rock and roll fan. It was an obscure Perkins original that never made the charts but had achieved legendary status for its raunchy lyrics and wild guitar riffs.

"Would the Beatles do *Dixie Fried*?" Bobby asked.

George's eyebrows flexed into a one eye up one eye down pattern that played havoc with his long brown bangs. It was a face Beatles fans knew well.

'Not with Eppy around. He'd nip that one in the bud, I'm afraid. Not the right image and all that sort of thing. Clovis is lucky that he's got complete and total musical freedom."

Clovis said, "Shit, I'd trade in all my freedom for a crack at your fame, pardner."

George shook his head.

"Don't ever say that, Clovis. One day you'll mourn the loss of it. I can't explain it to you but take it from one who's seen it from both ends."

Clovis scratched his head.

"OK, if you say so but I sure do dig that crazy fame and fortune scene. I'd like to find out for myself."

George smiled. "You'll get your chance."

Clovis showed Bobby how to wire George's electric guitar into his record player. Once connected George and Clovis jammed on their guitars all night. Clovis knew every Hank Williams, Carl Perkins, Buddy Holly, Eddie Cochran, Chuck Berry and Bo Diddley song in the universe; all of which he revealed to George.

Later when the guitars were put away and George prepared to leave for the airport he told Bobby.

"That guy is right amazing. He knew every bloody song. I learned a lot here tonight. My guitar playing will improve after this. If we ever get back here, I want to look that bloke up."

"Clovis Hicks is an amazing person. You should see his band, the Thunderbirds. They're really quite good although the only gig they can get is backing up strippers."

George laughed. "I've done that. It's definitely something I'll tell my grandchildren about."

George, Peter and Bobby loaded suitcases into Bobby's trunk. Cricket came out with tiny Winston in her arms. George touched the baby's nose. Winston responded by crying.

Cricket said, "Oh, poor baby. He's just had his bath. I'm afraid he's not very happy at the moment."

George nodded thoughtfully.

"Yes, but he's very clean."

Cricket comforted Winston. George leaned closer and looked closely at Winston's face.

"Looks a bit like Churchill, he does. I'd say you've done right well, Dust Bin Bob."

Cricket said, "Who's Dust Bin Bob?"

"Your husband. It's the only name I've ever known him by, Dust Bin Bob."

Bobby shrugged. "John gave me that nickname. I've been cursed ever since."

"It's cute," Cricket said.

"I hate cute."

"You don't hate me, and I'm cute. At least that's what you always say."

"Your cute is different than his cute."

George cleared his throat. "I think it's time to go."

Bobby pointed at George.

"Oh, sorry. You see how it is around here? A Liverpool boy can really get deep in the soup."

George and Peter said their good-byes.

"Thanks for taking us to the show and thanks for taking us to the Hi-Dee-Ho Soul Shack. It was fab. I'd love to bring the lads back with me next time. John and Paul would go barmy in there. I can't wait to tell them about it. Thanks for letting us stay here even though we kept you up all night."

Bobby smiled. "You're welcome. Maybe some day you'll tour here in the States."

"Not bloody likely. We'd have to have a number one first."

CHAPTER TWENTY-ONE

JFK

"Can you find me another one exactly like it?"

Bobby tried not to inhale the deadly perfume of Diane Danforth, the elderly president of the Baltimore Antique Society. She'd recently discovered Dingles of Read and bought all of Bobby's best Persian rugs. Bobby erased all incredulity from his voice. He answered casually taking time to lengthen and strengthen his words. His English accent helped.

"As you know, every handmade rug has its own unique pattern. When this rug was manufactured a hundred years ago in what is now Iran, each loom, each weaver was different. I strongly doubt if another one exists."

"Oh, pooh," said Mrs. Danforth. "I need two for my living room."

The phone behind the counter rang. Bobby answered it on the second ring grateful for the diversion.

"Hello. Dingles of Read."

"Bobby?"

Cricket's voice sounded strained. Bobby immediately knew something was wrong.

"Yes? What is it, honey?"

Bobby heard crying over the phone. He snapped to attention.

"What's wrong? What is it?"

Through the sniffles, Cricket said, "You gotta come home right now."

"OK, but what is it? Honey, tell me. What's wrong? Is it Winston?"

Oh, God.

"No..."

"Winston's OK?"

"Yes..."

Bobby exhaled. "OK, then, what's the matter?"

"It's the President. He's dead."

"What?"

"The President's been assassinated. Come home right away."

"The President? I just saw him on Greenmount Avenue six months ago."

"He's been shot. Close up the store and come home right away. I don't know what's going to happen."

Bobby's eyes were as wide as teacups.

"I'm on my way."

Bobby hung up the phone and faced Mrs. Danforth. He heaved a sigh and collected his thoughts.

"Mrs. Danforth, there's a problem. I have to go home right away."

"Now? But it's the middle of the day."

Bobby walked to the door and hung out the closed sign. He glanced outside. Traffic seemed to be moving normally. People didn't seem panicked.

"My wife just called with some shocking news. President Kennedy has been assassinated. He's dead."

Diane Danforth's jaw dropped.

"You can't be serious."

Bobby locked the door and turned on the radio. WCAO had interrupted their afternoon pop music show with news bulletins. The vacuum tubes warmed up and radio gained volume catching the newsman in mid-sentence.

"...today in Dallas, Texas, the victim of an assassin's bullet. Police do not have a suspect at this time. I repeat, John F. Kennedy, President of the United States, is dead. He was shot while traveling in a motorcade in Dallas, Texas. Mrs. Kennedy was at his side. Texas Governor John Connally was also shot. Vice President Lyndon Johnson is on route to Dallas."

Bobby looked at Diane Danforth. The voice on the radio sounded hard and callous. The news it delivered was unbelievable. Suddenly, Bobby felt cold.

"I think we should leave. I think we should all go directly home."

He hurried Mrs. Danforth out the door, locked the store and walked briskly to his car. He passed people on the street who seemed dazed. Some clearly did not know yet. Others wept openly. Traffic moved sluggishly up and down the street.

Bobby started to drive, feeling uneasy. The notion that something was terribly wrong hung in the air. People looked desperate and confused. Bobby himself fumbled at the controls. He missed his turn and had to double back. He finally parked the car on Southway and bounded up the steps to his front door.

Cricket was watching television and sobbing. There in shades of black-and-white, the tragedy played out. As the world slowed to a halt, Bobby sat down to watch it all.

His hand went to the telephone. For a moment he considered calling John. He knew from the latest *Mersey Beat*, that the Beatles were in Newcastle today about to start a major autumn tour. He grasped the receiver then stopped. Why would John care about JFK? As far as Bobby knew, the Beatles had no politics. Still he wanted to talk to John. Something monumental had happened in world history and Bobby felt bereft. He had no countrymen with which he could reflect. Surely John would have something revolutionary to say. Something to put it all in perspective. The thought seemed silly to him a moment later.

For the next twelve hours they watched TV together, numbly staring at the unthinkable images.

"Do you think we'll have a war?" she asked.

"I don't know."

"Do you think the Russians did it?"

"I don't know."

"Johnson's the President now. What will he do?"

"I don't know."

"It has to be the Russians. Who else would do such a thing?"

"I don't know."

"The Cubans don't have any missiles since the naval blockade, right?"

"I don't know."

"Maybe it was the Chinese."

"I don't know."

Bobby felt physically ill.

"I can't believe it. I just can't believe it."

* * *

In the days that followed, Bobby, Cricket, and the rest of the world watched one incredible event after another. The nation grieved. The police arrested Lee Harvey Oswald. Jack Ruby shot Oswald in the basement of the Dallas Police Department. The President's funeral played in slow motion. Bobby didn't return to his shop for a week.

Clovis and Erlene dropped by one night with some wine and a Joan Baez album. They tried to not mention it, but all conversations led back to JFK.

"They'll probably kill his brother next," Clovis said.

"Oh, shut up," Erlene snapped.

"Has the whole country gone crazy?"

"I think so."

"What next?"

Bobby just sipped his wine and concentrated on Joan Baez singing about the banks of the Ohio.

The world was painted black.

*   *   *

Clive Dingle and his cell mate escaped from prison a month after JFK's assassination. Police were unable to explain how two residents of Liverpool Prison had chipped through crumbling cement, climbed through an air duct, and escaped into the night. Clive had vanished.

CHAPTER TWENTY-TWO

AMERICAN RADIO

Bobby Dingle listened to the Beatles night and day. Their second long-playing album had been released in England the day JFK was shot. Bobby received his copy of *With The Beatles* signed by John with the note, 'Not bad for a bunch of working-class Liddypool laddies, eh, Dusty?' John's cheeky predictions didn't seem that outlandish anymore.

Bobby proudly noted that the album contained two of his recommendations: *Please, Mr. Postman* by the Marvelettes and *Money* by Barrett Strong. Their first album, *Please Please Me*, released in March had also contained two of his Hi-Dee-Ho Soul Shack specials: *Anna* by Arthur Alexander and *Twist and Shout* by the Isley Brothers.

Bobby followed all the Mersey Beat groups. The Beatles, Gerry and the Pacemakers and Billy J. Kramer and the Dakotas all had chart singles. Brian Epstein had created a little empire of Liverpool bands, and the British beat scene had exploded.

He continued to send records to Mendips. He put "Dust Bin Bob" on the return address to separate it from the other fan mail. He didn't feel like Dust Bin Bob anymore, but John loved to call him that and Bobby indulged him.

The Dingle family prospered in Baltimore. Bobby's Liverpool accent began to fade. Baby Winston grew like a weed. The cicadas sang in the summer. In winter everything froze.

One day while taking a bath, Bobby heard a Beatles record on the radio. He stood in the tub. *The Beatles! How was it possible?*

He shouted through the door, his voice echoing off the tiny octagonal white marble tiles.

"Honey? Did you hear that?"

"Hear what?"

"The Beatles. On the radio. Just now."

"I thought they were a Liverpool band. Why would they be on the radio in Baltimore?"

"I don't know. It was a new song. Something about holding your hand I think."

"Why don't you call the radio station?"

Bobby took a towel and dried himself. He wrapped it around his waist and walked into the kitchen. Cricket wore a blue cotton shirt tied at the waist over faded blue jeans.

"Here's the phone book, honey. I have to feed Winston."

Bobby looked up the number for WCAO and dialed the request line. The voice on the other end sounded professional.

"WCAO request line. Johnny Dark speaking."

"Did you just play a record by the Beatles?"

"Why, yes, I did. Is that an English accent I hear?"

Bobby suddenly felt self-conscious.

"Yeah..."

"Hang on. I'm gonna put you on the air."

It was too late. Bobby could hear Johnny Dark back-announcing the last few songs.

"That was *Our Day Will Come* by Ruby and the Romantics and Dion doing *Ruby Baby*. I've been getting many calls about that new group from England, the Beatles. Everybody wants to know about 'em. I've got somebody from England on the line right now. Who is this?"

Bobby didn't realize he was on the air.

"Ahh, excuse me?"

"What's your name?"

"Bobby."

"And you're from England, right?"

"Yes."

"Do you know about the Beatles?"

"Yes, of course. They're very big in England."

"What part of England are you from?"

"Liverpool."

"That's where the Beatles are from! You hear that, folks? We got somebody from the Beatles hometown! What can you tell us about their haircuts?"

"Haircuts?"

"Yeah. They have those weird haircuts."

"It's not so weird really. Lots of guys in Liverpool wear their hair the same way."

"What do you call it?"

"There's no name. I guess you could say they're regular Beatles haircuts."

"Hey, that's great! Do you have a request?"

"Yeah. I'd like to hear that one about holding hands again."

"All right! One more time! By special Liverpool request. The Beatles!"

I Want To Hold Your Hand started again and Bobby hung up. He looked at Cricket.

"The Beatles are on American radio. Amazing."

There seemed to be no end to what the Beatles could accomplish. Bobby decided to call John and tell him the good news. He dialed the number for Mendips and Aunt Mimi answered.

"Robert? I'm afraid John is off somewhere being a Beatle."

"Could you tell him I called to say I've just heard his record here in America."

"You don't say." She didn't sound very happy. "I'll give him the message."

Bobby hung up and scratched his head. Something fundamental was shifting in the world of rock and roll. An English band was bringing the music back to its American roots.

*   *   *

It soon became impossible to ignore the Beatles. They were everywhere. The radio buzzed with excitement. First *I Want To Hold Your Hand* released by Capital Records rocketed up the charts, followed by the previous releases on Swan and Vee-Jay. Bobby realized that the Beatles had suddenly become the hottest thing in pop music with several records in the top twenty. Even Preston Washington admitted he hadn't seen anything like it.

The American press went crazy with pictures, interviews, anything they could find about the Beatles. Beatlemania, as George had described it, was setting the American cultural landscape ablaze like nothing since Elvis. Then came the news that the Beatles would appear on Ed Sullivan.

"I don't believe it," Bobby said. "The whole world has gone wiggy. It's hard to imagine the same penniless urchins who hung around my stall at the flea market, begging for a listen to Chuck Berry, are now the top of the pops."

Clovis' once magnificent blond pompadour was gone, replaced by a Beatles-style haircut that hung down over his ears. Beneath the fringe of hair, Clovis' clean-shaven face smiled as he sat in Bobby's living room.

"And you actually know 'em! That makes you the most popular man in Baltimore."

"It's funny, really. These guys didn't have a pot to piss in when I first met them. All this has happened so suddenly."

"Overnight success, man. Happens all the time."

The TV flickered a grayish-white image of the four lads from Liverpool landing at Kennedy Airport in New York. Their press conference showcased John's biting wit which made Bobby feel nostalgic for the old days in Liverpool.

Clovis said, "You think they'll call you now that they're here?"

Bobby looked up from the TV screen.

"I don't know."

He half-expected John to call but part of Bobby knew the kind of fame the Beatles were experiencing warped existing relationships. They were almost too big. Now that they were rock royalty, the Beatles would shed their old friends like snakeskin.

"I'll betcha they won't even remember you," Clovis said. "Look at 'em."

Bobby's eyes wandered back to the TV screen. The press were bombarding the Beatles with questions.

"Are you going to have a haircut while you're in America?" one reporter asked George.

"I just had one yesterday."

A ripple of laughter went through the room.

"Would you sing something for us?"

"We need money first."

More laughs.

"Was your family in show business?"

"Me dad used to say me mother was a great performer."

"Are you part of a teenage rebellion against the older generation?"

"It's a dirty lie!"

Bobby chuckled at their responses but Clovis just stared, wide-eyed at the screen.

"These guys are so cool," he whispered.

The next day Bobby received a phone call from New York. A hoarse voice croaked into the phone.

"Dusty? Is that you?"

Bobby listened to the voice. It didn't sound like John.

"It's George."

"What's the matter with your voice?"

"I've got a sore throat."

"Oh, no. The Sullivan show is only a few days away."

"I know. I'm sick as a dog. My sister Louise is coming from St. Louis to take care of me."

"How bad are you?"

George coughed.

"Not very good, I'm afraid. I know Louise will heal me. She's always had the knack."

"Have you seen a doctor?"

"Brian had the house doctor look at me. They're doing everything they can, but I have to tell you... it's a madhouse here. Kids are outside surrounding the building. Cops are trying to hold them back. It's even worse than it was back home in England. It's completely out of hand."

Bobby heard a touch of sadness in George's voice. George coughed again.

"It's driving me crazy."

"Just hang in there, George."

"These Americans are scaring me."

Bobby didn't know what to say.

George continued. "Louise will be here soon, but there's so much hysteria around the hotel, I don't know if she'll be able to get in."

"Do you need my help?"

George's voice sounded like sandpaper.

"Yeah, would you?"

"Of course. I can take the train up from Baltimore straight away."

"I need you to help Louise. She has no idea how crazy the fans can be."

"I can be there by tonight."

George coughed violently. "I don't know anyone else to call, and you were so good to us when we visited. I haven't forgot that."

"What's your hotel?"

"We're at the Plaza on Central Park. But the whole place is surrounded by mobs."

"What room number?"

"We have the whole twelfth floor."

Bobby wrote the information on a piece of paper.

George's voice was fading. "Tell the men from the Burns detective agency that you are with us. Ask for Neil or Mal. Hopefully they'll let you in."

"It's great to hear from you, George, but I expected John to call."

George paused. "John and Paul are preoccupied. I'm sure he hasn't forgotten about you. It's just that the demands on his time have become ridiculous. He's trying to keep his head above water. We all are. Overwhelming, it is. None of us were ready for this."

Bobby threw a few items in his overnight bag and explained to Cricket where he was going.

"Be careful, honey," she said.

"I will. What can happen?"

Cricket shrugged. "Who knows? It's New York. Anything can happen. Just remember what I taught you."

Bobby nodded. Cricket had been teaching him the rudiments of competition style Judo since they'd begun living together. Bobby had progressed rapidly.

Bobby took the train from Baltimore's Penn Station to Grand Central Station in Manhattan. He grabbed a cab to Central Park but couldn't get closer than two blocks from the Plaza Hotel.

"Something big is goin' on," the cabbie said. "I think Khrushchev is in town."

Bobby paid the fare and walked the last blocks to the Plaza. He was not prepared for the scene.

The street was overrun by thousands of teenage girls. They buzzed and swarmed in unbridled frenzy. A movement in an upper window would prompt a teenybopper to scream as if she'd been stabbed. Then a thousand more would join the chorus. The sound of their combined shrieking made Bobby's blood run cold. En mass the girls were mindless and dangerous.

A dozen mounted policemen, along with an army of foot patrolmen, kept the crowd at bay. A blustery winter wind helped to slow them. Bobby skirted the mob.

He tried to enter the front door but was turned away by a gruff policeman who warned him to stay on the other side of the street. Bobby tried the back entrance but found a similar scene. Surprised to find the delivery entrance unguarded, he slipped into the building and made his way up the back stairs.

Winded from the twelve-floor climb, Bobby opened the stairwell door a crack and peered down the hall. As he caught his breath he surveyed the situation. The hall looked clear except for one older man standing near the elevator. Bobby opened the door and strode down the hall. He passed the man at the elevator and headed toward George's door. He could hear the television playing inside. Bobby knocked discretely.

"Who is it?" a female voiced said.

"It's Bobby Dingle, ma'am. George sent for me."

"Hold on."

A few moments later, George's sister, Louise, opened the door and Bobby stepped into the room. George was sitting up in bed watching TV with a cup of tea in his hand.

"Dusty! You've come! How did you get through the crowds?"

Bobby smiled. "I came up the back way. I'm a Merseyside lad. We're used to skulking about."

"Did you see the mob?"

"See it? I was in it."

"Frightening, isn't it?"

Bobby nodded. "I've never seen anything like it. The hotel is under siege."

"It's like this in England just not as bad."

"This country's been through some shocks lately. They just lost a popular President. They're still in mourning. People are just a bit excitable right now. I think the Beatles are the tonic. They're bound to calm down."

Louise poured another hot cup of tea for George and told him not to talk so much.

"You have to save your voice for Mr. Sullivan."

"They rehearsed without me today," George said glumly. "Right now they're off taking pictures in Central Park."

"Don't worry, George. You'll be back with the boys soon."

George sipped his hot tea.

"I felt bad in Paris. This has been building for a long time."

Louise frowned. "Just listen to you! You'd think you'd been kicked out of the band!"

Bobby changed the subject.

"Have you ordered any chicken soup? I hear that's good for a cold."

Louise shook her head.

"They didn't have it on the room service menu."

"That's odd."

George sneezed.

"Do you think you could get some?"

Bobby laughed. "This is New York. I'll find your chicken soup."

"What about the mobs?"

"I got in, didn't I? I'll get out too. I'll be back in no time with a hot, steaming bowl of Jewish penicillin."

"Jewish penicillin? Why didn't Eppy tell me about that?"

CHAPTER TWENTY-THREE

ED SULLIVAN

George perked up as soon as Bobby brought the chicken soup. The rest of the band returned from Central Park and crowded into George's room to cheer him up. The boys had interconnecting suites so they wouldn't be exposed to the other guests; ten rooms in all. Mal Evans and Neil Aspinall, the Beatles road managers and fearless veterans of British Beatlemania, planned it that way.

As soon as they saw Bobby, they began to shout.

"Dust Bin Bob! Dust Bin Bob! Dust Bin Bob!"

Ringo and Paul hugged Bobby and began trying to describe the incredible events of the past few days. None of this had happened before. Words fell short.

Bobby stood in front of John. An awkward moment passed before the two men embraced. Something had changed. Bobby sensed it. Something small and indefinable had shifted between the two of them. Bobby looked into John's eyes and searched for the friend who saved Stu at Lathom Hall. The same friend who stood up to Clive and opened his home to Bobby. John's smile broke the mood.

"Dusty, you old wanker! Come, give us a hug!"

Bobby threw his arms around John.

John turned up his scouse accent all the way. "We all knew yer when ya 'ad 'oles in yer kecks. Now look at ya! All presentable, you are. Gentlemanly like."

Bobby laughed. He hadn't heard the sing-song poetry of real Liverpool scouse since Mrs. Swithins.

Bobby said, "Honored, I am, to be makin' yer Lordship's acquaintance."

"Gawd, you sound like Ken Dodd!"

"Welcome to America, land of unlimited refills. Quite a change isn't it?"

"It's a bloody loony bin."

Paul and George clapped their hands.

"Hurray for Dust Bin Bob! Pride of Liverpool! Three cheers!"

John raised his hand and said, "I discovered Dusty."

Paul looked wounded.

"He's a friend to all of us, John. Remember the day we went up to his room and learned *Money*? That was the day we met his charming brothers. I'd say he's a treasure to be shared by all."

"You're right. Sorry if I got on your wick about it."

Bobby shook his head.

"Cheeky as ever, aren't you? I remember when you were Long John and the Silver Beetles."

Paul and George laughed.

"How are your wonderful brothers?"

"Mick's dead and Clive's in prison. Actually, he was in prison until a few days ago. He just broke out."

"I read about that. A big scandal, it was. Liverpool Prison?"

Bobby nodded.

"Wasn't Clive the one who swore he'd get us someday?" said Paul.

"One and the same. I have no idea where he is right now, but I'd keep a sharp eye out for him. Clive's a violent lad; thick as a brick, but he knows how to hold a grudge."

John snickered. "I don't see how anyone could penetrate the security we've been under. It's like a bloody jail."

Ringo said, "It's for your own good, John."

"That's what they say."

"Have you seen much of America yet?"

"We've seen a plane, the inside of a car and a hotel room. Not exactly what I call doing the town."

Bobby pointed at John.

"How are you holding up under the strain of it all?"

Paul answered for John.

"It's completely insane all right, but it could be over any minute, so we've got to make money while we can."

Two fellows Bobby didn't recognize were staring out the window at the mob of young girls below.

"I think it's got a way to go yet," said one.

John waved his hand.

"I forgot to introduce our zoo keepers, Mal and Neil. They let us out once a week for exercise."

Mal Evans casually saluted and Neil Aspinall nodded.

"Good to meet you, mate."

"This bloke has known us since before the beginning. He's a Liverpool legend."

Mal smiled. "A countryman is always welcome. These New Yorkers are insane."

"How long are you here?" John said.

"I thought I'd help Louise look after George until he's feeling better. What's your schedule?"

Paul said, "The Sullivan show is tomorrow. Then we fly to Washington to play a concert, then it's on to Miami for another Sullivan show."

Bobby said, "It's supposed to snow for the next few days."

"We've dealt with snow before."

"This is American snow. It's different."

"Yeah, it's dirtier."

*   *   *

The Ed Sullivan Theater on West 53rd Street only held seven hundred people but the show had received about fifty thousand applications for tickets. Cops lined the street in front. Bobby thought the Beatles were keeping remarkably calm.

Ed Sullivan himself greeted the band, waving a telegram from Elvis Presley.

"He wishes you luck," Ed said proudly. "Elvis and the Colonel both wish you success in America."

All four band members nodded, impressed that the King of Rock and Roll would acknowledge their presence.

Bobby stayed out of the way and accompanied George's sister Louise to her seat. Bobby saw a dense crowd of teenage girls squirming in their seats. The atmosphere crackled with electricity. TV cameras waited.

At last the stiff, uncomfortable image of Ed Sullivan appeared. After a rehearsal John had said Ed walked like he had a pole up his ass. Bobby could now corroborate this although no pole was visible. The red lights above each camera flickered on; the time was at hand.

Ed welcomed the viewers, made a few remarks, then introduced a brief commercial. A minute later he returned to a breathless audience. He must have known his words would go down in history, yet he rushed through them in the excitement of the moment.

"Now, yesterday and today, our theater has been jammed with newspapermen and hundreds of photographers from all over the nation, and these veterans agree with me that the city has never witnessed the excitement stirred by these youngsters from Liverpool who call themselves the Beatles. Now, tonight you'll be twice entertained by them, right now, and in the second half of our show. Ladies and gentlemen, the Beatles!"

Paul counted off the song and went into the first line of *All My Lovin'*. As soon as the band joined in, shrill keening filled the air. The sound shook the theater walls, echoing across America and raised the hair on the back of Bobby's neck. Hysterical screaming drowned out the music washing over them like a sonic tsunami. Louise clutched Bobby's arm.

The response to the Beatles was thunderous. The manic behavior of the audience frightened Bobby. Faces around him seemed twisted and desperate. The screaming rang in his ears. Tears rolled down the cheeks of the female audience members. Bobby found himself swept up in it and realized he too was shouting at the top of his lungs.

The Beatles seemed above it all, delivering their music to the frenzied masses in a thoroughly professional manner. The harmonies in *All My Lovin'* were perfect; the vocal blend was as natural and smooth as the Everly Brothers. Bobby was impressed that the group could play that flawlessly with relentless screaming in their ears.

All My Lovin' ended and *Till There Was You* started with another Paul vocal. Bobby thought it odd that they would follow *All My Lovin'* with another ballad sung by Paul but realized it was probably a group decision with Brian Epstein and Ed Sullivan approving the choice.

The third song, *She Loves You*, galvanized the audience and caused the greatest reaction of the set. Bobby considered *She Loves You* the ultimate Beatles song. Its "yeah, yeah, yeah" chorus and high pitched "whooo" at the end of the verses made it instantly recognizable.

When it ended the theater seemed to deflate. When the Beatles left the stage a huge vacuum sucked up the atmosphere.

Bobby looked at Louise. She blinked unbelieving.

"Good Lord. I don't believe it."

"It's beyond anything we could imagine," Bobby said.

They hardly noticed the next act, a man in a tuxedo doing card tricks.

Bobby's mind went back to the Beatles. He wondered what they thought of it. They were used to British Beatlemania, but this was... well, this was out of control. Bobby wondered where it would all lead.

The cast of the Broadway show *Oliver* followed, but Bobby couldn't focus on the song. Frank Gorshin did impersonations of celebrities Bobby never heard of, but Bobby enjoyed the man's elastic face and wild body language. Tessie O'Shea stood larger than life, strumming her banjo and belting out show tunes, but it seemed boring and ordinary to Bobby. The Beatles made everybody sound boring and ordinary.

An odd comedic team did a skit about a boss and his secretary, and Bobby found himself glancing at the clock, counting the minutes before the Beatles returned. At last they were back, and the screaming began anew.

"One! Two! Three! Fah!" Paul barked the count and Bobby instantly recognized the guitar intro to *I Saw Her Standing There*.

George played his dark brown Gretsch Country Gentleman guitar held high, picking the notes to the solo with a flourish. Bobby wondered why he wasn't using the black *Rickenbacker* he'd bought in St. Louis. John was playing his. Bobby imagined the matching black guitars would have looked cool on television. *I Want To Hold Your Hand* finished the set and caused the audience to expend what little energy they had left screaming and stamping their feet.

The sound of America screaming reverberated in Bobby's head, frightening him and at the same time filling him with excitement.

Louise said, "Well, that's it then."

Bobby nodded. "The genie is out of the bottle. Hang on to your hat."

Back at the hotel, Bobby slept on the sofa while soft snow fell gently across the city. He dreamed of Liverpool and Nancy Garlton.

In the morning Central Park was blanketed in white and the sounds of traffic were muffled. The group stared out the windows and blanched. They'd been on flights during inclement weather and knew the risk factors. Never a confident flier, George began to complain. Soon John and Paul joined in. Brian Epstein appeared to deal with the mutiny.

"It's a fookin' blizzard out there!" John said.

"I'm not getting on any planes today," George said, "No chance."

"We've got to get to Washington for the concert, George. Do you propose we drive? The roads are bad too. In a plane you'll fly above the storm."

"I'm not going," George said emphatically.

Louise looked worriedly around the room.

"If George isn't going, neither am I," John said.

"That's it, then," Paul said.

Brian wrung his hands.

"Boys, please. Listen to reason."

Bobby raised his hand as if in school. Brian looked at him, annoyed. "Yes?"

"You could take a train. It's an easy trip from New York to Washington. Trains don't usually have a problem with snow. That's how I was planning to go back to Baltimore."

Brian's voice had a crisp, upper class quality.

"A train? Why didn't I think of that? In America one assumes that one will be traveling by air. The distances seem so vast. Washington is not that far, is it?"

"The train is far more pleasant than a plane."

Brian turned to his female assistant.

"Call the train station. Find out the schedule to Washington."

Bobby said, "Would you like me to contact the Station Master? I'll see if a private car is available."

Brian fixed his gaze on Bobby.

"Who are you exactly?"

"He's the famous Dust Bin Bob from Liverpool," John said.

"Didn't I once see you at the Cavern Club?"

"Yes, sir."

"What are you doing here?"

"I'm an antiques dealer. I've been living in the States."

"He's gone and married a Yank," George added.

"I see," Brian said thoughtfully. "Why don't you get on the phone and see what you can do? I have to make a decision within the hour."

"I'm not flyin' in this fookin' blizzard," George repeated. "Train or no train."

Bobby spent the next hour on the telephone. Through patience and luck, he arranged for a private car for the world famous Beatles and their entourage.

Brian smiled. "Well done, Robert. That was good thinking. What are your plans for the rest of the week?"

"I'm not doing much."

"Would you like to work for me temporarily? We could always use another pair of hands. We've got a crazy week coming up, and it's absolutely imperative that we get the group from point A to point B on time. Since you already know the boys, you would be a natural."

Bobby grinned. "How would the band feel about that?"

Paul and George both nodded. Ringo gave the thumb's up. Only John didn't smile. Bobby stared at him, waiting for an answer.

"Well?"

"If you want to be one of Eppy's boys, it's your choice, not mine."

"If working for Brian would get in the way of our friendship then I won't do it. It's that simple."

John stared off into space.

"Come on, John," Paul said. "It'll be fun."

John stood.

"Look, Dusty, I don't think you working for Brian will be a problem at all. I wonder if you want to expose yourself to all the madness. It's bloody awful, running from place to place, people going daft all around you. It can be violent at times. Do you want to have to deal with all that?"

Bobby looked into John's eyes.

"Yes. I'm not sure why, but yes."

John shrugged. "It's off we go to Washington."

CHAPTER TWENTY-FOUR

BEATLEMANIA

Despite the snow Central Manhattan crawled with Beatles fans. Bobby helped Neil and Mal load luggage into the trunk of the black decoy limo. The band snuck out the back door and piled into in another vehicle. The advance team had already gone to Penn Station to smooth the way. Three dozen police officers held back a crowd of Beatlemaniacs. The girls' squeals were muffled in the frosty air.

As the decoy pulled up to the station, the girls began to scream. When they saw that the cargo was suitcases and not Beatles, they quickly calmed. The three men hoofed it through the station, pushing carts overloaded with luggage and guitar cases. Bobby struggled to keep up with Neil and Mal.

Bobby was the organized one so he drew the assignment of counting the luggage as the porter checked them one by one. Bobby wrote the name of each piece on the individual claim checks. That way he'd know which was which in case of a problem.

The private car was a beautifully restored Edwardian sleeping car from the old Richmond, Fredericksburg and Potomac Railroad.

John's wife, Cynthia, arrived in another limo with the New York disk jockey Murray the K. Cynthia, disguised in a brunette wig and dark sunglasses, didn't appear too pleased with the arrangement. Bobby escorted her to her seat then returned to Mal and Neil. They stood together, bracing for whatever might come.

A sound reverberated through the cavernous station walls. Bobby and Neil looked up.

"Looks like the boys are here," Mal said.

"Better get ready," Neil added.

Bobby wondered what that meant as he watched the four band members sprint toward the car.

"Come on!" Mal shouted. "Hurry up!"

John, Paul, George, and Ringo piled through the door.

"Quick! To the back!" Mal said, motioning the group toward the rear of the car. They stood on the small outdoor platform at the end of the car. The frigid New York air chilled Bobby's cheeks; his heart pounded. Here he stood, at the nervous heart of Beatlemania.

John winked at him. "Close one, eh, Dusty? Better get used to it. It's like this every bloody day."

"These people are downright crazy."

"Wait until the gig in Washington. You'll really see some insanity," George said.

The Beatles smoked cigarettes and joked among themselves. They stayed outside until the train began to move.

As it lurched down the track, Ringo shouted, "All aboard! The Beatles express!"

"Next stop, Hipsville, Flipsville, and Washington, A.C.D.C.!" John added.

Bobby threw his cigarette into the snow and turned his collar up.

"We might as well go in and have a cuppa," George said. "It's a bit chilly out here."

"Cold as a witch's tit," Bobby mumbled, repeating a line he heard from Clovis. John heard the phrase and laughed.

"That's damn cold, man," John replied.

Bobby glanced back into the car.

"Who's in charge in there?"

"Probably Brian Summerville," John yawned. "He's press liaison on this trip."

George wiggled his eyebrows.

"My vote is for Murray The K, the DJ. He's the geezer with the grotty clothes and the silly sayings."

"The one that calls everybody 'baby'?"

"That's him. He calls himself the fifth Beatle."

John snorted. "There's only one fifth Beatle."

"Dust Bin Bob is the true fifth Beatle," George said.

"Agreed," said John. "He was there for us in the beginning."

Bobby blushed. "Thanks... I don't know what to say... Just thanks..."

The Beatles, plus Bobby, Neil, and Mal entered the train car to a round of applause. Bobby noticed Brian Epstein standing with a gaggle of photographers at the end of the car. His immaculate clothes set him apart among the rumpled masses of American media. He waved at Bobby. Bobby waved back and threaded his way through the crowd to Brian.

"The concert is sold out and according to the promoter there are several thousand kids without tickets already standing outside the hall. I fear there may be some violence."

"How're you going to get the band in and out?"

Brian shrugged. "We've used different plans back in England including an armored truck. The boys hate the truck because they feel trapped."

"Do you worry about the band's mental state with all the madness surrounding them?"

Brian seemed surprised by the question.

"No. I tell them whatever is happening will pass and years from now we'll look back on these times with fondness while we sit about in our country estates counting money."

Bobby chuckled. "That seems right enough."

"This is success, Robert. Success beyond compare. You can't be afraid of it. People struggle their whole lives to get just a fraction of what these boys have achieved. This is what we've been working for, to make it in America. They'll just have to cope with it. A little inconvenience is a small fee to pay for financial security for the rest of their lives."

"What might it do to the boys? Couldn't it sour them on the whole idea eventually?"

Brian stared wistfully out the window.

"I doubt it. The Beatles aren't like the rest of us."

Bobby considered the statement. It seemed true enough.

"You seem like a bright boy, Robert. Do you have any plans for after the tour?"

"I have an antique shop in Baltimore."

"It may seem a bit dull after all this."

"I dare say it will. But that's what life is all about, isn't it? The dull bits? That's the way we live our lives, right?"

"Not the Beatles."

Bobby watched Ringo horsing around with the photographers. He'd draped about ten cameras around his neck and was pretending to take pictures.

"I guess you're right."

"Of course, I'm right. These are extraordinary times, Robert. It's a great moment to be young."

*   *   *

Beatlemania hit Washington, D.C. like a blizzard. When they arrived at Union Station thousands of teenagers screamed and pushed against the barricades. The Beatles ran to a waiting limo. Bobby stayed behind with Mal and Neil helping with the bags and equipment. He didn't see the band again until the concert.

Jellybeans rained down on the stage even before the Beatles started. Bobby stood in the wings. Brian Epstein came up next to him and set a hand on his shoulder.

"Neil tells me that the equipment has to be moved periodically during the show to allow for the theater in the round. You'll be helping John and George move their amps. Neil will help with Ringo"s drums and Mal will handle Paul's bass amplifier. Neil will give you a signal when the time comes."

"I'm ready," Bobby said.

"Good. I have a feeling that this could be one of the wildest shows yet."

Brian wasn't exaggerating. The Beatles took the stage to deafening shrieks and steady pelting of jellybeans. The Coliseum Sports Arena shook under the stomping feet and hysterical screaming of thousands of Beatles fans. The sound actually caused Bobby to shake in his boots. From the first note the Beatles were buried beneath a mountain of noise and hysteria.

If the Ed Sullivan Show had been the beginning of Beatlemania in the States, this could only be described as the peak. The fans were delirious. The building trembled. The display of rock and roll insanity frightened Bobby. Without the lines of uniformed policemen and efforts of a small army of ushers, the Beatles would have been torn limb from limb.

They exploded into the opening riff of Chuck Berry's *Roll Over Beethoven* and then followed with *From Me To You*. Ringo tried to sing *I Wanna Be Your Man* but the orgy of screaming drowned him out.

Bobby turned around to look at Brian and he saw tears in his eyes.

"Are you OK?" Bobby asked.

Brian nodded, dabbing his eyes with a handkerchief.

"It's beautiful isn't it? This is beyond anything we could have imagined."

Neil signaled to Bobby that it was time to reverse the equipment. Neil helped Ringo move his drums to face the opposite direction. John and Paul spoke to the crowd but their words were drowned out. John did his spastic dance for a few moments.

Being onstage with the Beatles gave Bobby a new perspective. He stole a glance at John who seemed impatient to restart the music. John noticed Bobby and grinned.

"Hey, Dusty, welcome to the monkey house."

Bobby barely heard the words. Jellybeans bounced off his back and one stung his ear, making him jump. He avoided looking directly at the audience. The stage, like a small ocean island, it seemed threatened by the storm surge of drowning worship. The excitement thrilled Bobby in a way he'd never experienced.

As soon as Ringo's drums were ready, Paul counted off the next song. Screams began anew. Bobby recoiled. The screams rang inside his ears, shaking his brain. He listened but heard nothing.

The band raced through *Please Please Me, Till There Was You, She Loves You,* and *I Want To Hold Your Hand.*

As soon as the last note faded, Neil and Mal hustled the boys off stage and into their vehicle for a mad dash to the hotel. Bobby stayed with the equipment. He found that the guitars and amplifiers were almost as famous as the band itself. Young girls were willing to dive through the arms of burly police officers or climb lighting towers just to touch Paul's guitar case.

"Next time maybe the band can stay home and the equipment can go on tour," Bobby said, but no one was listening.

CHAPTER TWENTY-FIVE

INSTANT PSYCHIATRIST

A visit to the British Embassy in Washington D.C. was not a popular idea with the band and they only agreed to do it to make Brian Epstein happy. Their philosophy was to avoid all things political. Apart from the occasional mayor welcoming them to a city, they had nothing to do with politicians. Publicist Brian Sommerville thought visiting the British Embassy would be good for their image.

Ambassador Sir David Ormsby-Gore met the band upon their arrival. When they entered the main reception area, a gaggle of diplomats and their wives, stiffly-dressed and already half-drunk on free booze, descended on the band, pressing them for autographs.

As George scrawled his name on an embassy napkin, someone behind him remarked, "Can they actually write?"

The attitude of superiority among the embassy staff made the band feel uneasy. People didn't ask for autographs here; they demanded them. The wife of one staffer snuck up on Ringo with a pair of scissors and snipped a lock of hair. Ringo reacted with a shout and a curse, refusing to sign more autographs.

"I've never been fawned over and insulted at the same time," George said. "It's weird."

John spoke conspiratorially. "We're the enemy to these types. They thrive on the class system while we tear it down."

George looked around.

"This is extremely unpleasant."

"Let's blow."

"They want us to announce prizes to a grotty embassy raffle!" Paul moaned.

"Is that why they asked us here?" George said.

"Apparently so."

John folded his arms.

"Sod the raffle. I'm leaving."

George signaled to Bobby.

"Tell Neil we're leaving."

"No, you're not!" an embassy staffer said. A group of six men in black suits surrounded the band. It reminded him of the night when John had come to Stu's rescue at Lathom Hall. If these straight-laced embassy types wanted to mix it up, Bobby was sure the Beatles, along with Neil and Mal, would prevail. The very thought seemed ridiculous. *A cock-up at the embassy?* he thought. *Never.*

Ringo put a hand on John's shoulder.

"Let's just get it over with."

"Ringo's right. Let's get it over with before they flog us with their jewelry," George said. "It's not worth an ugly scene."

The Beatles went back to their hotel in a foul mood. John Lennon threatened to write a song about it.

*   *   *

Brian Epstein put the phone down.

"All flights are cancelled due to the snow. We'll have to take the train back to New York."

"That's all right by me," John said.

"I'll be glad when we get to Miami. A bit of a holiday in the sun would be nice right now."

Bobby stood at the window of one of the Beatle suites on the seventh floor of the Shoreham Hotel. He watched the big flakes fall. Washington was beautiful in white, its streets nearly empty of cars. Bobby wondered what Southway looked like today. He visualized Winston bounding into the snow, squealing with delight. He wished he could be there now. The idea of traveling back to New York with the Beatles didn't seem as attractive as it might have few days earlier.

Another train ride, another mob scene. Beatlemania exhausted him. He couldn't wait for the tour to be over. Winston and Cricket needed him, even though Cricket had given him her blessing. After two shows at Carnegie Hall, there was only the trip to Miami for the second Ed Sullivan Show. Then it would be back to England for the Fab Four and back to Baltimore for him.

Bobby listened as Brian Epstein operated on the phone, setting up more concerts, TV appearances, recording sessions, making deals all over the world.

He looked at George who always seemed to have a guitar in his hands. George fingerpicked something like the old folk song *Barbara Allen*. George used the guitar to turn away from people, grabbing a moment's privacy in a world of distraction. He would bend his neck and bring his head down near the sound hole, listening as he fiddled or tuned. Whenever things got too intense, George retreated into his guitar. The people who knew him respected that.

A knock at the door signaled the arrival of breakfast. Bobby opened the door. As his eyes went from the cart full of food to the man who pushed it, his jaw dropped.

"Hey, Robby! Guess who?"

"Clovis! But how did you...?"

"I called your old lady who told me you were here. I brought breakfast!"

Clovis rolled a serving table full of covered dishes into the room. He vigorously chewed a wad of pink bubble gum.

"Any jelly butties in there, mate?" asked Paul.

Clovis chewed. "What's that?"

"He means jelly sandwiches."

Bobby said, "Clovis, how did you get past the cops?"

"I bribed the room service guy to let me bring this up here. It was easy."

Bobby laughed. "You are amazing."

George recognized Clovis and jumped up to embrace him.

"Hey, man! The guy who took me to see Sam Cooke!"

George turned to the others.

"This is Clovis, Dust Bin Bob's friend from Baltimore. He's a great guitar player. He plays *Dixie Fried* perfectly. He's Carl Perkins's spiritual brother."

The others nodded, impressed. Carl Perkins was the mystery man of guitarists. To know the secrets of Perkins was to know the secrets of the universe. Clovis looked like he knew.

"I just come down to see y'all and say hi to Georgie here. I figured you might need some help dealin' with the natives. That's my specialty. I know how to deal with people. I'm a people person."

"Who is this man?" Brian asked Bobby.

"He's a very resourceful musician friend of mine."

George said, "Can you come on the train with us? I'm so bored. We could jam all the way back to New York."

Clovis blew a bubble and popped it with a loud snap.

"Hot damn! Where do I sign up?"

"Just a minute," Brian said.

"He's my friend," George said, "and Dust Bin Bob's friend as well."

"Any duly authorized friend of Dust Bin Bob and George can't be all bad, Brian. We have room for one more. Why not?" Paul said. "I say, keep the band happy. A happy band is a productive band. Right, Eppy?"

Brian Epstein smiled shyly.

"Yes, of course, Paul."

＊　　＊　　＊

The train rocked gently from side to side as the click and clack of the wheels defined an easy rhythm. Clovis held George's acoustic guitar.

"I know every song ever written. Go ahead, ask me."

"All right," John said, "*Blue Moon Of Kentucky*."

"Bill Monroe or Elvis Presley?"

John grinned as if to say *Maybe he does know everything*.

"Elvis."

Clovis strummed the chords on the guitar, playing it exactly like the record which was the B side of *That's All Right, Mama*, Elvis' first single for *Sun Records*. He even sang like Elvis. It was perfect.

"The James Burton guitar solo on *Travelin' Man* by Rick Nelson," Paul said.

He had upped the ante considerably. It was a difficult solo and would truly put Clovis to the test.

"Ricky Nelson! Very close to my heart."

With John, Paul, and George watching closely, Clovis played a flawless solo.

John, Paul, George and Ringo played "Name That Tune" for over an hour until Clovis leaned over and whispered something to George. George smiled and whispered something to Paul who whispered to John. Bobby asked Clovis what was going on.

Clovis answered the question by slipping a hand into his breast pocket and flashing a pair of beautifully rolled joints. Clovis winked.

"Time for some instant psychiatrist."

John howled with laughter.

"Instant psychiatrist! Bloody brilliant!"

"You can't be serious," Bobby said.

Clovis leaned forward and dropped his voice. "Outside a moving train? I've done it lots of times. No one will ever know. Follow me."

Clovis rose and Bobby and the band followed him out to the small platform outside. Shielding the joint against the wind, he lit it and passed it around.

"This is great," John said. "Half the bleedin' press in America just a few feet away and here we are, smokin' a gasper right under their noses."

"What would they do if they found out?" Bobby asked.

John's throat constricted as he answered in a strange voice.

"Nothin', probably."

"The Beatles smoking weed? Come on. A scandal like that wouldn't be front page news?"

John exhaled slowly through his nostrils.

"If they did that their little party would be over. As long as we're news, they have a job. If they destroyed the Beatles who would they photograph and interview? They need us as much as we need them. Maybe more."

Bobby scratched his head.

"That makes sense."

"It's true. In England, Fleet Street absolutely loves us. They wouldn't dare say anything bad about us. We're good for business."

John handed the joint to George.

"I needed this," George said. He inhaled deeply then coughed violently.

Clovis patted his back as the train jolted.

"Easy there, Kemo Sabe."

"Thanks, Clovis. You really know how to make a train ride exciting."

George handed the joint to Clovis. Clovis sucked on the joint, taking in a huge toke.

"That's my style."

"Is it true that your girlfriend's a stripper?"

"Yeah. Top notch. She's got humongous ta-tas like you wouldn't believe, man. I used to back her up. Hell of a gig. I stared at her ass for eight hours a night."

Clovis took another hit and passed the joint.

"You're a cross between Jack Kerouac and Carl Perkins," John said.

Clovis nodded. "When it comes to strippers and pickers, I'm your man."

"Where'd you get this grass?"

"From some Jamaican cats."

The Beatles looked at Clovis as a genuine American hero: a guitar player with extensive knowledge and technique, good weed and a girlfriend who was a headlining stripper. He embodied the American myth of the rugged individualist. And he could play *Dixie Fried*.

*   *   *

The concerts at Carnegie Hall were as chaotic and intense as the one in Washington. Jellybeans rained, screams filled the air, and the band soldiered on. It was getting impossible for the boys to hear themselves, but it only bothered the Beatles. The fans loved the sound of their own screams.

Celebrities vied for tickets and demanded backstage meetings with the Fabs. Brian Epstein continued sheltering the boys as much as he could, but the New York notoriety had their emotional roof sagging. The band seemed frayed.

New York's first lady, Happy Rockefeller, waited with her two children at a backstage door while Shirley Bassey, (soon to have her own monster hit, singing the theme to *Goldfinger*) called between shows to congratulate them.

John and Clovis talked about music all night. In the morning, Bobby wanted to leave. He missed Cricket and his son. All he could think of now was going home. A great wave of guilt washed over him.

After room service tea and toast, the Beatles drifted into their main suite to receive their new itineraries. Brian read the schedule to them and answered questions. Afterward, Bobby and Clovis said good-bye to everyone and wished them well. Brian cornered Bobby before he could make his escape.

"Robert, you should really think about relocating to London. The scene is exploding right now. There are fortunes to be made. You could open an antique shop in London. I could introduce you to some people there. You really should consider it."

John tapped Brian on the shoulder.

"Don't waste your time, Eppy. He's married."

"I really should be going," Bobby said. "Thanks for everything."

"Are you sure you don't want to go to Miami? I hear the weather is better there."

"No. I really need to get home."

"You'll be missing the second Sullivan show."

"I'll watch it on TV."

Bobby left quickly, pausing only to embrace the boys.

"I'll see you on the next trip."

"We'll expect it. Bring Clovis along too."

Clovis saluted.

"You got it, pardner! I'll schedule a visit with the psychiatrist too."

Brian forced a weak smile.

"I beg your pardon?"

John said, "Forget it, Eppy. It's an inside joke."

The snow stopped falling. Bobby walked away from the hotel through the place where the crowds had gathered. It was nearly deserted now that the Beatlemaniacs had departed. He wondered where it would all wind up. The Beatles made history but none of them seemed to care. To them it was just the rush from gig to gig, hotel to hotel, pursued by mobs of screaming fans. They lacked the luxury of perspective.

Bobby took a cab to Penn Station.

Clovis split to look up some friends in Greenwich Village.

*　　*　　*

Baltimore had received its share of snow. Bobby's train arrived without fanfare, a welcome change from traveling with the Beatles. Bobby relished returning to the anonymity of life on Southway.

But the world had changed since he left. The voracious press coverage of the Beatles continued through the week. Bobby eagerly devoured every story and studied every photo. There were pictures of them arriving at airports, waving to crowds, cavorting on the beach, clowning with Cassius Clay, mugging for the cameras around a hotel pool. It looked like fun, but Bobby knew how claustrophobic the real picture was.

On Thursday George called to say hello and regale Bobby with stories of Miami Beach. The excitement in his voice tickled Bobby's ear.

"The police assigned a special bodyguard just for us. His name is Sergeant Buddy. He smuggled us out of the hotel through the kitchen in a meat wagon. Brian nearly had a cow. We spent the day at the beach. Then we went out on some millionaire's boat and the guy let Ringo drive. He plowed right into the dock! Then Sergeant Buddy took us home to dinner. His wife cooked a great meal; much better than room service food."

Bobby laughed. "Sounds like the time of your life."

"It is. Be sure to drop us a line back in England. We appreciate you, Dust

Bin Bob. Don't take anybody's shit."

"Thanks. Don't worry about me, George. You just keep the Beatles out of trouble."

Bobby hung up and sighed. On Sunday night he watched the Ed Sullivan Show broadcast from the Mau-Mau Room of the Deauville Hotel in Miami Beach. The southern screams were even fiercer.

CHAPTER TWENTY-SIX

THE BEATLES IN THE BIG B

In the year that followed, Beatlemania hit maximum insanity. The band's records dominated the charts while dozens of other talented British groups exploded onto the American scene. Brian Epstein's stable of Liverpool bands swelled, each one scoring hits. London bands like the Dave Clark Five and the Rolling Stones topped the charts. Manchester had its Hollies. Newcastle let loose the Animals. British rock and roll was finding its place in the world. In the months when the madness should've been fading, the boys still caused riots wherever they went.

On the American front, the Beatles had turned the record business upside down. Pressing plants struggled to keep up with the demand. At one point every record pressing plant in the country was turning out Beatle records. American musicians either adjusted or got out of the way.

In March Bobby saw Pete Best appearing on the TV Quiz Show *What's My Line*. Even former Beatles had a whiff of the magic. Following his friends through the media, Bobby marveled at every outrageous success. They might be the Beatles to the rest of the world but to him they were still four scruffy Liverpool lads who'd desperately wanted to hear his records.

Bobby read about the Beatles' breakneck schedule. In between their seemingly endless tours, they were now scheduled to begin work on their first feature length movie at Twickenham Studios with Richard Lester directing. Lester was American born but had gained a reputation for directing scathing BBC satires. John published a book and won an award. The Queen Mother was a fan. What else was left?

Then came word of a massive summer tour of America. Bobby's heart leapt at the news. The Beatles were coming to the Baltimore Civic Center on September 13th! Big B, meet the Beatles!

Bobby secured tickets the moment they went on sale. He contacted Brian Epstein to request a backstage pass. In the weeks preceding the concert, Bobby watched his adopted town go ga-ga over the Beatles.

Even Preston Washington down at the Hi-Dee-Ho Soul Shack took notice.

"I can't believe that little skinny white boy you brought in here is one of them Beatles!"

"Yeah."

"I saw 'em on Ed Sullivan. They got a pretty good thing goin', don't they? Damn! I shoulda took a picture."

Bobby grinned.

"Maybe you'll get your chance when they come to town in September."

"You don't say? They comin' here?"

Bobby nodded. "George already told me that he wants to come back to buy some more records when he's in town. I have a feelin' that the whole band might show up."

Preston thrust his stomach out and snapped his suspenders.

"Ain't that the shits?"

"The shits? Nice expression, Mr. Washington. Yes, it's the shits indeed. The Beatles probably won't have much time so I was wondering if it would be too much to ask if you could open the store just for them late at night? I could sneak the boys in after their gig. We couldn't tell anyone. I believe they would make it worth your while. Are you willing?"

"Willing? Yeah, I'm willing. I could make a nice chunk of change. You think they might sign a few items while they're here?"

"I don't see why not. Within reason, of course."

"Oh, yes. Of course."

Preston put a huge hand on Bobby's shoulder.

"You need some new vinyl, man? You look a little peaked. I got something new by a local group, The Royalettes. They got somethin' goin', man."

"I like local talent."

"Yeah, remember the Lafayettes? White kids from Baltimore on RCA

Records? *Life's Too Short*? Best record of the year if you ask me. You bring those Beatles down here and I'll fill 'em up with stuff they can't get nowhere else."

Preston took a record off the counter and handed it to Bobby.

"The Van Dykes on Atlantic Records. Atlantic's a cool label, man. They got Ray Charles and the Coasters. This is the Van Dykes doin' *Stupidity*. It's an instant classic. Once the rest of the country catches up with this record, it's gonna be school's out."

Preston put it on the turntable and jacked up the volume. The song poured out of big speakers fronted with chicken wire. A stompin' beat and a strong horn line made Bobby's feet move. He listened to the lyrics and marveled at the perfect groove. Preston sang along with the record, his smoky voice cracking like a preacher.

"Hey! Everybody! All around the world! Every boy and every girl! Take a lesson from me! Doin' the stupidity!"

Bobby laughed out loud. Preston started dancing like a circus bear. His singing voice was somewhere between James Brown and Bugs Bunny... and he was loud. His voice ricocheted off the walls.

"My poppa says I look pretty silly! My momma says I look like a fool..."

Bobby clapped his hands.

"Great record!"

Preston kept singing. "Come along with me! See how much fun it can be! Take a lesson from me, doin' the stupidity!"

"Get down, brother!"

"The Van Dykes. Local band, man. Atlantic records. Dig it."

The song ended and Preston put the record back in its sleeve.

"There's a bunch of local talent here in The Big B. You got the Lafayettes, the Van Dykes, the Royalettes, Tommy Vann and the Echoes, Bob Brady and the Concords, the El Corals featuring Little Wimpy Johnson and the El Coralettes, the Admirals..." Preston snapped his fingers. "Hey! Have I shown you this yet?" He handed Bobby an album.

"What's this?"

"My recommendation. *James Brown Live at the Apollo*. Best live record I ever heard. Fantastic. You'll think you're there on stage with 'em. It's powerful stuff."

"You've never been wrong before. You were right when told me *Doug Clark and the Hot Nuts On Campus* was a ripper."

"That's right." Preston began to sing again, "Hot nuts! Hot nuts! Get 'em from the peanut man!"

Bobby eased the record out of the sleeve.

"It's all one long cut."

Preston nodded. "Just one long show, man. No gaps. It's a revolutionary approach to making albums. Only James could do it. You gotta listen to the whole thing, see? None of this one song at a time bullshit. That's a man's album. Ain't for babies."

"I'll take it."

"Good. And you bring them Beatles down here and they can just go nuts, y'hear?"

*　*　*

Other English beat groups appeared on the Ed Sullivan show but none of them moved Bobby in the same way.

The summer weather in Baltimore became hot and sticky. In July Cricket's father invited the entire family to Ocean City, Maryland. He rented a huge old house called the Landmark at Eight Street on the Boardwalk.

Bobby loved the Landmark at first sight. This sagging, rambling seaside home boasted eight bedrooms and a huge plantation-style front porch overlooking the Atlantic Ocean. Its warped, weather-beaten wood peeked out from beneath layers of peeling white paint. The Landmark smelled of mildew and dead sand crabs.

Decades of ocean moisture had warped every board in the building leaving no right angles in the Landmark. Every door squeaked, every floorboard creaked, and sand was everywhere despite Mrs. Samansky's best efforts. After dinner the whole clan sat in the line of rickety beach chairs facing the Boardwalk. The world paraded past their reviewing stand.

Ocean City reminded Bobby of Blackpool, only busier. These Yanks took vacations seriously. Mr. Samansky often made a daily schedule, keeping to it as closely as a drill sergeant. The entire family came: Grandma Samansky, Aunt Julia with her three teenage daughters, Cricket's brother, Arthur, with his wife and two kids, plus the family dog. The Landmark held them all.

Ocean City, Maryland was a sand bar a few blocks wide and ten miles long. To the east was the Atlantic while the west was bordered by the Isle of Wight Bay. Mr. Samansky led crabbing expeditions on the bay side. The aspiring crabbers tied fish heads to string and dropped them over the side of their rented rowboat. They watched as lethargic crabs woke up to the presence of the fish heads. As the crabs took the bait, Mr. Samansky gently pulled them up and slipped a crab net underneath them. This simple exercise was amazingly effective allowing them to fill three bushel baskets with snapping blue crabs by early afternoon.

Cricket's mom spiced them with Old Bay Seasoning as they steamed in a giant pot. The Samanskys served them on newspaper, providing wooden mallets to crack the shells. The Maryland blue crab was quickly becoming Bobby's favorite crustacean.

In the mornings Cricket and her father practiced Judo on the beach. Bobby learned the rudiments. He marveled at Cricket's ability to toss him over her shoulder repeatedly without breaking a sweat. Mr. Samansky showed Bobby how it was done and made him practice until he learned each technique.

They went boating, water skiing, or fishing nearly every afternoon. At night Bobby lay in a sagging iron bed and fell asleep to the sounds of pounding waves mixing with the carnival blare of the Boardwalk. Ninth Street, the hub of the town, was only a block away. The ringing of the pinball machines sounded vaguely like the Reeperbahn in Hamburg. The jukeboxes were all playing Beatles music now. A few of the more adventurous kids had already adopted Beatles haircuts. The boys' influence was everywhere that summer.

Bobby took Cricket for long walks along the beach. They waded in the foaming surf and watched seagulls pinwheel in cloudless blue skies. On the Boardwalk they bought saltwater taffy at Dolles or French fries with salt and vinegar at Thrashers. At a place called the Safari Shop, Cricket bought Bobby a leopard-print necktie. Bobby combed the cutout bins of variety stores for records and found several Bo Diddley and Chuck Berry sides. The thick 45-rpm singles had white labels. The man at the counter said they had been used as promo copies. At three for a dollar Bobby didn't care about their original purpose. He just wanted to hear the songs.

In the evening the Samanskys played miniature golf and went to Dumser's for exotic ice cream sundaes. Bobby sent colorful postcards to his father and Mrs. Swithins. In the postcards the beach was filled with hundreds of umbrellas. Each hotel or rental stand had its own color design. When you looked at them from the porch or a window, the umbrellas formed beautiful patterns that appealed to Bobby's eye. Bobby came to love Ocean City.

After the Beatles hit, Clovis Hicks disbanded the Thunderbirds and joined a new band, the Telstars, who had a summer long Ocean City engagement at a place called The Beachcomber. The Beachcomber allowed teenagers to drink a beverage called "near beer" which tasted vaguely like beer but contained no alcohol. The waitresses wore white hip-huggers and halter tops that glowed in the ultraviolet lighting of the dance floor.

The Beachcomber was inland next to the bay. Bobby took Cricket there to see Clovis. Suntanned kids wearing madras shirts and white Levis loitered by their cars in the large parking lot in front. They smoked and laughed in the humid ocean breeze. The place was packed.

Music pulsated, vibrating Bobby's inner organs. He flashed back to the Star Club in Hamburg and the Cavern in Liverpool. The same vibe of expectancy charged the air. Bobby knew that the atmosphere in any room was dictated by the music. The Telstars were rockin'.

Bobby recognized the song, *One Too Many Mornings,* originally written and recorded by Bob Dylan. Somehow the Telstars had taken this quiet piece and supercharged it with a Beatles-like intensity. It jangled with the Rickenbacker guitars and pounded with the Ludwig drums. *Dylan folk songs played with a rock beat. Brilliant idea,* Bobby thought.

The Telstars blasted from a small stage directly in front of a scuffed linoleum dance floor at the end of the main room. People jammed themselves into every available space. It took a few minutes for Bobby and Cricket to jockey into position to actually see the band. All the band members wore matching gold suits.

Bobby laughed out loud when he saw the strange new haircut Clovis had adopted to fit in with the Telstars. The bizarre pompadour arched over Clovis' head like an angry cat.

As the song ended, Bobby pulled Cricket toward the stage. The next song started. It was *Mr. Pitiful* by Otis Redding. The keyboard player moved over to sax. He cranked out a horn line that was outrageous.

That had to be Clovis' influence; an eclectic choice of cover material from folk-rock to soul. It showed tremendous range, Bobby thought. The band played a tight version of *Louie Louie* then slammed through six Beatles songs in a row. The crowd responded by clogging the dance floor and surging against the stage. When the set ended Bobby approached and shook Clovis' hand.

"I had to give up my Beatle cut for this damn thing." Clovis pointed to his head. "But that was the deal with the Telstars. It's a steady gig and I'm finally makin' some money. It's only for the summer and then I'm startin' my own band, The Moss. I met a guy who has a club down in Georgetown. They've got a scene there, he says. He told me we could have a long run if the people dig us. And you know they will. If things get bad I can always put Erlene out in front of the band to flash her tits."

Cricket laughed.

"I think he's serious," Bobby said.

"I am. Hell, if your woman's a stripper, you gotta be proud of her natural assets. Those titties put food on the table. God bless 'em. You can't knock what God has created, can ya? In many ways, Erlene is out there spreadin' God's will. She's showing the great perfection of God's hand to those who come to worship at the altar of her hooters."

"That's beautiful," Cricket said. "Erlene's lucky to have a man like you, Clovis."

"Why, thank ya, ma'am. I do appreciate it."

*   *   *

One night in Baltimore, the phone rang. George's unmistakable voice crackled over the wire.

"Sir Dust Bin Bob? This is Sergeant Harrison of Her Majesty's Clockwork Rattle and Pinch Brigade reporting in."

"At ease, Harrison. How goes the campaign?"

"It's been like a bloody war out here. Every night something happens. Poor Ringo had it really bad. In Seattle a girl crawled through an airduct over the stage. When she reached the vent it broke and she fell twenty-five feet, landing right in front of Ringo. Ringo asked her if she was all right and she got up and ran away."

"It's a miracle she wasn't hurt."

"Yeah, but these fans, they don't get hurt. They can hide in a closet for twenty- four hours. They lay across the roof of the limo. They climb up fire escapes. And that's just the beginning. In Denver we couldn't breathe. They had to give us oxygen. How can you build a city where there's no oxygen?"

"Well... I don't know. But there's air in Baltimore. I breathe it every day. You're coming here on the thirteenth. I'll be there."

"We're in Boston the night before. I'll call you from the hotel. Hey, John's here. He wants to say hello."

Bobby listened to the shuffle as George handed the phone to John.

"Dusty? How are things on the outside?"

"Just great, John. How are you holding up?"

John sounded tired. "I don't know, man. Every day brings more madness than the day before. Bloody spooky, it is. In Canada Ringo got a death threat.

This guy was 'gonna kill the English Jew' which is really barmy because Ringo's not a Jew. So the cops put an armed detective on Ringo and he stayed by his side the whole time even on stage. Ringo played the entire show crouched down behind his drums. Nervewracking, it was. In Florida we played outdoors in a hurricane. Ringo's drums almost blew away."

John sighed. "Looking forward to seeing you, mate. Here's George."

When George was back on the line Bobby told him about the plan with Preston Washington.

"He's gonna open the shop for you after the show. No one will know. You can get all the records you want."

"That's fantastic! I'll let Neil and Mal know. John's gonna want to go too. I think we leave town right after the show that night. I can probably get them to push back the departure to give us an hour in the shop. You think that'll work?"

"Yeah. Tell Mal not to take the limo in that neighborhood. It's sure to draw a crowd. I'll take you in my truck. You can get in and out without anyone knowing."

"Perfect. I can't wait to see the Hi-Dee-Ho man again. The other guys are gonna love it."

*   *   *

The two concerts at the Civic Center were Baltimore's event of the year. Packed with screamers, Bobby watched the first show from the orchestra, front and center. Compared to other Beatles performances he'd seen in Hamburg and Liverpool, Bobby felt the show was fair. Screaming drowned out the band most of the time but even through the din, Bobby could tell that the Beatles still sounded tight.

From where he sat, Bobby saw disdain in John's eyes. He could see John's resentment of an audience that wanted to scream more than listen.

They opened with *Twist and Shout* then went into *You Can't Do That*, and *All My Lovin'*, their first song on the Ed Sullivan Show. The screaming peaked on *She Loves You* which was followed by *Things We Said Today*. George did his vocal on *Roll Over Beethoven*. They seemed to rush through *Can't Buy Me Love*, *If I Fell*, and *I Want To Hold Your Hand*. Ringo sang *Boys*, his reedy voice barely audible over the screaming. They finished with *A Hard Day's Night* and the Little Richard hit *Long Tall Sally*. It was all too loud yet over too soon.

After the show they escaped to the Hi-Dee-Ho Soul Shack. Preston Washington greeted them at the door.

"You boys be sure to check out the new one by King Curtis," he told them. "It's sure to make your liver quiver."

"I don't want my liver to quiver just yet," Ringo drawled. "I've just got here."

John stared at the walls of Preston's temple to soul music.

"I've never seen anything like it. It's the bloody Holy Grail."

"I told ya," George said.

"Would you like a few recommendations?" Preston asked.

"Yes." Ringo and Paul said in unison.

John said, "We don't know where to start. It's a bit overwhelming."

Preston rubbed his hands together.

"All right! Let me spin a few for you and see how you like 'em. We'll start with a little Otis Redding, James Brown, Wilson Pickett, James and Bobby Purify, and Sam and Dave. Then we got some nice Carla Thomas as a chaser. You in?"

"Go, man, go!" Ringo said.

Preston held up a single with a bright blue and green label that said Tri-Phi Records. It was *Any Way You Want It* by someone named Harvey.

John said, "Who's Harvey and what's his game?"

"It's Harvey Fuqua of Harvey and the Moonglows. He's Berry Gordy's brother-in-law. His game is blowin' your ever-lovin' mind."

"Berry Gordy? The guy who started Motown?"

"Yep. Shall we begin?"

Preston put the record on and the Beatles started grooving to the sound of Harvey.

"It's like nothing I've ever heard before," John said. "This is exactly what I've been lookin' for all my life."

Harvey's vocal scatted all over the song, singing and making nonsensical sounds. There were no lyrics, only Harvey shouting "any way you wanta!" and making monkey noises. At one point he sang "sucky, sucky, sucky, sucky!" The track percolated along behind him, drums bashing and horn line honking. It was magic.

Ringo threw his hands up and shouted, "That's it! I surrender! Give me five copies!"

Two hours later the Beatles, weighed down with boxes of records, left the store. Bobby said good-bye and wished them well.

"Look at it this way. It can't get any crazier," John said.

Bobby smiled. "That's a good attitude."

"The worst has to be over."

"One would hope so."

John sighed. "I miss the old days. I miss the Cavern and those wild nights in Hamburg. We're trapped now. It's just one hotel room after another. The whole thing's gotten out of hand."

Bobby put a hand on John's shoulder.

"Nothing lasts forever, John. Eventually things will die down. Then you can sit at home and count your money."

John said, "You'll never know what it's like to be me. No one's ever done what we're doing. There's no precedent. Think about that. No one's ever done this shit before. We don't know where it's all going to end up."

"How many bands can say they are actually too popular?"

John lit a Marlboro and blew smoke at the ceiling.

"I used to think it was impossible to be too popular but I've had to toss that silly old notion out. It sounds barmy, I know, but right now the Beatles are just too fookin' popular."

Bobby shook his head.

"When we first met who woulda thought someday we would have this conversation?"

"Ha! Remember what I said at the time?" John asked.

"That the Beatles would be bigger than Elvis?"

John nodded. "I rest my case. God help us all."

CHAPTER TWENTY-SEVEN

SWINGIN' LONDON

In October, Bobby received word from Mrs. Swithins that his father had taken a turn for the worse. He made arrangements to bring Cricket and Winston to Liverpool. He prayed that his father would live until he arrived, but according to Mrs. Swithins, his father was fading fast.

"It's another stroke, La. His old heart just can't take it anymore. You'd best come quick and take your leave of him or they'll be no leave left to take if you catch my meaning."

"Thank you, Mrs. Swithins, and God bless you. I'll be there directly."

Cricket packed their bags and Mr. Samansky drove them to the airport. Winston slept most of the way. Bobby checked them into the newest hotel in Liverpool and they took a cab to the hospital. They found Bobby's father lying there, tubes all over. The old man seemed much smaller now as if life had sucked him dry. Bobby's father didn't move.

"Dad? Can you hear me?"

His father's eyes remained closed. Monitors showed numbers that tracked his vital signs. Cricket and Winston watched silently. Bobby leaned closer, fighting back tears.

"Dad, it's me. Bobby. I came back and I brought my wife and son with me. Why don't you open your eyes and see them? The boy's name is Winston, Dad.

You always fancied Winston Churchill. It's a good name. He's your grandson. My wife is here too. Her name is Cricket. Well, that's her nickname. Her real name's Bernice. Why don't you open your eyes and take a look?"

Bobby's father didn't move.

"Dad, can you hear me?"

Nothing stirred.

"Well, they're here. I... just wanted you..." Bobby's voice cracked. He couldn't finish.

Mrs. Swithins appeared at the door. "He can't hear you, La. He's beyond that now, poor dear."

Bobby's hands shook as he wiped away his tears.

"Oh, God. I feel so damn helpless."

"We all do. It's only natural. He's in God's hands. There's nothing we can do. Look at him, laying there, so peaceful. His suffering is almost over."

"What should I do?"

Mrs. Swithins shook her head slowly.

"Nothing, La. The doctor said he wasn't gonna make it through the weekend and that was five days ago. He's livin' on borrowed time. Why don't you go on back to your hotel, and I'll tell the hospital to call you immediately if there are any changes. You can't do anything here. Your old man's a tough old bird; he's liable to hang on for a while. Take your sweet wife and baby away and rest. You all look tired."

Bobby nodded. Mrs. Swithins was right.

He deposited his weary family back in their room and went for a walk. Merseyside had changed little. He walked down Mathew Street and checked out the Cavern Club. It was still there but Bobby didn't recognize any of the bands on the playbill. The Beatles had moved to London along with Brian Epstein and the crew at NEMS, Brian's management company.

The streets seemed empty and cold. He stopped at The Grapes for a pint and ran into some Beatle fans he knew from the old days. They drank and talked for an hour.

A guy said, "It's all different now. The record companies came up from London and signed anybody with a guitar. It's sad, really. In the beginning the Beatles were our band, our very own Liverpool boys, but now they belong to the world. We have no hold over them anymore. My sister cried like a baby when they announced their move to London with that Liverpool traitor, Brian Epstein. All his fault, it is. It came like a slap in the face. All the original fans felt betrayed."

The bartender said, "You can't expect them to stand still now, can you? Be realistic. This town isn't likely to see the likes of the Beatles ever again. They're goin' where the money is. Smart, that is. You can't blame 'em. They've got to make as much money as they can right now. It's only natural they would move to London."

The other guy said, "You think they'll ever come back?"

"Not bloody likely."

Bobby drained his glass and walked back to the hotel. He didn't need the locals to tell him; the dream was over for Liverpool. He could smell it in the salty air and see it in the eyes of the people he passed. A miracle had taken place here, but the miracle had moved on. Bobby understood it was a natural thing. He had moved on too.

Back at the hotel Bobby received the news he'd been dreading. While he was out his father had died. Bobby cried and beat his fist against the door. Now his father was the one who'd moved on. As memories washed through him, Bobby understood that his whole life had changed. He could never go back.

Mrs. Swithins made the funeral arrangements while Bobby and his family mourned. Old Robert Dingle had outlived most of his friends. Only a handful showed up at the service. Afterward they went out for chips. Bobby felt numb.

"I suppose you'll be rid of the store now," Mrs. Swithins said.

Bobby shrugged. "I'd like to. But it's been on the market for a long time and nobody's shown the slightest interest."

"Maybe you should lower the price."

"The price is already low. The truth is I can't imagine anyone wanting that old place."

Mrs. Swithins put her teacup down and cleared her throat.

"I might want it."

"You?"

She nodded. "I've got some money stashed away, La. I could make you an offer. Not what you're asking, mind you, but an offer nonetheless. Your father and me done a lot of business over the years, and I know he wouldn't mind me making a penny or two from the old place."

"Why don't you just take over the shop? You don't have to buy it from me. I'll let you use it for free."

"No. I want to buy it fair and square. Of course, it wouldn't be a fortune, but it wouldn't be skint neither. My old bones are getting too tired to be draggin' me goodies all over town. I could use a permanent place to hang me hat, La."

"You've already done so much for me, Mrs. Swithins. I'd be embarrassed to take your money. Can't we work something out?"

Mrs. Swithins' had a twinkle in her eye. Her wizened face seemed to pucker up.

"Shut yer gob a minute and let me make my offer."

She squinted at him, a weird smile on her face. Her voice became businesslike.

"I'll give you half of what you're askin', cash on the barrel head. I'm serious, La. Half in cash. Right now."

"It's a deal." Bobby shook her bony hand. "And the best of luck to you, Mrs. Swithins."

He put the money in a Liverpool bank and looked up private investigators in the phone book. In England they were usually called "private enquiry agents." He searched the listings until he found one he liked. The ad read, "Enquiry Agent and Detecting Services" Missing persons our specialty! If I can not find them, they can not be found!"

He called the number.

"Henry Yee, Enquiry Agent. How may I help you?"

"You're Chinese?"

"Yes. Is there anything wrong in that?"

"No. It's just that we don't get many Chinese detectives in Liverpool.

"My father was a Merchant Marine," said Yee. "We traveled extensively. My family settled here many years ago. We are a respected, established Liverpool business. What can I do for you?"

"Sorry," Bobby mumbled. "I have a missing person I need found."

"Why don't you come to my office and we'll discuss it."

Later that day, Bobby told Henry Yee the situation. Bobby needed to get Clive his half of the money from their father's estate. It wasn't much after the creditors but half was Clive's. No one had heard from Clive since his successful prison break. Henry Yee accepted a retainer and promised to give Bobby the first report in three weeks. Satisfied, Bobby made arrangements to travel to London.

With Yee's help, Bobby would do his best to find Clive. If nothing developed, he would leave Clive's money in the bank.

* * *

London was like New York. Bobby might have been overwhelmed if it weren't for the presence of his famous friends. He called Brian Epstein's office and spoke with Mal and Neil who were there making travel arrangements for the next tour.

"The boys are still raving about the Hi-Dee-Ho Soul Shack," Neil told him over the phone. "John never stops playing those records, especially the one by Harvey. He's been driving us nuts with it."

Bobby chuckled. "It's good to know one's work is appreciated."

"Why don't we meet for a pint? There's a pub round the corner. I'll give you the address. I'll ring up the boys. As you can imagine, they don't go out in public much."

"I'll be there in an hour."

Bobby wrote the address down on a scrap of paper. An hour later he met Mal and Neil at the Courage Of The Fighting Cock Pub.

"You've never seen anything like what's been goin' on here in London, Bobby-boy. We're a couple of country bumpkins from Liverpool, right? Northern hicks, we are. When me and Neil got here our eyes just bugged out. Man, what a scene."

"Women, unbelievable women, throwing themselves at you day and night! They wear skirts here that are so short you can see their panties! Imagine. It's daft. And here we are right in the middle of it. We get to go to nightclubs and fancy restaurants every night. We got limo drivers. We get to be big shots when we're not out on the road. It's absolutely fantastic. Makes you wonder how long it's gonna last."

"Long enough," Bobby said with a smile.

Mal took a sip.

"There's an actual scene goin' on here. You can see it everywhere. It's swingin' London, man. Music, fashion, art, movies, photography; everything's exploding right now. You walk down the street and you see boutiques, art galleries, bookstores, mod shops, rocker shops and beautiful girls in miniskirts. It's bloody amazing. People are making fortunes overnight. This is the place to be."

Mal nodded. "We'll take you for a little tour around town... show you where the action is."

Mal phoned John from the pub, and John invited them to come over. John and Bobby drank lager and listened to Hi-Dee-Ho Soul Shack records for hours. Harvey had become a band favorite, and John played *Any Way You Want It* several times. John also had some other local Baltimore bands among his collection. Bobby saw the Lafayettes' *Life's Too Short* and the Van Dykes' *Stupidity*. John asked about Clovis. He was fascinated by the strange man whose wife was a stripper.

"You should all move to London right now," John said. "I'm serious. Clovis could start a band and his wife could strip. And you, Dust Bin Bob, you should open your very own shop among the trendies and sell lots of magical things."

"I'd love to, John. But it really depends on what the retail rates are and the availability of space."

"You sound like a bloody businessman."

"That's because I am."

"I thought you were Dust Bin Bob from the flea market."

"I haven't been Dust Bin Bob for years."

John looked down. "I haven't been John Lennon for years either."

"That's it then. Neither one of us is who we used to be. But here we are."

John smiled. "Dustman, I promise you. If you move here and become part of the scene, you'll be successful beyond your wildest dreams. This place is gold. There are stores on every block. Money is everywhere."

"I'll certainly think about it."

"It might be your fate."

"Fate is a funny thing, eh, John? You ever think all this is fate?"

John nodded. "Definitely. How else can you explain it? We must have been fated for all this. Otherwise it would be happening to somebody else. But it isn't. It's happening to us. Fate is as good a word as any."

"That's a soulful way to look at it."

John looked through his record shelves.

"What do you think soul is?"

"What? You mean like Ray Charles?"

"Yeah, sort of. That's soul music. I'm talkin' about the soul of a man. What do you think that is?"

Bobby raised his eyebrows.

"A tough question. I think maybe it has something to do with overcoming adversity and beating the odds. You know, the ability to bounce back when you're down."

"Bounce back, eh?"

"Yeah, like rubber. Like a rubber soul."

John's face lit up.

"Rubber soul! Brilliant! I have to write that down. Bloody perfect, that one is."

John played a stack of Motown records and commented on the way the drums snapped. He also loved the bass sound on the American soul singles. He played *Do You Love Me* by the Contours on Gordy Records over and over again. The false fade delighted him and he loved the vocals.

John also played the B side, *Move Mr. Man.* He loved B sides and knew them all; every artist, record company, and songwriter in R&B.

He pointed out Steve Cropper's guitar work on some Otis Redding records. Bobby loved talking about music with John.

When Bobby returned to his hotel he found Cricket breathless with excitement. She'd taken Winston all over London and she was amazed at what they'd seen.

"It's so colorful here. I love it. Everybody is so glamorous. I've never seen anything like it. So many boutiques! I want to buy a mini-skirt to show everybody back home."

Bobby chuckled. "I'm all for that."

*   *   *

They stayed in London another week. He and Cricket fell in love with the town and discussed the possibility of opening a store there. It wouldn't be a real antique store; more of a curio shop tailored to the fashionable Londoner. Cricket loved the idea. Bobby asked Brian Epstein about it and Brian referred him to the right people.

Bobby found an old chemist shop on Newburgh Street and signed a lease. The second Dingles store was born in a trendy London neighborhood. Bobby and Cricket would split their time between Baltimore and London, keeping both stores open and profitable.

Located just a block from Carnaby Street, Dingles of Newburgh had an esoteric collection: Victorian snuffboxes, antique wooden airplane propellers and century-old clocks were soon joined by American items from Dingles of Read. Stateside curiosities proved to be popular in London. Bobby sold American stuff to the English, and English stuff to the Americans.

The area, bounded by Charing Cross, Shaftsbury Avenue, Regent Street and Oxford Street was bursting with boutiques. Crazy shop names like *I Was Lord Kitchener's Valet* and *Kleptomania* were all the rage. Dingles of Newburgh fit right in. Brian Epstein's NEMS office was only a short walk away on Argyil Street just across from the famous London Palladium.

The Beatles were Bobby's first customers dropping in before opening day to avoid the crowd. John bought a leather World War One flying helmet with built-in goggles and an antique circus poster. George bought an authentic Indian sitar and a cowboy hat. Paul bought the same antique harmonium that had been in Bobby's father's shop in Liverpool.

Ringo bought rings.

CHAPTER TWENTY-EIGHT

DINGLES OF NEWBURGH

Bobby and Cricket found an apartment not far from the store and moved in. Winston took his first steps in London. Cricket thought she could hear a British accent in his baby talk.

"Well, Mr. Dingle. We moved half way around the world. We just can't seem to sit still, can we?"

"It's our nature, Mrs. Dingle. Our heritage, our pioneer spirit. We have the urge to constantly move forward."

"My family thinks I'm crazy."

Bobby smirked. "That's nothing new. Some of them thought you were crazy when you married me."

"You're one thing; moving to London is another."

"We haven't moved here full time. We still go back for half the year. Besides, business couldn't be better. I know your father appreciates that."

Cricket grinned. "I don't care what Daddy says. I love it here. I've never felt more alive, more jazzed. I'm thinking of getting into photography. I took some courses at the Institute so I know the basics. I just need a good camera."

"It seems like everybody in London has a camera these days."

"There are a lot of pictures to take."

The phone rang. When Bobby answered he recognized the voice of the detective, Henry Yee, his enquiry agent.

"Mr. Dingle? This is Henry Yee. I have your first report ready. I'll be in London on Friday. Can we get together? I'd like to explain in person and show you what I've done."

"Great! What about Clive? Have you found him?"

Henry's voice was professionally even.

"No. But I do have some interesting information that may lead to finding him."

"OK, Friday it is. Why don't we meet at my shop? I have a private office there where we can talk. Let's say around noon?"

Bobby gave the address to Henry and hung up. Cricket looked at him inquisitively.

"That was the enquiry agent I hired to find Clive. He's got something though he hasn't located him."

"What happens if they never find him?"

Bobby shrugged. "After seven years he's presumed dead, I think. If that happens I'll put the money in the bank for Winston's future."

At noon on Friday, Henry Yee strode into Dingles of Newburgh wearing a bowler derby and carrying a briefcase. Bobby waved him past the counter and into the office.

Henry sat down, opened his briefcase, and pulled out a manila folder.

Bobby said, "What have you learned?"

Henry Yee handed the file to Bobby and cleared his throat.

"It's all in the report. Clive Dingle broke out of prison along with his cellmate, a man named Eusebio Ragasa, AKA Ebong Ragasa, AKA Bong-Bong."

"The guy's name is Bong-Bong? What kind of name is that?"

"It's Filipino. Filipino nicknames often use the second syllable of a given name like Ebong, double it and turn it into Bong-Bong. Don't let the childish name fool you. This man is smart, dangerous, and most likely planned the escape."

"That makes sense," Bobby said. "I doubt if Clive would be capable of planning anything."

"The police suspect they had some people on the outside once they got past the walls."

"Yes," Bobby said. "I recall speculation about that. They would need someone to hide them."

"Exactly. Otherwise the police dragnet would have picked them up.

Associates of Mr. Ragasa one would think. Through some paid informants I
was able to find out that Mr. Ragasa has ties with organized crime figures in
Japan, the Philippines, Taiwan, and Thailand. Your brother probably left the
country with Mr. Ragasa."

Bobby raised his eyebrows.

"Clive and the Asian mafia?"

"He may be in Bangkok."

"You're joking."

"I never joke. Look at the last page of the report. There's a picture attached.
Tell me if one of the men in the picture is Clive Dingle."

Bobby turned to the last page and looked at the picture.

"Is it him?"

"It's definitely him."

"What about the others?"

Henry Yee handed Bobby a small magnifying glass to study the photo
closer.

Bobby gasped. "I've seen these guys before."

"Can you identify them?"

"The tall guy is Donovan. He once roomed with me in Hamburg at the
British Seaman's Mission years ago. He had a partner, a guy named Archie
Stillman who was murdered in that room. The police suspected Donovan but
he was never found."

Bobby looked up.

"When Archie Stillman was murdered, I was not only questioned by the
local police but by Interpol. They were very interested in Archie. The German
Interpol agent gave me his card and told me to call him if I ever saw Donovan
again. That was years ago."

"Do you still have his card?"

"I don't know. It might be in a box in my office in Baltimore. Should I
contact Interpol about this?"

Henry Yee raised his hand.

"I'll do it for you. I have friends there."

Bobby pointed at another face.

"I've seen this other guy too."

"Where?"

"In Hamburg at the Kaiserkeller where the Beatles were playing, it was
the same night that Stillman was killed. All of this was in the Reeperbahn.
I saw that guy hanging around with the Kaiserkeller's owner, uh, Bruno

Koschmider, if I recall correctly. I think Bruno was a bit of a gangster himself. At least the Beatles used to think so."

"That doesn't surprise me," said Yee. "Few Reeperbahn businessmen are completely on the up-and-up."

"Where did you get this picture?"

Henry leaned forward.

"My contacts are confidential, Mr. Dingle. I'm sorry but the source of that particular bit of information will have to remain anonymous."

Bobby looked at the picture again and shook his head.

"I can't believe it. My own brother mixed up with Asian gangsters from the Kaiserkeller. It's like something out of an Ian Fleming novel."

"The other guy in the picture is Bong-Bong Ragasa."

Bobby squinted at the picture.

"Why would these guys be in Hamburg and then hook up with my criminal brother later on?"

"Each question brings a new question."

Bobby examined the picture again. There were palm trees in the background.

"Where was this taken?"

"Thailand."

"I smell a rat."

Henry Yee nodded gravely.

"Rat has a pungent odor. Once smelled, it's seldom missed."

Bobby slid the picture back into the file.

"You've done a fine job, Henry."

"I'll contact the Interpol office here in London and see what they have on Ragasa and Donovan."

*   *   *

The Marquee Club on Wardour Street had a reputation for great bands. The Stones and the Yardbirds had played there. Two young employees of Dingles of Newburgh, nineteen-year-old Patti and eighteen-year-old Nigel had convinced Bobby and Cricket to go to Soho and stand in line in the rain to see a new band they liked. The Who.

"Who are The Who?" Bobby asked.

"The Who are cute," Patti said, "especially the lead singer."

Nigel made a face and said, "Don't listen to her. They're actually very good.

It's Pete Townsend, Roger Daltry, John Entwhistle and Keith Moon. Four really great musicians. If we're lucky maybe they'll smash their equipment."

"I beg you pardon?" Bobby said.

"They smash their stuff. It's cool. I hope they do it tonight."

"Do they do it every night?"

"Usually."

Bobby looked surprised.

"That's a lot of equipment. How do they afford it?"

"Who cares? I just want to see some stuff get smashed."

Bobby shook his head.

"I'm already out of touch and I'm only a few years older than you guys."

Nigel checked out some passing girls.

"Native wildlife seems to be doing well. Those birds were heavily plumed."

Cricket said, "Don't you have a girlfriend, Nigel?"

"Not at the moment. But there will be tons of chicks at the Who show. I guarantee it."

Cricket tugged at Bobby's sleeve.

"Don't you get roving eyes, hotshot."

Bobby chuckled. "I already have the most beautiful woman in London. I'm married to her."

Cricket kissed Bobby.

"You're so sweet."

Cricket looked great in a miniskirt. Her lithe body seemed tailor made for the latest fashions. Bobby was surprised that she dressed up so much in London. The art school clothes were gone in favor of colorful paisley print minis. Since she'd become a Londoner fashion had become important to Cricket.

The Who turned out to be even better than advertised mixing fascinating melodies with cranked up rock and roll arrangements. After the show Bobby sat in a taxi with Cricket, their ears ringing. In the quiet cab Bobby recalled his earlier meeting with Henry Yee and felt uneasy.

When they got back to their apartment, Cricket paid the babysitter and poured some wine. They took their shoes off and sat together on the sofa, but Bobby couldn't stop thinking about Donovan, Clive, and murder. There were too many unexplained links. The idea it might be coincidence was even more unsettling. The night Archie Stillman died, he and Donovan had been hanging with Ragasa and Bruno at the Kaiserkeller. It all seemed too unlikely to be random.

What Yee had done was shine a light on the connection between Bobby and the Beatles on one side and Clive, Donovan and Ragasa on the other. That thought chilled Bobby. *These evil people must never get anywhere near the Beatles,* he thought. *But the Beatles are so big, how can they avoid attracting Clive, Ragasa, or Bruno?*

*   *   *

Bobby and Cricket enjoyed more and more London nightlife. Often double dating with George and his glamorous new girlfriend from *A Hard Day's Night,* Patti Boyd. Bobby and Cricket enjoyed the perks of celebrity with few drawbacks. When they walked into the *Ad Lib* all eyes were on them. Everyone treated Bobby and Cricket like royalty because they were with the Beatles. Bobby felt a trifle guilty about it.

Dingles of Newburgh had drawn praise as one of the new, hip and successful businesses in London. Bobby seemed to sense what items he should stock. Because Dingles wasn't a clothing store, it drew a more eclectic clientele than other Carnaby Street shops. Bobby's unusual line of antiques were the kind young mods and rock stars could appreciate.

John loved the store and often shopped there after hours. He always found something he liked. One after hours night while George and Ringo were hanging out, Bobby invited them into his office for some jam butties.

"You're a rich man, Dust Bin Bob," Ringo said.

"Not as rich as you," Bobby replied.

"You'd think so, eh? Truth is we don't have much spending money. Everything goes through the office and we get a living allowance."

Bobby put a plate with bread on his desk.

"Jam butties, anyone? I've got a nice bottle of strawberry in my desk."

"I never have much money in me pockets," Ringo said.

"But you're selling millions of records."

Ringo nodded. "We're the Fab Four and all that, but Brian says we have to save our money for taxes."

"The taxman cometh," George said.

"Do you trust Brian?"

Ringo and George looked at each other.

George said, "He's like an uncle. Of course we trust him. He took us from the Cavern Club to the Palladium. Brian would never cheat us."

"You're lucky."

Ringo shook his head.

"Eppy's the man, man. You can't knock what he's done."

George reached for the jelly.

"You know, I shouldn't complain about success, but..."

As Bobby waited for George to finish the thought, Ringo interrupted.

"Mark my words. There's a day comin' when the Beatles won't be able to tour. I can see it up ahead. It's bloody near impossible now."

George said, "Brian knows it too. He's seen what we have to go through. We cause disruptions everywhere we go."

Ringo tapped his knees like a bongo drum.

"Barmy, ain't it?"

Bobby watched two of the most famous people in the world spreading jelly. Ringo finished building his sandwich and chewed thoughtfully. Bobby remained silent.

"We've gotten too big," George said. "Take a look at this proposed itinerary for next year."

George handed Bobby several pages stapled together. As Bobby read, Ringo summarized.

"Tour America, tour Asia, make another album, make another movie, more TV, more tours of Europe. When does it end?"

George shrugged. "It doesn't."

"Have you asked Brian to scale back?"

"We already know what he'll say."

Ringo wiped his mouth with a white napkin.

"We used to think, let's do it all 'cause it'll be over before you know it. We used to expect the bubble to pop any time. But, it hasn't.'"

"It's spooky," George said. "We're further down this road than anyone's ever been."

"What about John and Paul? What do they think?"

"It's different for John and Paul. They write the songs. They're getting royalties."

"We've talked among ourselves," Ringo said. "We all feel the same way. Nobody wants to tour until they drop but for now we go along with it."

Bobby pointed at the itinerary.

"This looks like a lot of work."

George managed a wan smile. "I really don't want to go."

CHAPTER TWENTY-NINE

NOTHING TO GET HUNG ABOUT

The Beatles became a national treasure. Bobby Dingle became an entrepreneur.

When word got out that the Beatles shopped at Dingles, it became the in place on Newburgh Street. Business boomed. The pricier antiques were usually purchased by rock stars who Bobby dealt with directly. They appreciated Bobby's coolness. He never fawned over them, never became too chummy, never gossiped and discretely billed their management. Watching how Brian Epstein ran the NEMS office on Argyll Street had educated Bobby. Bobby could deal with a stoned Brian Jones or a drunken Keith Moon and never resort to trickery. Bobby was one of them. He'd come up the hard way and earned their respect. Besides he was from Liverpool and knew the Beatles personally.

At Dingles you could buy a genuine wooden merry-go-round horse, a colorful American roadside Burma Shave sign, a Samurai sword, an Afghan Prayer mat, a Joe Louis boxing poster or Groucho Marx glasses. Bobby had everything a hip Londoner could ever need.

The phone rang and Bobby answered.

"This is Henry Yee."

"Oh, Henry! How is everything?"

"Fine. I'm calling to offer the services of a colleague of mine in Asia. He's a licensed investigator who occasionally works for my office. He's quite good and very reasonable. If you want to continue the search for you brother, this is the man for the job."

"What happened with Interpol? Did you tell them I recognized Donovan?"

"Yes. They were very appreciative about that but strangely noncommittal. I got the feeling that they aren't as interested in him as they were a few years ago. But they wouldn't give me any information. To find your brother, we need our own independent investigator; someone who knows the cities and has inside contacts."

"What's this man's name?"

"Faustino Magsaysay. He's an ex-police captain in Manila who knows people all over the Pacific Rim. He's got contacts in all the places we're interested in: Bangkok, Tokyo, Hong Kong—all the Asian capitals."

"What's it gonna cost me?"

Henry told him. Bobby accepted. Faustino Magsaysay was on the team.

* * *

When Mr. and Mrs. Samansky visited London Bobby and Cricket showed them around.

"These boys look like girls," her father said, looking at the hair and clothing. "And the girls look like boys. What's goin' on here?"

"Dad, it's the new fashion. Someday it'll spread all the way to Baltimore."

"That'll be the day."

"They call it unisex."

Mr. Samansky rolled his eyes. He'd seen great changes in his time, but none so swift and pervasive as the Beatles. Like many parents of the Beatle era, he'd struggled to come to grips with it. Deep down he knew there was no antidote.

Mrs. Samansky tolerated what she didn't understand. Cricket was her pride and joy and if being married to Bobby and living in London made her daughter happy then that was the way it would be.

The day after the Samanskys left, John Lennon appeared at Dingles.

"Dust Bin Bob! Grab your coat and hat. We're going for a drive!"

Bobby went with John. The Rolls Royce's chauffeur said nothing as they sped away from the city. At last they turned into the driveway to a large estate in Weybridge.

"Whose house it this?" Bobby asked.

"Mine," John said, "and I need somebody to visit."

"You need... John, you're a Beatle."

"I know, I know. I need some Liverpool soul, man."

"Some Liverpool rubber soul?"

John laughed. "Exactly. The only people I can hang with these days are George, Paul and Ringo, and you."

Bobby blushed as the big car rolled to a stop in front of an impressive Tudor mansion.

"Thank you."

"It's the truth. You don't want anything from me like the rest of those London wankers."

Bobby looked up at the ivy covered walls.

"It's magnificent."

John didn't smile but Bobby could tell that he was proud of the big house.

"It's called Kenwood. I had to buy it for tax reasons. We're all buying houses now."

"Aunt Mimi must be proud."

"I wouldn't know."

"Haven't you called to tell her? This is big news."

"Aunt Mimi doesn't approve of me being a Beatle."

"That's ridiculous. She wanted you to make a decent living. You've accomplished that."

"Yeah, I guess. But we rarely talk these days."

Bobby noticed a Jaguar and a Mini Minor parked in the driveway.

"I've got three cars," John said sheepishly.

"You don't even drive."

"I'll learn. Let's go in and have some lunch and then I want to show you something."

Inside the house, Bobby admired the décor. Someone had selected the furniture with great care. Everything was the best in its class. Bobby had sold items like these but never new.

They stopped in the kitchen and made sandwiches.

"Cyn and Julian are shopping in town. Let's go into the den."

John led Bobby through the house to his music room. Bobby saw the antique circus poster he'd sold John framed and hanging prominently. He stopped to admire it.

"I love that poster," John said.

"It's wonderful, isn't it? I wonder who these people were? Pablo Fanques and Mr. Kite?"

"The real star is Henry the dancing horse."

John plugged in a hot plate and brewed some tea.

"I don't have to go all the way down to the kitchen for a cuppa."

"All the latest modern conveniences. You've got quite a pad here."

John didn't answer. Instead he handed Bobby a piece of official looking paper. Bobby read it carefully.

"Good God, John! The Queen has awarded you Membership in the Most Excellent Order of the British Empire!"

John nodded. "It's too much. I thought you had to win a war to get an MBE. All we did was play rock and roll."

Bobby was astonished.

"John, this is a great honor. You'll get to meet the Queen."

"I've met her before."

"Don't you see? The Queen recognizes all you've done for England and she's bestowing a title on you."

John shrugged. "It must be for generating bloody tax revenues. God knows we pay a fortune."

John took a beautiful wooden box from the bookshelf and put it in front of Bobby.

"Could you roll us a joint?"

"You can't roll your own?"

"I'm out of practice. It's always done for me."

Bobby examined the contents of a plastic bag inside the box.

"It's a good thing Clovis taught me. This looks like good stuff."

"The best money can buy."

"Is this the only reason you brought me here? To roll you a joint?"

John nodded. "Several, if possible."

Bobby rolled five large joints and lit one. John seemed content to smoke and stare out the window. Afterward they had tea.

John made a great show out of putting one sugar cube in each cup. Bobby thought nothing of it. An hour later Bobby began to feel strange.

"My hands are getting big," John said. "Really big."

Bobby looked at John's hands. They didn't seem any bigger than normal, but the skin on them seemed to be translucent. Bobby thought he could see right through John's skin at the blood pumping through his veins.

"I can see your insides," Bobby said. His voice sounded constricted and

Donald Duck-like.

"What's going on?"

John's smile seemed to roll off his face.

"Acid, my friend. LSD. It was in the sugar cube."

Bobby panicked. He'd read that LSD scrambled your brains.

"What? You can't be... serious... there's nothing... I can do... about... it?"

"About what?"

"About this."

John began to laugh hysterically.

"There's always something you can do."

"John, I'm serious."

"Serious, is it? You want serious? Take a look at this."

John put Bobby in front of the antique circus poster he'd bought in Bobby's shop. It began to swirl and move.

"See anything different?"

"I see everything different."

Bobby turned to look at John. As their eyes met, Bobby suddenly screamed.

"Your face is melting!"

John grabbed Bobby's arm.

"Cool out. It's just the acid, man. Nothing to get hung about. Relax and float downstream. It's quite pleasant when you get the hang of it."

Bobby's heart pounded and his eyes felt like hot oysters.

"I don't feel right."

"Why don't you sit down and we'll play some music. Some music to soothe the savage beast. We can cool out a bit."

John led Bobby to the couch and put on one of the 45s from the Hi-Dee-Ho Soul Shack. He cranked the volume and dropped the needle. The diamond stylus hit the groove in the vinyl with a sound like a distant rifle shot.

John said. "I give you the great Harvey."

Any Way You Want It exploded from the speakers and Bobby nearly jumped out of his skin. It had the effect of an M-80 firecracker exploding in his face. Bobby skittered halfway down the couch, adrenaline coursing through his veins. He yelped like a struck dog and gripped the edge of the cushion tightly.

"Oh, God!"

The opening drum riff boomed like thunder and the horns honked like a battalion of cartoon roosters. Harvey's crazed voice vibrated Bobby's internal organs. The first note seemed to take a half an hour. With new LSD ears Bobby heard the familiar refrain. Harvey started low and kept going up. "Awwwwwwwwwwwwwwww, SHUCKS!"

Bobby was either laughing or crying. He didn't know which. There seemed to be moisture on his face. John was singing along with Harvey and doing silly spastic dance steps.

"Sucky, sucky, sucky, sucky! Any way you want it!"

John laughed hysterically between each line. Bobby began to giggle too. It seemed incredibly funny. The genius of Harvey was perfect when channeled through John Lennon. John was one of the most creative men in the world, but here he was shouting, "Sucky, sucky, sucky, sucky!" at he top of his lungs.

Bobby went from clutching paranoia to uncontrollable laughter. The trip's mood shifted. Now he was groovin'... groovin' with John Lennon. The insanity of Harvey infected their entire world. The fancy coffee tables vibrated to the bouncing bass line. Mr. Kite, Pablo Fanques, and Henry the horse all danced to Harvey's beat.

By the time the song reached its exotic monkey shout and its "a-nong-nong-nong-nong-nong-nong anyway" chorus, the whole universe was dancing. Bobby imagined one of Mrs. Swithins' ceramic toads singing and dancing on an English music hall stage with the voice of Harvey coming out of it.

They laughed long after the record ended and the needle was skipping on the last groove. They kept laughing for what seemed like hours. Time became distorted.

Bobby found himself in John's garden, crawling on the grass examining each blade like a scientist. Somewhere in the distance a dog barked and Bobby thought he could understand it. As he listened to the dog, he became aware of something else, something disturbing. He thought he was getting smaller. Bobby looked at his hands and they seemed very far away.

"I'm shrinking."

He crawled a few inches.

"I'm definitely getting smaller."

The idea that he was actually shrinking like Alice in Wonderland took hold. Bobby felt himself shrinking more with every heartbeat. He got down to the size of sparrow then he went microscopic.

Entering a door to a new universe, he became a giant reaching across light years. He then shrank back to normal size as if nothing had happened. But something had.

"Infinity," said Bobby.

Someone else spoke. "Finicky?"

Bobby looked up to see an elf with a bright red hat on.

"Who are you?" the elf asked in a strange, high-pitched voice.

Standing behind the elf was a woman with blinding blond hair, glowing like the sun. Rays of light shot from her eyes. Bobby thought she was an angel. She smiled.

"You must be Bob," said the angel.

Bobby blinked.

"Yes. I must be."

"Are you all right?"

Bobby considered the question. He didn't know how to answer.

"I said, are you all right?"

Bobby's tongue felt thick and dry. "I can't tell you."

The angel looked at him strangely.

"John said I'd find you out here."

"John?"

The angel reached out her delicate white hand.

"This is Julian. Say hello, Julian."

"Hello," the elf said.

Bobby gazed at them. Their faces vibrated like tuning forks.

"John said to come fetch you for tea."

Bobby said the only word he could get out of his mouth. "Yes?"

Bobby spent the night at Kenwood, tripping and grooving with John. Bobby was completely wrecked, but John seemed be able to handle it. He played records and watched TV, made drawings and wrote poems. LSD only stimulated John.

When the sun came up, Bobby came down.

"Holy shit, man. Did you get the number of the truck that hit me?" he asked.

John grinned. "Welcome to the club. Now you can say you've tripped."

"You tricked me."

"It was the only way. No harm done, I hope?"

"I've got to call Cricket. She's probably worried to death."

"I had Cynthia call her."

"Good." Bobby rubbed his face. His cheeks hurt from smiling for ten hours. He felt disoriented.

Bobby felt dazed for days.

He stayed away from the shop but eventually he had to go back in. The acid had changed something. Everything seemed a little less real, a little more dream-like.

London crackled with energy, and the Beatles kept pace. *Yesterday*, by Paul featured a revolutionary George Martin arrangement using a string quartette. The new movie *Help* was underway, and its title song was number one around the world. The Beatles showed no signs of slowing down.

Bobby gathered his family for the trip back to Baltimore. It was hard to leave London. They would miss the energy. But they'd promised Cricket's mom that little Winston would spend half his time there.

Upon arrival Bobby plunged into business determined to keep both stores successful. He had an offer to buy a quantity of antique Japanese silk kimonos from an estate sale. Though the price was high, he bought them and placed several in the window. They sold immediately so he replaced them with another set which also sold immediately. Bobby kept selling the kimonos, the price increasing as the supply ran out. He went looking for more kimonos but none were available.

He found a dealer in Tokyo and made arrangements to import some. The problem was he couldn't see them in advance so he had no idea what they would look like before he bought them. If he couldn't see something, he couldn't estimate its worth.

When the shipment arrived Bobby was disappointed. The quality wasn't as good as the earlier batch. The colors weren't as vibrant. It took longer to sell them.

"You should go to Tokyo on a buying trip," Cricket said. "It would pay for itself. You could pick out a whole bunch of stuff."

Bobby considered it but decided to wait. Weren't the Beatles going to Japan this year? Maybe Bobby would coordinate his trip with theirs.

CHAPTER THIRTY

WE CAN WORK IT OUT

Back in Baltimore, Bobby thought the Beatles influence might have waned but nothing showed the slightest hint of slowing down. Like every other city in America, Baltimore had been changed by them. The first thing he noticed was that Read Street had become hipper. Several curious shops with names like *The Bum Steer* and *The Psychedelic Propeller* had opened in Bobby's absence. He noticed more young people with shaggy Beatle-style hair. The American cultural revolution was in full swing.

The Beatles rolled on. By year's end they released their new album *Rubber Soul*.

Faustino Magsaysay, Henry Yee's investigator in Manila, called Bobby in Baltimore a few months later. His accent was thick but Bobby could understand everything he said. The long distance phone line sputtered and crackled.

"Mr. Yee told me to report directly to you so I am calling with my case summary. I hope you don't mind. I will mail you a copy also."

"Tell me everything, Faustino."

"I checked up on those people in the photograph. Bong-Bong Ragasa is well-known here. It's assumed that he works for Ferdinand Marcos."

"The dictator?"

"Yes. Marcos employs a lot of tough guys for his private security force. If you cross these people you take your life into your hands. They are very aggressive. Here in Manila if you want to do business on any level you have to cut the Marcos family in. Those who resist come to a bad end. To ensure that happens quietly and efficiently, he keeps men like Bong-Bong on the payroll."

"How does anything legitimate get done?"

"Things get done. It's just a very complicated system of payoffs and graft. Once in a while somebody gets killed. Assassination is a common political strategy here these days."

"Go on."

"Your brother has been located in Bangkok. Big, white Englishmen stand out there."

"They don't come any bigger and whiter than Clive."

"He was spotted immediately after I put the word out. He and Donovan were in the company of a local gangster."

"What does an Asian gangster want with an English white guy?"

"From time to time they need a Caucasian face and their preferred brand is English," said Magsaysay.

"What about Donovan?"

"Interpol wouldn't give me any information on Donovan but they obviously have something."

Bobby shook his head.

"Can my brother be contacted?"

"I might be able to arrange for a hand delivered message, for an additional fee."

Bobby groaned.

"Tell him his brother Robert is trying to contact him. Tell him his father is dead and his share of what's left of the money is waiting for him back in Liverpool. Sign it with my name. Tell him to contact your office."

"I understand."

"You've done a fine job, Faustino. I'm impressed."

"Any client of Mr. Henry Yee gets the best treatment."

*   *   *

Bobby worried that business at the London store would slack off. Sales dipped slightly when Bobby wasn't there. Much of the success of Dingles was due to Bobby's charm. Without his personal touch things were not the same. As a result, he found himself traveling more frequently back and forth alone which strained his marriage. The two worlds tugged against each other. Being out of town so much, Bobby missed a birthday here, a holiday there and he felt guilty about it. When he came home he tried to make up for it.

Life on Southway had a soothing effect on him. Bobby loved lazy afternoons on the quiet, tree-lined street. Winston played with his toys, and Bobby played with his.

On a quiet winter afternoon Cricket flopped down on the couch next to Bobby. Winston piloted a truck around on the rug at their feet.

"I miss the London scene," Cricket said. "I hate to say this, but I'm bored here in Baltimore."

Bobby looked surprised.

"That's funny because I was thinking about the same thing except I was worried that too much of the London lifestyle would change us for the worse."

"The worse? London is great and I'm starting to think we should spend more time there."

Bobby paused. "I'm tired of going back and forth. Business slacks off whenever I'm gone from either store, and it's wearing me out."

*　*　*

Clovis Hicks and Erlene came to dinner occasionally and Bobby marveled at Clovis' ever changing visage. Lately he looked exactly like Brian Jones of The Rolling Stones. He sported a big blond bowl cut; long bangs, long back and sides, and sideboards like lamb chops. Erlene dressed like a Vegas showgirl with stretch pants in colors that do not appear in nature. Together they were traffic stoppers.

Clovis and his new band, The Moss, were part of a Georgetown rock scene in D.C. that included half a dozen clubs. They had a gig nearly every night of the week. Inspired by John, Clovis had started writing songs. He'd even cut some demos at a tiny recording studio on Biddle Street in downtown Baltimore.

Clovis waved his hands excitedly.

"The new stuff sounds great. I just did some vocals and a sitar part on this new song I wrote. I think it's a hit, man."

"I can't wait to hear it, Clovis."

"If it's good enough maybe you could play it for the Fabs and see what they think."

Bobby tried not to show his annoyance. He hated requests that exploited his friendship with the Beatles.

"The Fabs are a bit busy these days. They start a big something-or-other next week. They're always starting a big something-or-other."

Clovis put his hands on his hips.

"Well, suck my left nut, pilgrim. Here's what you're supposed to say."

Clovis imitated Bobby badly with a corny English accent. "Play your song for the Beatles, Clovis, dear buddy? Of course I will. Nothing's too good for a friend like you."

Clovis's voice dropped back into its normal range.

"That would have been the proper response. Let's try it again."

Erlene kicked Clovis hard enough to make him yelp.

"What?"

"Quit askin' for favors."

She kicked him again.

"I don't want you to ask our friends for favors, y'hear? Cut that shit out."

"But, honey bun, I..."

She started to kick him again.

"All right! All right!"

"That's better."

Bobby laughed. Erlene would have been a great slapstick comedian in another life.

"You always keep him in line like that?"

"You mean the swift kick? Yeah. It usually works."

"His shins must be black and blue."

Clovis rubbed his leg.

"You ain't kiddin', pardner. They're quite a sight. I go to the beach with these shins and I scare little children."

Bobby said, "Clovis, I'm not just trying to put you off. You helped them out when they were here and I'm sure they'd remember it, but I haven't spoken to the boys for a while. They're moving at the speed of light. I'll play your tape for them when the opportunity arises."

Clovis grinned. "That's more like it."

"John told me you should move to London and start a band there. He said Erlene could strip while you're playing."

Clovis' mouth dropped.

"Are you serious? John Lennon said that? He mentioned me by name?"

"It was back when he was trying to talk me into moving."

"Damn!" Clovis turned to Erlene. "Honey, we gotta pack."

Bobby said, "Hold on. That's no reason to suddenly pull up stakes and move to London."

"It's not? Well, what the fuck is?"

Bobby cleared his throat.

"He didn't say he would help you or get you a record deal or anything like that. It was just a casual remark. He may have been kidding for all I know. He's seen you play and he knows you're good. George knows it too, but that's no guarantee that they'll help. One of the reasons I've been able to remain friends with them is that I never ask them for anything. I give them something just about every time I see them. It began with records. Our relationship is based on me being cool about stuff like that."

Clovis frowned.

"I just want to play some music."

Bobby said, "I don't want you to suddenly move to London on the strength of that story, that's all. I don't mean to be an arse but that's the way I feel. Besides, you don't know anyone over there."

Clovis looked wounded.

"I know you."

Cricket said, "But we aren't always there. How do you feel about it, Erlene? You ever wanted to live in London?"

Erlene fluttered her eyelashes.

"I rightly don't know. Can a girl make a livin' peelin' off her clothes there?"

Clovis stood and began pacing.

"I don't know why I didn't think of this before. It was right under my nose the whole time. Move to London. Of course! It makes total sense. London is the center of the music world right now. I'll bet I can get a record deal over there! Hot damn, I'm gonna go for it!"

"Clovis, cool out."

"It's my destiny, man."

Bobby sighed. "I'm not getting through to you, am I?"

Clovis continued. "Erlene can get a job at one of those fancy nightclubs. I can get a group goin'. We'll get a little place and start rockin'. I'll get a record deal and we'll make a whole bunch of money. Then we can start a family. Right, honey?"

"That's real nice, hon, but don't put your friends on the spot."

Cricket said, "Maybe they could stay at our place for a few weeks while they're getting settled."

Bobby looked at his wife with despair.

"For God's sake."

Cricket's eyes had a twinkle in them.

"Just think about it."

Bobby tried to smile.

"I'll think about it."

Clovis pumped his fist in the air.

"All right!"

* * *

Bobby wasn't happy about it. He didn't understand why Cricket had suggested it, but that spring Clovis and Erlene appeared at their door in London.

"Damn, man! This place is cool. We just rode on the Underground."

Bobby felt great trepidation as he led them into his apartment. Cricket, ever the perfect hostess, set them up in Winston's room, moving the child into their room. Bobby had to be careful not to wake his son coming and going. Clovis got on his nerves immediately.

He complained to Cricket.

"How much longer are they gonna stay here? They're always around. I need some peace and quiet. I've got a business to run. Clovis is after me to play his tape for the boys. He's guilt tripping me into talking to Brian."

"He's your friend, Bobby. Couldn't you at least try?"

Bobby snorted. "I have to try. If for no other reason than to get him off my back."

Bobby explained to Clovis that he couldn't go to the NEMS office. Clovis wasn't having any of it.

"I gotta go, man. It's my life. I'll bring my guitar and audition right there in the guy's office."

Bobby shook his head.

"I go alone or I don't go."

"Don't be such a hardhead."

"They don't know you there."

"I met them guys on the train, remember?"

"Clovis, you were one of thousands of people they met on that trip. I don't want to argue about it. Do you want me to go or not?"

"OK. Go."

Bobby walked from Dingles to the NEMS office with Clovis' demo tape in his hand. He entered the reception area and asked for Brian.

"Tell him Robert Dingle is here to see him."

Ten minutes later he was ushered into Brian's office. After a few minutes of polite small talk, Bobby got to the point.

"I know you've been signing quite a few bands lately, and I thought you might be interested in an American chap. He's quite good. George and John have already jammed with him, so they can vouch for him. You've met him, actually. He was the room service guy from the hotel in Washington on the first American tour. He traveled on the train with us. I've brought an audition tape with me."

Brian held up his hand.

"I can't manage an American act."

"He's here in London."

"Does he live here?"

Bobby swallowed hard and said yes.

"I see. Put the tape on and let's give it a listen."

Bobby handed the reel-to-reel tape to Brian and he threaded it up on his office Ampex machine.

Brian cranked the volume and Clovis' voice and guitar leapt from the speakers. Bobby didn't own a tape recorder so he was hearing the tape for the first time. What he heard surprised him. It sounded like something recorded at Sun Studios in Memphis.

Brian said nothing until the song was finished. When the tape recorder was rewinding, he cleared his throat.

"It's not my cup of tea, actually."

Bobby's face fell.

"I'm sorry I wasted your time."

"It's all right, Robert. People do this all the time. You'd be surprised how many people have come out of the woodwork since the Beatles hit it big."

"I know what you mean."

Brian straightened his tie.

"Tell your friend that I have a policy of only signing British groups. Sorry but that's the way it is. I can recommend you to some other people who may be able to help."

"Thank you. That would be appreciated."

Bobby stood and retrieved the tape.

Brian said, "Are you doing anything now?"

Bobby shrugged. "Not really."

"Would you like to have lunch?"

Surprised at the invitation, Bobby hesitated.

"Why not?"

"Good. There's a new place just down the street I want to try."

Bobby followed Brian out of the office and down Argyll Street to a small bistro where Brian ordered an expensive lunch.

"How's the antique business?"

"Good. I've noticed the differences in doing business in the States and here in London."

"What is the difference?"

"I can sell antique silk kimonos in Baltimore like they're going out of style. But here, nothing."

Brian chuckled. "Supply and demand. Now you can appreciate what I'm doing with the boys. I know they're tired of touring. Who wouldn't be? But the Beatles have a limited time at the top, and I owe it to them to maximize their earning power now while they're still profitable. They'll thank me later."

"What about their safety?"

Brian sipped a cup of tea and looked detached.

"I worry about that all the time. Each tour has been more and more bizarre; the fans, the press, the venues, all of it. It's not so bad in England because the boys feel safe here. But elsewhere things are not quite as civilized. Sometimes I fear for their lives. If anything ever happened to them I don't know what I'd do."

"Don't you have an Asian tour coming up?"

"That's a good example. I can't mind every detail so I count on the promoters to keep things from going to pot."

Bobby nodded.

"Seems like a tall order."

"It is. I have an idea. You mentioned kimonos? Why don't you come along with us to Japan? You could get kimonos there."

Bobby was surprised.

"Why would you want me along?"

Brian's smile was warm.

"The boys like you, Robert. You're from Liverpool. You have a calming influence on them, especially John. You could help out Mal as well. What do you say?"

Bobby scratched his chin.

"I'd have to ask my wife."

"Of course. I don't need an answer right away."

When Bobby got home he told Cricket about Brian's offer.

"He seemed serious about it. Should I go?"

Cricket didn't hesitate.

"Yes."

Bobby thought for a moment.

"Maybe I will."

CHAPTER THIRTY-ONE

BEYOND NEXT MONTH

Henry Yee swept into Dingles of Newburgh carrying his briefcase.

"Can we talk privately?"

Bobby led the way. As soon as the door clicked shut behind them, Henry opened the briefcase and handed Bobby a sheet of paper.

"Please read."

Bobby read aloud, "This being a message from Clive Dingle to his brother Robert. Sorry to hear of Dad's death. It's a sad day. How much money is there? Contact me via this address." Bobby saw an address in Tokyo.

Bobby looked at Henry.

"It's short and to the point."

"What's important is we have established contact."

"I thought he was in Bangkok."

"The Tokyo address is as good a place to start as any. I'll tell Faustino to ask for a meeting. Let him handle the details. Tokyo is a good choice."

"This Faustino Magsaysay guy is good."

Henry beamed.

"Faustino is my best agent. He speaks five languages. I've tried to convince him to move to England and open an office but he won't leave his beloved Philippines. He's happy there. I wish I had a lot more like Faustino."

"I wonder how he got the message through."

"He's got contacts at every level throughout the Pacific Rim. It's simply a matter of paying off the right person."

Bobby reread the message.

"Looks like Clive wants me to come to him and hand him his money."

"Charming chap, your brother."

"Can you write this down?"

Henry pulled out a ballpoint pen and clicked it. He opened a small leather bound notebook.

Bobby said, "This being a message from Robert Dingle to his brother Clive. Dear brother, father is buried next to your mother. God rest his soul. After the creditors, your half comes to five thousand, seven hundred and ninety pounds. I am holding it at a bank in Liverpool. I might consider a meeting with restrictions. Please advise."

Henry read it back.

"Perfect. Send that to Faustino and we'll see what happens."

Henry closed his notebook.

"Do you mind if I ask you a question?"

"Not at all."

"What do you hope to accomplish here?"

"I'd hope Clive would have a change of heart and give himself up, pay his debt to society and go straight. I seriously doubt that will happen. If I get his share of Dad's money to him, then I'd wash my hands of the whole affair."

"He's a fugitive from justice."

"Yes."

"Are you serious about a meeting?"

Bobby sighed.

"I don't know yet."

*   *   *

"If you're ever going to take this trip, now is the time," Cricket said.

"It's so far." Bobby's voice had a whiney edge.

Cricket stood with her hands on her hips.

"Quit it, will you? It's just a couple of plane rides. You're making excuses. If you don't go now you'll never get this thing with your brother off your back. I've seen what it does to you. Now you've got a great chance to kill three birds with one stone. Close it out with Clive, buy the kimonos, and be with the boys. You said yourself there won't be many more concerts so you better take advantage of this while you can. Winston and I can handle everything here. We're Londoners now. We're completely acclimated."

"What about the store?"

"The store can get along fine for a week or two without you."

"I don't know."

"You'll never get another chance like this again. Your adventurous nature got you this far in life, honey. Don't abandon it now. Deal with it like you always do, and get Clive out of your hair once and for all."

"You really think so?"

"Go, you big dummy."

*   *   *

The Beatles tour started in Munich. As Bobby stepped from the plane and squinted across the tarmac, waves of Beatles fans lined the terminal roof, the rest spilling into the parking lot. Their collective scream was like an amplified banshee wail. It rivaled the sound of the jet engines.

"It's great to come back to Germany as conquering heroes," John said. "How does it feel to be back on the road with the Beatles, Dusty?"

Bobby surveyed the crowd.

"I'd forgotten how insane it can be."

"Welcome to the traveling monkey house."

George said, "I wonder if the old gang will show up when we play Hamburg."

Bobby thought of Bruno Koschmider, the owner of the Kaiserkeller. The man he saw with Donovan the night Archie was murdered. He wondered what he would say if Bruno showed up at the Hamburg gig.

A white Mercedes whisked the band away to the Bayerischer Hof Hotel where they had a rare day off. On their way from their suite on the fifth floor to a press conference in the lobby, the Beatles' elevator stalled.

"What's this, then?"

"A broken lift, I think."

John frowned. "That's a bad omen."

Bobby said, "No, it's not. It's just a stalled elevator. I'm sure they'll fix it straightaway."

Five minutes went by and nothing happened. The air in the elevator became stagnant. The Beatles, plus Bobby and Mal stood together, staring at the lighted floor display above the door.

"How much longer?" John said. "I'm feeling claustrophobic in here."

"It can't be too long," Mal said, "We're due at the press conference."

"I hate this."

"I hear something," Bobby said.

Voices shouted in German.

"The Krauts are trying to communicate with us. What's Kraut for 'stuck'?"

Paul didn't worry about language barriers.

"We're stuck in here!" he yelled.

"Let us out!" John shouted.

The voices stopped.

George turned to Bobby.

"See how it is? It's like this every day. How can a man live like this?"

"Hang on," Bobby said. "It'll just be a few more minutes."

"I'm not talking about the bloody elevator!"

John said, "He means touring. It's horrible. We can't stand it."

"Have you told Brian?"

John looked at George conspiratorially.

"Brian is interested in making as much money as he can."

"He'd never let you suffer. He loves you, all of you. If you told him how you felt..."

Mal cleared his throat.

"Brian's aware of the band's unhappiness. We have contracts to fulfill. Once this tour is over, he'll sit down with everybody."

The elevator lurched then dropped a few inches.

"Oh, bloody hell!"

The sound of machinery starting below echoed up the shaft. A moment later the elevator shuddered then began to descend.

"Hurray! We're moving again!"

The elevator door opened a moment later. Standing in front of the elevator dozens of shoving photographers unleashed a flurry of flashbulbs. The strobe-like effect of the flashes blinded Bobby. Reporters began shouting questions before they even left the elevator. The flashes wouldn't stop, and Bobby saw what John was talking about. The boys worried it would never end.

The next day they rehearsed for their gig at the Circus Krone.

"We sound bloody awful," George said to Bobby before the concert. "Musically we've gone all to hell. Don't listen to us tonight, OK?"

Bobby shrugged. "OK."

"We're recording it for German TV. God knows how it's going to sound."

Bobby thought George was exaggerating. He broke his promise and listened. He decided they sounded all right. It wasn't their best gig but far from disastrous. When it was over the band, still sweating, was hustled into a limo. The mood back at the hotel was one of exhaustion- and the tour was just beginning.

The next day they boarded a special ceremonial train previously used by the Queen. The Beatles had their own suite of rooms complete with a private dining car.

They enjoyed a relatively relaxing train ride to Essen where they performed at the Grugahalle. The band sounded better, Bobby thought, and they seemed more cheerful.

They had dinner in their dressing room and did a press conference between shows. It was hard work. After the show they waited for the crowd to disperse, and the limo spirited them back to their special train. The train's gentle rocking soon put Bobby into dreamland.

At six the next morning they arrived at Central Station in Hamburg and saw the same platform they had walked as paupers. A sullen young man who looked remarkably like Stu Sutcliffe asked for an autograph. John signed it without comment.

Speaking to Bobby, John's voice was low.

"I have many ghosts here."

"I expect they'll all be at the show," Bobby replied.

*   *   *

Bobby slept until one and quickly showered and shaved. He wanted to go into town with John and Paul. They were all staying thirty miles outside of Hamburg at the Schloss Hotel in Tremsbuttel.

"Meet me in the lobby in ten minutes," John told Bobby on the hotel line. "We're going to see Astrid."

They took a cab into Hamburg where they found Astrid, pale and melancholy, her room covered with pictures of Stu. She clung to John like a frightened cat.

"You've got to let go," John whispered. "He's gone. Let it go."

Astrid sobbed. Bobby couldn't swallow because of the lump in his throat. The last time he'd been in her house had been the day of the Beatle haircuts. He remembered how moody Stu seemed in Germany. His brooding intensity and Astrid's joy had collided like two trains.

They invited Astrid to visit backstage after the concert.

"Let's have a jolly party backstage tonight," John said. "We'll get all the old gang together. It'll be fun. Come on, Astrid."

She wiped away a tear.

"I will come if you want me to."

"Of course I want you to! George and Paul want to see you. Call all the exis and tell them to come. Their names will be on the backstage list."

"OK, John."

"Give us a smile," John said. "Come on, just a little tiny smile."

Astrid managed a smile.

John did a little dance.

"All right then. It's off to the British Sailors Society to visit old Jim Hawke! Can you call us a cab?"

They drove to their old haunt. As soon as Bobby walked into the four story Sailors Society, the memories overcame him. He remembered slipping on Archie Stillman's blood, and Jim Hawke's calming words and take-charge manner. Bobby had replayed that scene in his brain countless times.

"Let's have a proper plate of chips," John said as they entered the dining hall.

Bobby looked at the vacant eyed seamen slumped around the room and thought of his own time.

"I'm glad we got this chance to come back," John said. "The way my life is going, I'll never be able to do this kind of thing again."

Suddenly there was Jim Hawke, smiling at them. Hawke squeezed John's shoulder.

"Welcome back," he said softly. "Glad to see things worked out for you, son."

*   *   *

Ernst Merck Halle was packed. Hamburg welcomed the Beatles as their own. The German version of *She Loves You* had made them heroes. *Paperback Writer*, their latest single was flying up the charts.

The Beatles were better here, Bobby noted. The boys strove to capture the magic they'd so easily created at the Kaiserkeller.

The set started with *Rock and Roll Music* by Chuck Berry, rolled through *She's A Woman* and *If I Needed Someone*. It accelerated with *Day Tripper* and *I Feel Fine* then slowed as Paul sang *Yesterday*. Ringo picked up the tempo with *I Want To Be Your Man*. Then came *Nowhere Man* and *Paperback Writer*.

The closer was *I'm Down* with Paul shouting his voice raw.

At the backstage reunion party, Bobby saw many familiar faces. Bruno Koschmider was not among them nor was Hosrt Fascher, the Kaiserkeller bouncer. No one said "Mak Shau." Bobby felt relieved.

Bettina who worked behind the bar at the Star Club made a great show of hugging all the Beatles.

"Beatles vont Prellys?" she asked with a laugh.

"Actually, yes," John replied. "You got any?"

Bert Kaempfert, the bandleader who first recorded the Beatles backing Tony Sheridan, smiled and shook everyone's hand.

"We were billed as the Beat Brothers back then," Paul quipped.

Astrid looked beautiful as she glided into the dressing room. The band crowded around her. The good feelings in the room seemed to revolve around her. She and the Beatles talked for hours. It was as if they'd found a memory and couldn't let go. No one was looking forward to the long flight to Tokyo.

*   *   *

Back at the hotel someone had left a note for George under his door. He read it several times before calling Brian Epstein.

"It's a death threat," George said, his voice cracking. "A bloody death threat!"

"I'm sorry," Brian said. "It's not the first."

"But they're usually those idiotic scrawls in the mail. Whoever sent this got past all your security efforts and slipped it under my bloody door, right here where I'm sleeping tonight."

Brian read the note and handed it to Mal Evans. Tony Barrow, the Beatles press officer, stood looking over his shoulder.

Mal read aloud. "You won't live beyond next month."

"That's it?" Tony asked.

"That's it," Brian said soberly.

When Bobby entered the room, Mal whispered to him, "George just got a death threat. It was right under his door."

Bobby went numb.

"Oh, my God."

Brian said, "Gentlemen, we have no recourse but to take this threat seriously. I'll contact the proper authorities, but from now on we have to be wary. We'll have to tighten security at every level. We have to keep cool about this. Chances are it's a hoax."

George looked mortified.

"What if it's serious? Somebody was serious enough to sneak up here. What if they really want to kill me? All it takes is one maniac."

Mal said, "Do you have any idea who wrote this?"

George shrugged. "It's Hamburg. We have a lot of strange friends here. It could be somebody from the old days who thinks we crossed him, but I can't recall any bad blood like that."

Bobby raised his hand.

"Brian doesn't know about my brother. It's time we told him."

Brian raised an eyebrow.

"You have a brother?"

"Yes. In all likelihood he's the man who killed Stuart Sutcliffe. It happened before you met the band."

"Do tell."

Bobby told the story of Clive and the Beatles and how he'd kicked Stu in the head at Lathom Hall.

"The last time I saw him, he was in prison. He's since broken out and fled the country. I hired a detective to track him down so I could give him his share of the family inheritance. He's in Tokyo. I don't know how much of a threat he is, but I think we should keep a sharp watch. He hates the Beatles."

"You think he did this?" Mal held the note aloft.

Bobby shook his head.

"It's not his style. Clive is more of a thug than a note writer, and he's on the other side of the world."

"That's where we're going," said Brian.

Bobby said, "The thought of Clive and the Beatles in the same city makes me nervous."

Brian put a hand on George's shoulder.

"It's probably nothing, George, but, we're going to take appropriate measures. You know I would never let anything happen to you."

George stared glumly at the floor.

"I better get some sleep."

"Good idea. We'll put you in different suites on another floor and double security. Then we can all get some rest. We'll talk on the plane tomorrow."

Once everyone was settled, Bobby lay in his bed and tried to sleep. Though he was dead tired, his mind refused to slow down. He tossed and turned until the wake-up call.

The Beatles didn't like long plane rides. They read, smoked, and fidgeted. A few hours into the flight, Brian Epstein called for an impromptu meeting.

"We've all been under a lot of stress lately and I just want to say how much I appreciate everyone's efforts. The police have the note and they're doing everything possible to find the author. We've radioed Tokyo for additional security. The promoter there is working with the police to ensure our protection. I've spoken to the British Embassy. Our Ambassador is aware of the situation. I want you all to feel safe. Our job is to get you boys on and off the stage with complete security. Your job is to play the music your fans want to hear."

Brian paused. Bobby saw a flicker of self-doubt in his eyes, but it was gone in an instant, replaced by a boyish smile.

"I know you've all been wondering about the future of the Beatles touring. I know how you feel."

"Do you?" said John, his voice dripping sarcasm.

George, who hadn't said a word for the entire flight, cleared his throat.

"I can't speak for the others but I'm finished. I can't handle another tour after this. It's become too much."

"It's not the Beatles without George," Paul said.

John said, "If George is out, I'm out."

"Where does that leave me?" said Ringo. "You guys get all the songwriting royalties. I get none of that. The only real money I get is from live shows."

Brian said, "You've got performance royalties coming from the record company, Ringo."

"You know what I mean, Brian. It's not the same."

George sighed. "It's not the money. I just can't stand it anymore."

"It's not fun anymore," John said. "We sound bloody awful."

"What I'm saying is that I don't want to do the American tour," said George.

A moment of silence passed.

Brian said, "If you're absolutely sure you won't go and there's a group consensus then I'll have to cancel it. We'll lose millions of dollars. I've already accepted deposits that will have to be returned."

John and Paul exchanged glances.

"Millions?"

"I'll call the American promoter and find out how much it would cost to cancel the tour. If necessary, I will pay it out of my own pocket. I won't make you do something against your will."

John said, "Let's wait until after this tour and decide when we get back to London. There's only two stops left. It's less than a week. Fair enough, George?"

George nodded. "OK."

The captain announced that due to a typhoon in Japan, they were rerouting through Alaska where they would refuel. Flying into Anchorage, Bobby watched pristine wilderness give way to cinderblock and asphalt. He hoped it wasn't a bad omen.

* * *

Emerging from the cramped plane in Tokyo after a seemingly endless flight, the Beatles, rumpled and tired, watched as Japanese riot police pushed back a crowd of hysterical fans. The specially trained cops flanked the Beatles and cleared the way whisking them into limos that sped to the Tokyo Hilton.

The Beatles went directly to their suites to rest. Brian Epstein looked through his messages. He handed most of them to Tony Barrow with the usual instructions; no political visits, no exclusive interviews, authorized press conferences only, privacy.

Bobby had messages from his kimono contact and Faustino Magsaysay. Bobby was about to call them both when the phone rang.

"Hello? Bobby Dingle here."

"Mr. Dingle, this is Faustino Magsaysay."

"That was fast. I just checked in."

"I'm staying in the same hotel. I've been in contact with your brother. He wants to meet with you tonight."

"Tonight? I'm a little jet lagged, but I want to get this done."

"Timing is everything, Mr. Dingle. I will phone you in two hours. Please be ready to go. Do you have the money?"

"In cash."

After Faustino hung up Bobby called the kimono dealer and made an appointment for the next morning. Bobby would have his kimonos shipped directly to London and Baltimore.

* * *

The meeting took place in the *Roppongi* district of Tokyo. Faustino drove a rented car through tiny streets lined with restaurants, bars, and nightclubs. They made a myriad of turns but eventually came to a narrow cobblestone street no larger than an alley. Faustino parked the car and pointed to a small café across the street.

"That's the place. I'll go in first and you come in five minutes later. Clive's not due for thirty minutes so I want to check things out."

Bobby nodded. "I'm not much good at cloak-and-dagger."

Faustino grunted and got out. Bobby watched him enter the café. After five minutes Bobby went inside.

The café was tiny even by Tokyo standards. Faustino stood at a square bar set up against one wall. There were only four tables. A trio of Japanese businessmen sat at one. The rest were vacant.

A small Hibachi blazed with Chicken Yakatori. The aroma filled the air. A beautiful vintage American Rockola Juke Box sat in an alcove just inside the door. Bobby wondered where the owner had found it. He walked over and examined the selection. There were a dozen Beatles songs.

Bobby stopped at the bar. He put a coin on a napkin and wrote a short note, slipping it silently to Faustino. Bobby went to a table and ordered sake.

Twenty minutes later, Clive walked in. He spotted Bobby and sat down.

"Me little bruvva come all this way to see me. It's enough to bring a tear."

"Hello, Clive."

"Did you bring the money?"

Bobby reached inside his shirt and withdrew an envelope. He held it out to Clive.

"Five thousand, seven hundred and ninety English pounds. That represents your half of the inheritance."

Clive took the envelope and looked inside.

"Thank you, little bruvva." He thrust his nose into the envelope and inhaled.

"Smells like good old British pounds sterling! How I've missed 'em."

Bobby held up his hands.

"I've done my duty."

"That you have, lad."

"Why don't you use the money to start a new life and go straight?"

Clive laughed.

"That's a good one. I'll go straight, all right... straight to the whorehouse."

"Dad wouldn't approve."

"Fuck Dad. He's dead. Life goes on for the rest of us, eh? But tell me, little bruvva, what possessed you to come all this way?"

Bobby shrugged.

"I have some business in Tokyo. I just wanted to do the right thing. That's what Dad would have wanted. I thought maybe we could bury the hatchet. We are the only two Dingles left."

The sake arrived. The waitress poured two cups and withdrew.

"I'll drink to that."

They raised their cups and knocked back the contents. While they drank, Faustino slipped from his place at the bar and put a coin in the Juke Box. *Paperback Writer* by the Beatles began to play. Clive frowned when he heard it.

"The bloody Beatles are everywhere."

"Yes..." Bobby stopped himself from saying more. He studied his brother's face. There was nothing to be read.

"Still holding a grudge?" Bobby asked.

Clive grinned like a pirate. "What do you think?"

*　　*　　*

Bobby told Brian everything.

"I had Faustino play a Beatles song on the Juke Box so I didn't have to broach the subject. I thought it would spark a reaction."

"Did it?"

Bobby shook his head.

"If he had anything to do with the Hamburg note he didn't act like it. I asked him him if he still held a grudge. He wouldn't give me a straight answer."

Brian's tired eyes flashed.

"I'll contact the promoter to have the police pick up Clive and detain him until after we're gone. I don't want him within ten miles of the Beatles."

Brian looked worried. Bobby wondered what other problems the Beatles' manager had on his mind.

"We've had some other threats," Brian said. "Apparently the Budokan Hall where we're playing is a sacred place for the martial arts. There are some purists who object strongly to our presence. Security here will be unprecedented for an entertainment act. It'll be more along the lines of what they'd provide for a president or a prime minister. I've set it up so the Beatles will be safer here than they have been anywhere."

The Beatles had become prisoners of their own fame. Bobby knew that Paul and John had tried to sneak out of the hotel twice and both times they were caught and returned. On Brian's orders their translators scolded them.

The Japanese promoter gave everyone a brand new Nikon camera. He brought merchants into their suite to display their wares. The Beatles spent money but never ventured out.

In the face of more death threats, the British Embassy fielded a special Beatles detachment. Riot police kept them surrounded. The promoter told Brian that if anything happened to the Beatles on his watch, it would bring dishonor to all involved. The Beatles' disposition sagged under the strain of increased security.

CHAPTER THIRTY-TWO

THRILLA IN MANILA

The first show at the *Budokan* was strange. The Beatles performed the same show they had done in Germany. But the audience did not scream. The band could actually hear themselves. Playing every night with a roar as loud as a 727 in their ears had left them sluggish. Their singing was off, their instrumentation sloppy. Bobby could tell that it bugged them and watched as they tried to pull it together. By the second show things had improved dramatically.

The police detained two men who fit Clive's description, a German footballer and an American hardware salesman, but the real Clive had disappeared. At the show it seemed as if there were as many cops as fans.

John complained all the way back to the hotel.

"We go out there night after night and do a dog and pony show for a bunch of screamin' maniacs. Back in the Reeperbahn we were unknown, but at least our music was real. Now we're just shuck and jive showbiz pop stars. I wish we could go back in time."

"We were happy then," George said.

Paul snapped his fingers.

"What's the problem? We're getting paid a fortune! I think we can grin and bear it for another couple of days. I know I can. After that, we can go back to making albums."

John said, "At least the recording studio is pure. We can still make art there."

Paul said, "We made the promotional films for *Paperback Writer* and *Rain* right? That's the way of the future. We stay home and let the film go on tour."

John looked at Paul.

"You know what I think? I think we should go back and make the greatest fookin' album of all time, our masterpiece. Then the punters can listen to that instead of screaming their heads off at a gig. We'll do things that could never possibly be recreated live."

Paul said, "Come on, lads. Let's finish this run with some dignity."

George fixed his weary eyes on Paul.

"Let's. But after this we've got to start a new era."

"Gentlemen, start your engines," Ringo said. "The new era is upon us."

The driver of their limo honked his horn to alert a slow moving delivery truck up ahead. As they rounded the lorry, they could see his load of two live donkeys. The donkeys looked up at the Tokyo skyline and brayed in terror. They came from another world. All four Beatles understood.

"Gentlemen, mount your burros," Ringo said.

*　　*　　*

Bobby sat with Neil and Mal on the plane to Manila. From the window they could see thousands of kids and hundreds of riot police. It looked like the airport was under siege.

As soon as they got off the plane, Neil and Mal turned their backs for a moment and the Beatles were shoved into a car and driven away. It happened so quickly no one had a chance to object. Suddenly the boys were in a limo and the limo was gone. Neil and Mal stood on the tarmac shouting and waving but the car with the Beatles receded in the distance.

"Wait! Stop! You can't do that! We have to stay with the band!"

Neil ran after the car.

"Stop!"

Mal pulled Bobby aside and whispered in his ear.

"You see those four leather overnight bags?"

Bobby nodded.

"Keep your eye on those bags. They have weed in them. This could be a bust."

Bobby opened his mouth to speak but Mal cut him off.

"When nobody's looking, toss them in the boot of whatever car we get in."

"Got it."

Neil hustled off looking for someone with a car. No one seemed to be in charge. Mal argued with a uniformed military officer. Brian ran around looking for someone in authority and Bobby just stood and worried. Were the Beatles in the right car or had they been abducted?

Mal saw one of the men who had manhandled the Beatles into the car. He grabbed the man by the arm.

"Where are they taking them? Where are they taking the Beatles?"

"Yes," said the man. "They take them. The Beatles are safe, very safe."

Mal was nearly shouting now. "Who are 'they'?"

"Protective security. They keep the Beatles safe, very safe. Don't worry."

Mal was beside himself.

"We can't have this! Bring the Beatles back here this minute!"

It was no use. The Beatles were not coming back anytime soon.

"Can we please have a car?" Mal shouted. "Hello? A car? We need a car."

Another car appeared. Bobby threw the luggage and guitar cases into the trunk with the bags of weed stashed among them.

"Take us where you've taken the Beatles! And hurry!"

Bobby climbed in behind Neil and Mal as the car lurched forward. As they pulled away, he looked at the frowning faces of the guards being left behind. The attitude of the Filipinos was all wrong. Instead of being gracious these people were bullying tyrants. They all had guns and they made sure everyone knew it. Could the boys already be victims of a kidnapping?

After driving through Manila the limo parked at the end of a long pier. Neil and Mal got out and looked around.

Mal said, "Where are they?"

The driver pointed to a boat out in the middle of the bay.

"There."

"Where?"

"In the boat."

"In the boat? That's insane! Why are they on a boat? This is all wrong. We have to go out there and get them. The Beatles cannot stay on that boat. They must be taken to their hotel immediately! Do you understand?"

The driver wrung his hands and looked worried. Mal tried another approach.

"The Beatles are on the boat, right?"

The driver nodded.

"Who owns the boat?"

The driver shrugged.

"Is it the promoter?"

The driver shook his head. "No."

Mal turned to Neil and Bobby.

"The Beatles have been taken by somebody who is not the promoter. We've got to get a boat.

"I don't like any of this. Everybody's got a gun. Their lives could be in danger out there."

Brian arrived along with his own people, and Ramon Ramos, the local promoter. Brian was livid.

"Damn it! My boys are out there!"

"Relax, everything is fine," said one Filipino.

"Everything is not fine! If you want the Beatles to play you better take me out to that boat right now!"

"But the contract..."

"The contract doesn't say anything about kidnapping the band and holding them on a boat!"

"They are not kidnapped. They are completely safe in protective custody."

Bobby watched Brian shout at the man. It reminded him of an argument he saw at a baseball game at Memorial Stadium in Baltimore. The Oriole's manager got within inches of the umpire's face and berated him unmercifully. The manager had been ejected. How would Brian do?

A speedboat pulled up to the dock. Brian wasted no time getting in.

"Mal, Bobby, come with me. Neil, you stay here and coordinate transport to our hotel. I'm going to get my boys."

Bobby jumped in behind Brian. Brian turned and addressed the group.

"If we're not back in twenty minutes call the British Embassy. Call the embassy anyway. I want to talk to our ambassador. This is not only disrespectful, it's dangerous and illegal."

With that, Brian, Mal, and Bobby took off for the ride of their lives. The pilot liked speed. They skimmed across the water, bouncing high. Bobby held on for dear life. Brian squinted into the wind and spray, his eyes fixed on the yacht ahead.

As soon as they neared the yacht, another speedboat buzzed them. Bobby could see four men armed with automatic rifles. They tried to pull close, but Brian's boat was too fast. The deck of the yacht was ringed with armed, uniformed men. Bobby couldn't see the Beatles.

Brian waved to the pilot house. At that moment all the guns on deck swung in his direction. Bobby heard a familiar voice shout from somewhere on the big boat.

"It's Eppy! He's come to save us!"

"Hurray for Eppy!"

After considerable shouting, Brian managed to convince the yacht's captain to let him aboard though he needed help from John.

"He's Brian Epstein," John snapped. "He's our manager. Let him come on board. He's with us."

Flustered and uncharacteristically disheveled, Brian climbed on board with Mal and Bobby right behind.

George shouted, "Eppy! Mal! Dust Bin Bob! Thank God you've come!"

Brian looked at each of them.

"You're all fine?"

They nodded.

"No one's been hurt?"

"We just want to get off this boat and go to the hotel."

John put his hand on Brian's shoulder.

"I've never been happier to see you, man."

"Why did they bring you here?"

George said, "We have no idea. We stepped off the plane and this guy started yelling at us, 'Get in this car! Don't touch those bags! They shoved us in so quickly we didn't have time to think. We expected Mal to pop up any second, but the car just took off. We shouted to the driver to stop but he ignored us. We didn't know if we were being kidnapped. Frightening, it was."

John said, "They brought us here and put us on this yacht with all these armed goons. The mosquitoes have been feasting on us, it's hotter than hell, and these guys are scaring the shit out of me."

Brian listened, furious, but he kept his cool around the band.

"It'll never happen again, lads. I promise."

John wiped his brow.

"It better not."

"It won't, John. I give you my word."

Bobby cleared his throat.

"Would you like me to ring up the captain, Mr. Epstein?"

"Yes, Robert. If you would be so kind, do call the captain for me."

Bobby fetched the ship's captain and Brian had the Beatles off the boat and on their way to the hotel in no time. They drove back in tense silence, staring out at the alien cityscape. So far Manila had been a disaster.

At the hotel the Beatles settled into their usual isolation. When Paul and Neil managed to sneak out and go for a drive, everyone freaked out. Bobby understood how they felt. The hotel rooms were closing in on him. He had to get out.

He decided to call Faustino Magsaysay who'd returned to his office in Manila. They arranged to meet at a local café. It was a sunny day so Bobby decided to walk. On the way he passed a corner where six girl scouts stood. They carried lethal looking automatic rifles with pistol grips. Bobby tried not to stare. They couldn't have been more than fifteen or sixteen years old.

Faustino was waiting for him at the cafe. They shook hands.

"You really are traveling with the Beatles?"

"Yes, I'm afraid so. This trip has been a mess."

"I heard about the boat incident. The yacht belonged to Don Manolo Elizalde, a millionaire. It could have been a power play."

Bobby shook his head.

"Shit was happening all around."

"Manila can be a funny place. Sometimes things happen that make no sense."

"It's certainly been an adventure. There are two shows at the stadium tomorrow and the next day we leave. Let's hope it goes without incident."

Faustino leaned forward.

"If you need my help call my office. They can always reach me, day or night."

"Thanks, Faustino. I appreciate that. You're the one guy I can trust here."

*   *   *

While the others were still asleep the next morning, Ringo wandered out of the room he was sharing with John and tried to order breakfast. As he dialed room service, a loud, insistent knocking started at the door. Bobby answered.

The promoter, Ramon Ramos, stood in the doorway looking very ethnic in a translucent white Barong Tagalog dress shirt.

"Is it room service?" shouted Mal from somewhere back in the suite.

"No," Bobby called.

Ramos said, "We're here to take you to the palace. Are the Beatles ready?"

Bobby told Ramos to wait then found Mal who hurried to the door.

"What's this all about?"

"Madame Marcos invited the Beatles to the Malacanang Palace for a special reception this morning," Ramos said. "We are here to pick them up. We need to hurry to avoid being late."

Mal shook his head.

"The Beatles received no invitation to the palace. And even if they did, Brian Epstein doesn't allow them to attend foreign diplomatic functions. They can't be seen endorsing this government or that government. It's not their policy."

"Madame Marcos sent me. She said it was all set up. She's got some kids who want to meet the Beatles."

Mal frowned.

"They can't go. Tell whoever is in charge that the Beatles don't do this sort of thing. It must be cleared in advance by Mr. Epstein. We have to be out at the stadium in a few hours. Our first show is at four and we arrive two hours before. You should know that, Mr. Ramos. Whoever arranged this had no knowledge of our schedule."

"What do you want me to tell Madame Marcos?"

"Tell her no. I'm sorry about the misunderstanding."

Mal closed the door.

"Bloody strange."

"I think we should wake Brian and tell him something is afoot here."

A short time later someone pounded on the door. It was Ramon Ramos again. He seemed very agitated.

"Turn on the TV! Turn on the TV!"

Bobby switched on the big color console unit in the living room. The rest of the Beatles wandered out of their rooms to see what was going on. As the picture came into view, Mal gasped. On the TV screen was a crying child.

The camera panned across a large banquet table with a group of children sitting around it all crying.

The announcer said, "We're still waiting for the Beatles to arrive. No word yet on when that will be."

Everyone gathered around the TV. Imelda Marcos came on. She was crying too.

"They let me down! They let me down! They let the children down! They let all of the Philippines down!"

The announcer's voice returned.

"Will the Beatles show up? Will they choose to snub the First Lady? Stay tuned. We are coming to you live from Malacanang Palace."

"Holy shit!" Mal said. He ran to wake Brian.

A few moments later Brian was shouting at Ramon Ramos.

"How could you let this happen? Tony Barrow sent a telex from Tokyo declining the offer! We never agreed to do this! You should have told them that we don't make official visits."

Ramon stood his ground.

"You have to go now."

"It's out of the question."

Ramon Ramos shook his head.

"No, no, no. You must go. It's very important. They are waiting for you."

"The Beatles don't do official functions with government leaders, damn it!"

Paul stepped forward.

"We know it's a great honor and everything, but we just can't do it. We've got two shows today."

Ramon's jaw clenched. The muscles on his face stood out.

"It's just a short limo ride. The car is downstairs. We can make it if we leave now."

Brian sighed. "The answer is no."

Ramon Ramos left without another word. As the door closed, all four Beatles began to chatter.

"Can you believe that?"

"The nerve of these people!"

"Who do they think they are?"

The phone rang and Mal picked it up and listened for a moment.

"It's the Embassy. They want to talk to Brian."

Brian took the receiver.

"Hello? Yes, Mr. Ambassador. Thank you. To tell you the truth, we're having a bit of a problem right now."

Brian listened for a few minutes, then cupped his hand over the mouthpiece.

"He says, turn on Channel Two."

Neil switched the channel and they all watched a middle-aged anchorman.

"The Beatles snubbed First Lady Imelda Marcos today. They were scheduled to appear at a special children's luncheon at Malacanang Palace this morning but did not show up. Hundreds of children were crying. The disappointment on their faces was evident. When asked if they would come, a representative of the group said 'the answer is no.'"

Brian's facial expression sank.

The announcer continued.

"They are scheduled to play two sold out shows at Rizal Memorial Football Stadium this afternoon. No word from the Palace on what the reaction will be."

"Good Lord... what next?" Brian muttered.

Into the phone he said, "Yes, Mr. Ambassador, I agree. It was all a misunderstanding. I had telexed our regrets on not being able to attend, but there seems to be some confusion over that. It's possible they never got the telex. The Beatles don't do that sort of thing. It's our policy."

Brian listened for a while.

"Why would they schedule a luncheon on the morning of the show? It doesn't make sense. The promoter really screwed this one up, and now we're in trouble with Madame Marcos."

Brian listened again for a few minutes, then said good-bye.

"You won't believe this, but the Ambassador advised us to go to the palace. He said the Marcos family should not be stood up. They are too powerful. His position is that we're here because of their generosity. I told him no. I will not be strong-armed. Then he said we need to do some damage control. He suggested a public apology."

"What a load," George said.

"Why should we apologize when we haven't done anything wrong?" asked John.

Brian said, "I'm going over to the television station in between shows to broadcast the apology. The Ambassador thinks that will help. He said he'd make the necessary calls to set it up. I'll take Tony with me. Mal, you stay with the band. Make sure nothing else happens."

When they arrived at the Stadium they were shocked. The expected crowd of seventy thousand had swelled to well over a hundred thousand. Brian immediately started calling for Ramos to amend the contract. The extra people were not part of the original accounting. Ramos stood to make a fortune at the Beatles expense.

Their dressing room was a mess, and no explanation was offered. Bobby assumed it must be the work of Marcos loyalists.

Brian moaned.

"Now they're trying to cheat the boys on thirty thousand gate receipts. Times two shows that makes sixty thousand unaccounted tickets."

"Ramos is nowhere to be found," Mal said. "They say they can't locate him."

Brian looked as if he might explode.

"Why did I accept this booking?"

Mal said, "Because it's the biggest concert the boys have ever done."

John shouted, "I hate this place!"

Despite the bad feelings, the Beatles played to a sea of hot-blooded Filipinos under a blazing tropical sun. Bobby stayed next to Neil and Mal. Everywhere he looked, hostility bubbled just under the surface.

Between shows they watched Brian Epstein on the backstage TV. Brian came on and began to read the apology that Tony Barrow had prepared. Static blocked the reception, persisting until the end of Brian's statement. As soon as he finished, the static disappeared.

Neil said, "They sabotaged Brian."

"Those dirty bastards."

Neil looked at his watch.

"We'll be out of here in eighteen hours, twenty minutes."

George sighed. "If we survive that long."

*   *   *

The second show went without incident. When it was over the Beatles returned to their hotel. As thousands of Beatles fans clogged the streets, the Filipino police got brutal. Though these fans were no worse than any others, the Beatles watched helplessly as the police went on a rampage.

Ringo ordered a room service dinner. It arrived rancid as if they'd scooped it out of the garbage.

"Don't eat anything!" Ringo said. "They're trying to poison us."

The phone rang and Bobby answered thinking it would be the hotel manager apologizing for the meal. Instead he heard Faustino Magsaysay.

"Mr. Dingle? I must see you right away on a matter of great urgency."

"What's going on?"

"I must see you now."

"How about dinner? They've cut us off here at the hotel. I'd like to eat."

Faustino gave Bobby directions to a restaurant owned by one of his many cousins. They met there an hour later. Faustino looked worried.

"What's wrong?"

Faustino looked around to see if anyone was listening then leaned across the table.

"Donovan wants a meeting. It has to be early in the morning because that's the only time he can make it. He gave me an address. I know the place.

It's safe."

"Donovan? Why would he want a meeting?"

Faustino whispered, "The Beatles."

Bobby frowned and wrinkled his nose.

"What about the Beatles? They're leaving the country in a few hours. What could Donovan want with them?"

"He says it's urgent."

"Urgent?"

Faustino nodded. "A man like Donovan doesn't request a meeting unless he has a very good reason. He says he wants to help the Beatles."

"Why would Donovan want to help the Beatles?"

"I don't know," said Faustino, "but he said I should tell you this, word for word, 'Music is more important than Clive.'"

CHAPTER THIRTY-THREE

BEATLES ALIS DAYAN

Bobby recognized Donovan in the back booth of a dingy bar in a bad neighborhood. Three grizzled alcoholics nursed shots and beers curing their morning shakes. Bobby and Faustino walked through cigarette haze, past a bored waitress to Donovan's table.

"I had to be sure it was you," Donovan said to Bobby.

"It is," Bobby replied.

"Sit down and buy me a drink."

Faustino moved to another table to give them privacy.

Bobby said, "What's going on? I know very little about you. I haven't seen you since the night Archie Stillman died. I could be aiding and abetting a criminal."

Donovan looked around again.

"Archie Stillman was a communist pig. He was a petty thief who stole to bankroll dictators. The British government wanted him dead."

Bobby's eyes got wide.

"You?"

Donovan glanced nervously at the door.

"I'm a double agent," he whispered. "Shut up and listen to what I have to say."

Bobby swallowed hard.

"This meeting never happened. Do you understand?"

Bobby said, "Yes."

"I'm only going to say this once."

Bobby nodded.

"Somewhere between the hotel and the airplane one or more of the Beatles will be assassinated."

Bobby's jaw dropped.

"Are you sure?"

"Absolutely."

"Clive?"

Donovan nodded.

"That's why I gave a message to your detective. Clive's armed and ready. I told him I didn't think it was a good idea. It would cause an international incident. He didn't care. He's crazy."

"Why are you still in touch with Clive?"

"Ragasa recruited him to work for the Marcos family. I'm investigating them."

"Why?"

"I'd rather not say."

"Clive is here? I just saw him in Tokyo."

"Manila's always been a great town for murder," Donovan said.

"Why are you telling me all this?"

Donovan smiled.

"I thought you would've figured that out. I'm a Beatles fan."

*   *   *

Faustino sped back to the hotel with Bobby. Brian, Mal, press officer, Tony Barrow, and driver, Alf Bicknell had already left for the airport with the Beatles. Bobby ran through the lobby to find Neil loading the last of their bags onto a pushcart.

"Thank God I found you! Have they all gone?"

"Yeah. Where were you? We were worried."

"I don't have time to explain now. I have reason to believe that there will an assassination attempt against the Beatles before they get to the plane."

"Are you serious?"

"Yes, I'm completely serious. It comes from a very reliable source. My brother is in Manila."

"Jesus Christ! What can we do?"

Bobby looked around.

"Where are the military guards?"

"Gone! I came down to the lobby this morning after nobody responded to my calls. The whole place has turned against us. I saw the newspaper headline *Beatles Snub President* and thought, oh shit, let's get out of here. So I roused the troops and they've just left. It's incredible, the hostility we're getting. They withdrew all the security leaving us completely vulnerable. No limo, no guards, no nothing."

Fear shot through Bobby.

"We gotta get to the airport fast!"

"We'll have to get a cab."

"Faustino Magsaysay will take us!"

"Who?"

"Follow me!" Bobby shouted as he pushed the luggage cart out onto the sidewalk.

Faustino drove like a maniac as Neil told the rest of his story.

"No one helped with the luggage. The food was spoiled. Checkout was a nightmare. They were so rude you'd think we hadn't paid our bill. The limos were not available, we couldn't get another car. Finally we got some weird little guy to charter some cabs. I was the last one out. Lucky for me, you came along."

"I hope we're not too late."

Faustino turned to Bobby.

"I have an idea."

*   *   *

A rock whistled through the air and hit the wall directly behind John Lennon.

"Bloody hell! Now they're throwing things!"

A shouting mob of Filipinos surged from behind huge plate glass windows of the Manila International Airport terminal onto the main concourse. The Beatles ducked as bottles sailed over their heads and exploded against garbage cans. Mal nudged them along toward the boarding gate. A half dozen angry men broke away from the mob and charged at the band.

"Run!" Mal shouted. "They've gone crazy!"

The greatest band in history ran for their lives. They rounded a corner and raced toward the escalators to the main level. Alf and Mal created a human shield behind them. As they approached the escalator George shouted.

"They're not working! The escalators are shut down!"

The panic in George's voice galvanized the rest of the band. They were carrying their own luggage. That and the heat wore them down. As the boys stared up at the unmoving metal stairs, they heard the mob nearing the last turn.

"Go anyway! Go!"

They stumbled up the oversized steps, dragging their baggage as they gasped for breath. Hundreds of people jeered and threw any projectile they could find. The jeers hardened into a threatening chant.

"What are they saying?" John asked.

George shook his head.

"Sounds like gibberish to me."

John turned to Ringo.

"Maybe they're unhappy with the drumming."

The mob chanted, "*Beatles Alis Dayan! Beatles Alis Dayan!*" It didn't take long to catch on. Beatles go home.

The main concourse opened into several corridors leading to the departure gates. A gaggle of Beatles fans began to scream hysterically. The mob stormed up the escalators with the fans following. Chaos. The band didn't know which direction to run. Mal pointed at the overhead airlines flight directory.

"KLM flight 862 to New Delhi, Gate 23! This way!"

They sprinted down the corridor. A sign pointed down a flight of stairs to Gate 23. By the time the band had traveled halfway down, the mob was upon them. Alf raised his arms to block them, but he couldn't hold back a riot. Somebody pushed Alf into John who nearly fell.

"Keep movin', lads!" Alf shouted. "The punters are out for blood!"

"Where are the cops?"

Alf glanced over his shoulder.

"All the security is gone. It's just us."

The confusion on John's face might have been comical in another setting. All four Beatles suddenly realized they could actually die here.

Mal took charge.

"Brian's got the tickets and hopefully he and Tony have things sorted out at the gate. We just have to make it there in one piece. So let's keep moving."

Angry Marcos loyalists and hysterical fans spilled into the stairwell, straining to grab the Beatles. Alf took a punch to the face then a kick in the knee and stumbled backward. John shouted at the crowd, but they could see the fear in his eyes. The almighty Beatles could be taken, and the mob knew it.

The band ran down the remaining steps and into the boarding area. John saw a group of nuns standing together.

"Get behind the nuns!" he shouted. "They wouldn't hurt nuns!"

*   *   *

Bags in tow, Neil jumped from the car at the departures sign.

Bobby shouted after him, "Warn the boys!"

Faustino stepped on the gas. They rounded the terminal and drove along the frontage road next to the runway. Faustino drove around the building and swung the Caddy into the maintenance area on the opposite side of the terminal.

Faustino said, "I investigated several assassinations at this airport. The moment of most vulnerability is the walk across the tarmac to the airplane. They'll be completely exposed for a hundred feet. Snipers always shoot from the roof."

He nodded at a metal ladder running up the side of the warehouse.

"That's where we're going. To the roof."

"There's two!" said Bobby.

"You take this one, I'll take the other."

Bobby got out of the car. Faustino drove off before Bobby could ask him what to do once he was up there. Faustino parked next to the second ladder.

Bobby started up the ladder. It rose five stories above the tarmac, straight up. Within twenty seconds Bobby was higher than he'd ever climbed on a ladder. By the time he neared the top he was terrified, forcing himself up one rung at a time.

He glanced over at Faustino climbing opposite him. The detective was already scrambling over the top. Once Faustino was upright, he reached inside his sport coat and pulled a blue steel .45 automatic. Faustino crouched and edged along the roofline.

He's got a gun. Bobby thought. *What do I have? I have to stop my brother from shooting at the Beatles with my bare hands? This is insane.*

At last Bobby landed on the roof. It was the size of a football field. Air ducts and pipes dotted the tar and gravel expanse. There were plenty of hiding places.

"Shit," Bobby said.

He ran along the edge of the rooftop, making his way among the outcroppings. Bobby knew the Beatles were flying on KLM Airlines to India. He saw four KLM 747s parked in a row below him.

One had its baggage doors open.

*   *   *

The Beatles huddled behind the nuns. Still the fans and thugs found them. No matter where they went the crowd pressed in.

"You will be treated just like any other passenger!" an airline employee shouted at John.

"Do you assault all of your passengers?"

In a desperate negotiation Brian had begged the KLM pilot to hold the plane for the Beatles.

"I'll wait, within reason," the pilot agreed.

"Where's Dust Bin Bob?" John asked when they finally reached the departure lounge.

"He didn't show up for check out," Mal called. "Wasn't in his room…"

"I hope he's all right."

Neil arrived, gasping for breath. He'd managed to pile all the extra bags on a rented cart and he pushed it all the way to the gate. Now he looked ready to collapse.

"Mal," he uttered. "Mal, I must talk to you!"

"What is it?"

Mal pulled Neil aside and let him catch his breath.

"Bobby got a tip… there's going to be an assassination attempt on the boys before they reach the plane."

"Oh, my God."

He looked over at the Beatles. Finally having a moment when no one was trying to assault them they were surrounded by fans all jabbering away.

"What happened to Bobby?"

"I think he's gone after the assassin."

"That's preposterous!"

"He's with a Filipino detective. They've gone after his brother, Clive."

Mal shook his head.

"This is insane. I better tell Brian."

*   *   *

Bobby slipped between the obstructions. He glanced over the edge. Below he could see guitar cases being loaded into the belly of one of the jetliners. Passengers were boarding via a set of movable stairs at the front of the plane.

Bobby rounded an air duct and saw his brother's head peeking up. Clive aimed a sniper's rifle.

*   *   *

"Are you sure?" The color drained from Brian's face.

"No," Mal said, "I'm not sure."

The public address system crackled to life with a metallic female voice.

"KLM flight 862 to New Delhi is now ready for boarding. All first class passengers, please have your tickets, passports, and boarding passes ready for inspection."

Brian looked as if he were about to cry. The shoving and punching had paused, but the thugs wouldn't give up. Held back by security, they still spit insults at George and John. Brian hurried to the front of the line.

"Boys! Listen to me! You could be in danger! I want you to run, not walk, to the plane. Understand? Run as fast as you can and keep moving until you're inside the plane."

John stared at Brian.

"What now?"

Mal said, "Your friend, Dust Bin Bob, heard about an assassination plot. This is the last piece of Filipino real estate you have to cross but it might be the most dangerous. Once you're on that plane, you're safe. Now let's all stay together and move as one, quickly and efficiently to the plane!"

"Are they trying to kill us?" Ringo said.

Brian tried another approach.

"It's just a precaution. I suppose we could stay here and perhaps the authorities will come to help us."

John said, "No! I want to get out of here!"

"Me too," said George. "Let's just make a run for it."

Brian organized Mal, Neil, Alf, Tony, and himself as human shields for the band. They all moved through the checkpoint and began a mad dash across the tarmac to the plane.

*   *   *

As the Beatles emerged from the terminal, Clive stood and took aim. The fear in Bobby's body dissipated. Clive didn't know Bobby was there. Bobby focused on Clive's back. He no longer felt like Bobby. He thought of Cricket confronting the muggers on the first night he'd met her and John standing up to Clive. Bobby couldn't let the Beatles die.

He stepped forward stealthily. Clive's eye was to the sight. Clive pulled back the bolt and a bullet snapped into the chamber. Bobby felt tingling in his arms. As Clive curled his finger around the trigger Bobby launched himself. He caught Clive in a blindside tackle. The gun leapt from Clive's fingers, forced up by Bobby's blow. For an instant, time stopped. Bobby watched the rifle hover motionless in the air then disappear over the edge. Clive groped for it but it was gone. One second passed. Then two more. Amidst the airport din came something that sounded like a shot as the gun hit the ground.

Clive realized who'd stopped him.

"What the hell? You?"

Clive punched Bobby's face. Pain flared. Bobby's head snapped back and he fell onto his ass. He stared up at his brother.

"Shit! You ruined my shot! What are you, the big hero? Come to save your precious Beatles?"

Bobby spoke with a hoarse, disembodied voice.

"I'm protecting my friends."

*   *   *

John thought he heard the crack of gunfire but it was lost in the noise from the jet engines. John lurched forward and ran up the steps. George was a step behind. Brian, Mal, and Neil surrounded the band, hoping no one would shoot. Everyone made it to the top of the stairs and onto the plane.

George crossed the threshold, shouting, "We made it! We're safe!"

They took their seats, all of them shaking. Relief spread through the group. A cheer went up.

"Where's Dust Bin Bob?" John asked.

"I don't know, but I am not getting off of this plane, no matter what," Paul said.

John said, "This place is a bloody dictatorship, and as long..."

Before John could complete his sentence, the public address system buzzed.

"Will Mr. Epstein, Mr. Evans, and Mr. Barrow, please get off the plane?"

Brian, looking terrified, called the stewardess.

"What's this about?"

The stewardess shrugged. "I don't know. Something to do with taxes, I think. You'll have to exit the aircraft, sir. I'm afraid there's nothing we can do."

Mal Evans, sitting in the row in front of Brian, turned and looked at the band. His face was pale and sweaty.

"Tell my wife I love her," he croaked. "This could be it, boys. God help us."

"Do we have to go?" Brian asked the stewardess.

"They won't let the plane take off unless you comply."

Brian sighed. He rose slowly from his seat and walked toward the door.

"What if they're not allowed to leave the country?" John said as he watched the three men leave.

An official of the Philippine tax authority met them on the tarmac. His assistant made the introductions.

"This is Misael Vera of the Philippine Tax Authority. He says you have not paid all the taxes required before you can leave the country."

Brian clenched his jaw.

"My office in London will handle any additional tax bills."

Mr. Vera shook his head.

"I show a balance of seventy-four thousand, four hundred and fifty pesos still due. I'm afraid we can't let you go until you've paid it in full."

Brian tried to sound authoritative.

"This is outrageous! You pull us off the plane and demand more money or we can't leave? That's robbery!"

"Are you insulting Mr. Vera?" the assistant snapped.

Tony tapped Brian on the shoulder.

"Just pay it and let's get out of here."

Brian stared straight ahead.

The assistant said, "Also you forgot to sign some immigration papers which will further delay your departure."

"Pay the money, Brian. I'll sign whatever they want. Let's not invite any more trouble."

Brian blinked. "The amount is seventy-four thousand, four-fifty? That's the amount we earned at the concert."

"Pay it, Brian. Let the lawyers suss it out."

Brian straightened.

"If I pay, will the Beatles and their party be allowed to leave on that plane?"

Misael Vera said something to his assistant in Tagalog. After a short, animated discussion, the assistant spoke.

"If you pay that amount, and sign the papers, you can go."

"I'll pay the tax, but I do so under protest."

*　　*　　*

Bobby froze. His brother loomed in front of him, touching a bloody cut on his face.

Bobby got up.

"Why are you doing this, Clive?"

"Because I hate the bloody Beatles! I hate them for what they did to you!"

"To me?"

Clive sneered. "Look at yourself! You look like a bloody fairy! Long hair like a girl, poofy little velvet suit, high heeled boots... Where's your Dingle toughness? It's all because of the Beatles. They ruined you. Before you met them you were a half right guy, but they've turned you into a sissy."

Bobby shook his head.

"You've lost your mind."

"Lost my mind? The Beatles ruined everything! Not just for us, but for the whole world!"

Clive charged at Bobby. They rolled across the roof, punching and gouging. Bobby broke free and jumped to his feet. Clive came after him like a bear. Bobby tried to get back to the ladder. Clive grabbed his shoulder and swung him around. They were dangerously close to the edge.

Clive swung a big roundhouse punch. Bobby, trained by Cricket's father, stepped inside the arc of Clive's swing, put his shoulder into Clive's chest and used leverage to flip the big man head over heels. The last Bobby saw of his brother was Clive's startled expression as he screamed and flew over the edge.

What have I done?

Clive was gone.

Bobby peered over the edge and saw the body below, arms and legs akimbo on the concrete.

"I killed him!"

"It was in self-defense," said a voice.

Bobby turned to see Faustino standing with his gun drawn.

"He was trying to kill you," Faustino added.

"Oh, God!" Bobby wailed.

The sound of revving jet engines filled the air, drowning out Bobby's voice. Wind heated his face.

Faustino came to Bobby's side and looked over the edge.

"He was going to do that to you!"

"He was my brother!"

"Brothers have killed brothers since biblical times. You did what you had to do. It was self-defense. I'm a witness."

Bobby started to shake.

"I didn't think he was gonna go over the edge. I swear I didn't."

"I believe you."

KLM flight 862 backed away from the terminal. Bobby watched as it turned and rolled down the runway. When its nose rose into the air and the great silver bird took wing, he began to cry. He stood for a moment, overcome with emotion.

"What have I done?"

"You just saved the Beatles, that's what."

EPILOGUE

The Beatles never returned to the Philippines. After their plane took off, President Ferdinand Marcos issued a statement saying, "There was no intention on the part of The Beatles to slight the First Lady or the Government of the Republic of the Philippines."

The Filipino newspapers printed the apology Brian had tried to make through TV static. According to one report the Manila City Council voted to ban the sale, display, or playing of any Beatles record in any public place. Beatles movies were pulled from the theaters.

Imelda Marcos said, "I never liked them anyway. Their music is horrible."

The British Embassy lodged a formal protest over the airport tax incident. The local promoter Ramon Ramos and his production company filed for bankruptcy.

The Beatles' next single was *Nowhere Man*.

Upon their arrival in England the Beatles held a press conference and complained about their treatment in Manila.

Ringo said, "The Philippines was the most frightening thing that's ever happened to me."

John said, "No plane is going to go to the Philippines with me on it. I wouldn't even fly over it."

The Beatles legal team tried to recover the money they'd lost to the Philippine Tax Authority. Brian handed over seventeen thousand dollars in cash that day. Whether or not he got a receipt is still in question. The only ones who came out ahead were the lawyers.

The Beatles did one final tour of America. Their last concert was at Candlestick Park in San Francisco.

Beatlemania did not die with the end of touring. Some people, including Charlie Manson, heard strange messages in the music.

Miraculously Clive Dingle survived his fall but never walked again. The Beatles broke up in 1970. Ferdinand Marcos was driven from power and forced into exile in 1986. His wife Imelda still has the largest collection of shoes in the known universe.

Clovis Hicks never became a rock star but had a successful career as a studio musician and record producer. He and Erlene had seven sons.

Bobby Dingle returned to England and remained close to the Beatles. He opened several record shops based on the Hi-Dee-Ho Soul Shack, and even hired Preston Washington to manage them. He also opened several art galleries where young artists could exhibit their work including an ambitious Japanese conceptual artist named Yoko Ono. Cricket became a popular fashion photographer and designer of album covers.

Dust Bin Bob lives on.

ABOUT THE AUTHOR

Greg Kihn has been called "Rock's True Renaissance Man." His career stretches from the dawn of punk and indie rock to the discos of the 80's to the glory days of MTV.

He's had hit records, appeared on Saturday Night Live, opened for the Rolling Stones, jammed with Bruce Springsteen, won the ASCAP and MIDEM Awards for his worldwide #1 hit JEOPARDY and THE BREAKUP SONG, was parodied by Weird Al and lived to tell about it.

In the 90's he turned his attention to writing fiction and published four novels: HORROR SHOW, SHADE OF PALE, BIG ROCK BEAT, and MOJO HAND, a handful of short stories, and edited a compilation of stories by famous musicians CARVED IN ROCK. HORROR SHOW was nominated for the Bram Stoker Award for Best First Novel.

It was also in the 90's that Greg began his radio career and spent sixteen years as the host of the morning show on KFOX Radio in San Jose/San Francisco.

Greg was inducted into the San Jose Rock Hall Of Fame in 2008 and the Bay Area Radio Hall of Fame in 2012.

He still plays with his band featuring his son Ry Kihn on lead guitar. Greg grew up in Baltimore and moved to California in 1972.

Greg's manager is Joel Turtle. You can contact him at Joelturtle@yahoo.com

Rubber Soul Representation by Judy Coppage at The Coppage Company.
You can contact her at Coppage@aol.com

CPSIA information can be obtained at www.ICGtesting.com
Printed in the USA
BVOW08s0633101013

333366BV00003B/8/P